Face the Wind

BOOKS BY CAREN J. WERLINGER

Novels:
Looking Through Windows
Miserere
In This Small Spot
Neither Present Time
Year of the Monsoon
She Sings of Old, Unhappy, Far-off Things
Turning for Home
Cast Me Gently
The Beast That Never Was
When the Stars Sang
A Bittersweet Garden
Invisible, as Music
Face the Wind

Short Stories:
Twist of the Magi
Just a Normal Christmas
(part of *Do You Feel What I Feel? Holiday Anthology*)

The Dragonmage Saga:
Rising From the Ashes: The Chronicles of Caymin
The Portal: The Chronicles of Caymin
The Standing Stones: The Chronicles of Caymin

Face the Wind

the

Wind

CAREN J. WERLINGER

CORGYN
Publishing

Face the Wind
Published by Corgyn Publishing, LLC.

e-Book ISBN: 978-1-953070-00-5
Print ISBN: 978-1-953070-01-2

E-mail: cjwerlingerbooks@yahoo.com
Web site: www.cjwerlinger.wordpress.com

Cover design by Patty G. Henderson
www.boulevardphotografica.yolasite.com

Cover Photo: Yaroslav Gerzhedovich/Shutterstock

Interior decoration: Can Stock Photo/Red Koala

Book design by Maureen Cutajar
www.gopublished.com

This is a work of fiction. Names, characters, places, and incidents are the product of the author's imagination or are used fictitiously, and any resemblance to actual persons, living or dead, businesses, companies, events, or locales is entirely coincidental.

To all of my mothers

Acknowledgements

Trying to remember the people and influences that helped to shape a new novel can be tough, because sometimes those prompts happened years before the book actually got written.

In this case, though, it's much simpler. I'd never written a true sequel. I don't count The Dragonmage Saga, as it was always intended to be a trilogy (or more... someday). But readers responded so warmly to *When the Stars Sang*, seeming to fall in love with Little Sister Island as much as I did, that they got me thinking. There were more stories to tell, more characters whose lives were left in limbo at the end of that book. When fellow author Debra Holland took the time to write me and suggest a sequel, the idea seriously took hold, so a huge thank-you to Debra.

My thanks, also, to Kassie and Denni, who graciously read the first several chapters of the (very rough) first draft, and provided me with feedback and guidance for the discussion of the Coquille tribe. I'm so appreciative of their willingness to take this on as the pandemic began raging.

Speaking of the pandemic, the world will probably always now be divided into "BC" (before coronavirus) and "AC" (after coronavirus). I started writing this novel late in 2019, well before the virus was even on our horizon, and I saw no need to alter it. I don't know if or when I'll write a book set in this new world we live in. The next few in the queue are set further back in time, so I probably won't be delving into the pandemic any time soon. I think I'll prefer to go the escape route with my reading, as well.

Thank you to my editor, Lisa, who always helps me make my stories better (and helps me realize how many times I overuse the same words. You'd think I'd have learned by now!). Thanks as well to Danielle for her eagle proofreading eyes.

And to my spouse, Beth. Your encouragement, especially when the doubts begin to take root, has meant the world to me.

To my readers, I wish you all good health and safe times with family and friends. Take good care.

Prologue

10th October 1760

WIND SHRIEKED THROUGH THE seams around the porthole, and waves pounded the ship with a roar that drowned out voices. Ida clung for dear life to the wooden side of her bunk as the ship rolled impossibly high and then dropped with a sickening plunge. Her other arm was wrapped around her little brother, Thomas. Across from her, others' mouths were open in screams she couldn't hear, barely visible in the gloomy semi-darkness of the passenger hold. The whale oil lamps had guttered out long ago, and what little could be seen through the porthole was almost as dark as night.

Water poured through the cracks of the trapdoor at the top of the ladder, splashing to the floor of the hold to mix with the vomit that swilled about with the pitching of the boat.

One man, panicked, crawled out of his bunk. Unable to keep his footing on the wet boards, his feet flew out from under him as the ship tilted again. He slid on his back, grasping at anything he could reach. The boat tipped the other way, and he tumbled toward the ladder. Seizing it, he hauled himself up the rungs and pounded on the trapdoor.

"Let us out!" he bellowed. Another wash of water sluiced through the cracks, splashing into his face and causing him to choke. He gagged and spat, hammering on the hatch. "We'll die down here!"

Ida watched, as did the others, waiting to see if anyone would open the hatch door. Above them, she heard muffled shouts.

The boat heaved again, rising almost vertically before falling to crash with an ominous crack of timbers. The man on the ladder lost his grip and fell heavily, landing on his shoulder. With a howl of pain, he grabbed his arm, now twisted grotesquely.

The ship pitched sideways, and there were renewed cries from above decks. A groan from overhead grew louder until the wall opposite Ida's bunk suddenly caved in with a deafening explosion. She threw herself over Thomas to protect him. When she opened her eyes, an enormous mast lay atop the bunks, crushing the boy lying in the upper one. She got only a momentary glance at his lifeless eyes staring skyward before water began gushing through the opening, filling the hold. Other people clambered and wriggled out of the bunks now submerged under the deluge.

With the extra weight of the water coming in, the boat could no longer right itself and began to list heavily. All of the people tumbled out of their bunks, linking arms as they scrambled for the ladder. One young man wrenched a splintered board loose from where the mast had come through and used it to hammer the trapdoor until it burst upward. The climb up the ladder was precarious as more water cascaded through, beating on their heads, trying to bear them down. But down was certain death.

Ida shoved Thomas ahead of her, up the ladder, but before she could climb through the hatch opening, he was swept across the deck by another wave.

"Thomas!"

Her scream was lost in the storm. All about her, sailors clung to ropes and rigging as they fought to bring the sails down. The broken mast had sailors trapped in its lines. They flailed helplessly, waves washing over them as they tried desperately to free themselves. One man, already dead, flopped flaccidly with the churning of the ocean.

Ida squinted through the stinging rain, searching for her brother. She caught sight of his white face, his arm wrapped about the splintered side rail.

"I'm coming!" she yelled at him, letting go of the side of the hatch to allow herself to slide sideways across the wet decking until she skidded into a large coil of rope.

Squatting inside the coil, she took the free end and threw it in Thomas's direction. "Grab hold!"

But another wave washed over the deck, full into her brother's face. When the water cleared, Thomas was gone.

All around her, men shouted, women and children cried and clutched to one another. The ship rode lower as it took on more water. She thought she saw Thomas's starkly pale face bobbing in the waves beyond the boat. She hesitated a moment more and then stepped out onto the slippery deck, letting herself slither closer and closer to the edge. When the next wave hit and took her with it, she wasn't prepared for the battering force of the water, driving her under.

She fought her way toward the surface, but another wave crashed upon her, tumbling her through the water so that she didn't know which way was up. Her lungs were ready to burst when her head broke free into air. She drew in a quick breath just before another wave pummeled her, crushing her with pulverizing force. Clawing at the water, she swam toward the surface. A chunk of wood slammed into her head, nearly knocking her unconscious. She grabbed at it, hauling herself partially onto it, and tried to clear her foggy vision.

"Thomas!" she cried. "Thom—"

Another wave washed over her, filling her mouth. Her stomach convulsed and she threw up all the salt water she'd swallowed. Exhausted, she dragged herself further onto the wooden beam she desperately grasped. In the distance, faint screams came to her through the raging storm, but she could no longer see the ship.

The endless night seemed to stretch on, and she wondered vaguely if this was eternity, if she was in one of the places in hell the priest back home had threatened them with.

Through the gloom, she thought she saw movement. She squinted into dark faces, bobbing on the water atop strange floating logs. They spoke words she didn't understand.

Her eyes closed, but she dreamed that hands reached out of the darkness, dragging her to safety and warmth.

Chapter 1

MOLLY COOPER SHIVERED IN the pre-dawn darkness. Maybe Kathleen had been the smart one, still home, snuggled in a warm bed. Even Blossom had given her only a waggle of his tail before curling more tightly into his dog bed.

Every year, Molly recalled, she did this. Just because the calendar said April didn't mean the weather—or the water—at Little Sister Island was ready to welcome spring. But, after a long winter of rowing indoors, the itch to get out on the ocean was so strong, Molly couldn't resist.

She tugged the oars out of the Toyota's cargo hold, locking them into the scull resting on the sand. She briefly debated not shedding her extra layers, but she knew if she dressed too warmly to begin, she'd be overheated halfway through her row, and then the cold air would chill her sweaty body that much faster. Gritting her teeth, she stripped down to tights and a couple of wicking layers for her upper body. She zipped up a fleece vest and buckled on her inflatable life jacket over top. The sand crunched icily as she shoved the scull sideways into the water and stepped in, managing to do it with only one wet shoe.

A few minutes later, she was pulling with long, even strokes, propelling the scull over the calm water. Behind her, the sky lightened, gradually throwing her shadow onto the water in her wake.

She soon warmed and was glad she'd bitten the bullet for those cold initial minutes. *God, I love this.* Her indoor rower, though it was a lifesaver during the long, cold months of a Maine winter, couldn't compare to the freedom of getting out on the water. She heard a few gulls mew in search of breakfast. Her own stomach rumbled. She paused her rowing, reaching for an insulated bottle filled with a warm power drink. The scull bobbed on the gentle swells, and Molly watched the black hulk of Little Sister slowly come into full view as the line between sunlight and shadow lowered. The trees that clung to the bluff were still leafless this time of year. She was far enough out that, in the distance, the granite Head was visible with its wind turbines catching what breezes were beginning to blow. Last, the narrow beach from which she'd launched gleamed gold when the sunlight touched it.

A shadow moved there. Molly narrowed her eyes and smiled to see Kathleen and Blossom on the sand. Kathleen waved in her direction. Molly waved back and picked the oars up. She watched them walk on while she resumed her course, just a little while longer away from the island before she turned around. It was hard to remember when she used to daydream about rowing away and never coming back. Now, her reasons for coming back disappeared into the trees.

She had a few oil deliveries to make today, and that nearly always involved having to clean and repair and restart a few furnaces. She was proud of the fact that the islanders' oil consumption had dropped by more than half from last winter, thanks to the efforts they'd all made to add solar to most of the houses. They still relied on oil for heat in the deepest cold, but the memory of the shortage they'd faced last year thanks to the hostile actions of Kathleen's father—Molly stopped that train of thought. It always got her riled up, and she didn't want to spoil this first time on the water. It would be the only time she got to herself all day.

Maybe Kathleen would have pancake batter mixed and ready to go by the time she got home. Her stomach rumbled again, her back and arms aching in a familiar, pleasant way. Just as she decided to turn the scull and head back, Little Sister shimmered, like a desert mirage. A moment later, a ripple ran through the ocean, a small tidal wave racing in her direction. When it reached her, the scull rose and then fell back to a calm sea.

"What the hell was that?"

Molly squeezed her eyes shut for a few seconds, but when she opened them, everything looked normal. The island solid and real, the water around her undisturbed. She shook her head and dug one oar in to turn around.

By the time she rowed back and got the scull and oars loaded, the sun was fully up. She cranked the ignition and bumped the 4-Runner over the rocky terrain. At the road, she hesitated before turning toward town.

Her hunch was justified when she saw her mother's SUV parked at the diner. Reaching for her jacket, she hurriedly parked beside her mom. Inside, Wilma was behind the counter, pouring coffee into a line of white mugs while Kathleen carried them to where a couple of tables had been hastily pushed together. She flashed a smile when she saw Molly.

"We wondered if you'd find us," she said.

Blossom trotted over for a pat and then hurried back to the tables.

Molly quickly took in the odd crowd assembled. Her mother, Jenny, slid a mug of coffee over to Louisa Woodhouse, whose silver hair was hanging loose over her shoulders, the first time Molly could remember not seeing it primly tucked into its usual bun. Wilma whisked away the breakfast plates of the last couple of men sitting at the counter, shooing them out the door. With a curious glance at the women bustling about, they scooted.

In the kitchen, Nels bent down to the pass-through and called to his wife. Wilma took the heaping platters of eggs and bacon and toast that he'd prepared. She set everything on the counter alongside a stack of plates.

"Let's all just help ourselves."

While Jenny filled a plate for Louisa, the door opened and Miranda Shannahan came in, closely followed by Siobhan Greyeagle.

"What the bloody hell was that?" Siobhan asked, looking annoyed as she tried to finger-brush her mane of wild, red curls into some semblance of tameness. Giving up, she accepted a cup of tea from Wilma.

"You sit down," Wilma said with a calming pat on the shoulder. "We all felt it."

Molly loaded a plate and made a quick bacon sandwich with some of the toast. Shoveling eggs into her mouth with the fork in her other hand, she alternated eggs and sandwich while the others got situated.

"Hungry?"

Molly glanced up at Kathleen, standing beside her. "Starving," she managed to mumble around a mouthful.

Kathleen set a steaming cup of coffee in front of her and bent to kiss her cheek. "Salty."

Molly gave an apologetic shrug.

"We're just waiting for—"

The door's bell tinkled again.

"Well, that didn't take long." Rebecca Ahearn nodded approvingly at the group gathered. She took her gloves and jacket off, depositing them on an empty table before quickly filling a plate herself.

Molly shifted over to make room for her aunt.

"Eat while everything is hot," Wilma said.

For a few minutes, the only sounds were the metallic clinks of forks against plates and the intermittent thunks of coffee mugs being set down on the tabletops.

Rebecca was the first to finish. She cradled her cup in her hands, surveying the women assembled. "I assume we're all here at this hour because we all felt the same thing."

Molly quickly scanned the table as everyone nodded. "What did you feel?"

"Didn't you?" Rebecca's sharp eyes probed.

"I was rowing."

"What did you feel, then?"

Molly paused her eating to try and figure out how to describe it. "It was more what I saw. The island kind of... shivered."

Everyone froze mid-drink or mid-bite.

Jenny frowned. "Shivered."

"Yeah. You know how things," Molly waggled her fingers, "kind of shiver in heat waves, like in those movies set in the desert? That's what it looked like. And then came the wave."

"What wave?" Kathleen asked.

"A wave. Like a tidal wave, only small." Molly tilted her head, trying to remember. "I think it spread out from the island like a ring." She glanced around. "Why? What did you feel here?"

"The ground shifted," Jenny said. "Or it seemed to."

"Like an earthquake?"

"Maybe. But nothing in the house was damaged."

"I came through the market on my way here," Miranda said. "Nothing was disturbed on the shelves."

Molly gestured toward the counter with her cup. "The men who were here, didn't seem like they were talking about this. Didn't they feel it? Whatever it was?"

Wilma glanced toward the kitchen. "Nels didn't feel it, either."

"Even I felt it," Kathleen said. "We'd just seen you from the beach and were walking the trail through the woods. The trees shook with it, but nothing fell."

"So why just us?" Molly asked.

They all turned to Rebecca, who said, "I don't believe it was just us, but it was just the women of the island. There are others, still at home."

"I don't understand," Kathleen said. "Is this some new island ritual I don't know about yet?"

Rebecca shook her head. "It has nothing to do with that, but I am a bit surprised you felt it, as you've only been back a little over a year."

Molly rephrased her question. "Then why only the women?"

"Because the island is our mother," Siobhan answered, fingering a white crystal pendant hanging around her neck. "Even those of us who haven't borne children are connected to her in ways men are not. She's telling us something."

"What?" Jenny eyed her sister. "You know."

Rebecca shook her head. "I don't know what, but Siobhan is right." She fixed her gaze on Louisa. "I've only read about this happening three times in the island chronicles."

Everyone turned to Louisa, who folded her hands, looking as if she were about to lecture a class. "As the eldest here—actually, I'm the eldest on the entire island—I suppose I'm the only one to remember. The rest of you are too young. The last time this happened was June 1954."

The others all shared puzzled glances.

"How do you remember that so precisely?" Kathleen asked.

Louisa pursed her lips for a moment. "Because a couple of months later, that August, Hurricane Carol hit further south, mostly Massachusetts and Rhode Island, killing sixty-eight people. Only a couple of weeks after that, Hurricane Edna hit. We lost six islanders in that storm. Ian Whitefeather and his five sons."

Molly leaned forward. "I don't even know that name."

"You wouldn't," Rebecca said. "After the storm took Ian and his sons, Mary Whitefeather lived out her days. You know the house now as the O'Malley place. Niall won the lottery after Mary passed."

"Land sakes, an entire line, gone in one storm," Wilma murmured.

A heavy silence followed.

"So, wait," Kathleen said. "You said this has happened only three times—"

"Three times that are recorded," Rebecca corrected. "There may have been others that the Keepers of the Record didn't recognize or make note of."

"But what does it mean?" Jenny asked. "Does it mean another storm is coming?"

"It's obvious, isn't it?" Louisa said, her voice sharper than Molly remembered hearing before. "When I—" She paused. "I'm the last Woodhouse. Another line is coming to an end."

She pushed to her feet. "I'm going to walk home. The air will do me good."

Molly opened her mouth to protest that she'd drive her, but Rebecca laid a hand on her arm.

"Let her go."

"HERE YOU GO, DADDY."

Louisa shifted a wooden box nearer a window, where the sunlight highlighted the deeply carved name, *Walter Woodhouse*. She placed a second box next to it.

"Ollie, you sit here and keep him company."

She'd been slightly mortified to get home from the diner to realize she'd left them both behind in her haste. She hardly went anywhere without them. When Olivia was alive, she and her sister had taken their daddy with them everywhere, strapping his box into the back seat of their Ford Fairmont, the last new car Daddy had bought, back in 1978. When it was new, its blue paint had gleamed, and Daddy used to wash and wax it regularly, but now...

Louisa blinked when the clock chimed and realized she'd been standing there lost in thought for more than fifteen minutes. It was happening more and more lately. She could remember the tiniest details of something that happened forty years ago, but couldn't remember what she'd come into a room to do.

"Need to stay busy," she said to herself, something else she was saying more frequently.

If her body gave out, if she just dropped dead, the way Ollie had done, she could accept that. But she dreaded her mind going, leaking out of her head a little at a time, until she was just an empty shell. That would be worse than death, to her way of thinking.

So she forced herself to do everything she and Ollie used to do together. Not that there wasn't plenty to do here. This old house really was more than she could keep up with. Molly kept patching and repairing the roof with new shingles when old ones blew off in storms, but the entire roof needed replacing. And the house desperately needed to be painted. It did have new solar panels and a small house-sized wind turbine, as did most of the houses on Little Sister now, churning out and storing enough electricity to reduce the islanders' dependence on the diesel-fueled generators that had provided their power for decades.

Today, she decided it was warm enough to hang some washing outside to dry. She washed her sheets and towels—it had taken her a while to stop stripping all three beds every week, until Katie had pointed out that she was wasting hot water, washing what didn't need washing.

"Dear Katie," Louisa said with a smile as she carried her wet sheets outside to the clothesline. "You'd be proud of her, Maisie." It didn't matter that Maisie Halloran had been dead for almost three years. She could hear her, Louisa was sure of that.

The poor thing had been through a lot—first to get back home to Little Sister, and then to stay here, what with her broken family. But now she had Molly and the rest of the Coopers and all of the islanders as the family she'd never had growing up.

Louisa finished with the last sheet, smoothing a wrinkled corner, and climbed the steps to sit on the back porch. It was time to turn over the compost heap, getting it ready to spread in the garden for the spring planting. The peas and carrots would need to be put in soon. How could it be April already? She made a mental timetable of all the spring chores that needed to be done.

For a moment, it all felt like too much. For that moment, Louisa wished she could join Ollie and Maisie and her parents.

"Don't be foolish," she said impatiently. Brushing tears from her cheeks, she got to her feet and reached for a rattan basket from a stack on the porch. She went around the house to the wooden cellar door to get some of last year's carrots and potatoes for a fresh pot of stew.

In the kitchen, she tipped the contents of her basket into the sink to scrub and peel everything, but her mind was still on Molly and Katie. It made her happy that Molly now had the thing that had been missing from her life, but it hadn't always been like that. That girl had given Louisa more sleepless nights than almost any of her former students. From the beginning, Molly had had a restless, independent streak—she'd had to with those three brothers of hers. Louisa had known she needed the opportunity to get off Little Sister, to go to college and make something of herself. She'd argued to the island council, had pushed Molly, tutored her to help her get the marks she needed on her entrance exams. When word came that Molly had been accepted at Vassar, Louisa couldn't have been prouder. And no one was more disappointed when Molly came back. She knew she hadn't hidden her displeasure from Molly.

"Hide it? You didn't hide it a'tall."

"Be quiet," Louisa said.

"You tried to make her do what you really wanted to."

Louisa tried to ignore her sister's voice, but Olivia wasn't going to let it go.

"It wasn't until I told you, I said, 'Molly isn't you, Lou.' Remember when I said that?"

Louisa nodded, her head bowed over the cutting board. "I remember. And you were right."

"Sorry. What was that?"

Louisa's mouth curled into a grudging smile. "I said, you were right."

"You had to wait until I was dead to say that?"

"You said Molly needed to stretch her wings, but was always going to migrate back home."

"What else did I say?"

Louisa didn't answer for a moment. "You said..." Her voice cracked.

"I said I knew something else, some storm had chased you back, or you wouldn't have come home. But you never said what."

Louisa lifted the cutting board to scrape the cut potatoes into the pot.

"You need to put the meat in the bottom, not the potatoes."

"It's my stew, Ollie. I like the potatoes in the bottom."

"But then the meat doesn't cook properly."

"When the meat is in the bottom, it falls apart," Louisa complained.

"The way it should. I'm right about that, too."

Louisa whirled around to the empty kitchen. She stood there a moment before going to the refrigerator to get the roast.

"Think I don't know how to make stew," she muttered, but she laid the beef in the bottom of the slow cooker and layered the potatoes and carrots over top.

Chapter 2

EREDITH WAS BENT OVER a book, taking in every detail of an old illustration, hoping for something that would look familiar. Suddenly, the overhead lights flicked off.

"What? Hey!"

"Who's there?" came an answering voice.

"It's me," she responded as the fluorescents flickered back on.

A face appeared around the corner of the tall bookshelf. "Meredith. I didn't realize you were here."

"Sorry, Barb." Meredith glanced at her watch. "I don't mean to keep you. Didn't see how late it was getting."

Barb leaned over the table and picked up one of the books scattered there. "*Shipwrecks of the North Pacific.* Research?"

"Kind of," Meredith said with a shrug. "Can I check these two out?"

"Sure." Barb reached for them. "I'll do it now."

"Thanks."

A few minutes later, Meredith sauntered out of the school library, her heavy tote slung over one shoulder.

She descended the stairs to the atrium where a large banner hung, urging the baseball and softball teams to victory. The double bank of windows reaching almost two stories floor-to-ceiling spilled warm sunshine across the marble floor. She paused for a moment, her face lifted to the light.

"Hi, Miss Turner," said a teenage girl carrying a pair of track cleats by the laces.

"Meet today, Surina?"

"Yes. I'm in two of the relays," the girl said.

"Great day for it," Meredith said. "Go Bobcats!"

"Thanks. See you Monday."

"Don't forget, we're having an exam on *The Scarlet Letter*."

Surina smiled. "I've already started studying."

Meredith gave her a thumbs up and headed out to the parking lot. The interior of her car was pleasantly warm thanks to the spring sunshine.

In the few minutes it took her to drive from the school to her small house in Pacific City, a marine layer had rolled in, obscuring the coast in cold fog.

A plaintive whine greeted her before she could even get her key in the door.

"Did you miss me, Jasper?" she crooned to the shepherd-lab mix who jumped up to place his paws on her chest.

He woofed in reply, carrying on a non-stop scolding as she deposited her tote on the kitchen table and draped her purse over the back of a chair.

"Okay, okay." She bent to give him a good scratch, sending one hind leg into a frenzy of kicking when she found a ticklish spot on his flank.

When she stopped scratching, he trotted to the door, sitting and glancing back at her with an expectant stare.

"All right, let me change."

She quickly switched from her teaching clothes to jeans and a warm sweater. Pausing to snag a rain jacket off the hooks near the door, she slipped into boots and clipped a leash to Jasper's collar.

No matter what time of year, when this fog blanket rolled in, it was cold. Droplets condensed on her jacket and hair as she and Jasper strolled down the hill toward the ocean. Once they had crossed the main road and climbed the low dune to the beach, she let Jasper off the leash.

He bounded off, barking and chasing gulls, acting more like a puppy than a ten-year-old senior canine. She draped the leash around her neck and tucked her hands in her pockets. Down here, near the surf, the fog felt like a living thing, undulating and flowing as unseen breaths of wind pushed it around her. Out in the sea, like a disembodied specter, Haystack Rock appeared as the mists thinned momentarily, only to disappear again into the gloaming. She stood, just beyond where the ocean's fingers could reach her, hearing in her head the screams and crashes and shouts of her shipwreck dream.

What must it be like? she wondered. *How does anyone survive something like that in such a vast ocean?*

That dream had haunted her sleep as a child, night after night, causing her to wake with tears running down her face. Then, when she was about eight, it had faded so that she rarely woke to that nightmare. But in these last several months, it had returned, more vivid than it had been. The girl, the one in the dream, kept reaching out to her, as if she expected Meredith to save her.

Pale face, black hair, frightened blue eyes—that face was burned into Meredith's memory. Without realizing it, she sometimes found herself scanning the faces of people she passed, searching...

A wet dog nose pressed into her palm startled her. She opened her eyes to find herself standing with one arm outstretched to the empty ocean. Embarrassed, she dropped her arm and looked around.

Other than her and Jasper, the beach was empty. Unless the mist was hiding more than her dreams.

"Come on," she said, rubbing her hand along his wet coat. "Let's go get some dinner."

Back at the house, she kicked off her boots, leaving them on the rubber mat by the door. Jasper sat on his towel, patiently allowing her to dry one paw at a time and then rub the towel roughly over his back and belly.

"You love this part, don't you, old man?" Meredith asked.

Jasper gave her a doggy grin.

She scooped some fresh kibble for him, adding some chopped-up carrot. Leaving him to eat, she opened the fridge, weighing scrambled eggs versus last night's leftover pizza. She opted for the pizza and flipped the oven on to pre-heat.

By the time the oven was ready, she'd changed out of her damp clothes into warm sweatpants, thick socks, and a heavy fleece, and Jasper was curled up in his own fuzzy round bed. She slid the pizza in to warm up and poured herself a glass of water—"why not?" she said, spying the half-bottle of Riesling in the fridge—and another of the wine.

Taking them both to the table, she opened her tote and retrieved a stack of papers to grade. She graded while she ate, but the shipwreck books kept diverting her attention. She brushed the last of the pizza crumbs from her fingers and slid the papers aside. She tugged one of the books out of the tote and repositioned her lamp. She'd lived in Oregon for most of her life, but she'd never realized how many shipwrecks there'd been off the coast. It seemed most of them didn't involve loss of life, just ships running aground. But some, like the *Lupatia* in 1881, were tragic. Sixteen lives lost, all except the ship's dog.

She frowned. She wasn't sure why, but 1881 seemed too late. Plus, there was nothing in her dream to indicate the wreck had taken place here, *but where else would I start?*

She caught herself and sat back. "It's a dream." Jasper raised his head. She looked at him. "Why am I acting as if this was real?"

She closed the books firmly and refilled her wine glass before returning to her papers.

Her cell phone rang. Glancing at the number, she accepted the call. "Hi, Mom."

"Your father and I are going to some beer festival this weekend—"

"Irene, I told you, it's ale, not beer!" Meredith heard her father say in the background. "Ales are completely different from lagers."

"Anyway," her mother said, lowering her voice. "Roy insists this is something we have to do. I think you should join us."

Meredith smiled. "You mean, you need someone to talk to while Dad drinks ale."

She frowned at the muffled sounds coming from the phone, and it was a moment before her mother said, "I had to go out on the porch. Please, come. He has taken it into his head that turning our house into a home brewery is a good project now that he's retired. He's going to drive me crazy!"

Meredith stifled a laugh. "We knew it was going to be an adjustment for both of you when he retired."

"Well, I wasn't counting on this much of an adjustment. I need reinforcements."

"Okay. Jasper and I will drive up Friday after school."

"Oh, thank you, honey. See you Friday."

※※※※※※※※※※

THE SETTING FOR THE ale festival turned out to be a charming farmstead. Multiple local brewers had put up tents outside, plus many more had set up stands inside the barn. The competing aromas of the food vendors made Meredith's mouth water.

"What is it about fried dough and Italian sausage that smells so darn good?" she asked, inhaling deeply.

Her mother chuckled. "Your father said that about the beer. Ale. Whatever."

They left him to wander on his own while they bought a couple of steak-and-cheese sandwiches—"and an elephant ear," Meredith insisted—and found an empty spot at a long row of picnic tables set up under another tent.

"Lucked out with the weather this weekend," she commented.

"Yay."

Meredith couldn't help snorting at her mother's scorn.

Jasper lay under the table at Meredith's feet.

"Oh, my gosh, this is good!" Irene closed her eyes as she chewed.

Meredith just grunted in agreement, tearing off a bit and slipping it down to Jasper. "So, you and Dad. Marital bliss is in jeopardy?"

Irene's eyes snapped open. "Do you—" She stopped and scanned the crowd near them to make sure Roy wasn't within hearing. Still, she dropped her voice to a whisper. "Do you know what he did the first week he was home after retiring?"

Meredith shook her head, hoping this didn't involve an affair or porn or anything like that.

"He rearranged my kitchen!" Irene's nostrils flared. "Said my kitchen was inefficient. Just because he's an *engineer*—" The last word was emphasized with air quotes. "He thinks he knows better than I do how to organize *my* kitchen. He didn't have any problems with my efficiency in cooking his dinner the last thirty-nine years. But all of a sudden, he knows better than I do."

Meredith tore a large piece of elephant ear loose and slid it in her mom's direction. "Here. You need fat and sugar."

Irene grabbed the fried dough and shoved it into her mouth, leaving telltale powdered sugar on her lips. "I have to go back to work, or I may kill that man."

Meredith paused with her own piece of dough almost in her mouth.

She lowered it. "Really?"

"Really." Irene tilted her head. "Do you think they'd hire an old art teacher who hasn't taught in eight years?"

Meredith considered how to answer. "Things were a little different when you retired, Mom. Even in elementary schools, they're now using smart boards and PowerPoint and stuff like that."

Irene's face fell. Meredith studied her mother's features. She hoped this was what she'd look like in twenty-five years—dark hair turning silver, fine lines at her eyes and mouth in an otherwise smooth face, still petite and slim.

"Why don't you substitute for a while?" she suggested. "That way, you can see how things are done now. Get a feel for whether you really want to go back into education. And if you don't feel like working on a given day, just say no."

Irene chewed thoughtfully. "That's a good idea."

"There are only a few months left in the year; you can try it out."

"And not divorce your father."

Meredith laughed, popping the last of the elephant ear into her mouth. "That, too."

"Speaking of which, have you spoken to Grant?"

The bite she'd just taken got caught in her throat as Meredith tried to swallow. Her eyes watered. She reached for her water and forced it down. "No," she rasped. "Why would you—"

She narrowed her eyes. "He called you, didn't he?"

Her mother, she noted, had the decency to at least look abashed.

"Well," Irene said, "he said you weren't returning his calls, and he wondered if maybe..."

Her eyes flicked to something behind Meredith.

"Oh, you didn't."

"Hi, babe."

Meredith stiffened as Grant sat beside her on the picnic bench. Under the table, she felt Jasper shift to huddle between her knees.

"I think I'll go find Roy," Irene said, jumping up with her plate and cup.

Meredith glared after her for a moment before turning with a resigned sigh. "Hello."

Grant smiled, as handsome as ever, his Vineyard Vines polo the perfect blue to match his eyes, the collar popped below his wavy blond hair. Meredith was certain, if she looked, he'd be wearing Sperry Top-Siders and rolled chinos, looking more suited for the cover of a yachting magazine than an ale festival.

"Can I buy you an ale?" he asked, lifting his own cup filled with a foamy brew.

"No, thanks. I'm good."

"How've you been?" he asked, reaching for her hand.

She looked down, trying to remember when she'd enjoyed being near him, walking hand in hand, or cuddling against him with his arm wrapped around her, especially after sex. But that was before.

She withdrew her hand. "Why are you here, Grant?"

"Oh, c'mon, babe."

"Don't call me babe."

Grant's smile faltered. "We were so good together. I know I was stupid, but can't we let that go?"

She searched his face. He was serious. "No. We can't. You want to play? Go play. But don't come back to me when you're done."

He shifted to face her, straddling the bench. "Five years is a long time to throw away."

She nodded. "It is, isn't it. Maybe you should have thought about that before you decided to go party in Vegas with your buddies in the accounting department."

"I just needed guy time to blow off some steam. It didn't mean anything. You spend time with your girlfriends."

She stared at him. "Don't insult me. We're not talking about a ball game or camping trip with your friends. You hooked up with someone. And I don't trust that you were safe." She shrugged. "You're not coming near me again, Grant. And that's that. Go find someone else. Or don't. It's really none of my business. And my life is none of yours."

She got up from the table. Jasper wriggled from under the bench to join her. She spied her mother, standing in the entrance to one of the beer tents. Furious at her mom's interference, she stalked by, out to the field being used for parking the cars. She wandered for ten minutes before remembering she'd come with her parents in their Audi.

"Damn."

Too proud to go back and find them to beg the car keys, she settled under a tree that gave her a view of the car. Jasper lay beside her, his head resting on her thigh. She blinked back tears. Five years had been hard to walk away from. Five years of being a fixture at Grant's side at his office functions, of having her teacher friends commenting on what a beautiful couple they made, all of them wondering when a ring was coming.

Meredith had had her disappointments when birthdays and Christmases and weekends away had come and gone without a proposal. Thank goodness it never had.

"But better to know now," she muttered.

There'd been only one night of tears after Grant had confessed to what happened, and even those tears hadn't been of the broken-hearted variety. *That should have told me something,* she reminded herself.

Her friends were beginning to notice that Grant hadn't been around the last couple of months, but Jan was the only one she'd actually told. Sooner or later, she was going to have to tell them, but she dreaded it—the pity, the having to explain.

She dug her fingers into Jasper's thick ruff. "You'll never cheat on me, will you? From now on, it's just you and me."

"HOW COULD YOU DO that to me?" Meredith demanded a couple of hours later as she stormed into her parents' house.

The ride home from the ale festival had stretched on interminably. She fumed in the back seat while her father, seemingly oblivious to the tension filling the car, rambled on about the new ale-brewing kit in the trunk.

"But honey," Irene protested, following Meredith into the kitchen, "he seemed so worried about you. And you never really did say why you broke up. I think he'd like to make it up to you."

"Oh, I know he would," Meredith spat. She closed her eyes and took a calming breath. "Look, Mom, I know you meant well, but it's over between Grant and me."

She went to the refrigerator to get a pitcher of water and poured herself a glass.

"Was it..." Her mother hesitated. "Was there someone else?"

Meredith stood with her back to her mom. *Why am I covering for him?* "Yes. There was someone else."

"And you can't forgive—"

Meredith whirled around. "Forgive? Why would I?" She slammed the refrigerator door. "If he would cheat on me now, why would I ever trust him again?"

Irene sighed and pulled out a chair. "I suppose. I just hate to see you alone."

"I'm not alone. I have Jasper. I have friends. I have my students." Meredith took a sip of her water and forced herself to smile. "And I have you and Dad."

"You won't forever."

Meredith frowned. "What does that mean? Are you—"

Irene waved a dismissive hand. "No, we're fine. It's just that ever since your grandfather passed last year, I've been thinking more and more about family, about what we leave behind. It's only me and your uncle now from our generation. But you'll be alone when we're gone, honey."

Meredith joined her mom at the table and took her hand. "Just because it didn't work out with Grant doesn't mean there won't be anyone else." She gave her mother's hand a squeeze.

Irene smiled. "Well, I do expect grandchildren someday."

"Don't need a husband for that," Meredith said.

Irene's eyebrows shot up. "Have you been thinking about—"

"No," Meredith said with a chortle. "But if my clock starts ticking, I may."

"Let's go see what your father is up to. It worries me when he's this quiet."

Meredith looked around. "And Jasper's with him."

They headed down the hall toward the basement steps, but Meredith stopped short at the door to her mother's studio.

"Mom."

"What?" Irene retraced her steps to where Meredith was pointing. "What is that?"

"Oh, nothing." Irene went to her easel where a large pad was propped with a charcoal sketch of a ship in a stormy sea.

"It's not nothing," Meredith said softly. "I've seen this ship. In my dreams. People screaming as a mast breaks..."

"...and floods the hold."

"And the girl," Meredith said, seeing her as clearly as she saw her mother.

"Black hair?"

Meredith nodded. "She stares at me, every time I have this dream. Like she's trying to speak to me."

Meredith and her mother stood in front of the easel.

"How could we both be dreaming about the same thing?" Irene asked. "And such a specific, odd thing."

"This can't be just a coincidence." Meredith murmured, touching a finger to the sketch. "Is it the same dream, every time?"

Irene nodded. "How long have you been having it?"

Meredith thought. "I used to have this exact dream when I was a little girl. It felt like a nightmare then. But it went away for years. And then it came back." Meredith squinted at the sketch. "Christmas a year ago. Remember? I had a bad cold. I just thought I was having weird dreams from the medicine. But it kept coming back, at first only now and again. But it's been coming more regularly lately. Almost every night."

Irene gasped. "Me, too. All my life, it would come for a few months and then go away for ages before coming back again. What can it mean?"

Meredith shook her head. "I don't know."

Chapter 3

KATHLEEN SHIFTED THE TABLE lamp a little closer as she pored over yellowed pages filled with line after line of minuscule writing. She adjusted her glasses, her other hand absently playing with the shooting star necklace dangling from the open neck of her cotton polo.

She flipped the page and froze. "Here it is."

Rebecca came into the back room from the front part of the island's library. "Read it to me."

"3rd June 1954," Kathleen read, "A most unusual thing happened today before the sun was fully up. I was awakened by a curious sensation, as if the entire island was quaking. However, when I got up, not a thing was disturbed nor broken. When I came into the village, nearly a score of the women had felt the same thing. Strangely, none of the men seemed to have felt it. None of us can recall such a thing happening before, nor do we know what it signifies."

She took her glasses off and sat back, rubbing her eyes. "But no mention of it happening previously. Like Louisa did for us last week."

Rebecca scanned the other books lining the shelves in this back room, their ancient leather covers scuffed and scarred. "I think it may be that the last time before that pre-dated any of those women."

"You mentioned that this shaking or quaking had only been recorded three times."

Rebecca nodded. "But I can't remember the dates. I think we should start at the beginning. Find the quakes, and then look over the entries for the following few months, see if there were other big events like the storm Louisa described. Search for a pattern."

"Clear back to 1760?" Kathleen's shoulders sagged.

Rebecca fixed her with those startlingly light blue-green eyes—eyes so like Molly's, eyes that used to seem at odds with their dark First Ones complexions—and said, "Do you have a better idea?"

"No." Kathleen sighed. "But I think I'm going to have to get 3x magnifiers to read this script."

Rebecca nodded her agreement, holding up her own reading glasses. "It gets easier with practice. When I first started studying with Naomi to become Keeper of the Record, I had a horrible time deciphering the writing in these old annals."

Kathleen slid her glasses back in place. "Do you think Miss Louisa was right? Does this mean the end of her line is imminent?"

"We already knew that, didn't we? With Miss Olivia gone, Louisa's the last Woodhouse. I don't know why the island would need to tell us that." Rebecca frowned at the books as if she could force an answer from them. "I have a feeling this means something else. Not sure what."

Kathleen closed the book she'd been studying. "Mind if we pick this up again tomorrow? I'm in the middle of an edit with a deadline coming up next week."

"No problem. I can start if you're busy."

"No," Kathleen said quickly. "I need to learn these journals if I'm to become the next Keeper, but I've got to balance it with my day job. Tomorrow afternoon work for you?"

"Sure." Rebecca rose. "See you tomorrow."

Blossom scrambled up from where he'd been sleeping in the sunshine streaming in through the window.

"Stay close," Kathleen said, swinging a leg over her bicycle. Most of the islanders had taken to biking or walking on their errands around the island as often as they could. Not only did it save gasoline, she figured most of them had probably lost weight and were getting healthier. Of course, with no doctor on Little Sister, that was only a guess.

Before she was halfway home, she was cussing in sync with her labored breathing. "Damn...Why... do I always... forget... how uphill... the way... home is..."

Even with the granny gears on her bike, her legs spinning like a pinwheel, the trip back to the cottage was always so much harder than the mostly coasting cruise into the village. Blossom, on the other hand, loped effortlessly alongside her snail-like pace.

By the time she propped the bike against the front porch, she was sweating. Blossom sat at the front door, his tongue lolling. When she opened the door, he trotted through to the kitchen to lap up half a bowl of water while she gulped down a glassful herself.

She refilled her glass and went out to the living room where her grandmother's old rocker sat alongside Molly's recliner and her own re-upholstered armchair and ottoman.

She dropped into her chair. This cottage had almost not stayed in the family, she recalled. If she hadn't returned to Little Sister just prior to the one-year anniversary of her grandmother's death, the cottage would have gone to the island's lottery system for leasing it to a new family. She remembered how odd it had felt to learn that no one on Little Sister owned any land or the houses—a tradition passed down by the First Ones who had rescued the Irish survivors of the shipwreck just off the island's coast in 1760.

Ignoring for the moment all the work waiting for her upstairs, she sat back and propped her legs up. Blossom sat, leaning against her, his head resting on her thigh. She played with his soft ears, thinking.

It was impossible to picture the sprawling Woodhouse place without Miss Louisa puttering around it, tending her garden. What must it feel like for her now? To have lived her entire life on Little Sister. To be the last of the Woodhouses. To know that, when she died, so would their line.

Even though Kathleen had been studying the island's family histories under Rebecca's tutelage, she hadn't really paid that much attention to those lines that had died off or moved away. Since no one could live on this island unless they came from an island lineage, she'd been focusing on the families currently living on Little Sister, learning which ones had children off to college or other relatives on the mainland.

She was kind of looking forward to the day when she got to perform her first Passing, the ritual she herself had had to go through to prove she came from an island family that could trace its roots back to that shipwreck and the blended Irish and First Ones lines that had resulted.

With Kathleen's grandmother deceased and no other family here when she decided to return, Miss Louisa and Miss Olivia had taken her in, made her feel welcome.

"We need to do something for her," she said. Blossom raised his head. "Come on."

By the time Molly's 4-Runner rumbled into the drive, Kathleen had been busy in the kitchen for hours, editing on her laptop as things baked and bubbled.

Expecting to hear the front door open, she was startled when Molly appeared on the back porch. She got up from the table to find Molly stripping down outside. The sight of that long, lean body, nearly naked on the porch made her smile.

"Were you in the mood for a quickie al fresco?" she asked, stepping through the back door. But almost as soon as the words left her mouth, she stopped short, her nose wrinkled. Even Blossom skidded to a halt, his nose quivering at the strange scents emanating from Molly.

"I don't think you'll want to get that close." Molly slid her underwear down to join the pile of clothing she'd shed.

"What happened?" Kathleen tried valiantly to maintain a neutral expression.

"I was replacing Emma Riley's toilet. Turned out the old one wasn't as empty as I thought." Molly held her arms away from her sides. "I can't stand myself. And the Toyota is gonna need a good airing out, too. Left the windows down. Hope it doesn't rain any time soon."

"Then I'll drive." Kathleen held the screen door open for Molly.

"Where are we going?" Molly stopped as soon as she stepped into the kitchen. "Oh, my gosh, it smells like heaven in here."

"We're taking dinner to Miss Louisa."

"Spaghetti?" Molly sniffed again. "And orange-cranberry bread?"

"Yep. I know it's not as good as she can make, but I wanted to do something for her. Go shower. A long, hot shower. With lots and lots of soap."

Molly grinned and hurried upstairs.

▧▧▧▧▧▧▧▧▧

"YOU GIRLS SHOULDN'T HAVE done this," Louisa said as she bustled about the kitchen, getting down plates and glasses.

"You and Miss Olivia did this for me plenty of times," Kathleen reminded her. "Remember, you brought me a loaf of this bread my first day in Nanna's cottage."

"I remember," Louisa said. "Maisie would have been so happy to know you were back."

Molly came inside, Blossom on her heels. "Miss Lou, you've got a couple of broken shutters on the east side of the house. Probably blew loose in the last storm. I'm going to patch those up for you before they come off completely."

"Molly, you don't have to do that."

"Sure it's no trouble. Better to fix them now than to have to replace them later. And if we get a big blow, you'll want to be able to pull them shut. I'll get to it this week."

"I remember many a big storm, sitting inside with the hurricane lamps, windows shuttered to protect the glass—it was dear and hard to replace when we were young. Mama would tell us stories to keep us from getting scared."

Louisa got the garlic bread out of the oven while Kathleen drained the spaghetti.

"Oh, Katie, this all smells so good. You've turned into quite a cook."

"I'm not complaining," Molly said, giving Kathleen a kiss on the cheek as she spooned a large helping of spaghetti onto a plate and passed it to Louisa to add her own sauce.

Once they were seated—with Olivia and Mr. Woodhouse's boxes on adjacent chairs near the table—Kathleen said, "I found the entry for the quake you told us about. Just like you said. June 1954."

Molly slowed her twirling of her spaghetti. "Do you think it was an earthquake?"

Kathleen shrugged. "I've been calling it a quake just because I don't know what else to call it." She turned to Louisa. "Did you feel that one?"

Louisa held up a finger and didn't answer immediately, swallowing first and dabbing daintily at her mouth. "I was fourteen. We were stair steps. One year apart. I was born in '40, Maisie in '41, then Ollie in '42. I remember wondering about that, because Maisie and I both felt it, but Ollie didn't. I don't think any of the younger girls did, either."

Molly frowned. "Is it an age thing? You have to be a teenager?"

Louisa shook her head. "I don't know. Perhaps. Or have started our periods?"

"Blood again," Kathleen said morosely. "Why does every important thing on this island have to do with blood?"

"If you're going to be Keeper, you'd better get over that," Molly said with a shake of her head.

Kathleen gave her a poke with her foot. "Anyway, back to 1954. When the storm came in August, who put that loss together with the quake? How did you know they were related?"

Louisa tore a piece off her bread, chewing thoughtfully. "I don't think anyone did immediately. We were all so devastated for the Whitefeather family. Or, I should say, just Mary, since she was the only one left. But when Gladys Greyeagle—she was Keeper then—went to record the deaths, she was the one who remembered the tremor. It wasn't until after that we started to believe it had been a portent, the island warning us of such a terrible loss. Maisie took it especially hard."

Kathleen pushed her spaghetti around to spread the sauce more evenly. "Why? Was my grandmother especially close to the Whitefeather family?"

"No." Louisa sighed. "It had only been a year since Mick died."

Kathleen glanced at Molly, but she looked just as confused as Kathleen was. "Mick who?"

Louisa stared at her for a moment. "You don't know Mick? Michael Ross. Your great-uncle. He was four years older than Maisie. She adored him. He was killed in Korea. That left Maisie the last of the Ross line until she bonded with Séan and took the Halloran name."

Kathleen sat back. "How did I not know this? I've been so busy studying other family lines, I haven't studied my own."

"Your father was named for him," Louisa said.

"You mentioned that Keeper, Gladys Greyeagle," Molly said. "Related to Siobhan?"

"Siobhan is her granddaughter," Louisa said. "You probably knew her mother, Serena. Siobhan looks so like her. There were no Keepers in the family after Gladys, but they're all witches."

Kathleen remembered that it wasn't so long ago, when Louisa made a similar statement, she'd been incredulous at such a suggestion, but no longer. This island had magic. It was magic. *Why shouldn't it be capable of trying to tell us things?*

⁂

A LOUD CREAKING ECHOED through the boathouse as Molly gingerly pried at a rotted board in the hull of the '55 Capri she was restoring. This and a couple of others her dad, Joe, had brought back last fall from Big Sister Island had been their winter projects. Molly's specialty was antique boats. Her younger brothers, Joey and Matty, preferred working on newer boats with bigger, more powerful motors. The boat repair work got them through when they couldn't fish.

Molly grunted, and the board gave way with a sudden crack. "Shit." She held the splintered mahogany. "So much for one piece."

Joey had shoved off before daybreak to meet Matty at Big Sister's marina. It was funny to think that her baby brother was now expecting his first baby. Brandi was due in July, and Jenny was over the moon at the thought of her first grandchild, even if it would live over on Big Sister, where Brandi worked in her family's restaurant.

"I have a feeling we'll be running up quite a fuel bill," Joe kept muttering, but only when Jenny couldn't hear him.

But when Joe wasn't around, Jenny confided her own plans to Molly. "I keep hinting to Brandi that they should be bonded and live here."

So far, Brandi seemed content with the more conventional wedding she'd had on Big Sister—where money and pomp ruled. But she offered little indications that the earthier traditions of Little Sister were appealing to her, asking questions about how lineage worked.

"I don't think she'd consider it unless they could have a house of their own here," Molly had cautioned, but she wasn't sure her mom heard.

A soft squawk announced the arrival of a gull who fluttered to a landing on his one leg.

"Good morning, Cap'n Jack," Molly said. She tossed a bit of peanut butter toast in his direction. "Saved you a little breakfast."

He snatched it up and settled with a rustle of his feathers, his head tilting as he watched her pry the remainder of the rotted board out, using a bit more force now that the board had snapped.

When she got the remnant out, she set it over top of a fresh length of mahogany to use as a template.

The hint of spring that had tempted her out onto the open water had given way to a new wave of frigid air. Winter wasn't quite ready to let go. She'd pulled out the old oil-filled heater to keep the boathouse warm enough to work in. The water lapped softly at the pilings, and the boats rose and fell gently.

She cut several new boards to the correct width and put them in the steamer so she could bend them to the proper curve for the hull.

Outside, she heard a deep horn. Cap'n Jack flapped his wings indignantly when she jumped up and rushed out of the boathouse to greet the ferry as it chugged into the marina.

She helped her dad secure the gangplank. A quick scan confirmed there weren't any passenger cars this trip, just supplies. She ran on board and threw herself at her older brother as he climbed down from the pilothouse.

"Aidan!"

He gave her a tight squeeze. "Hey, Mo. Dad."

"Where's Bobby?" Joe asked.

"He had to cover a run to Big Sister today. Just me and Fred."

Aidan cocked a thumb over his shoulder at the rotund older man maneuvering a forklift under a pallet of supplies for the market.

"They let you drive unsupervised?" Molly asked.

"Captain Aidan," Fred called over the noise of the forklift. "Thinks he's a big deal now."

"Really?" Molly gave him a punch in the arm. "That's great." She reached up to tug on the beard covering his jaw. "And what's this?"

He ran his own fingers through it. "Figured I might as well look like a seaman."

"More like a lumberjack," she teased.

He plucked her up and slung her over his shoulder as she beat on his back until he dumped her unceremoniously into the bin of paper and cardboard waiting to be recycled.

"I can still whoop you," he said over his shoulder.

Scowling, she clambered over the bin. "Brute."

He just laughed as he walked away.

As if some message had gone around, islanders showed up to help unload the ferry of its cargo: fresh supplies for all of the shops on the island, plus food Wilma and Nels had ordered for the diner. In the month since the last ferry run, the recycling bins had filled. Working together, they got everything destined for the mainland reloaded onto the ferry in just a few hours.

When they were done, Fred went to the diner for lunch while Aidan accompanied Joe and Molly home, where Jenny had a huge pot of soup waiting for them.

"Kathleen!" Molly said in surprise when she stepped into the kitchen to see Kathleen taking a pan of cornbread out of the oven.

"Had to come and see my brother-in-law." Kathleen gave her a quick kiss and then reached for Aidan. "You doing okay?"

"Yeah." He hugged her. "You?"

"Good."

Molly's heart swelled watching them. She knew she'd never fully

36

understand the bond they shared over the drowning death of Kathleen's brother more than twenty-five years ago, but it had brought healing they'd both desperately needed. For that, she was grateful. It meant she didn't have to watch her brother drink himself stupid anymore, and she didn't have to wonder if Kathleen would ever let her in.

"Where's Blossom?" Molly asked.

"Guess." Kathleen nodded toward the living room where Blossom sat next to the sofa, nosing Minnow, the orange tabby, who was sprawled on her back, pretending she wasn't interested in playing.

"Sit down, everyone," Jenny said, dishing out bowls of thick potato and broccoli soup. "Eat while it's hot."

"Saw Matty last week on the Big Sister run," Aidan said. "He sends his love. Brandi's good. They're putting together a nursery." He shook his head. "Matty a father."

"I know," Molly said, digging a spoon into her soup. "Can't believe it. Guess we're all really and truly grown up now."

"Speak for yourself," Aidan said with a grin.

"When will you be back?" Jenny asked.

"We should be able to start weekly runs now winter's broke."

"Makes it feel like spring, when the ferry starts coming weekly." Jenny gave his arm a squeeze. "Winters are long enough, but I never will get used to going so long without seeing you or Bobby."

"Speaking of growing up," Joe said, clapping his son on the shoulder, "Aidan got to pilot the ferry all by himself today. Your brother must have done a good job training him."

"Really?" Jenny asked.

Aidan couldn't hide an embarrassed smile. "Got my captain's license last month."

"Honey, that's wonderful," Jenny said proudly.

When lunch was done, Aidan pushed back from the table. "Mom, this was great. Thanks." He gave her a tight hug. "Dad, can you give me a lift back down the marina? Got to get underway."

Molly and Kathleen both said good-bye to him, and then helped Jenny clean up. She sent them off with a container of soup. Blossom galloped ahead to hop into the back of the SUV when Molly opened the door for him.

Kathleen buckled up in the passenger seat. "Aidan seems really good."

"Yeah," Molly agreed, cranking the ignition. "He does."

Kathleen took Molly's free hand. "It's so nice to see him happy."

"The whole island," Molly said. "Everyone's healthy and happy. No worries about oil or power. Everything feels... settled. Content."

Later, Molly would think back on that conversation, wondering if they somehow jinxed things.

Chapter 4

THE BELL RANG, SIGNALING the start of Meredith's free period. She bypassed the English office, heading to the library.

There were several students milling around the checkout desk. She slipped into the stacks unnoticed by any of them and made her way to the Oregon history section. Browsing the shelves, she picked out a few more books on shipwrecks and coastal history and carried them to a table.

As she read, she rubbed her forehead. This damned headache wouldn't go away.

"Back again?"

Meredith jumped at Barb's sudden appearance beside her. "Yeah."

"More research?"

"Kind of."

Barb tilted her head. "No offense, but you look like hell." She pulled out a chair across from Meredith. "What's up?"

Meredith glanced around, but there were no students nearby. "Just having some weird dreams. Not sleeping well."

"Sounds mysterious. Care to share?"

Meredith opened her mouth but then closed it when a student rounded the corner with a question. Barb held up a finger to signal Meredith to wait. She led the student to the appropriate shelves.

"Come on back here." She gathered Meredith's books and led the way around the checkout desk into her office. "Now what's so intriguing?"

"You'll think it's crazy," Meredith said.

Barb simply raised one eyebrow, and Meredith suddenly found herself spilling everything.

"Wait," Barb cut in. "Your mother is having the exact same dream?"

"It seems so. From her drawing and her description."

"So that's why you were researching shipwrecks?"

Meredith nodded. "I was hoping something would click. A ship's name or a description of how it went down, survivors, anything."

Barb drummed her fingers on her desk. "We could ask my grandmother."

Meredith frowned in bewilderment. "What's your grandmother have to do with anything?"

"She's a healer."

When Meredith continued to stare, Barb said, "You didn't know I'm Coquille?"

"No. And I thought it was pronounced *ko-keel*."

"The town is pronounced that way." Barb rolled her eyes. "French trappers. But the tribe call ourselves *ko-kwell*."

She tilted her head. "I've always wondered what tribe you are."

Meredith stared. "Me? I'm not Native."

Barb frowned. "Really?"

"What would make you think that? I mean," Meredith added quickly. "I'm not offended. In fact, I think I'm flattered. But why?"

"If you're not Native, you may think I'm crazy..." Barb hesitated. "But there's a feeling I get about people sometimes."

"What kind of feeling?"

Barb gave an embarrassed half-laugh. "My grandmother would say she's rubbed off on me, but sometimes I can kind of see something—like an aura—around people with Native blood."

Meredith's mouth hung open for a moment. "And you see this... aura thing around me?"

"Yeah. Like a shimmer in the air around you. Not all the time, but just a moment ago, when I saw you at the table. It was there."

Meredith digested this. "As far as I know, I'm just Scots and English. Why only Native people?"

"I'm not sure. Maybe because I am, too. Maybe because we've maintained a closer connection to the earth and nature than most Europeans. My grandmother says it's my power speaking to their blood memory."

"Blood memory."

"Yes. It's like genealogy, I guess, but echoes of the past, carried in someone's genes, in their blood."

Meredith grinned. "Well, I think I triggered a false alarm."

"Maybe," Barb said doubtfully. "Anyway, would you like to speak with my grandmother?"

"Um, not just yet. I'll keep researching. See what turns up."

"Okay. Hope you find what you're looking for." Barb stood to follow Meredith out of the office. "If you change your mind, let me know."

The rest of the day passed in a blur for Meredith, partly because of her headache, partly because her mind was filled with her conversation with Barb. She'd never considered that her family was anything other than what her parents said—Scots and maybe some Irish on her dad's side, and English on her mom's. How could Barb think she had any Native blood in her family?

By the time she got home, all she wanted was ibuprofen and sleep. She let Jasper out, promising him a walk later, and lay down. Almost as soon as her head hit the pillow, she began to dream.

⁂

ALL AROUND HER IN the dark movie theater, people laughed or ooohhhed or aaahhhed at the rom-com flashing across the screen. For Meredith, it only reinforced how lonely she felt. It wasn't the adorable couple in the film falling in love and having mind-blowing sex contrasted with her complete lack of same. And it wasn't Grant she was missing. She was sitting beside her closest friend, Jan, who was obviously enthralled with the male lead, so it must just be her, caught in some kind of funk.

Snap out of it, she told herself, trying to laugh along with everyone else.

But after the movie, over a beer at a brewpub near the theater, Jan set her glass down with a thunk on the wooden tabletop.

"Okay, what gives?"

"What do you mean?" Meredith asked, setting her own glass down and wiping the foam from her lip.

Jan dipped a tortilla chip in some salsa. "You've hardly said three words since we left. The whole drive to McMinnville, I talked, you grunted. So, what gives? And don't say nothing."

Meredith gave her a grudging smile. With her white-blonde hair and blue eyes, Jan was as fair as Meredith was dark. She knew Meredith inside out, and she was the one person who knew what had happened with Grant.

"Is it the jerk?" Jan guessed. "Has he tried calling?"

"No, I mean, yes."

Jan's eyebrows raised. "Come again?"

Meredith took another swig of beer. "He has tried calling, and he sabotaged me by calling my mother to arrange to meet us when I was with them."

42

"Your mother?" Jan said, lowering her voice to cover her outrage. "That is low."

"I know."

Jan's eyes narrowed. "Don't tell me you caved and forgave him."

"Oh, God no." Meredith shook her head. "It was strange. Seeing him for the first time since... well, for weeks, I felt... nothing. Isn't that sad? Five years of my life. A man I thought I could marry. And now, I don't feel anything. Not sad. Not relieved. Not angry. I'm just numb. What's wrong with me?"

Jan squeezed her hand. "Meredith, there's nothing wrong with you. I think it's a protective mechanism. Like a scab."

Meredith snorted, almost choking on her beer.

Jan grinned, reaching for another tortilla chip. "So, if you're not pining for Grant, why do you look like you haven't slept for three months?"

"Probably because I haven't slept for three months," Meredith replied drily. "At least not well."

Their server delivered a plate with a huge chicken quesadilla.

Jan waited until he left. "Go on."

"I've been having this weird dream." Meredith hesitated. "Don't think I'm crazy or anything." And she launched into a vivid description of the storm and the shipwreck. "I've been researching the wrecks along the Oregon coast, but nothing seems familiar."

"Familiar." Jan picked a few jalapeños off her slice of quesadilla and deposited them on Meredith's plate. "You think this is real?"

"I don't know." Meredith stuffed the extra jalapeños into her own slice. "My mom is having the same dream."

Jan's mouth was open for her next bite, but she lowered her fork. "Say again?"

"I saw a drawing my mom did—oh, wait till I tell you about my dad—anyway, it was a drawing of a ship caught in a storm at sea. And I knew. When I asked her about it, she's been having the same dream."

"Holy shit."

"Yeah."

"How is that even possible?"

Meredith shook her head. "Barb Tilko wants me to—"

"How does Barb know?"

"She found me researching shipwrecks in the school library. Anyway, did you know she's Coquille? I didn't. But her grandmother is a healer, and Barb offered for me to talk to her and see if she knew what it meant."

Meredith gave an embarrassed laugh, but Jan wasn't laughing.

"Are you going to?"

"A second ago, you didn't think this was real."

"A second ago, I didn't know your mom was having the same dream. This is definitely *Twilight Zone* kind of weird."

Meredith heaved a sigh of relief that Jan didn't think she was crazy.

"If you do the healer thing," Jan said, picking another jalapeño off her quesadilla, "can I come?"

By the time Meredith got home after dropping Jan off, she felt relieved. She'd told two people, and they'd both believed her.

Jasper danced around when she entered the house.

"All right."

She leashed him up, and he almost pulled her down the hill to the beach. She unclipped the leash, and he took off at a gallop. She followed, her hands in her jacket pockets, enjoying the unpredictable sunshine. Offshore, Haystack Rock rose out of the water, almost beckoning to her. She stepped closer to the surf, staying just beyond the reach of the waves as they washed ashore. She never went into the water.

Her friends had always made fun of her, from the time she was young—she was irresistibly drawn to the ocean, choosing to live next to it as an adult, but never went in. She argued that the Pacific was so cold, no one but crazy people would choose to don wetsuits—and make themselves look like seals to passing pods of orca—to swim or surf.

But it was deeper than that. The ocean whispered to her, she could almost hear it calling her name in the sighs of the wind, in the rhythm of the waves. And she was afraid.

Squatting down, she dipped her hand into the water. Almost instantly, she felt the icy spray of huge waves, so dense it was blinding, salt stinging her eyes amid the utter chaos on deck, deafening roars from the storm drowning out all sound except the splintering of the wooden ship. With a gasp, she fell back onto her butt in the sand.

She scrambled to her feet and whistled for Jasper, who came galumphing back, dragging a long stick of driftwood, a prize he'd found. When he dropped it at her feet, she bent to look at it. It looked like a board, not a branch or other part of a tree. A board. From a boat?

"Let's go."

She clipped his leash on and hurried back home. The mail had come, and the box was stuffed, one cardboard box along with several bills. Inside, she dried Jasper and put the kettle on while she changed into dry clothes.

Settled on the couch a few minutes later with a steaming cup of Constant Comment tea, she turned her attention to the box. It was from her mother. Inside was a note.

Meredith,

I thought it would be fun for all of us to do one of these DNA kits. I ordered one for each of us, and sent one to your Uncle Art, too. Follow the instructions, and send yours in. We should have the results by your birthday. I want to start putting together a family tree. Plan on spending the whole weekend here!

Love,

Mom

Meredith smiled. Her mom always insisted on making a big deal of her birthday. May 1st, a Mayday child. Her birthday would be on a Friday this year. She still had two personal days she hadn't used this school year. She picked up the DNA kit. This might be fun.

Chapter 5

THE SUN WASN'T FULLY up, but Molly kissed Kathleen's cheek, shaking her awake in the pre-dawn gloom.

"Wake up. Time to get ready."

"Ready for what?" Kathleen managed to say through a yawn.

"Big Sister, remember? We're going to visit Brandi."

Kathleen groaned and turned over.

"Mom's been waiting all winter to get over there," Molly said, tossing back the covers. "Get going. You shower and I'll make the coffee." She gave Kathleen a light swat on the butt.

Blossom raced her down the stairs. She let him out. With a smile she heard footsteps stomp across the floor upstairs. A moment later, water gurgled through the pipes as Kathleen got the shower running. Molly scooped coffee into the maker, tossing in an extra scoop to make it strong enough to brace Kathleen for the cold boat ride.

Kathleen was more awake by the time they drove down to the

marina where Joe was fueling up the launch. Jenny had a picnic basket packed with what Molly hoped were muffins and cookies.

She stowed the basket and helped steady the boat for Kathleen while Blossom leapt in. Jenny kissed Joe and stepped down into the boat.

"Give Brandi my best," he said, untying the mooring line from the cleat and giving the launch a little shove as Molly slid the throttle forward.

Blossom jumped up to plant his paws on the dashboard.

"Good to have a co-pilot," she said with a grin, giving him a rub. Over her shoulder, she said, "Bundle up."

Behind her, Kathleen and Jenny settled into their seats with hats and scarves snugged tight, the basket between them. Blossom curled up on a blanket. As they chugged slowly between the buoys and out of the marina, Kathleen handed her a blueberry muffin and a travel cup of coffee to hold between her knees.

Overhead, the sky had lightened further, but a cloud layer obscured the sun. Once in open water, Molly pushed the throttle and let the boat settle into a rhythm, bouncing gently over the swells.

Behind her, she caught snatches of conversation as her mom and Kathleen talked. From the bits she heard, Kathleen was telling Jenny about what she'd learned regarding her own family tree, about the great-uncle who'd been killed in the war.

Molly sipped her coffee, trying to remember the last time she'd been off Little Sister. It must have been last fall. After she and Kathleen had bonded, they'd taken a trip to the mainland. It was a kind of honeymoon, but mostly turned into a shopping trip for some new furniture for the cottage and some new computer stuff for Kathleen's work.

It was almost hard now to remember when she'd felt she was being ripped in two. At eighteen, she'd left for college, certain she'd never live on Little Sister again, but after a few years, the island called to her, pulling on her heart. Even after she'd returned, giving up thoughts of grad school and a career on the mainland, after she'd finally come to terms with living on Little Sister as the part-time sheriff and handywoman, it had been lonely. Part of her had chafed and fought it. Not even the comfort of having Siobhan as a lover for a time was enough. She'd been hit with powerful bouts of restlessness. Her rowing kind of saved her, let her feel as if she were escaping, but the island was always there to welcome her back.

She smiled into her coffee. Funny how love had changed all that. Kathleen, the woman she'd resented, the one she'd been certain wouldn't stay. Molly now couldn't imagine her life without Kathleen and Blossom and the little family they'd created.

The clouds were breaking up by the time they neared Big Sister, its beach diminished by the mansions looming over it. She shook her head at the waste. A few rich people getting to own and control the entire island. She whispered a prayer of gratitude to her ancestors for having the foresight and wisdom to prevent that from happening on Little Sister.

She guided the launch into a slip at the marina and jumped out to tie up. She offered a hand to her mom and then Kathleen, who clipped a leash to Blossom's collar.

"What time's his vet appointment?" Molly asked.

"Not until ten-thirty," Kathleen said. "We have time to do a little shopping, and I need to go to the bank."

"We'll meet you at The Lobster Pot at noon," Molly said to her mother.

"Don't be late," Jenny called after them.

Kathleen replenished her cash supply at the bank, and then purchased some art supplies at a shop that doubled as a gallery. By then, it was nearing the time for Blossom's appointment.

"I've got a few errands I need to run," Molly said. "I'll meet you at the restaurant."

"You didn't say anything about errands," Kathleen said suspiciously.

Molly grinned and kissed her before jogging away. Once she was certain Kathleen had veered off the main street toward the vet's office, she made her way to a jeweler. She knew from Matty that this was where he'd gone to have Brandi's engagement locket made as well as both wedding rings. She tugged a folded piece of paper from her pocket.

The bonding ceremony meant more to her and Kathleen than marriage. The connection, not just to each other, but to the island—by ancestry, by the letting of blood, by the ceremony itself—it went deep. But she wanted an outward sign of their bond. Kathleen had never mentioned wanting a ring, but Molly had an idea.

When Molly got to the restaurant, Kathleen and Blossom were already there. Kathleen eyed Molly questioningly, but Molly pretended to ignore her in the flurry of greetings with Brandi, who was as pretty as ever, just beginning to show. Her joy was palpable, as was Jenny's. Molly knew her mom had been wanting grandkids more than anything. It wasn't going to happen with Aidan from the look of things, and she doubted if Joey would ever move out on his own, with or without a wife. And she—her mind ran into a brick wall at the thought.

"Are you all right?" Brandi asked.

"Yeah, fine," Molly said. "Just hungry."

"I've got a table reserved for us in the back."

The food, as always, was wonderful. Brandi had made the chowder herself, her family's recipe. She served a smorgasbord of broiled swordfish, lobster rolls, and crab cakes. After lunch, she showed them the nursery, painted a pretty pale green.

"That was my bassinet," she said.

"And you don't know if it's a boy or girl?" Kathleen asked.

"No." Brandi rubbed her stomach. "We want to be surprised. All we're asking for is healthy."

"Well, you'll probably have more knitted and crocheted baby blankets and hats and sweaters than this baby will ever use," Jenny said. "I think every family on the island is making something."

Brandi beamed. "That makes them all special. And Matty has already bought an antique crib he wants to refinish."

Molly shook her head. "Matty, a dad. It's kind of like watching Peter Pan finally grow up."

⬚⬚⬚⬚⬚⬚⬚⬚⬚⬚

THE SUN WAS GENTLE on her back as Louisa bent over her freshly tilled garden. Tim Shannahan had come by with his rototiller last week to turn the earth for her.

"It's no problem, Miss Louisa," he'd insisted over her protests. "I've been tilling my garden for the market anyhow. Wait until you see how much fresh produce we have this year, between the garden and the greenhouse."

"Thank goodness for these people," she said now to Olivia and Daddy, both of them sitting in the grass while she planted seed potatoes, gently patting the soil over top of them. "I'll have to remember to bring them something."

The next section held the carrots she'd planted a couple of weeks ago, tender green shoots already poking through to drink up the sunshine. Soon, the peas and turnips would do the same. She had her tomato cages all ready, and poles with string for the beans down the end of the garden.

"You're planting those potatoes too deep."

"Ollie," Louisa said, "you never liked planting or digging potatoes. Don't tell me how deep to plant them."

"That's because I had to do them myself all those years you were away."

Louisa stood up, stretching her back. "It wasn't so many years. Just the years I was at college."

"Four years without you here felt like forever."

Louisa heard the slight note of accusation.

51

The island teacher back then, Mrs. Stickley, had had her hands full with the younger children. She often gave Louisa charge of the teenagers, trusting her to tutor them and set their assignments. Maisie and the others didn't mind so much, but Ollie had hated it. Of course, Maisie was already sweet on Séan Halloran by then. They all knew they'd get bonded, but for Louisa, the thought of bonding and never leaving Little Sister had chafed her almost raw. Mrs. Stickley had already been planning that Louisa would become the island's next teacher, but Louisa had different ideas.

Louisa adjusted her floppy straw hat and bent over the potatoes again.

"I didn't think you were going to come back," Olivia prodded.

Shuffling along the row, Louisa admitted, "I almost didn't."

"Was it so bad here, sister?"

"Not bad," Louisa said. Sudden tears blurred her vision, and she had to straighten again to wipe her eyes and dab at her nose. "I just wanted more."

"More than family? More than home?"

Louisa plucked up both boxes and carried them inside. She set them in a window warmed by the sun and went to pour herself a glass of lemonade. When she returned to the garden to finish planting her potatoes, she went alone.

<hr/>

REBECCA HAD BROUGHT EXTRA lamps into the library's back room to give them sufficient light as they bent over the old texts. Kathleen wore flip-up magnifiers over top of her glasses. Molly hadn't been able to suppress a snort of laughter the first time she'd seen her wearing them.

"Your eyes are huge! You look like an owl."

But they helped as Kathleen tried to decipher the scratchy writing, marred by time, ink blots, and strange spellings. So far, Rebecca had found one other mention of an island tremor, in October 1799, but they were searching for what it meant, "if anything," Rebecca had cautioned.

"You're right," Kathleen conceded. "We have to try and stay unbiased."

It was so easy to look at any unusual entry as "proof" the quake event had signified something.

The Keepers had been fairly diligent in making regular recordings of island events—births, deaths, the very rare instances of strangers arriving on the island—but in March of 1800, "I think this is it," Kathleen said softly.

Rebecca leaned over her shoulder as they both read the entry.

An unusually mild winter, without the cold we moste often experience. We celebrated Imbolc with great anticipation of Spring, but then the fever came, spredding wildely. It affected the First Ones the moste, with twenty-three souls lost to us.

Kathleen covered her mouth. "Twenty-three. Here's the list, names and ages."

Blossom whined and came to sit with his head on her thigh.

Rebecca bent nearer. "Four under the age of three."

Kathleen sat back. "Does the quake always signify something horrible?"

Rebecca laid a reverent hand on the list of names. "We don't have enough data yet. But we need a break."

Kathleen nodded numbly. She took her eyeglasses off and unclipped the magnifiers. Rubbing her eyes, she said, "We think life here is hard now sometimes. When storms keep the ferry from coming. When someone gets sick. But it's nothing to what they lived with."

Rebecca marked the place where Kathleen had found the entry about the fever. "I need to pray. You should meditate."

Kathleen made a face. "I know you've been trying to teach me how to empty my mind when I meditate, but as soon as I try, it just fills up with tons of little things I can't get rid of. And Siobhan has been teaching me yoga, trying to get me to do the same thing, focus on my breathing and feel the Spirit working through my body and blah, blah, blah."

Rebecca smiled. "Do whatever works for you." She gestured toward the books. "But we both carry the burden of the past. We need to let it go."

They left the library. Rebecca veered toward her house while Kathleen and Blossom headed out of the village, walking toward their cottage. She waved to a few islanders who passed on bikes or in cars. Molly, she knew, was building a new bathroom for Tim and Miranda Shannahan. When she got to the entrance to their drive, she wasn't ready to go in despite the three books waiting for her to come up with proofs of cover designs. Rebecca was right, she needed to clear her mind. The April sun felt good despite the chill of the air. She called to Blossom, who was already on the porch, and they continued up the ring road to where a trail veered into the woods.

She hiked to the bluff, high above the waves that crashed against the granite base of the island. She perched on one of the rocks, and Blossom hopped up to sit beside her. She draped an arm over his back, pulling him close.

"This was where you first let me touch you, remember?"

He nuzzled her cheek.

She gazed out at the water, almost hypnotized by the sunlight sparkling off the waves. She was no longer afraid to be on the water, not like she had been when she first came back to Little Sister. But sometimes, she couldn't help thinking about her brother, what it must have been like for Bryan, out there, beyond sight of land, when he and Aidan had dared each other to a race. Storms could blow up quickly out here, and they'd been caught by a fierce one. The times she'd been rowing with Molly, she felt like such a small speck on the ocean, but they'd only gone when it was calm. What had it been like for him when he realized he wasn't going to make it back?

Death. Loss. It was the story of this island. She hugged Blossom more tightly. *But so is love, and family, and new life.*

"You can't have one without the other."

Maybe she was actually absorbing some of the lessons Rebecca and Siobhan and Louisa and Jenny had been trying to teach her. Hell, the entire island was a constant lesson in how to live in the moment. Know that sadness will inevitably come, but take joy where it could be found. It was almost carved in the very rock the island was made of.

She closed her eyes and tried to quiet her mind, lose herself in the sounds of the ocean below, the glow of the sunshine through her eyelids, the solid certainty of the rock beneath her. It seemed voices floated on the breeze that tickled her cheeks and tugged at her hair, whispers from the past. She tried to make out what they were saying, but it was always just beyond...

Her eyes opened slowly. Blossom had shifted to lie beside her, and the sun had moved toward the southwest.

"Let's go home."

She got up stiffly, scoffing when Blossom bounded off the rock. "Show off."

They made their way home. Kathleen's heart dropped when she saw that Molly's SUV wasn't there yet. Inside, she sat down at her computer, forcing herself to get some work done, but one ear was tuned for the familiar rumble of the 4-Runner. When she heard it, she ran downstairs to throw herself into Molly's arms as soon as she got out.

"You okay?" Molly asked.

Kathleen nodded against her neck, breathing her in. She smelled of sawdust and outdoor air and, under it, that scent that was uniquely hers.

Molly tried to draw away to look into Kathleen's face, but Kathleen clung to her. "Just hold me."

"What happened?"

"I'll tell you later. For now, I need to feel you."

Molly's arms tightened. "Always."

LATER THAT NIGHT, MOLLY lay spooned in behind Kathleen, her body still tingling pleasantly from their lovemaking. She felt the rise and fall of Kathleen's ribs as she breathed. Molly took a deep breath and tried again to go to sleep, but her mind wouldn't quiet.

When Kathleen had told her what she and Rebecca had found, Molly was dumbfounded. She knew, all the islanders did, that there had been harsh winters, sickness, boating accidents, but she couldn't think of any other event that had taken so many. Kathleen had tried to reassure her that they were much healthier now than those ancestors in 1800 had been. But still.

Twenty-three dead that spring. Twenty-three bodies, having to be stored until the ground thawed enough to dig twenty-three graves. Twenty-three people whose blood most likely ran through the veins of islanders living here today, maybe even hers. For all they celebrated the First Ones and Irish ancestors who'd lived and worked and loved and died on Little Sister, it seemed they didn't really know the island's history as well as they thought. She'd never really wandered to that oldest part of the cemetery. She knew where those stones were, small and weathered.

Even though the islanders lived mostly outdoors and were active and probably pretty hardy, they were also relatively isolated. One vicious flu or virus brought here could spread like wildfire.

Just today, building that new bathroom for the Shannahans, little Ellis had decided to be her helper. A few months shy of two, he was talking non-stop and was fascinated by her tools. Miranda kept apologizing, coming back to collect him, but she was seven months pregnant with her second and wasn't moving nearly as quickly as Ellis.

"Have you..." Miranda had hesitated.

Molly had glanced up from where she was joining the drainpipe for the new tub. "What?"

"Ever since that morning, down the diner, when we all felt something." Miranda laid a hand on her stomach.

"Are you all right?" Molly had asked quickly.

"Yes, yes, I'm fine. It's just..."

"What?"

"It feels like something's about to happen." Miranda had blushed and laughed at herself. "Look at me, being all hormonal. It's nothing."

Molly had agreed, only to set Miranda's mind at ease, but she felt it, too. She caught herself sometimes, looking to the sky, wondering if a storm was catching them unawares, but everything was calm. Nothing out of the ordinary.

She rolled over and tried again to go to sleep.

Chapter 6

CHECKING HER LESSON PLANS one last time for the substitute, Meredith made sure everything was in place in her desk drawer, including a folder containing a quiz for each class. Satisfied that nothing could go wrong—*but I think that every time,* she recalled wryly—she went down the hall to Jan's Spanish classroom.

"*Hola.*"

Jan glanced up from her computer. "All set for your big weekend?"

"Yeah."

"And you still haven't peeked at the genealogy results?"

Meredith shook her head. "Promised my mom so we could all open them together. My uncle will be there, too."

"You've got more willpower than I have," Jan said.

"What's there to get all excited about?" Meredith shrugged. "I know pretty much what mine will say. The more interesting thing is we did the wider database to look for other relatives and check for medical stuff."

"Really?" Jan powered off her computer and opened her desk drawer for her purse. "I'm not sure I'd want to know if I had a cancer or Alzheimer's gene."

"I thought about that," Meredith admitted. "Seems like it could become a self-fulfilling prophecy, but Mom wanted to know."

They walked out to the parking lot where Jan gave Meredith a hug. "Happy Birthday. See you next week, and we'll go celebrate." "Deal."

Meredith got into her Forester and drove home. An hour later, changed and loaded with everything she and Jasper would need for the weekend, they headed to Portland. The worst of the rush-hour traffic was over by the time she pulled into her parents' house in Arlington Heights.

She got out of the car to see her dad in the garage, standing on a stepstool perched on top of two upturned plastic totes, trying to reach some loose wire near the ceiling.

"Hi, Dad," she said, hoping not to startle him.

"Hi, Meredith," he said, glancing under his arm in her direction.

"You focus on what you're doing," she cautioned. "We'll be inside."

She found her mom in the living room, reading the paper. "I don't know what Dad is doing, but it has Aflac written all over it."

Irene rolled her eyes. "I've told him again and again, we can hire someone to come and do things, but he insists. I just can't even look anymore."

She stood to give Meredith a hug. Jasper plopped down to stretch out on the rug, looking exhausted.

"You'd think he'd just run five miles," Meredith said. "When do Art and Kenny get here?"

"Tomorrow afternoon," Irene said. "I'm so glad you took the day so we could spend your birthday together. This will be fun."

Meredith wasn't so sure that was the word she'd use for turning thirty-six, but she forced a smile for her mother's sake.

"Has Dad given up reorganizing the house?"

Irene's pursed lips answered that question. "Let's just say, I laid down the law that certain parts of this house are off-limits to him. We've achieved a truce."

Meredith grinned. "So no divorce plans?"

"Or immediate funeral expenses." Irene shifted to face Meredith. "You haven't opened your packet, have you?"

"Scout's honor," Meredith swore, holding up her hand. "No peeking." She tilted her head. "You're really curious about this, aren't you?"

"You aren't?"

"Not really. Don't we already know what we are?"

"But there's so much more to learn!" Irene's eyes lit up. "I've been watching those genealogy shows on TV. Almost no one knows anything further back than their grandparents. I certainly don't. So instead of going back to teaching, I think this is what I'm going to do. Work on our family tree."

"Cool."

"Come and see what I've been doing." Irene grabbed Meredith by the hand and pulled her down the hall toward the bedrooms. "Hope you don't mind sharing."

Meredith's old room now held a desk set up with a computer and several old-style composition books.

"I'm going to use one book for each side of each branch of the family," Irene said. "There's so much information out there. Census records, immigration records, birth and marriage and death certificates. Newspaper clippings."

Meredith smiled at the excitement in her mother's voice. "You're really into this."

Irene's excited expression altered, became more serious. "That dream we've been sharing—you're still having it?"

Meredith nodded.

"Me, too." Irene took Meredith's hand. "It means something, honey. I know it does. Maybe this," she gestured toward the desk, "will help us figure out what."

⬭⬭⬭⬭⬭⬭⬭⬭⬭⬭⬭

MEREDITH FELT KIND OF silly, with all the fuss over a birthday at her age, but the day had been fun. She and her mom had gone shopping, then out to lunch, followed by more shopping.

"Let's hope your father doesn't burn the house down while we're gone," Irene had said ruefully as she backed out of the garage. "He's been talking about putting an addition on the house for his micro-brewery, and he thinks he can do the electrical wiring himself."

"So that's what he was talking about last night," Meredith said. "I thought he was buying into one."

Irene had given a long-suffering sigh. "If only. But let's forget about that. This is your day."

And it had been. Meredith couldn't remember the last time she and her mother had spent an entire day together, just the two of them. Irene had insisted on buying Meredith three new outfits, over Meredith's protests.

By the time they got home, Art and Kenny had arrived. Meredith gave her uncles each a tight hug. Art was a little paunchier, probably owing to Kenny's love of baking, but "happy fat" she knew he'd say with a laugh.

Kenny held her at arm's length, looking her up and down. "You never change."

"You know that's not true." But she laughed anyhow, pleased by the compliment.

For some reason, this birthday was getting to her. Not that thirty-six was old, but forty was only a few years away. This felt like some kind of tipping point, as if she needed to make something happen in her life if it was ever going to happen.

62

Everyone pitched in to make dinner. Art and Kenny squabbled over how much garlic to put in the guacamole while Irene scrambled eggs with onion and crispy strips of corn tortilla. Her dad insisted everyone had to try one of his ales, but her mother sent Art to bring in a case of Dos Equis from the extra refrigerator in the garage. Meredith bravely tried to drink her father's brew as she shredded lettuce and diced tomatoes, but she reached for a Dos Equis at the first opportunity.

Meredith could tell her mother was squirming impatiently when everyone went back for seconds, but the moment the dinner dishes were cleared away and the birthday cake had been cut, Irene said, "Okay, ancestry time, everyone!"

She retrieved the stack of envelopes containing their results, checking to make sure they were all still sealed and that no one had cheated.

"I really don't think I should have been included in this," Kenny said.

"Nonsense!" Irene waved a dismissive hand. "You've been part of this family for almost forty years."

"And what if we have children?" Art asked.

Kenny gave him a fake punch in the arm followed by a quick kiss. "I'd be the father of your children any day, sweetheart."

Meredith grinned at the familiar teasing.

"Stop stalling," Irene said, nearly bouncing in her seat. "All together. Three... two... one."

In unison, they each opened their envelopes. For a long moment, there was silence as everyone read the enclosed reports, then they all began speaking at once.

"Native American!"

"Italian and Greek? How can I—"

"This is impossible! There must be some mistake."

"Almost all Scots/Irish. Just what I expected."

"Wait," Irene commanded. She held up a hand. "One at a time. Roy, what's yours?"

He turned his color-coded chart around for the others to see. "I'm about seventy-five percent Scots/Irish. With some other European genes thrown in. No surprise there. What's this about Native American?"

"In a minute," Irene said, holding up a finger. "Art, what about you?"

Art looked utterly bewildered. "This says I'm Italian and Greek, with some Ashkenazi Jew. How can that be?"

He and Irene stared at each other.

"Mom?" Meredith prompted. "What does yours say?" Her own heart was pounding, looking at her results.

Irene frowned at her paper. "This says I'm almost thirty percent Native American. And Irish and German." She raised her eyes to her brother. "How?"

Kenny reached for her paper and held it next to Art's. "If this is accurate, you two aren't related at all."

"That's impossible." Irene shook her head. "I'll call them. There must be some mix-up. We got someone else's results."

Kenny held up his paper. "Mine is what I expected. Scandinavian with a smidge of other European thrown in." He glanced in Meredith's direction. "How about yours?"

"Mine is a mix of Mom's and Dad's. Native American, Irish, Scots, German, some other European." She looked at her mom. "Where did Native American come from?"

She was reminded suddenly of her conversation with Barb.

Art must have noticed. "What?"

"It's just... I recently had a co-worker assume I'm part Native. She is, and she said she gets this... kind of sense about other people with Native blood."

"Like gaydar." Kenny nodded. "Only Naydar."

"Yeah, but I laughed at the time, figured her Naydar was way off."

"Maybe not," he said. Looking worriedly at Art, he laid a hand on his arm. "You okay?"

Art's eyes glistened. "I don't understand."

"From what little I know," Meredith said, "these tests aren't always accurate."

"We're not talking about the chance of inheriting baldness from grandma's side of the family," he snapped. "I'm sorry, Meredith." His jaw worked. "If this is even remotely accurate," he turned to Irene, "you're not my sister. We know nothing about our family."

"Now, wait just a minute, everyone."

Roy's tone startled them into attention.

"First of all, we don't have enough data to jump to these kind of conclusions," he said firmly, and Meredith suddenly appreciated his logical mind. "We need information from the company that we can't get right away. Second, what's the worst possible scenario, even if this data is accurate?"

The others all looked at one another in bewilderment.

"It's entirely probable that one or both of you were adopted," he said.

Art's mouth fell open in a perfect O. Meredith fought the sudden urge to giggle.

"That's not—" Irene began.

"Honey," Roy cut in. "Don't say it isn't possible. Right now, anything is possible. As for you two not being sister and brother, since when has this family been determined by traditional norms? Even if you're not related biologically, you were raised together as siblings. You'll always be family. You know better than that."

His scolding had the desired effect. Art looked chastised.

"I'm sorry, Reney," he said, stretching a hand out to Irene.

She took it. "We'll figure it out, Art. I promise."

THEY MADE IT AN early night to stop everyone rehashing what the genealogy results could mean. Meredith lay in her old room, a couple of socks placed over the blue lights of her mother's computer equipment to give her some welcome darkness for her thoughts. Those reports had shaken them all.

We're exactly the same people we were. One minute, we were certain about who we were, individually and as a family. The next, nothing seems certain. I wish we'd never done the damn things.

When at last she drifted into sleep, it was restless, barely skimming beneath the surface of wakefulness. She felt more awake than asleep as she began to dream—but not the shipwreck dream.

In this dream, people were gathered on land, standing in an intimate circle around a bonfire. Overhead, a half-moon floated in the sky. She listened hard, trying to make out what they were singing. And then she realized there was the sound of ocean waves in the background. The people were on a beach, and the singing sounded... Irish. Like the kind of songs she'd heard on travel shows about Irish pubs, but not rowdy. These were heart-wrenching songs of longing, of sadness, of loss.

On the other side of the fire, one man raised his eyes and seemed to see her. His gaze burned into hers, dark eyes in a strong face edged by a dark beard. For long heartbeats, they stared at each other until the people shifted position, dancing in a circle around the fire.

Then the eye contact was broken, and the dream began to fade, leaving Meredith with an ache in her heart that seemed to reach into her very core. When she turned onto her side, her tears soaked into her pillow.

Chapter 7

EVEN THOUGH SHE KNEW what to expect by now, Molly woke with a groan, her hands gripping her pounding head. For once, Kathleen was up before she was, already showered, though she didn't look as if she felt much better. Blossom followed Kathleen into the bedroom.

"Why do we do that to ourselves?" she asked, sitting beside Molly on the bed.

"Tradition," Molly groaned. "Bealtaine's one of our favorite festivals. You know, fertility and all that." She grinned through her headache, the memory of their wild lovemaking sending shivers of pleasure running down her body.

Kathleen smiled at her, running her fingers through Molly's black hair. "Well, we got that part right. Maybe I'm pregnant."

Molly snorted. "If you are, we're going down in the annals of medicine."

Kathleen leaned down and kissed her. "You ready for breakfast?"

Molly groaned again. "A small one. And then I need Miss Louisa and Olivia—" She stopped short.

"I know," Kathleen said. "I'll never get used to thinking of one without the other."

"I think this past Christmas was hard for her."

"First anniversaries always are," Kathleen said softly. "So are connections. My birthday will always be linked to Bryan's death. And Christmas to Olivia's."

Molly opened her mouth to protest, but it was true. "Did you notice..." She hesitated. "Last night. She came to the beach alone."

Kathleen nodded. "No boxes. I wonder if they're awkward to carry everywhere."

"She's been different," Molly said, taking Kathleen's hand to intertwine their fingers. "When I've been by to check on the house, sometimes I've heard her talking. Before she realizes I'm there."

"To herself? I do that all the time." Kathleen grinned. "Good thing there's no one to hear me except Blossom. And he won't tell."

At the sound of his name, Blossom hopped up to nose them both.

Molly scratched his ears. "Sounds like she thinks she's talking to Olivia."

"Oh." Kathleen frowned. "She must be so lonely. We should go by more often. We all should. I don't want her—"

Molly knew it still hurt Kathleen to think of all the years her own grandmother was alone, when none of the family had returned to Little Sister after Bryan's death.

"Miss Louisa isn't alone," she insisted. "Let me shower, and we'll go see her."

A half-hour later, her head somewhat cleared by a hot shower and a cup of strong coffee, Molly drove them to the Woodhouse place.

"I want to check her oil tank and furnace while we're there. Still likely to have some cold nights before things really warm up."

They found Louisa, wearing old Wellies with her flowered dress and a wool jacket to ward off the morning chill, watering the pansies in her window boxes. "Good morning, girls. I figured I'd be seeing you."

Molly winced when Kathleen slammed her door. "How many others have been by?"

"Oh, a fair few. Always got a bit of a head the morning after, don't we?"

She toed off her boots on the porch and slid her feet into fuzzy slippers to lead the way inside to the kitchen where a pot simmered on the stove. Molly noticed the two wooden boxes sitting on kitchen chairs when she pulled a seat out for Kathleen.

Louisa ladled some light green liquid from the pot into two mugs. "Here. This will fix you right up."

Kathleen closed her eyes and sighed as the liquid slid down her throat. "Oh, that's so much better. I don't know how you do it. Why does *poitín* affect us that way? Other liquor doesn't."

"Don't forget the pipe," Molly said.

"It's not just the *poitín* or the pot," Louisa said. "It's the magic."

Molly hid a smile when Kathleen opened her eyes and fixed Louisa with a dubious frown.

"Magic?"

"Now, Katie," Louisa said, adopting her best teacher tone, "you've lived on Little Sister long enough to know that things happen here that can't be explained. The First Ones always accepted the presence of the spirit world, blending with ours. And the Irish who stayed here after the shipwreck brought their beliefs in *Tír na nÓg*. All of our festivals are blends of pagan, First Ones, and Christian." She shrugged. "The *poitín* and the pipe open us to those things that can't be seen. There's a little price to pay for that gift."

"Doesn't feel like much of a gift," Kathleen grumbled.

"Didn't it let you see Maisie and Bryan your first Samhain back here?" Louisa reminded her.

"Yeah," Kathleen said, staring into her mug.

"It was so nice to have Aidan join us for Bealtaine," Louisa said. "I didn't expect him."

"Me, either," Molly said. "He got permission to overnight here and go back today. I didn't really get a chance to talk to him. Has he already been by for some of this?" She raised her mug.

"He came by to see me earlier," Louisa said. "But he didn't need any of the cure. He didn't drink last night. Or smoke. He's really turned his life around, thanks to Katie."

"I didn't do anything," Kathleen protested.

"Yeah, you did." Molly gave her shoulder a squeeze. "I want to check your oil tank real quick while I'm here, Miss Louisa. Be right back."

She went out to the SUV and retrieved her wooden pole from the cargo hold. When she inserted it into the oil tank on the side of the house, it measured less than thirty gallons.

"You're low, but you don't need a fill-up," she said when Kathleen and Louisa stepped onto the porch. "I'll bring you a few gallons later today."

"Oh, but..." Louisa twisted her hands together.

"Don't worry," Molly said, anticipating her reaction. "A few gallons won't be missed, but if your furnace goes dry, it's more work to get it fired up again."

"Thank you for your morning-after brew," Kathleen said. "We'll see you soon, Miss Louisa."

As Molly pulled away, Kathleen asked, "How much does she really need?"

Molly smiled. "Fifty, maybe seventy-five. That should get her through the coldest nights we'll still have. I'll talk to Dad."

She pulled into their drive. "I'll be working on the Capri all day today."

Kathleen leaned over for a kiss. "See you tonight."

70

Molly hurried down to the marina, hoping to catch Aidan before he shoved off. But as she turned the Toyota off and jumped out, the ferry was chugging away. She doubted Aidan was looking back in her direction, but she waved anyhow. Sometimes she missed having her big brother around more.

⁂

LOUISA SET THE TWO boxes side-by-side on the piano bench and moved through the parlor, dusting all the framed paintings on the walls, wiping down bookshelves, rearranging framed photos scattered across the tops of tables and mantel and piano.

She picked up one photo off the piano, wiping the glass tenderly, smiling at the three young faces that smiled back at her. She, Ollie, and Maisie—summer 1958, she recalled. Down on Little Sister's beach, after a chilly dip. They'd wrapped themselves in blankets and sat to soak up some of the sun. The summer before she'd left for college on the mainland.

"We were so young," she murmured.

"The last summer we were really together," Ollie said.

"I came home for holidays and summers after that," Louisa said.

"Not all of them."

There was no mistaking the accusatory note in Olivia's voice.

"I had to focus on my studies," Louisa said defensively. "So I could come back to teach."

For long seconds there was no reply, then, "You weren't going to come back. You told Maisie so. But you didn't tell me. You told her you wanted to go to a city like Boston or New York."

Louisa shrugged. "I was naïve and gullible. Saying it and doing it were two different things. I figured that out eventually."

"You only came back because Mama got sick."

Louisa frowned. "Well, I had to come back for that, to help you and Daddy take care of her. And then Little Sister needed a teacher."

71

"You weren't the same then, sister."

Louisa placed the photo back on the piano, moving on to plump the cushions and pillows on the sofa and armchairs.

"What happened when you were away, Lou?"

Louisa snatched up the two wooden boxes and placed them on the windowsill. "I think you'd both enjoy some time in the sun. I have to go down the market."

She quickly grabbed her purse and car keys and slammed the door behind her. Standing for a moment on the porch, she took a couple of deep breaths before going to the car. She had to turn the key three times before the engine started.

"Might have to get Molly to give you a tune-up," she said, giving the old Ford's dashboard a pat.

She drove down the winding island road into the village and pulled into a parking spot at the market.

"Hi, Miss Louisa!" Miranda said. She waddled from behind the counter, chasing Ellis who ran unsteadily in Louisa's direction.

Louisa bent to pick him up. "Hello, little man."

She handed him back to his mother, where he squirmed to get down. Miranda bounced him on her hip.

"Need anything special today?"

"Just a few groceries." Louisa reached for a cart.

"Holler if you need help."

Louisa chuckled. "If I need help, I think I'll be hollering for Tim."

Miranda grinned down at herself. "You're probably right."

Louisa pushed her cart through the market's aisles, picking up odds and ends: a new bottle of lamp oil, oatmeal, a few cans of navy beans for soup. In the produce section—nicely stocked with fresh vegetables from Tim and Miranda's solar-powered greenhouse—she was choosing some leaf lettuce when she heard, "Hello, Miss Louisa."

She turned around. "Rebecca. Hello. How are you?"

"Fine. I've been wanting to speak with you."

Louisa placed her lettuce in her cart. "What about?"

"A summer program at the library." Rebecca leaned over the bin of green beans, stuffing a couple of handfuls into a brown paper bag. "A librarian friend of mine is sending me a few boxes of children's books. I thought we might do a reading group this summer once the kids are back onisland. Just two mornings a week. I could use some help, especially with the younger ones who might need tutoring to get their reading up to speed. Would you be interested in helping out?"

Louisa's face lit up. "Reading? I'd love to."

Rebecca nodded. "Thank you. I'd value your experience." She peered into Louisa's cart. "All alone today?"

"Daddy and Ollie are enjoying a sunny window back home."

"Is everything else all right?"

Louisa blinked, suddenly very interested in the carrots. "Everything is fine."

Rebecca didn't say anything for several seconds. Louisa wished she would go away.

"Well, the books should be here on the next ferry," Rebecca said at last. "With the children home in less than a month, we should do some planning. Come by the library whenever you've an hour or two."

"Sure I'll do that."

Louisa breathed a sigh of relief when Rebecca finally moved on to another aisle.

"I can go places by myself," she muttered under her breath.

"What was that, Miss Louisa?" Miranda asked from behind the counter.

"Nothing."

A DELIGHTFULLY WARM BREEZE drifted through the open window, fluttering the edges of the pages. Under the table, Blossom snored softly. Kathleen laid a hand on the book to keep the page from moving as she traced a finger along the lines of a family tree. The Woodhouses were connected, over the past generations, to four other island families.

"What a history they had," she said. "And now, all of this will come to an end."

"Yes, it will." Rebecca held out a nibbed pen and a bottle of ink. "We should have recorded Miss Olivia's death long before now. You do it."

"Me?"

"If you're to be the next Keeper, you'll have to be doing all of this some day."

Kathleen took the pen and dipped it in the ink, but chose to practice first on a scrap of paper. This proved to be a good idea, as a large inkblot immediately bled into the paper.

"Why aren't we using a modern pen?" she mumbled, trying again to write legibly.

"For the same reason we demand a drop of blood when we do the Passing," Rebecca said wryly. "It's been done this way since the first shipwreck survivors began keeping records. And we're charged with continuing the tradition."

At last, Kathleen was able to get an even flow of ink from pen to page. She pulled the book near. Under the entry: *Olivia Flannery Woodhouse, b. 13th September 1942,* she added, *d. 26th December 2018.*

The only line remaining was Louisa's. *Louisa Flannery Woodhouse, b. 25th May 1940.* Only one entry left to be made someday.

"This reminds me, are you going to be at Miss Louisa's birthday dinner?"

"Yes," Rebecca said. "Told Jenny I'd come over early and help her get things together." She tapped the book. "We need to add Miss Olivia's biography to their family book. I'd like you to do it."

"Really?"

"We know most of her story, but it would be a good idea for you to talk to Louisa. Find out as much as you can and compose a fitting summary of her life."

It felt like a huge responsibility, to sum up a person's life in a few paragraphs, but it was one of the things Kathleen loved about studying these books. She felt she was gradually getting to know the islanders, past and present, more intimately than she'd ever known anyone before she came back to Little Sister.

"Rebecca," Kathleen said as a thought occurred. "When I first started studying the books, when I realized that Molly and I are, like, seventh cousins or whatever, you told me part of the Keeper's role is to check the lineage of islanders before they marry or bond."

"Yes."

"And you said it had happened a few times that people who fell in love were too closely related."

Rebecca's blue-green eyes crinkled in a knowing smile. "And you want to know how close is too close?"

"That and what we do about it."

Rebecca sat down across from Kathleen. "The First Ones who lived here actively sent young people to Big Sister or all the way to the mainland, and brought new people here to mate with us and live on Little Sister. They knew, in their ancient wisdom, that a closed gene pool was eventually a path to self-destruction. Our ancestors established a rule that the common ancestor between two people has to be three or more generations back, so great-grandparent or older."

Kathleen frowned. "So, what's the solution if they fall in love but the connection is more recent?"

Rebecca shrugged. "There were herbs that could act as contraceptives, but they weren't fool-proof. When surgical options came along, that simplified things. But it doesn't always end well. It hasn't happened since my parents' generation. Nathaniel Longtree fell in love with Sarah

Longtree, but they were first cousins. The island council met, but they couldn't give them permission to bond. It was a bitter fight."

"What happened?"

"Nathaniel ended up enlisting and was killed in Normandy. Sarah couldn't forgive the elders. She left Little Sister and never returned. From what I remember, she never married. Died alone."

"That's so sad." Kathleen stared at the page with the Woodhouse sisters' names. No mates. No children. No one after them.

"What about you and Molly?"

Kathleen jerked her head up to find Rebecca staring at her quizzically. "What about us?"

"Have you talked about children?"

"No! I mean," Kathleen searched frantically for a way to answer this. "We don't... we haven't..."

Rebecca chuckled. "Don't panic. I was just asking. It would be easy enough."

Kathleen stared at her for a moment, not sure she really wanted to pursue this line of questioning. "What would?"

"Molly has three brothers. Well, two who are available. You could—"

"Oh, my God, no!"

Rebecca shrugged. "Just a thought. The genes would match as closely as if you and Molly could have your own."

Kathleen slammed the book closed. "I have to go."

Blossom scrambled to his feet, and Rebecca's laughter followed Kathleen out of the library. Even outside, she could hear Rebecca's chortle through the window.

She stormed away, muttering to herself as she turned toward the village. She was still fuming when she got to the marina where Molly was working on the antique boat.

When she flung open the door of the boathouse, she startled a gull perched on one of the pilings. With a loud squawk, it flew away.

Molly looked up from the bench, where she was working on a board. "What's wrong?"

"Do you— Your—" Kathleen sputtered, pointing in the direction of the library.

"My...?" Molly held her hands up.

"Rebecca! Do you know what your aunt just asked me?"

Molly set her tools down. "Calm down. Come and sit with me." She took Kathleen by the hand and led the way outside.

They sat side by side on the dock, their feet dangling above the water, the sun warm on their backs.

"Now, what did she say?"

Kathleen took a deep breath. "We were updating the Woodhouse book with Miss Olivia's death date, and talking about family connections and the end of lines and..." She glanced at Molly and then fixed her gaze on a sailboat bobbing on the water. "She asked if we'd talked about children."

Blossom wriggled in between them.

Molly grinned and gave his ribs a thump. "I assume she didn't mean this kind."

"No," Kathleen said with a grudging smile.

"What did you say?"

"I said no, of course!"

"Mmmm." Molly stared down at the water lapping against the pilings.

"What does that mean?"

"Ever since... After that quake thing we all felt, and Miss Louisa said she knew what it meant, I've been thinking. About family. About going on."

Kathleen's heart thudded in her chest. "And?"

Molly shrugged. "Nothing really. I mean, looks like Matty and Brandi are going to continue our line. Can't see Joey ever settling down, or Aidan. That leaves me. Us. And you. You're the last Halloran."

Kathleen stared at her. "Do you want kids?"

"I don't know. Do you?"

"I've never... It was never even a question before. I've honestly never thought about it."

"Was that what upset you so much?"

Kathleen couldn't meet Molly's eyes. She fiddled with the tag on Blossom's collar. "Rebecca said..."

When Kathleen couldn't continue, Molly prompted, "She said what?"

"She said you have two brothers." She tried to continue, but couldn't.

Molly gave a funny kind of snort that turned into a snigger that turned into a full belly laugh. She was laughing so hard, she fell onto her back.

"What's so funny?"

"You and Joey." Molly wiped tears from her eyes.

Kathleen wasn't sure if she should be offended or not. "Aidan is more my type."

That shut Molly up. She sat upright. "You wouldn't..."

"No. But stop laughing."

Molly sobered. "If..." She reached for Kathleen's hand. "If you, I mean, if we did want a family, we could ask one of them to... and do it artificially."

Kathleen gaped at her for a long moment. "I... I don't even know what to say to that."

Blossom whined and sat up, nuzzling her cheek.

Kathleen's eyes narrowed. "Of course, it doesn't have to be me. You could get pregnant."

"Oh, hell no." Molly leaned over Blossom to kiss her. "This is all the kid we need. For now."

Chapter 8

ONE OF MEREDITH'S STUDENTS glanced up from his test paper, and she realized she was tapping her toe impatiently on the floor. She stopped, giving him a small smile, and tried to relax. She forced herself to sit quietly while the seconds ticked by, but when the students began to finish the exam and hand their papers in, she nearly snatched them from their hands. She whispered to each that she or he could leave the room quietly. By the time the last stragglers stopped erasing and changing their answers, she was ready to scream at them.

"Have a good weekend," she said instead, cramming the papers into her bag, though she doubted she'd get started grading them before the next week.

She hurried from her classroom and found Barb packing up in the library.

"All set?" Barb asked.

Meredith nodded nervously. "Jan's feeling left out. When I first told her about your offer to meet your grandmother, she asked if she could come. But that was before the ancestry thing. I can't leave my mom out of this."

"We can fill her in when we get back. I'm as curious as you are to see what Nonna will make of all this."

They walked together out to the parking lot. Barb followed Meredith home to Pacific City, where Irene and Jasper waited for them. Meredith made the introductions.

"Are you sure your grandmother won't mind us bringing Jasper along?" Meredith asked.

"Not at all," Barb assured her. "She has an old beagle who loves other dogs."

They packed the back of Barb's Tahoe with suitcases and dog supplies. Meredith insisted her mom sit up front in the passenger seat while she sat in back with Jasper, who stretched out with his head on her thigh.

"You will let us pay for all of your gas," Irene said firmly.

"Deal," Barb agreed. "But my Nonna has been reminding me for ages that I owe her a visit, so this takes care of that, too."

They took Highway 101 along the coast, heading south toward Bandon. As she drove, Barb carried on a conversation with Irene, mostly talking about the changes in education. Meredith only half paid attention, interjecting a comment every now and then, but mostly, she took in the scenery as she listened.

"We were all so shocked to get our results," Irene was saying.

That's an understatement, Meredith thought. But it was weird. Once they'd had the results, she could see things she'd never seen before. Her uncle's complexion, though dark, was more olive compared to the bronze her mom turned in summer. His profile looked nothing like Irene's, and she wondered how she'd never noticed before. Like it or not, what they'd learned had changed things.

Once the surprise had worn off, Irene had been thrilled to discover that she had Native ancestry. When Meredith had told her about Barb's offer to meet her grandmother, Irene had jumped at the opportunity.

They stopped to eat in Winchester Bay, and then drove on for a while before leaving the highway for Riverton.

It was dark by the time they pulled into the driveway of a cute Craftsman bungalow surrounded by large pine trees. Jasper leapt out of the SUV, trotting straight to a tree to lift a leg while they retrieved their luggage.

A mournful bay sounded from inside the house.

"Sally heard us." Barb chuckled. "She's getting on, but her nose and her ears are still as good as ever."

The front door opened, and a slightly built woman stepped out onto the porch. A fat beagle wriggled out of the storm door before it could close and raced down the steps to greet Jasper.

"Hi, Nonna," said Barb, climbing the stairs to give her grandmother a hug. "These are the friends I was telling you about, Meredith Turner and her mother, Irene. My grandmother, Jeanette Laborteaux."

"*Dai.* Welcome, all of you."

"Thank you so much for having us," Meredith said.

Barb's grandmother, with her short-cropped silver hair, jeans, and flannel shirt, was not the image Meredith had had of a healer.

Jeanette fixed her with bright eyes. "I'm fascinated by what Barb has told me. Come in."

The living room was furnished with comfortable-looking furniture in natural hues of blue and green and russet.

"Your home is lovely," Irene said.

"Thank you. Barb, why don't you take Irene and Meredith up to their room? I've got the kettle on. We'll have some tea to relax you before you go to bed."

An hour later, Meredith tried to settle her mind enough to sleep. In the twin bed beside her, her mom was snoring softly while Jasper added to the night sounds from his bed, where he must have been chasing a rabbit in his dreams, judging from the way his legs were twitching. As they'd been drinking their tea—a homemade brew that made Meredith wonder what was in it—Jeanette had avoided asking any probing questions.

But her eyes probed plenty.

Meredith had felt as if Jeanette could see right through her every time she glanced up to find those sharp eyes fixed on her. She almost expected to hear Jeanette's voice in her mind.

You're being ridiculous. Go to sleep.

She rolled over, certain it would be a sleepless night.

The next thing she knew, her mother was flinging open the curtains, and Meredith found herself blinded by the sunlight. She yanked the sheet over her head.

"Get up, sleepy!" Irene gave her rump a swat on her way to the bathroom.

By the time she got downstairs, the others were all gathered in the kitchen. Jeanette served up a wonderful breakfast of blueberry pancakes and strong coffee.

Meredith sighed contentedly, pushing her empty plate away. "That was really good."

"So," Jeanette said, getting up for the coffee pot. She returned to the table to refill everyone's cup. "Tell me about these dreams."

Meredith let her mom start, but interjected frequently. They described the storm, the scene in the hold, the panic of the people there as the ship began to founder. Irene had brought some of her drawings and went upstairs to collect them.

Jeanette studied them, her lips pursed. "You," she looked at Meredith, "recall having this same dream when you were a child?"

Meredith nodded. "Then I stopped having it. I'd nearly forgotten it until two Christmases ago. It started back up, and now it's nearly every night."

Jeanette turned to Irene. "What about you?"

"Mine never completely stopped, but also became more regular since that Christmas. And then, a couple of weeks ago, we found out we're Native American and—"

"You're not," Jeanette said icily.

Irene's mouth still hung open mid-sentence. Her eyes flicked to Meredith and back to Jeanette. "But our DNA results..."

Jeanette set the drawings down, a fierce look in her eyes. "Do you think our culture can be boiled down to a lab test?"

"I meant no offense," Irene said meekly.

Meredith felt a surge of anger at Jeanette's rebuke and opened her mouth to retort, but Barb laid a restraining hand on her arm.

"Don't blame them, Nonna. This is no different than how I would feel if I found out I had African blood I didn't know about."

Jeanette's expression softened. "I'm sorry. I didn't mean to insult you, a guest in my home."

"I can see Meredith's Native blood," Barb said. "I told her about what I see. And I see it with her mother as well."

Irene looked intrigued at this, but before she could ask questions, Meredith nudged her under the table to silence her. This entire visit suddenly felt fraught with the potential to cause a lot of pain and hurt feelings. She wasn't so sure this was a good idea.

"Having Native ancestors is not the same as being of our culture," Jeanette explained. "When was the last time one of you was called 'squaw' or 'Pocahontas'? What do you know of the traditions and rituals of any tribe? Do you even know what tribe you descend from?"

"No," Meredith and Irene said in unison, both looking shame-faced.

Jeanette folded her hands and said more gently, "You must understand, for us, most tribes have ancient stories of origin, of gifts given us by the spirits—the earth, the oceans, the animals. They aren't just stories, they're part of the fabric of who we are. More than genes. More than simply the blood we carry. In the days of invasion—"

"Nonna," chided Barb.

"It was so an invasion," Jeanette said. At Barb's continued stern look, she relented. "Okay, okay. In the days when Europeans came to our lands, our coasts, there were many conflicts, but ours weren't as violent as some places. Often, the whites taken in by Natives were adopted into our tribes, became part of our families, learned of our culture and rituals. They became Native in all the important ways, and blood didn't matter. With a few exceptions, the Natives who were abducted by Europeans were never accepted. They lived a half-life, never again fully Native, but never fully white, either."

"I never really thought about that," Irene admitted.

"This craze of genealogy research is a mixed blessing," Jeanette conceded. "It gives people a welcome sense of who and where they come from, I suppose. But we have always known where we come from. And no lab test will ever suddenly make someone Native."

"I think I understand," Irene said.

Meredith was still feeling apprehensive about whatever Barb thought this visit might accomplish, but Irene leaned forward.

"Can you help us understand this dream?"

"Perhaps." Jeanette got up and refilled the kettle, putting it on to heat. "No more coffee, either of you. You girls clean up, and I'll get ready."

"Ready for what?" Meredith asked, puzzled as to how any kind of healing ritual could help. "What are you going to do?"

"I'm going to hypnotize you."

Meredith and Irene both stared at her.

"What?" Jeanette looked from one to the other. "Didn't Barb tell you I'm a hypnotherapist?"

Meredith glared at Barb, feeling gullible and foolish. "She told me you were, are, a healer."

"Well, I'm that, too." Jeanette tilted her head, one eyebrow cocked. "I can wave feathers over you and bring out my peace pipe if that will make you feel better."

Meredith felt her face burn at the sarcasm. "I didn't mean—"

"Traditional medicine isn't so very far removed from the things you accept. We just work from the premise that the spirit and the body are inextricably intertwined. Where they go, the mind follows. You can't treat one without treating the others."

※※※※※※※※※

MEREDITH WAS EXHAUSTED, BUT Irene was exhilarated. "That was fascinating," she said, pacing around the living room.

Meredith rubbed her temples, where a dull headache throbbed, wondering how the herbal tea Jeanette had given them could have had such vastly different effects on her and her mother. Jasper whined and nudged her hand.

"You were much more open to my suggestions," Jeanette said. Nodding her head in Meredith's direction, she added, "But you, you were much tougher."

"Call me a skeptic," Meredith said with a droll smile, one hand scratching Jasper to reassure him she was okay.

"But you both recalled different details from your dreams," Barb said, running a finger down the notes she'd taken. "You," she glanced at Irene, "saw your rescuers approach in what sounds like a dugout log boat or canoe, but with some kind of outrigger that you had to climb over before they could pull you in."

Irene nodded. "It was heavy, thick, but definitely wood. They spoke a language I couldn't understand."

"While Meredith," Jeanette said, "recalled the name of a girl, Ida, and her brother, Thomas. It was almost as if you were watching things happen through Ida's eyes."

"I certainly felt her terror," Meredith said. "I think that's the worst part of this dream. Every time I have it, I relive the horror of that storm, her helpless feeling of being trapped down in that hold, as if I'm living it with her. I never seem to remember that she made it off the ship, that she was rescued."

"But was it real?" Irene asked.

Jeanette sat back, tapping her fingertips together. "I've used hypnosis several times to help people recall traumatic events that they've suppressed. You both recall more detail than most of those people. If I were pressed, I'd say it was real."

"But how is that even possible?" Meredith asked incredulously. "I mean, how can something like this be... transmitted or whatever to both of us?"

Barb set her notes down. "Many people believe that what some call reincarnation or past lives is just genetic memory, passed down from generation to generation. Your ancestors speaking to you."

Irene dropped heavily onto the sofa beside Meredith. "But now, it seems that connection back in time stops with me."

"What do you mean?" Jeanette asked.

"When we did the ancestry and DNA analysis," Irene explained, "we realized my brother and I aren't related genetically. Our parents are both dead. So far, we haven't found any likely explanation except that one or both of us is adopted, and our parents never told us."

Meredith took her hand. "We'll figure it out."

Barb set her pad down. "I think that's enough drama for one day. How about we drive into Bandon to eat and wander the shops?"

"That sounds great," Meredith said gratefully.

Barb drove into town, where Bandon was filled with people taking advantage of a beautiful, sunny Saturday. They settled on Foley's Irish Pub for lunch.

"This is lovely," Irene said, looking around at the bric-a-brac covering almost every surface: instruments, books, photos and paintings, flags pinned to the ceiling.

Meredith ordered an iced tea, not sure her headache would be helped by alcohol, but the others ordered Guinness or wine. They placed their food orders and sat back with their drinks.

Meredith found herself staring, frowning at a poster, an image of cliffs over a stormy sea, with something written in Gaelic. "They were Irish."

"What?" Barb said.

Meredith stared at her mom. "The people on the boat. They were Irish."

Irene's eyes widened. "You're right. Some of them were screaming and yelling in Irish, not English. Why are we just now realizing this?"

"You're still open," Jeanette said. "From our sessions this morning. Don't block it. There may be other things that will come to you."

Meredith pressed her fingers to her forehead, not sure she wanted to be any more open. It was disconcerting to be hit with sudden realizations like that. She tried to forget the dream and just enjoy her lunch. She listened to Jeanette speak of her work with various psychologists and therapists. In addition to her hypnosis, she ran a business making natural, herbal medicines.

After their meal, they wandered the Old Town area of Bandon. The shops, galleries, waterfront stands, it all acted as a balm to sweep away the remnants of the dream from Meredith's mind.

"The south jetty," Jeanette said, pointing toward a long wall of boulders and rocks helping to form a boundary wall in and out of the river's mouth, "was built from Grandmother Rock. From the beginning of time, she gave our people the stone we needed to make tools. Mostly blueschist, hard enough to carve wood before we had metal tools. She remains sacred to us, even though they disarticulated her to make their wall."

Meredith gazed in the direction of the jetty, wondering what it must be like to have such constant reminders of what used to be.

Irene wanted to go into most of the galleries, enjoying the variety of art for sale. "There are so many beautiful things here," she said, picking up a delicate blown glass sculpture.

Meredith agreed, moving on to look at an array of photos hanging on the wall. Her eye was caught by one image. Without warning, the room began to spin.

"Meredith!" Barb grabbed for her as she sagged against the wall for support. "Are you all right? What's wrong?"

"Too much psychic activity for one day," Jeanette said. "Let's go—"

"No." Meredith straightened, pointing. "That's it."

"That's what?" Barb asked in bewilderment.

But Irene had hurried over to them and was staring at the photo Meredith indicated, a sunset view of an island with a rocky hump on one side and a narrow ribbon of beach. Bending closer to peer at the photographer's penciled notation at the bottom of the matte, she read, "Little Sister Island, Maine."

Chapter 9

THE MARINA WAS QUIET by the time Molly finished a pre-dawn row, showered, and got to the boathouse. The early bustle of activity was over—the fishing boats fueled and long-gone, having to travel farther and troll deeper waters to find the fish and lobsters.

She found her dad in the office. "Joey already out?"

Joe nodded. "He and Matty have charters for the next few weeks. Halibut are running, and the big islanders pay good money to be taken out." He sat back. "The Capri is looking good."

"Thanks, but I'm going to need some help with the engine. You available in the next few days to help me tear it down?"

"Sure. I'll clear tomorrow." He stood. "I want to do some maintenance on the electric generators today."

Molly considered. She was at a point with the Capri where there was nothing more to be done until the engine was rebuilt. "I need to check the wind turbines. Hasn't been done since October."

"Not alone," Joe said sternly.

"Dad," Molly said. "I was up there a hundred times with the crew that installed them."

Truth be told, Molly was the only one who would climb the towers. She often thought if she ever took a trip out west, she'd want to try climbing an actual rock face.

"Come with me," Joe said. "We'll get both done today."

They loaded up the truck with the tools and gear needed and drove out to the Head where the wind turbines stood, helping to power the island's electric generators.

From up here, they had a wide view of the ocean, with Big Sister Island barely visible in the distance. Several boats, tiny from this height, dotted the water between the islands. The Head was always windy, one of the prime reasons this site had been chosen for the turbines. That and the solid granite bedrock here to anchor them.

While Joe shut down and locked the blades of the first turbine, Molly cinched herself into a climbing harness and scrambled up the rungs inside the turbine tower. At the top, she opened the hatch and stepped onto the deck. The wind was blowing about three times harder at this height. Clipped to the safety rail, she had a dizzying vantage point as she checked the blades, lubed the gearbox, tested the warning lights. She had to keep a wide stance to resist the constant buffeting of the wind. All appeared to be in good working order. She finished her maintenance and stood, gazing west toward the mainland, way beyond her visible horizon, even at this height.

Her walkie-talkie buzzed.

"All right up there?" Joe asked from the ground, one hand shielding his eyes from the sun.

Molly leaned over the side and gave a thumbs up. She raised the walkie-talkie to her mouth and pressed the button. "All good. Coming down."

Bending over to unclip the carabiner from the safety rail, she was hit by a sudden gust of wind that knocked all of her weight to one foot.

She fumbled to snap the carabiner back onto the rail as she fought to regain her balance. For one awful moment, she was staring over the edge of the tower's deck at a hundred sixty feet of empty air down to the rock below. Time slowed to a crawl. Another blast of wind toppled her just as the carabiner's latch slid over the rail and clicked into position. In slow motion, she went over the side, seeming to fall forever before the nylon safety strap went taut, stopping her descent with a snap of her spine that drove the breath from her lungs. Hanging horizontally, she spun uncontrollably and couldn't draw a breath.

The wind buffeted her about like a kite. She fought not to pass out, reaching for the strap, trying to pull herself upright and stop the rush of blood to her head. Finally, she was able to claw herself into a position where she was sitting in her harness, still swinging with each fresh gust of wind that banged her into the side of the tower. She closed her eyes and pressed her forehead against her hands, tightly clenched around the nylon. She prayed it wouldn't give.

Time resumed its normal pace, and she opened her eyes when she could finally breathe. "How the hell am I going to get back up top?"

"Mo!"

Her dad's face appeared over the edge of the deck. Hand over hand, he hauled her up until she could grab the rail and help pull herself to safety. His arms wrapped around her, and she clung to him, both of them kneeling on the deck, her body only now beginning to shake uncontrollably.

"I've got you," he whispered over and over.

"I'm okay." She took several deep breaths. "I'm okay."

She crawled on her hands and knees to the hatch, only unclipping from the safety rail when her feet were securely planted on the rungs of the ladder inside the tower. Joe climbed down after her, pausing to pull the hatch door into position and secure it.

At the bottom, Molly stepped outside the confines of the tower and let herself fall to the ground, her heart still beating a mile a minute as she lay staring up at the sky and the huge stationary rotors. Joe dropped to sit beside her.

"Three more to go," she reminded him.

"Not today," he panted. "Let's not tell your mother about this."

"Or Kathleen."

"Deal."

He offered a fist. She raised hers to bump it.

⁂

WEARING AN OLD PAIR of Olivia's dungarees tucked into her Wellies, her straw hat on her head, Louisa pushed the mower through the grass. No gasoline or electric. Just her own energy to keep the metal blades whirring. It didn't do the neatest job. Odd blades of grass got smushed down instead of being cut, and, once the danger was past, they sprung up, bravely waving in the sun again.

Kind of like me, she thought, pausing to look at the section she'd just mowed.

"Who ever smushed you down?"

Louisa closed her eyes for a moment. "Can't I have a private conversation in my own head anymore?"

"You didn't answer."

"It was nothing." Louisa resumed her mowing.

"Wasn't."

"Was."

"Did I smush you?"

Louisa didn't respond.

"Did I, sister?"

"You are so dadblamed stubborn, Ollie." Louisa paused the mower again. "Sometimes."

"Well, you're no bigger than a gnat. Probably couldn't help it." A throaty chuckle, so familiar, so dear, so missed.

"You and Daddy and..." Louisa stopped.

"And? Go on. Say what you're thinking."

Louisa left the mower sitting in the shade of the big oak in the yard and went to the porch, where the boxes sat in the sunshine. She sipped from a glass of lemonade she'd left there.

"I just wanted things..."

"What kind of things? Clothes? Books?"

"Not things," Louisa said impatiently. "Things out of life. For my life. I'm eighty years old now, but there are things that never happened. Never will."

"Thought you were happy here."

Louisa couldn't miss the hurt tone, the one that always twisted her heart when she and Ollie argued. "I was, mostly. I learned to be."

"But not completely?"

"Never completely." Louisa stared at the ice cubes bobbing in the glass. "Don't know why I'm thinking about this so much now, wondering..."

"Wondering what?"

Louisa drained her glass. "I've got to finish the yard so I can start working on Katie's birthday present."

No voices followed as she went back to the mower.

⬚⬚⬚⬚⬚⬚⬚⬚⬚

MOLLY COULDN'T STOP A groan from escaping when she tried to sit up on the edge of the bed.

"Your back still bothering you?" Kathleen asked, rolling over to slip a warm hand under Molly's shirt and rub the spasmed muscles.

"Yeah." Molly might have hidden how it happened, but there was no disguising the back pain. She hadn't been able to row or do much of anything the last couple of days.

"You shouldn't have tried lifting that radiator by yourself," Kathleen said.

"What?" Molly's mind fumbled for a minute before she remembered the story she'd made up. "Oh, yeah. That cast iron was heavier than I thought. Next time, I'll make sure I have help."

She pushed to her feet, hunched slightly.

"Why don't you stay in bed?"

Molly shook her head. "Hot shower will help. Besides, ferry comes today. I want to see Aidan."

"Okay. I'll have coffee ready. Call if you need me to put your socks on for you."

"Very funny."

But when Molly got to the bathroom and bent over to take her sleeping pants and underwear off, it didn't seem so much of a joke. She let the hot water beat on her back longer than usual and felt more limber as she dried off.

"You're standing straight," Kathleen said when Molly entered the kitchen. "Well, straighter. Still got a little hitch in your gitalong."

Molly nodded, lowering herself gingerly into a chair.

Kathleen set a mug in front of her. "Cereal?"

"That'd be great, thanks."

Blossom came over to lay his head on her thigh, his brown eyes concerned. She patted him.

"I'm okay."

He went back to his kibble while his humans ate.

"What do you have going on today?" Molly asked.

"I've got to finish that book cover I've been working on." Kathleen spooned up some bran flakes. "The publisher and author finally agreed on a font, so I can put everything together and get this sent off."

She eyed Molly. "You're not going to work on the boat today, are you?"

"No." Molly shook her head. "There's no way I could bend over the engine feeling like this. I'll take it easy."

"Good."

Kathleen cleared the dishes and washed them quickly. "I'll see you later." She gave Molly a kiss and went upstairs to her office.

Molly filled a travel cup with coffee and made her slow, careful way out to the Toyota. She passed only a couple of other vehicles on her way into town. She figured that would change this week. Though the ferry had begun its weekly schedule after Bealtaine, so far, there'd been no tourists. After Memorial Day, with the ferry running daily, they'd have lots more, but never as many as Big Sister. Most folks didn't want to travel the extra hour or two to get here, and didn't want to be bound to just one ferry a day. Big Sister had them coming and going four or five times a day during the high season. Day trippers, just out for a few hours on the island, then back to the mainland.

Here, folks had to stay the entire week until the ferry runs changed. It was kind of nice, getting repeat families who loved visiting Little Sister and came back year after year. Molly, as sheriff, often had to ride herd on rowdy tourists during the summer—yahoos who thought they could go boating while inebriated or wanted to speed around the island. But their regulars came back precisely because they enjoyed this island's slower pace. Wilma and Nels treated them like family at the hotel.

Every now and again, someone asked about buying a house here. The islanders all knew to give the simple answer that there weren't any houses for sale. It wasn't necessary to go into the real reason—that no one owned houses or land on Little Sister. It was a concept most people who weren't from Little Sister just couldn't comprehend.

She parked and let herself into her tiny sheriff's office on the village's main street. A small whimper escaped as she slowly lowered herself into her desk chair. She'd put off some of the paperwork she was supposed to produce—mostly safety reports detailing any homicides, car accidents, fires—all of which were non-existent, thank the goddess.

Even though there was nothing to report, she was several months behind on this stuff. She was so rarely in this office, between the scarcity of sheriffing work and the fact that she was much busier with her fixit jobs, that no one ever looked for her here. So she about jumped out of her skin when the door opened and Jenny stepped inside.

"Mom." Molly sat back with her hand over her pounding heart. "You scared me."

"Good," Jenny said, her mouth quirking into a grin. "I like to think I can keep my kids on their toes."

She opened the door wide. "It's too nice a morning to be sitting in this stuffy office."

"Just waiting for the ferry. I want to see Aidan."

"Me, too." Jenny took the seat opposite the desk. "I miss having a house full of noise and people."

It was Molly's turn to grin. "Thought you couldn't wait to get rid of us."

Jenny shrugged. "Seemed like a good idea when I couldn't keep you all fed. Felt like I was cooking for an army."

"I think Joey's eating enough for all of us," Molly said. "Looks like he's packed on a few pounds."

"Maybe, but I don't mind." Jenny tilted her head, surveying her daughter. "So, are you going to tell me what really happened the other day?"

Molly suddenly found the paperwork before her very interesting. "What do you mean?"

"I mean, the day your father came home looking kind of gray in the face." Jenny waited a beat. "The same day Wilma told me she thought she saw someone dangling off the side of one of the wind turbines."

Molly slumped in her seat. "She did?"

"You know, Mo," Jenny said wryly, "you'd better never go into undercover work." Her expression sobered. "What happened?"

Giving up, Molly told her. "But I was clipped in. Everything is fine." Her guts churned to remember how she'd carelessly unclipped her line before she was safely inside the hatch.

"Molly," Jenny said, focusing on her hands, clasped in her lap, "I've lived my whole life with the knowledge I could lose people I love. My dad and Bobby, out fishing when I was growing up. I was so happy when Bobby left to get his captain's license and pilot the ferry, but even that has its risks. When you all were little, and your dad was still lobstering, I never rested easy until he was nearly home. Then, when the boys got older and wanted to fish, it started all over again. And you. If you were a cop on the mainland, I'd worry myself sick. As it is, here, you're climbing up on roofs and now up on the turbines. It's a wonder I wasn't gray by the time I turned thirty."

"No one comes with guarantees, Mom."

"I know that." Jenny smiled sadly. "But not a day goes by that I don't whisper a prayer of thanks that I still have all of you."

The ferry's horn cut through the morning, and Jenny's face lit up.

"Let's go see your brother."

⁂

As ALWAYS ON FERRY days, there was a lot of hustle and bustle at the marina. Two couples from Ottawa were visiting for the week. Molly pointed them in the direction of the hotel. Fred gave her and Jenny a wave as he maneuvered the forklift under a pallet. Aidan, not bothering with the forklift, was lifting heavy cardboard boxes filled with supplies for the stores and Shannahan's market.

Molly watched him with a bit of envy as her tight back muscles gave her a little tweak, just enough to remind her that she wouldn't be lifting anything heavy any time soon.

"Who needs a gym?" she joked as Aidan squatted to set a load down.

"Hey." His bearded face broke into a huge grin. He gave Jenny a tight hug, dwarfing his mom. Molly gave him a punch in the shoulder.

"Will you have time for a short visit?" Jenny asked.

"Let me finish helping Fred unload," he said. "I'll buy you lunch at the diner."

"Deal."

Molly went to the boathouse to inspect the Capri. It sat on blocks, the engine hanging from a chain hoist, waiting to be rebuilt. The brightwork on this boat was in really fine shape and hadn't needed to be sent away to be rechromed. It was all carefully wrapped in oilcloth and stacked to the side, waiting for the other work to be completed. She'd hoped to have this beauty ready to be delivered by Memorial Day, but this stupid back injury was setting her behind schedule.

Still, there were some things she could do. She had new vinyl ready for the bench seat. That was something her back could handle. She spent the next hour stripping off the old, cracked vinyl and repadding the seat with new foam. It took more strength than she remembered to stretch the replacement vinyl taut.

"Need a hand?"

Aidan stepped up behind her and gathered the sheet of stiff material in his hands, pulling it tight for her. Together, they wrapped it around the seat so Molly could tack it into place.

"Thanks."

"Mom said you hurt your back. You okay?"

"Yeah. Just twisted it." She looked him up and down. "I meant it. You look like you're in great shape."

He ran his hand through his black hair. "Thanks. I'm working such long hours, there's no time to get to a gym. So I use the loading and unloading as a workout. Hits all the big muscles."

He ran a finger along the shiny vinyl and cleared his throat. "Hey, Mo, I've been wanting to ask..." He gave her a sheepish look.

"What?"

"On Bealtaine, did you see anything... unusual that night?"

Molly had to think back. When she did, she couldn't help but blush at the memory of the "fertility" ritual she and Kathleen had shared, but she just said, "No. Nothing unusual. Why?" She peered at him. "What did you see?"

Before he could reply, she laid a hand on his arm. "Miss Louisa said you didn't drink or smoke that night."

"I didn't." He held up his hand in their childhood swearing gesture. "Honest Injun. I won't. It was... something else." He lowered his hand. "Someone else."

Molly frowned. "What do you mean?"

He pulled two rolling work stools near, and they both sat. "When we were all dancing around the bonfire—and I swear, I didn't drink or smoke—through the flames, I saw a woman."

"What woman?"

He shook his head. "I don't know. She was a stranger, not an islander. But she was there. Patrick and Wilma and Nels were all on that side of the fire, across from me. And suddenly, her face was there, between Wilma and Nels. And she was looking right at me. Right through me."

Scrubbing his hands roughly across his face, he gave a half-laugh. "Sounds crazy, doesn't it?"

Molly shrugged. "On this island, we learn weird things can happen. What did she look like?"

"She was beautiful," he said softly. "Dark hair, dark eyes. About our age. But something in her eyes, like she was searching for something, and, when she saw me..." He stopped and gave another embarrassed clearing of his throat. "So you didn't see anything unusual that night?"

"No." She clapped him on the shoulder. "Like I said, weird things happen here, Aidan. Who knows?"

Another thought occurred to her. "Hey, I've been meaning to ask you, can you take a day or two off in June? Once the ferry is running daily?"

He met her eyes. "Already done. From now on, that day is Kathleen's birthday, not the day Bryan—"

She leaned against him for a minute. "Thanks, Aidan."

Chapter 10

"WAIT, SLOW DOWN," JAN commanded.

She had insisted that Meredith and Barb come out to dinner with her after school to fill her in on the weekend with Barb's grandmother.

"Your grandmother is a hypnotist? I thought she's a healer."

"She's both," Barb said, dribbling a little more dressing over her chicken pecan salad. "And she would tell you hypnotists are the Vegas stage-show people. She uses hypnosis as a therapeutic tool, like imagery or meditation."

"That's kind of what it felt like," Meredith said. She picked all the mushrooms off her salad, tucking them behind the bowl where she wouldn't have to look at them. "I don't think I was ever unaware of what was going on. She guided my mom and me through the dreams we already have, but her questions took us deeper into them, helped us remember more detail."

"Which I wrote down," Barb said. "So we wouldn't forget anything."

"This is so cool," Jan said, her eyes wide. "So what about this photograph? I thought this shipwreck stuff was supposed to be here, off our coast."

Meredith shrugged. "I had no idea where the dream took place. I was researching Oregon shipwrecks only because I didn't know where else to start. But as soon as I saw the outline of the island in the photo, I knew. That's it. That's where it happened. My mom recognized it, too."

"That is just crazy." Jan stabbed her fork into her spinach salad.

Meredith reached for her wine. "We're going."

Barb and Jan exchanged a quick glance.

"Going?" Barb asked.

"In June, as soon as school is out," Meredith said. "Portland to Portland. Isn't that strange? Then on to Little Sister Island. My parents are going with me. We'll drive and take Jasper. There's a ferry. I looked it up. We've got reservations at what looks like the only hotel."

"You're kidding," Jan said.

"About the hotel? No. The island looks pretty small, as its name implies," Meredith said.

"Not about the hotel," Jan said impatiently. "About going. What are you going to say? Hi, island people. We've been dreaming about some ancient shipwreck near this place and thought we'd come check it out."

Meredith laughed. "I hadn't thought about how to introduce ourselves, but that might work."

Barb cut another bite of her chicken. "How long are you going for?"

"No idea. Mom and Dad are retired, and I've got the summer off. Who knows?"

That prospect was about the only thing buoying Meredith through the last few weeks of school. Some days she thought she might scream in frustration. The pull of Little Sister Island, this place she hadn't even

102

known existed until a few days ago, it was almost frightening how strong it was. She hadn't been able to say it, even to Barb, but something inside her felt that she'd been destined to find this place. The photograph hung on her bedroom wall, where she could sit in bed and stare at it.

"Maybe it's where we're really supposed to be," she confided, but only to Jasper, who wagged his tail in agreement.

She'd actually started crossing the days off her wall calendar in the kitchen. She made arrangements for one of her neighbors to collect her mail for her and check the house every few days in case of a water leak or something.

She had no idea what the weather might be like, figuring that on any island, even in the Atlantic, it could be a lot like the unpredictable weather here. She'd packed two suitcases with a variety of clothes that could be layered. But she kept unpacking them, rethinking what she might need.

"You act like they don't have stores out there," Jan teased when Meredith confessed her indecision. "I'm pretty sure you could buy anything you need that you didn't bring with you."

Jan glanced around, but the teachers' break room was empty except for the two of them. "What about Grant?"

Meredith's expression darkened. "What about him?"

"Have you spoken to him? Does he know about this quest of yours?"

"No and no. It's none of his business. I have no idea what he's up to these days, and I don't want to know."

Jan stared hard at Meredith, her Diet Coke halfway to her mouth. "So it's really over?"

"Why? You want him?"

Jan nearly spit her Coke out of her mouth. "God, no. I just wondered if you were having any regrets or second thoughts."

Meredith shook her head. "Not one. Told you, I'm kind of numb about him. Just glad I found out what he's like before it was too late."

Her mind immediately went to the strange man she'd seen the night of her birthday. Something must have shown on her face because Jan immediately leaned forward.

"What?"

Meredith tried to deflect. "What what?"

"Don't even."

Meredith's shoulders sagged. "Okay, but don't get all weird on me." She quickly described her dream that night.

Jan was appropriately impressed, her mouth hanging open. "And you've never seen this guy before?"

Meredith shook her head.

"And what about those other people? Dancing around a bonfire? Do you think you were having another vision of the past? Like the ship?"

"I don't know. I didn't say anything to Jeanette. Or my mom. You're the only one I've told, so keep it quiet, will you?"

Jan crossed her heart. "But you have to promise to tell me if you meet this mystery man."

⬚⬚⬚⬚⬚⬚⬚⬚⬚⬚

WITH A HURRIED GOOD-BYE to the school secretaries, Meredith nearly ran out of the school on the final day. She'd already promised Jan and Barb updates when she had some to send. The Subaru was partially packed; she'd purchased a rooftop carrier so Jasper could have the entire cargo section to stretch out in on their cross-country trek.

She drove home to pick him up and finish packing, say a final thank-you to the neighbor who was watching the house for her, and set off for Portland.

When she pulled into her parents' drive, she recognized Art's Lexus parked in front of the garage door. Jasper trotted out to the lawn and then raced her inside to greet everyone.

104

"I didn't know you'd be here," she said, hugging Art and Kenny.

"We had to see you off," Kenny said, glancing in Art's direction. "And share some news."

"What news?" Irene demanded. "You've been here for two hours and haven't said anything about news."

"We were waiting for Meredith to get here." Art's expression was serious, triggering Meredith's heart rate to pick up.

"What's going on?" she asked.

"Let's sit down," Art said.

"With wine," Kenny suggested.

Roy brightened. "I've got a new batch of ale—"

"NO!" came a chorus.

"All right, all right," he grumbled.

Art went to the refrigerator for the wine while Roy got glasses from the cupboard.

When they were all seated around the table, Art began, "After the genealogy fiasco—"

"I'm so sorry," Irene cut in.

He shook his head. "It's not your fault. It was just such a shock." He paused to take a sip of his wine, and Kenny gave his back an encouraging rub.

Art took a deep breath. "I've been through so many emotions. Surprise, disbelief, and then anger."

"At me?" Irene's chin quivered.

"No, Reney." Art reached for her hand. "Not at you. At Mom and Dad. They lied to us. Our entire lives."

"I only suggested the adoption possibility," Roy said. "We don't know—"

"But we do," Art said quietly.

Roy's mouth hung open for a moment. "Oh."

Irene frowned. "What do you know?"

"My birth certificate is from Massachusetts," Art said.

"And mine is from New Hampshire," Irene said. "They moved when you were three. We knew that."

"But when I contacted Massachusetts," Art explained, "they confirmed my birth certificate is an adoption certificate. They wouldn't tell me any more. They said there's an application for a pre-adoption birth record. I filled it out, and now I'm waiting."

Irene stared at him for a moment. "I wonder what New Hampshire's law is?"

Kenny reached toward the counter beside the table for an envelope Meredith hadn't noticed and slid it across the table to Irene. "This is the New Hampshire application, if you want to fill it out. We don't know what the status of your birth certificate is. If you're also adopted, Irene, there are separate registries where, if both adoptee and biological family sign up, they'll put them in contact with each other."

Irene stared at the envelope. "So, our mother and father..."

"Weren't really our, or at least my, biological mother and father," Art said.

Irene's eyes filled with tears. "But they loved us."

"Just not enough to tell us the truth."

Meredith had never seen Art this hurt or angry. Her uncle was usually the joker in the family, the one who soothed rough patches. Kenny sent her an apologetic smile that told her he'd been the soother for this rough patch.

"Adoption in the 50s and 60s was completely different than it is now," Roy said. "A lot of people kept it secret. I had a cousin who was adopted. Her parents chose to tell her, but I remember arguments when the family got together about whether they should have."

Art swirled the wine in his glass, watching the ruby liquid sheet the glass and then dissolve into drops. "I'll get used to the idea, I suppose. It's just that we can't ask them questions now. There are things we'll never know."

Meredith was reminded of what she'd realized the night of her birthday after they'd all received the surprising results. "We're exactly the same people we were before we knew. You're my family."

"But you belong to your parents, love," Art reminded her. "You don't have to wonder why they gave you away."

⬚⬚⬚⬚⬚⬚⬚⬚⬚⬚⬚

MEREDITH SAT IN THE passenger seat, keeping her dad company while her mom slept in the back seat, Jasper's head on her lap. Despite Meredith's careful plans to keep the cargo area clear for him, he'd whined and looked so pitiful, that with Roy's first nod of the head, Jasper had clambered into the back seat to sleep with whoever was resting there. They'd been taking turns driving for about four hours each to get twelve hours in each day. A seventies station played on the radio as they drove through northern Indiana.

She couldn't remember ever living anywhere but Oregon. Her father's engineering career had brought her parents to St. Louis when they were first married, and it was where she'd been born. Then Art and Kenny had coaxed them into visiting Portland. They'd fallen in love with the Northwest and had moved when Meredith was four. Grandma and Granddad had left New England and followed everyone else, so Meredith had had most of her family around her almost all her life. Her father's parents had retired to Arizona, and family vacations had always been to visit them.

She watched her dad now, studied him—his sandy hair, wireless glasses, the laugh lines around his eyes—and tried to imagine what it would feel like to learn that he wasn't her biological father. Though she looked so like her mother, she'd inherited Roy's crooked smile. She couldn't really imagine not loving—and feeling loved by—this man.

But would that change if he were my adopted father?

He'd been there for her, always. Granted, he'd thought trying to teach her the physics of momentum would help her learn to ride her bicycle more quickly. Math came as easily to him as breathing, so he was no help at all when she couldn't grasp algebra or trig. But he was also the one who always found her when she and her mom had had an argument.

"Two peas in a pod," he'd say, wrapping an arm around her shoulders while she buried her face against him. "I couldn't live without my girls."

Sudden tears blurred her eyes now, and she had a hint of what Art must be feeling. It was, she decided, the shock of learning that everything you thought you knew about yourself was wrong. Or at least not complete.

He glanced over and caught her watching him. "All right?" he asked, reaching for her hand.

She nodded, giving him a squeeze. "Just thinking about family."

He sighed. "This family has been through a shakeup, that's for sure."

She shifted in her seat. "How do you feel about all this?"

He didn't answer immediately. In his typical, thoughtful way, he had to frame his words. She'd learned to wait.

"I can see how important this is to your mother. I've known she has this dream, the one you share, but we never knew what it was connected to." He frowned. "I just worry that she and Art are attaching too much importance to what they learned."

"Art seems really shaken by the ancestry stuff," Meredith said.

"He is. Kenny said all he seems to focus on was that he was given up."

"But he was also chosen," Meredith said.

Roy smiled. "Maybe you should remind him of that when we get back."

"I will."

He released her hand. "How are you feeling about all of this?"

She watched the wildflowers planted in the median on the inter-state, such a nice display of color. "It's exciting, and kind of frightening."

"Frightening?"

"Yeah. I mean," Meredith paused, feeling silly. "I've been having this dream on and off almost my entire life, and now, I might learn what it means. I'm excited, but kind of scared at the same time. What if it changes everything?"

Roy thought about that. "It just might."

Chapter 11

KATHLEEN AND BLOSSOM ROSE with Molly before sunup. "Early or never" had become Kathleen's mantra for walking and marketing now that the ferry was running daily. Molly had always enjoyed rowing at dawn, when the water was at its calmest, but sometimes, Kathleen had to drag herself out of bed when it was still dark. The cool breeze coming in through the screen made her want to roll over and keep Molly's warm body in bed with her. Today, she sat up with a big yawn.

"What's on for today?" she asked as they both got dressed.

"First a row, now my back's finally better," Molly said, slipping a snug-fitting tank top over her head. "Then back here to shower. If the decking I ordered came in, I need to start rebuilding the porch and back deck on the Strongwind house. That's probably going to take me a good two weeks. What about you?"

"Thought I'd go by Miss Louisa's." Kathleen sat on the side of the bed to lace her sneakers. "See if she wants to go to market with me this morning. Then I've got a new edit to start on."

Blossom led the way downstairs. Molly let him out while Kathleen got the coffee brewing. Molly gulped down a half-cup.

"See you this evening," she said, giving Kathleen a kiss before heading out.

Kathleen had a more leisurely breakfast, enjoying two cups of coffee. Sometimes, it was hard to remember what life was like pre-island. She recalled hurried mornings—if there hadn't been an argument with her ex—usually grabbing a granola bar or fast-food breakfast sandwich on her way to the office, being jostled on the bus with all the other early-morning commuters. Same with lunch, rushing to a sandwich shop nearby so she could cram some food into her mouth and be back at her desk for four more hours before joining many of the same commuters, looking just as harried, on the crowded bus going in the other direction.

She sat back and cradled her coffee cup, listening to the quiet of the island, that same cool breeze wafting through the screens of the open doors and windows. It felt almost wrong to be this ridiculously happy. She wasn't making tons of money—maybe half of what she made at her job in Philly—but she had all she needed. Here, there was no push to get ahead. No one cared how she dressed—*or even if I dressed*, she thought with a chuckle. Folks here helped each other out, looked after one another.

"Which is why we're going to check on Miss Louisa," she told Blossom.

She collected a handful of cloth tote bags and snagged the car keys from the bowl near the door. Blossom hopped into the back seat of her Nissan. She immediately saw that she wasn't the only one with the idea of getting errands run early. Waving to a few familiar cars and other islanders on bicycles, she drove to the Woodhouse place where she was unsurprised to see a light already on. Before she and

Blossom could climb the porch steps, Miss Louisa opened the front screen door, a robe over her flowered housedress, fuzzy slippers on her feet.

"This is a surprise," she said, bending to pat Blossom, who was wagging his rump.

"Good morning, Miss Louisa. We're headed to the market early. Wondered if you'd like to come along."

Louisa beamed. "How thoughtful, Katie. Give me just a minute to dress. Come in."

They followed her inside. She trotted up the stairs, leaving Kathleen and Blossom to make themselves at home.

Kathleen wandered, looking at the dozens of photos scattered about, covering tables and the top of the piano. Many were of her grandmother with Louisa and Olivia when they were young. Kathleen cradled one of them, looking at the teenage versions of the three. There was another of the four Woodhouses together on the porch. Louisa was right; she did favor her mother, who was very pretty. Olivia, always stouter, took after their dad. Next to it was another of Olivia with Maisie and a handsome young man—Kathleen's grandfather, Séan. She couldn't remember him at all; he'd died of a heart attack when she was a young child.

She tried to picture herself and Molly as old women, still living in their cottage. Her own auburn hair was starting to show a few strands of silver, but Molly's was just as black as ever.

Her musings were interrupted by Louisa's return, now dressed in cotton pants and a linen shirt, her silver hair gathered into its usual bun.

Kathleen bent to pick up the boxes of ashes, but Louisa said, "Let's not disturb them so early. I'll make sure Daddy and Ollie get some sun later."

"Okay."

Kathleen glanced in Louisa's direction a few times as she drove them into the village. "When does the children's reading group start?"

"Tomorrow." Louisa's face lit up. "We decided the families needed a week or so with everyone home together before we began. Oh, Katie, I'm so looking forward to it."

"You've missed teaching, haven't you?"

"I truly have. It gave my life purpose."

Something in her tone made Kathleen reach for her hand. "You have purpose just by being here, Miss Louisa. Life on Little Sister wouldn't be the same without you."

Louisa gave her a small smile. "Thank you for saying that, Katie. But life will go on when I'm gone. Just as it does for all of us."

Kathleen didn't know what to say to that.

The market was crowded with islanders who all had the same idea of getting their shopping done before the tourists were up and about. Tim and Miranda were both helping people with groceries and supplies for summer projects. One of the things Kathleen loved about this market was that it was a mix of everything—lumberyard, hardware store, grocery store, even clothing store now that summer was here. She saw that the Shannahans, like most of the island shops and businesses, had hired a few of the island teenagers for the summer. They were busily ringing up and bagging purchases at the counter.

"Shouldn't you be resting?" Louisa asked Miranda.

Kathleen was thinking the same thing. Miranda looked ready to pop at any moment. Louisa bent to snag Ellis as he tried to race by her.

"That's what I said." Tim looked frazzled.

"I don't need to rest yet," Miranda insisted. "I'll be doing plenty of that in a couple of weeks."

Tim took Ellis, and Louisa continued down the aisle toward the meat. Kathleen accompanied her, picking out some chicken and bacon.

"Will she go offisland to give birth?" Kathleen asked. It hadn't occurred to her before. "How will she know when it's time?"

Louisa shook her head, placing a roast in her cart. "Lena Clearwater is our midwife. She's delivered most of the babies for the last couple of decades."

"But what if there are problems?"

Louisa moved on to the dairy section. "It happens sometimes. If they know ahead of time that it might be a difficult birth, or the baby has health issues, people make arrangements to go to the mainland. Luckily, that doesn't happen often. Most of us are pretty healthy."

When they were done with their shopping—*just in time*, Kathleen thought as a loud group of tourists emerged from the hotel—she drove Louisa home.

"You don't have to do that," Louisa said when Kathleen reached for her bags to carry them inside for her.

"I don't mind."

She carried the bags through to the kitchen.

"Thank you so much, Katie," Louisa said.

"Our pleasure." Kathleen paused in the living room, and picked up a framed photo. "Miss Louisa, how old were my grandparents when they bonded?"

"Maisie was nineteen, Séan twenty-one. He'd already been out of school and fishing for a couple of years."

Kathleen set the photo down. "Can you tell me about their bonding?" She turned to Louisa but stopped at the expression on her face. "I'm sorry if I'm being pushy."

"No," Louisa said with a shake of her head. "It's not you, Katie."

"It's just, I'd like to know and..."

"And I'm the only one left who can tell you." Louisa nodded. "Another day. I'm tired now."

"Okay," Kathleen said hesitantly. She patted her thigh, and Blossom trotted to the door. "We'll see you soon."

She glanced again in Louisa's direction as she started the car. Louisa waved from the porch and went inside.

※※※※※※※※※

IN THE HOUSE, LOUISA moved the wooden boxes to a sunny window-sill.

"Why didn't you tell her?"

Louisa tried to ignore the question, but Ollie never was one to let something go.

"You weren't there for your best friend's bonding. You'll have to tell her."

"I know I will," Louisa snapped. "But not today."

"You never told me why, either, sister."

"Did so. I told you I had to stay on campus that summer."

"All your years at that college, and that was the only summer you had to take courses? Maisie never understood, and neither did I."

"Why are you interrogating me? Why won't you leave me alone?" Louisa stomped through to the kitchen, but Olivia followed her.

"You know the answer to that. Some part of you wants me here. Secrets will out, Lou. They never stay secret forever."

※※※※※※※※※

SEVERAL GULLS CIRCLED OVER the marina, mewing, watchful for any food they could steal. Despite the "Do Not Feed the Gulls" signs posted at the marina and down at the beach for the summer, people still did. And the gulls, being the opportunists they were, learned quickly how to dive-bomb people and steal food right from their hands.

When indignant tourists complained, Molly shook her head and pointed at the sign. "It's there for a reason."

To herself, she frequently muttered things that wouldn't make for good PR for the island, things that usually included words like "stupid" and "idiots" and various curse words.

She'd taken to wearing her uniform shirt with her badge prominently displayed, and she'd washed and waxed the 4-Runner, parking it in front of her tiny office in the village. The stars on its doors were faded but still visible.

She popped in to Siobhan's shop. "Morning, Shauna," she said to the teenage girl behind the register.

"Hi, Molly," Shauna said.

Siobhan glanced over from where she was restocking a display of candles. "Good morning." Her eyes flicked down to the badge. "Sheriff."

Molly grinned. Several tourists roamed the shop. Business was good, judging from the large numbers of items in their arms.

"Siobhan," she said quietly, "I need—"

"Already wrapped it."

Molly frowned, perplexed. "Wrapped what? I haven't told you what it is yet."

Siobhan laughed and took Molly by the hand, leading her through the door behind the counter into her private living space. On the table sat a beautifully wrapped box.

"What the heck?"

Siobhan leaned near and whispered, "I am a witch, remember?"

Molly remembered only too well how Siobhan had bewitched her years ago—a time when both of them were lonely and had turned to each other. She inhaled Siobhan's unique scent now, felt the warm brush of soft lips against her cheek as Siobhan kissed her with a throaty laugh.

"But this box is for your beloved. Some oils and soaps and scented candles she mentioned she liked. I thought I'd go ahead and make up a birthday package for you."

Molly was touched. "Siobhan, that was really sweet of you." She kissed Siobhan's cheek in return. "Thank you."

She gathered the box and carried it out to the counter, where Shauna rang her up.

"Tell your mom and dad I said hi," she said as she handed the cash over.

"I will, Molly. Bye."

She loved that the islanders had an unwritten pact to hire as many of the island teens as they could. Most of the island businesses needed extra help during high season, but even the ones that didn't found chores and whatnot that could be hired out. It gave the kids extra spending money, and it boosted the unspoken hopes that these young people would want to settle here and make Little Sister their home again some day.

Of course, Molly and her brothers had always had plenty of work waiting for them—out on the fishing boats, upkeep at the marina, or things that needed doing around the house. Even in those days when Miss Louisa was still teaching and the children didn't leave for school, there'd been no shortage of things to keep them busy during the summers. She suspected her parents had adopted the "keep them too tired to get into trouble" philosophy.

Wilma and Nels by far hired the most summer help. With the ferry arriving before noon most days, and not departing until four, they had a tight window for getting rooms cleaned and ready for a new wave of guests each day, plus the extra traffic in the diner, which seemed to still be full this late in the morning.

She stashed Kathleen's present in the Toyota and went on toward the marina. Her dad was busy with a couple of people in the office, most likely wanting to rent boats for the afternoon. She went into the boathouse. The Capri, her engine rebuilt and reinstalled, was nearly ready to deliver. Another couple of coats of spar varnish, reattach the chrome, and she'd be done.

Every time Molly finished restoring one of these beauties, she felt a twinge of regret at having to let it go. So many hours of work, only to turn it over to someone else who got to enjoy it. Someday, she'd buy one to restore and keep.

The ferry horn sounded from outside. She watched it ease up to the dock. Through the window, she saw that it was her uncle who was piloting, not Aidan. Fred waved at her from the deck, and she helped secure the gangplank for the cars that were offloading.

She'd never written an actual ticket, but occasionally, she'd had to "jail" a tourist at the hotel until she could escort them onto the next ferry with a clear uninvitation to return. Out of habit, she found herself scanning the new cars arriving: black Ford Fusion, silver Tacoma, red Forester. Not like the parade of luxury cars over at Big Sister. She wondered sometimes if it was against island law over there to drive anything that cost less than a year's salary.

She snorted at the thought. Her salary was less than the cost of any of these cars. But she didn't care. Without mortgages, Little Sister islanders tended to be a content lot. The most expensive thing most people here owned were their boats, and even those tended to be older and well-maintained. Still, sometimes she thought about ferrying the aging Toyota over to Big Sister and driving around just to see the expressions of dismay.

She nodded to each car as it passed her. The woman driving the Subaru caught her eye, staring at her with an expression Molly couldn't read. She braked and rolled down her window.

"Could you tell us where the hotel is, please?"

Molly pointed. "Hard to miss. Biggest building in the village. On the whole island for that matter."

"Thank you." The woman continued to stare for just a beat longer and then drove on.

Molly's attention was diverted to Fred, who was loosening the straps tying down the cargo.

"Hey, Mo."

She gave him a hand. "Where's Aidan?"

Fred nodded in a generally northern direction. "He's working a few double shifts to Big Sister. So's he can take a couple of days off next week. How's things?"

119

"'Bout the same as always. Nothing much changes around here."

Fred laughed. "You got that right."

Chapter 12

J ASPER LAY STRETCHED OUT on his side on the floor of the hotel
room.

"You just slept for four days," Meredith reminded him. "How
can you be tired?"

His answer was one limp thump of his tail.

Shaking her head, she went to the window and gazed out toward
the ocean. It wasn't visible from the hotel, but she knew it was out
there. She reminded herself that she lived beside the ocean. *Why is
my heart racing?* An ocean was an ocean. But she was itching to get out
and explore the island. Her father's reply to that suggestion had been
firm.

"We've been on the road for days," he said. "I am stretching out
on that bed and not getting back in the car for the rest of the day."

She unpacked her suitcases, something she never did on vacation.
But this doesn't feel like a vacation. She couldn't articulate it better than

that. With her clothes tucked neatly into dresser drawers and hung in the small closet, she lay down on the bed and tried to rest. After fifteen minutes, she gave an impatient huff and sat up.

"We don't have to drive anywhere, but I'm not going to lie here and waste time."

Jasper, for all his appearance of exhaustion, leapt to his feet, instantly alert. He accompanied her out into the hall. Meredith paused outside her parents' door, wondering if she should knock to see if her mom at least wanted to explore with her, but she decided against that.

"Come on," she whispered.

Jasper raced down the stairs ahead of her. The hotel owner was at the desk, checking out another guest.

"We've enjoyed having you," she was saying as she handed the man his room receipt. "Come back to see us next season."

Meredith waited until they were done and the owner turned to her.

"Yes, dear? What can I help you with?" she asked.

"We've never been here before," Meredith said. "Is there a tourist office or brochures?"

"Land sakes," said the woman with a hearty laugh. "We're not so uppity as that. No brochures. Just plenty of friendly folk here. Island's too small to get lost, and if you get turned around, anyone can set you straight. Tell them to send you back to Wilma. Wilma Greatneck. My husband, Nels, does all the cooking in the diner. I do most everything else."

"I'm Meredith Turner." She shook Wilma's proffered hand. "What about the island's history? Is there someplace I can learn more about that?"

"Sure we have the prettiest little library," said Wilma. "Just across the street and back a block or so."

"Thank you." Meredith turned toward the door, but paused. "Wilma, when we arrived, there was a woman, I think she had a badge of some kind. Welcoming people as we drove off the ferry."

"Oh, that's Molly Cooper, our sheriff." Wilma laughed again. "Not that we need one most days. But I can track her down if you need her."

"No," Meredith said quickly. "No, thanks. If my parents come down looking for me, just tell them I've gone to that library."

"I'll do that."

Meredith stepped out onto the hotel's wide porch, several inviting rocking chairs scattered about. She took a deep breath. The air here smelled different from Pacific air. She clipped Jasper's leash to his collar, not sure if they had a leash law. Her head swiveled as she walked, trying to take everything in—the shops, the houses. She studied the people curiously, no idea who was a tourist and who was an islander.

Molly Cooper.

Something about her had looked so familiar. Meredith tried to recall more details of the dream she'd had the night of her birthday—the people dancing on the beach—and wondered if Molly could have been one of them.

The ferry, she knew, was scheduled to depart again about four o'clock. A few cars had already boarded. Their own hotel reservation had been made for two weeks.

"What in the world are we going to do there for two weeks?" Roy had asked, but Irene and Meredith were both adamant that they needed time. If he wondered what for, he didn't voice it.

She left the village's main street and wandered through what looked like a more residential area, large trees sheltering cute dwellings, some painted clapboard, some weathered shingles. There, among a stand of oaks, she found the Little Sister Library. It was charming—complete with its own little porch with two more rocking chairs. Behind the screen door, the wooden door was swung wide. Tentatively, she knocked. When no one answered, she tugged the screen door open.

"Hello?" There didn't seem to be anyone here. Jasper stepped through and began sniffing around.

Meredith jumped when a door behind the librarian's desk suddenly opened and another dog came trotting through.

"Hi," Meredith said. "I didn't mean—is it okay that we're here?"

The auburn-haired woman who'd followed the dog from the back room smiled. "It's fine. I'm Kathleen."

"Meredith." She gestured. "And this is Jasper."

He and the other dog were standing nose to butt, tails high and ears alert, but no signs of aggression from either of them.

"That's Blossom." Kathleen came around from behind the desk to shake Meredith's hand. "Welcome to Little Sister. Were you looking for anything in particular?"

"I'd like to learn more about the island's history," Meredith said. "We only just arrived. I'm here with my parents."

"Where from?" Kathleen asked, heading to a particular set of shelves.

"Oregon. Portland."

Kathleen turned around. "Wow, that's about as far cross country as you can go." She pulled three books off the shelf. "There isn't much published about Little Sister, I'm afraid. Here are some books on Big Sister. You passed it on the way here. I guess not many authors think we're worth writing about."

Something in Kathleen's secretive smile made Meredith think the smaller island's inhabitants were just fine with that.

"May I sit and look through these?" Meredith asked.

"Of course. Make yourself comfortable, in here or out on the porch."

Kathleen glanced at the dogs, who were starting to hop around each other playfully. "Will Jasper run off?"

"No."

"We can let them out to romp, if you'd like."

"That would be great," Meredith, bending to unclip Jasper's leash. "He's been cooped up in the car for four days."

They opened the screen door and let the dogs out to play a game of chase around the trees. Meredith sat in one of the rockers, and Kathleen took the other as they watched the dogs.

"Are you the librarian here?" Meredith asked curiously, taking in Kathleen's casual shorts and loose button-down.

Kathleen chuckled. "Kind of the librarian in training. Rebecca, the real librarian, is somewhere."

Meredith eyed her curiously. "Have you lived here all your life?"

"No," Kathleen said as she rocked. "My dad grew up on Little Sister, and I spent summers here with my grandmother, but I only moved back about two years ago."

She met Meredith's gaze. "What brought you and your parents all the way from Oregon? Not many people travel the extra distance to Little Sister. Most take advantage of Big Sister's location and shopping and restaurants."

Meredith broke eye contact, watching the dogs as they came trotting back, tongues lolling, to lap water from the big bowl on the porch. "We wanted something smaller, quieter."

It wasn't untrue, even if it wasn't the whole truth. How in the world could she explain what really had brought them here?

Kathleen tilted her head, studying Meredith more closely. "You're sure you weren't here last season? You sure look familiar."

"I'm sure."

"Right. Guess you'd remember, wouldn't you? Well, if it's small and quiet you're after, you're in the right place." Kathleen pushed to her feet. "I'll let you look through those. Just call if you need anything."

"Thank you."

The screen door slapped shut, leaving Meredith alone with the two dogs, who were sprawled, panting, on the porch. She sat, rocking, listening, just being. Here, at last.

MOLLY WENT OVER HER list again. Nels was making his special carrot cake, Kathleen's favorite. Jenny was roasting a few chickens with potatoes and turnips and carrots—Molly had spent part of the afternoon helping scrub and chop the vegetables. Miss Louisa was baking a fresh loaf of bread; Molly had arranged to swing by and pick her up at five. Siobhan had confirmed she'd be there, as had Rebecca. She knew they'd both bring something to share.

This wouldn't be as elaborate as last year's birthday—Kathleen's first since moving back, and her first celebration in twenty-five years, since Bryan's drowning on her tenth. Her *tar abháile* last year had been special, marking her homecoming back to Little Sister for good. But Molly wanted every birthday for the rest of Kathleen's life to feel special.

The ferry horn sounded, and Molly glanced at her watch. Departing on schedule. Aidan had done another Big Sister run with a fellow ferry captain today, and planned to boat here with Matty, Brandi, and Joey for the party.

She sauntered through the village, pausing to wave a car by. Tourist faces came and went; the day-trippers, only here for a few hours, barely registered. The ones who stayed for a week became familiar, though she rarely knew their names or anything about them. That one family, though, the Turners, they had caught her attention. Kathleen said the daughter—Marion or Marianne or something with an M—had come by the library a few days ago, and Siobhan and Wilma had both mentioned the mother and daughter asking lots of questions about the island. Wilma had whispered to Molly that they'd reserved two whole weeks at the hotel with the possibility of staying a month or longer.

No one ever stayed on Little Sister that long. There was absolutely nothing strange or suspicious about these people, but Molly had started looking out for them. Mr. Turner was on the hotel porch now, rocking and reading. She considered for a moment and then made her way to the hotel.

Taking the chair beside him, she said, "Good afternoon, Mr. Turner."

He lowered his book. "Sheriff."

"It's just Molly. Molly Cooper." She extended a hand, which he shook. "Are you enjoying Little Sister?"

"Very much. And I'm Roy."

He seemed to be a man of few words. Molly hid a smile. "Wilma says you're visiting from Portland, Oregon. We don't get many people from so far away."

He nodded. "I think perhaps we shouldn't be surprised that you know so much about us."

She rocked for a moment, watching the last couple of cars queue up for the ferry. Fred was waving them onboard. "Small island. Not much happens here that folks don't hear about. And not many visitors come for such an extended stay."

He mimicked her, rocking for several seconds before saying, "We didn't come here by chance. Or for the scenery."

She shifted her chair to face him obliquely. "I'm listening."

Her mouth fell open as she listened to his tale. Even growing up on Little Sister, where magic and their blended Celtic and First Ones' traditions always involved a bit of the unexplained, this was fantastic.

"I don't think your wife or daughter have told anyone about this, or I'd've heard."

He chuckled. "I think they're both afraid they'll get branded as weirdos if they do. They've been poking around, trying to learn more about the island and its history, to see if it could possibly match up with their dreams."

Molly tapped her fingers on the arm of the rocker. She hated to distract from the reason for tonight's celebration, but... "Roy, would

you—all of you—like to join us for dinner tonight? It's a birthday celebration, but there'll be more than enough food. And most of the
island's elders will be there. People who can answer some questions
for you."

He stared at her. "We'd be delighted. As long as you're sure we're
not intruding."

She reached into her back pocket for a small notepad and pencil,
usually filled with scribbles about the fixit jobs people were always
stopping her to schedule. She jotted down the directions to the
Cooper house and ripped the page out.

"Six o'clock. And your dog is welcome."

He accepted the paper. "See you tonight, Molly."

※※※※※※※※

JASPER SAT, TILTING HIS head with a bemused expression, as he
watched his human tossing clothes onto the bed and muttering to
herself.

"Why didn't I pack more clothes?"

Meredith had emptied what she had hanging in the closet, laying
everything out on the bed. The shorts and blouses she'd been wearing since they arrived on Little Sister didn't seem nice enough. She
hadn't even thought to pack any of her teaching clothes.

Irene had been as excited as she when Roy told them about Molly
Cooper's invitation. "This is wonderful, but aren't we intruding if it's
someone's birthday?"

Roy had shrugged. "She's the one who asked us."

"We should bring something," Irene decided.

Roy had chuckled. "From one of the shops they've never been to?"

That had brought her up short. "Oh."

He had been the one to suggest they go to Wilma to see if the
diner could supply them with something to contribute to the dinner.

Nels had quickly offered to prepare a container of his special pasta salad for them.

"I feel better not going empty-handed," Irene had said with satisfaction.

Meredith whirled around at a knock on her door.

"Ready?" came her mom's voice from the hall.

"Just about." She huffed in exasperation, finally choosing a pair of capris and a sleeveless blouse. Slipping into sandals, she ran a brush quickly through her hair.

She reflexively reached for her cell phone before remembering there was no cell service here. When they first got to Little Sister, she'd felt as if she'd lost a limb, not being able to text Jan or Barb, not hearing the ping of incoming messages. She'd never realized how often she checked her phone. She left it on the dresser.

"You look fine, Meredith," Roy said, anticipating her protests, and Meredith guessed he'd probably already been through this with Irene.

Her mom shrugged. "They might as well see us as we are."

Meredith thought her mother looked lovely, in a deep indigo tunic and white slacks.

Roy placed a hand on Irene's back, nudging her along. "Come on. We don't want to be late."

With Irene reading the directions—Meredith almost laughed to think they needed directions to any place on Little Sister—they headed out of the village, following the ring road. They'd done a good bit of exploring since they arrived, and had driven the circumference of the island several times. Smaller roads branched off the main one, but the majority of the houses seemed to be set back off this one road that encircled the island. When Roy pulled into the Cooper drive, Meredith realized they had passed this house several times. She knew Mr. Cooper owned and operated the marina, and she had learned that Molly, the sheriff, was his daughter—information cheerfully offered by Wilma.

When they got out of the car, Irene paused for a moment, and Meredith realized her mom was probably as nervous as she was.

"Ready, honey?" Irene reached for Meredith's hand.

Before they got to the porch, the screen door opened and Molly stepped outside. "Glad you could make it."

A spotted dog nudged past her leg.

"Isn't that Blossom?" Meredith asked as he sailed off the porch.

"Yes," Molly said, grinning when the two dogs immediately began a game of chase. "They'll be fine. Come on in."

Meredith followed her parents inside.

"Meredith, hi." Kathleen from the library came over to greet her. "This must be your mom and dad."

A flurry of introductions followed. Meredith struggled to remember all the names: Joe, Jenny, Rebecca, Louisa. Siobhan she recognized from her gift shop in the village.

"We're expecting a few more," Jenny said, leading everybody back to the kitchen. "They should be here soon."

"We brought some pasta salad," Irene said, holding the container.

"You didn't have to do that," Rebecca told her, taking it to place in the fridge for now.

"Nels made it," Roy said. "We're kitchen-less at the moment." He patted his stomach. "We've already learned you can't go wrong with his cooking."

Meredith said little, instead curiously observing the physical similarities between Molly and Rebecca—the black hair, those strange blue-green eyes.

Kathleen must have noticed. "I thought Molly must be Rebecca's daughter at first. Hard to believe Rebecca and Jenny are sisters. Bobby, one of the ferry captains, is their brother."

"I remember him," Meredith said. "And the big guy. Talks a lot."

Kathleen laughed. "Fred. Yeah, I think Fred learns everything there is to know about everyone on the way here."

"Whose birthday is it?" Meredith asked.

"Mine."

"Happy Birthday! You're sure we're not intruding?"

"We're sure. Around here, the more, the merrier."

Molly came over carrying two glasses. "Wine?"

"Thanks," Kathleen said, leaning over for a quick kiss.

Molly held out the other. "Meredith?"

"Thank you."

A radio on the counter crackled, and everyone hushed so that Joe could listen through the static to a voice. Meredith couldn't make out what it said, but Joe replied, "Thirty minutes. Got it."

"Everything's ready," Jenny said. "Why don't we all go sit on the porch and wait for them?"

Meredith didn't know who "them" was, but she followed everyone out to the porch. The older woman, Louisa, shared a two-seat glider with Rebecca. Jenny insisted Roy and Irene take the other two Adirondack chairs while Joe and Molly carried a few kitchen chairs outside. Siobhan somehow managed to float down to sit on the porch, her bare feet gracefully tucked under her skirt. Meredith had a feeling she could look elegant in sackcloth.

Jasper and Blossom came galumphing full-speed out of the trees to collapse at the base of the steps, tongues lolling. Kathleen brought out a bowl of water, which they both drank from noisily.

Meredith was just getting ready to ask about the two wooden boxes Molly had set on the porch beside the glider when Jenny asked, "So what brought you to Little Sister?"

Irene opened her mouth to reply, but before she could speak, Molly said, "I didn't invite the Turners here tonight just to be friendly."

Immediately everyone quieted, and Meredith had the strong feeling they'd all been waiting for this.

Molly settled on the top porch step. "Seems they have quite a story to tell."

Meredith gave her mother a small nod, and Irene began—the dreams, her drawings, the visit to Jeanette and the discovery of the photo of Little Sister.

"And we just knew we had to come here," she finished.

A stunned silence followed her story.

Kathleen was the first to speak. "Meredith, you're having the same dream as your mom? Of the shipwreck?"

Meredith nodded. "I had it when I was a girl, then it went away for years. And then it returned."

"When?" Rebecca asked sharply.

Meredith thought back to be sure. "Christmas a year ago."

Louisa gripped Rebecca's arm, hard by the look of her white knuckles.

"You're sure it was two Christmases ago?" Rebecca pushed.

Meredith thought again. "Yes. Because I spent that Christmas with my family in Portland, like I always do, but I was really sick, feverish with a cold, and Christmas night was the first night the dream came back. I remember waking up, feeling strange. Why?"

Louisa's face was white. "Because that's when my sister, Olivia, died."

"And it has continued since then?" Siobhan asked.

"Yes," Meredith said. "At first it was only every month or two, and then it became more frequent, until now, it's almost every night."

She glanced at her mother, who nodded her agreement.

"It started to feel more urgent," Irene said. She tilted her head. "But I just realized, I haven't had it once since we arrived here."

Meredith's mouth dropped. "Neither have I."

"Tell them about the ancestry reports," Roy said, speaking for the first time.

"What ancestry reports?" Rebecca demanded.

"I wanted our family to do one of those ancestry things," Irene said. "I thought it would be fun."

Her voice faltered, and Roy reached for her hand.

"We may have let the genie out of the bottle," he said.

"What do you mean?" Jenny asked. "What did you find out?"

"We don't know what it all means yet," Meredith said. "But my mom has a high percentage of Native American DNA, something we never knew about. My uncle doesn't have any. In fact, none of his matches hers."

"My brother, Art," Irene said, "checked with Massachusetts—where he was born—and confirmed he was adopted. I've sent away to inquire whether I am. I guess they can tell you if your birth certificate is an original or an adoption certificate. Our parents have passed, so we just don't know."

They were all distracted by the arrival of a car. It pulled to a stop as Jenny and Joe and the others jumped up to greet the latecomers. Meredith watched curiously as a pretty blonde woman, clearly pregnant, got out of the passenger seat, assisted by a young guy who could only be Molly's brother. The back door opened and two more men disentangled themselves from the rear seat. One of them went around to the trunk while everyone was busy greeting and hugging the new arrivals.

Meredith, Irene, and Roy stood politely as the scrum approached the house and a new round of introductions was made. Meredith shook hands with Brandi, Matty, Joey. Turning to the last person, his arms filled with boxes, she found herself face to face with the man from her dream.

Chapter 13

I T SEEMED TO KATHLEEN that they were caught up in one of her authors' bizarre stories; the Turners' tale was so unbelievable. Over dinner—once they got everyone settled at the table—Rebecca recounted to them some of the history of the island.

"So there was a wreck here," Irene said. "A ship with wooden masts, like in our dreams?"

"There have been many shipwrecks near this island," Rebecca corrected.

"But the one you describe in your dream sounds like the accounts of the survivors of the first recorded one, yes," said Louisa. "The *Connemara*. She went down in 1760."

"And the passengers were all Irish?" Roy asked.

"They were more like chattel," Rebecca said. "Poor laborers, most indentured to work their debts off over here. When they were rescued, the First Ones offered them an opportunity for a new life. Most took it."

"And you're all their descendants?" Meredith asked.

"Most of us," Jenny said. "Some, like Nels and Tim, have married into island families."

"Have any of you done the DNA tests?" Irene asked.

"We don't need DNA to tell us where we belong," Rebecca said sharply.

"I seem to keep offending people with that question," Irene said.

Kathleen leaned near. "Don't mind her," she said in a loud whisper. "She scared the bejeebers out of me when I met her, but her bark is worse than her bite."

Everyone at the table howled, making the dogs lift their heads from where they were stretched out in the living room. Even Rebecca had to smile.

"My apologies if I seem harsh," she said grudgingly. "But our entire history has been one of having to protect what we have from those who would take it from us."

"But what does any of this have to do with us?" Meredith asked in frustration. She cast a quick glance in Aidan's direction.

Kathleen caught that glance and noticed that Aidan's eyes were downcast. Now that she thought about it, he hadn't said a word since arriving. This was how he'd been when she first returned to Little Sister, when he was drinking, not dealing with the past, Kathleen recalled with a niggle of worry.

"I think," Roy said, laying a hand on Meredith's arm, "that we're being a little rude. Wasn't this supposed to be a birthday celebration?"

"You're right. I'm sorry," Meredith said contritely.

"Hey, we can do more than one thing," Joey said, raising his bottle of Smithwick's. "Happy Birthday, Kathleen!"

A chorus followed as everyone drank a toast to Kathleen. She couldn't help but bask in this. Prior to last year, it had been so long since anyone had acknowledged this day as anything but the anniversary of

Bryan's drowning. She caught Aidan's eye, and he gave her a little nod as he took a drink of his cranberry juice and ginger ale.

"Have you heard from your parents, Katie?" Louisa asked.

Kathleen nodded. "Got a card from my dad." He'd signed her mom's name, but it was a start.

"Is the nursery ready?" she asked Brandi, deliberately redirecting the conversation.

Baby talk took over for the rest of the dinner. Matty couldn't seem to wipe the dazed grin off his face.

As soon as dinner plates were emptied of second helpings—mostly Joey and Matty—Aidan was one of the first to help scoop dishes off the table to take to the kitchen. Kathleen was about to send Molly to talk to him when Molly gave her a tight smile, filling her hands with plates and silverware, and followed him to the kitchen. Siobhan and Louisa got up to help.

Kathleen stared after them and wasn't listening when Brandi spoke.

"Kathleen?"

She jumped. "Hmmm?"

"I asked how your book business is going?"

"Sorry. It's going great. Things have been steady."

"What do you do?" Irene asked.

"I edit and format," Kathleen said. "It was one of the best things about coming here. I can work remotely as long as I have an Internet connection."

"She's being modest," Louisa said, catching that last as she came back for more dishes. "She does the most beautiful book covers."

"Do you?" Irene's face lit up. "I'd love to see some of your work."

"Mom's an artist, too," Meredith offered.

Irene shook her head. "Just a retired art teacher. And definitely an amateur. Although there's enough inspiration on this island to keep a real artist going for the rest of her life."

"Did you bring any supplies with you?" Kathleen asked.

Irene shook her head. "We weren't sure what we'd find when we got here, or how long we'd stay."

"I can lend you a pad and pencils, or Miranda and Tim stock a little of everything," Kathleen said. "If you'd like, pick up a few things, and we'll go out for a sketching party one day."

"Oh, that would be wonderful."

Further conversation was interrupted by the arrival of the birthday cake, alight with thirty-six candles, and a loud chorus of "Happy Birthday."

Kathleen blew all the candles out and cut the cake, passing plates down the table. From the kitchen, the telephone jangled. Joe got up to answer. He returned a moment later and lifted his glass again.

"Another reason to celebrate!" he said. "Miranda went into labor a few hours ago. Lena helped her deliver a healthy baby girl, Charlotte."

Everyone drank a toast to the new arrival.

"What a nice birthday present, Katie," Louisa said.

"Do they need help at the market this evening?" Siobhan asked.

Joe shook his head. "Tim said they've got it covered for tonight with the kids they hired. I told him we'd all be by to sign up and help cover for the next few weeks."

Irene turned to Kathleen. "You're all just going to work at the market?"

Kathleen chuckled. "I know. When I arrived, I wasn't used to this, either. Everyone here helps everyone else. This will give Tim and Miranda time with the new baby, especially since it's high season. We'll all pitch in."

"Amazing," Irene said.

"Yes." Kathleen sighed happily. "It is amazing."

When she and Molly left the Cooper house an hour later, the June twilight was lingering in the west, Venus brilliant above the horizon. Molly parked in the drive but caught Kathleen's hand before she could climb the steps.

"One more thing."

Kathleen was totally bewildered as Molly retrieved a parcel she'd hidden on the porch.

"Come on," Molly said, reaching for Kathleen's hand and leading her toward the trail through the woods behind the house. Blossom, always eager for an adventure, galloped up the path ahead of them.

"Where are we going?" Kathleen asked.

Molly grinned. "You'll see."

When Molly was being all mysterious like this, Kathleen had learned to just go with it. "Did you talk to Aidan?"

"Yeah."

"What's up? He was weird at dinner. Everything okay?"

"Not sure."

"What does that mean?"

Molly slowed a bit. "At Bealtaine, do you remember seeing anything that night? Anything unusual? During the bonfire?"

Kathleen thought back. "You mean other than Siobhan going skyclad again? And you trying not to look at her."

Molly suddenly tripped over a root. "Shit!" She regained her balance as Kathleen doubled over, laughing. "Very funny."

"She is beautiful. You'd have to be dead not to notice."

"She is." Molly reached for Kathleen's hand again, pulling her close for a kiss. "But not as beautiful as you."

Kathleen leaned into the kiss, enjoying the effect Molly's lips and tongue had on her, promising more of the same later tonight.

"Come on," Molly whispered, tugging on her hand. "Anyway, Aidan—and he swears he didn't have anything to drink and he didn't smoke—he says he saw a woman that night. On the other side of the circle. Looking at him. He told me about her weeks ago. And tonight, he met her."

"Wait, what?" Kathleen's mind was in a whirl.

"Meredith."

They stepped out of the trees onto the rocky contours of the bluff. "Meredith was the woman he saw that night."

Kathleen gaped at her. "She was really weird with him, the way she looked—or tried not to look—at him."

The wind teased her hair, tossing it in little gusts as she gazed out over the ocean, black under the gathering night. Soon, the rising moon would sprinkle diamonds on the waves, but not yet.

She reached for Molly's hand, warm and sure and solid. "I realized tonight, it's not right to forget Bryan on this day any more than when my parents forgot me. And that includes Aidan. This day will forever be tied to all three of us. A piece of Aidan died that day with Bryan."

Molly gathered her in her arms, and Kathleen clung to her. "I wish Aidan could find what we have," Molly said, her voice muffled as she nuzzled into Kathleen's neck. "I wish he could find someone to fill that hole, make him complete again."

Kathleen sniffed and released Molly. "What are we doing here?"

Molly squatted down to where her parcel lay on the ground. She loosened the strings binding it, and rolled out a piece of paper.

"I was kind of thinking already about what you just said, about us not forgetting Bryan on this day."

Kathleen squinted through the deepening night. Molly reached into her pocket and flicked a wind-proof lighter.

"Is... is that a kite?" Kathleen asked.

"Yeah. Hold this, will you?"

Kathleen took the lighter from her. The wind made the flame flicker wildly as Molly assembled the sticks at the paper's edges.

"Everything is biodegradable," Molly said. "I used wood scraps I had in the shop. The string is water-soluble. And I used rice paper. So we can let this go and not worry. Had to make sure the wind was blowing in its usual direction tonight. This will go out to sea."

The tail was tied in several knots.

Kathleen sniffed. "Lamp oil?"

"Yep. And wax for a slow burn. Trade me." Molly stood and reached for the tail. "Make a wish, and get ready to play out the string."

She held the lighter to the cloth tail, and it ignited immediately. Kathleen sent a wish to Bryan and Nanna and let the wind take the kite out, away from the bluff, over the ocean. She gradually released a couple hundred feet of string, watching the flames slowly engulf the tail, knot by knot, until at last the kite itself ignited.

She let the string go, and the kite took off, burning brightly in the night sky before falling to the water in a shower of sparks.

⬛⬛⬛⬛⬛⬛⬛

WHEN THE FIRST RAYS of the sun lit the sky, pushing away the darkness of her room, Meredith was already awake. Aidan Cooper. She'd spent a restless night, barely dropping below the surface of sleep, only to relive that dream from the night of her birthday.

None of these incidents could be mere coincidence. There were too many of them—learning of their DNA, no matter what Jeannette said; the immediate recognition of the photo of Little Sister Island; meeting Aidan last night.

Something was pulling them here. She hadn't yet told her parents about her other dream and seeing Aidan. That was so inexplicable she wasn't ready to share it yet. But that didn't stop her stomach from fluttering at the memory of looking into his eyes last evening.

She got out of bed and flung the curtain open. He'd seemed just as flustered as she was, and she wondered if he could possibly have recognized her as well.

After a quick shower, she chose one of the books she'd borrowed from the library and headed down to take Jasper out and then get some breakfast. Her parents would be down whenever they woke. Their entire pace of life had slowed to a delicious crawl since coming here. She knew it couldn't last forever, but she was enjoying every second while it lasted.

"Good morning, dear," sang Wilma, automatically bringing her a steaming mug of coffee. "The usual?"

Meredith grinned. "Yes, please." Nels's banana pancakes were the best she'd ever had. Jasper curled up under the table.

She smiled in the direction of the counter, where she was learning to recognize the faces of the locals. Her smile froze on her face when she realized Aidan was sitting there, gazing at her. Her heart leapt into her throat when he slid off his stool and walked in her direction, but he stalked by without a word.

She stared into her coffee, willing her heart to slow down. *Stop behaving like a schoolgirl.*

She opened her book and read some more about the early development of Big Sister Island. She'd read and heard enough to know that hardly any of the original island families still lived on Big Sister, as land had been sold and offlanders—*I'm even using their language now,* she realized with a smile—had bought it up to build big, exclusive houses. That triggered a thought.

"Wilma," she said when her breakfast arrived, "can you tell me where I can find out what houses are for sale here on Little Sister?"

Wilma stared down at her, halfway through refilling her coffee cup. "For sale? Land sakes, there's no houses for sale here on Little Sister."

Meredith frowned. "None?"

Wilma cleared her throat. "I guess folks that live here want to stay here."

She moved on, collecting dishes and talking to the new hotel guests arriving for breakfast.

Meredith knew from her own area of Oregon that there were always houses for sale. People who thought living near the ocean sounded like a great idea were disillusioned by the constant upkeep required.

"There you are."

She looked up to find her dad pulling out a chair at her table.

"You're up early," Roy said.

"Couldn't sleep." Meredith took a bite of her pancakes. "What about you? This is early for you, too."

Roy nodded his thanks to Wilma when she brought him a mug of coffee.

"I'll have your eggs and hash browns up for you in a jiffy," she said.

"I find myself in a different rhythm here," he said when she left. "I'm in bed earlier, up earlier."

"I know," Meredith agreed. "It's... it's like we've always been here."

Roy took a sip of coffee. "I was talking to Joe Cooper last night. Thought we might take a boat over to Big Sister, check it out."

"Really?" She considered. "Have you talked to Mom?"

"She's excited about it. Joe said one of them would be going in the next few days, and we could go along."

"That sounds like fun."

Wilma brought a plate with two eggs, a large pile of hash browns, and toast. "Here you go."

"Thank you." Roy dug hungrily into his breakfast. "What's on your docket today?"

"I want to go back to the library," Meredith said. "Talk to Rebecca some more. What about you?"

Roy flushed a little, immediately looking guilty of something.

"What?" Meredith asked.

He shrugged. "I was talking to Patrick Flaherty, you know, the owner of the pub. He's doing some brewing of his own, ales mostly. Thought I might pass some time with him."

Meredith laughed. "Have you told Mom you're spending the day in the pub?"

He gave her a sheepish grin. "It's a small island. She'll figure it out."

143

"SOUND IT OUT," LOUISA said, sitting with an arm wrapped around eight-year-old Alexis Redhawk, who was struggling with her reading.

The summer reading group had been a success, with about twenty-five children attending, ranging from four to thirteen years of age. Some were just learning to read, but others, like Alexis, found reading and spelling difficult and were falling behind in their schoolwork.

"She's got the patience of a saint," Rebecca muttered to Kathleen.

"The kids love her," Kathleen agreed. "She keeps using those old mnemonics and rhymes I learned. I before E, except after C. They helped us learn. Why don't they teach those anymore?"

"I heard that," Louisa said, glancing at them. "I suppose they're as old-fashioned as I am." She gave a dismissive sniff. "But maybe we still have some value."

Kathleen had helped some, but it was Blossom who really enjoyed the reading group. He loved lying on the floor between a couple of the kids while they read aloud.

The screen door opened, and Meredith Turner stepped inside.

"I'm so sorry," she blurted. "I didn't mean to interrupt."

She grabbed for Jasper's collar. Blossom's tail thumped the floor at the sight of his playmate.

"You're not interrupting if you're here to read," said Louisa. "That's what we're all doing. And dogs are welcome, too, as long as they like to listen."

The kids looked up at Meredith expectantly as she hesitated.

"Then count me in." She plucked a book from the table in the middle of the room and sat down on the floor.

Jasper settled next to her, and one of the youngest children, little Isaiah Mulcahy, climbed into her lap.

"Read my book," he said.

Louisa smiled when Meredith set her book aside and began tracing a finger from word to word as she bent near Isaiah, reading to him quietly.

When the children's parents came by to get them an hour later, Louisa stood, stretching her stiff knees.

"You're a natural," she said.

Meredith smiled. "I haven't worked with this age group since my student teaching days."

Louisa paused in the midst of gathering the books scattered across the table. "You're a teacher?"

Meredith nodded. "High school English and literature."

"So you and your mother are both educators," Louisa said.

"Mom was actually thinking about going back," Meredith recalled. "She and my dad were clashing a bit once he retired. Too much togetherness after all those years."

Rebecca and Kathleen emerged from the back room, each carrying two mugs.

"Tea?" Rebecca asked, setting one mug in front of Louisa.

"Oh, thank you," Louisa said. "My throat was getting dry."

Meredith looked past Kathleen curiously. "What's back there?"

"Oh, just old books that need cataloguing," Rebecca said vaguely. "Sounds like things went well out here."

"Meredith is a teacher," Louisa told her.

"So I heard." Rebecca tilted her head. "You enjoy teaching."

"I do." Meredith bent to pick up a few books left lying on the floor. Both dogs jumped up, and she opened the door for them.

Louisa caught Rebecca's eye.

"Tell me about Aidan Cooper," Meredith said, coming to sit at the table.

"What do you want to know?" Rebecca pulled out a chair.

Louisa shifted her chair over as Kathleen joined them at the table.

"He's a ferry pilot?" Meredith asked.

"Yes. He's Joe and Jenny's eldest. Molly you've met. Then Joey, and Matty is the youngest." Rebecca's eyes narrowed. "Why?"

Meredith straightened a pile of books unnecessarily, her mouth opening and closing a couple of times as she seemed to grope for words.

"You saw him, didn't you?" Kathleen said.

Meredith stared at her. "How do you know that?"

"Wait," Rebecca commanded. "What do you mean, saw him?" She turned to Kathleen. "And how do you know that?"

Kathleen leaned her elbows on the table. "Because Aidan saw her, too. On Bealtaine. During the bonfire. He told Molly weeks ago. He didn't know who the woman was, until last night. It was you."

"How is that possible?" Louisa asked, but Rebecca held up a hand. "Tell us what you saw."

Meredith described the scene—the fire, people dancing, the beat of a drum, and Aidan's eyes staring into hers.

"When was this?" Rebecca asked.

"The night of my birthday, May first," Meredith said. "That was the night we opened our ancestry packets, and my uncle was so upset. We all went to bed early. And... I had that dream."

"If her time zone was three hours behind us..." Kathleen murmured.

"It may have all been happening at the same time," Louisa finished.

"I don't understand," Meredith said.

"That's how we celebrate Bealtaine," Kathleen explained. "We gather on the beach. Rebecca leads us in prayers, and we light the fire. There's music and dancing."

"But how could I have seen Aidan? And him me?" Meredith's tone was suspicious.

"Aidan didn't have anything to drink or smoke that night," Louisa reminded them. "Could he have been that open?"

Rebecca sat back, studying Meredith. "You said that was the night you opened your DNA results?"

"Yes." Meredith nodded. "It was the first time my mother and I realized we had Native American ancestry. Not," she added quickly, "that that makes us Native. I understand that."

Louisa frowned. "Are you thinking they could have First Ones' blood?"

Rebecca shook her head. "I just don't know." She tapped her fingers against her lips, deep in thought. "You said your mother and uncle were born in Massachusetts and adopted?"

"We only know my uncle was adopted," Meredith clarified. "My mom is waiting to hear back from New Hampshire."

"Why New Hampshire?" Kathleen asked.

"Because that's where she was born."

The room began to spin, and it seemed the light dimmed. Vaguely, Louisa heard the sound of porcelain shattering. Hands gripped her arms, steadying her.

"Miss Louisa!" Kathleen's lips were moving, but her voice sounded as if it were coming from underwater or something.

"I'm fine, Katie," Louisa said. "Just tired. Let me go rest."

"I'll drive you." Kathleen leaned down to help her to her feet.

"You don't have to—" Louisa started to protest.

"Yes, she does," Rebecca said firmly.

Louisa allowed herself to be assisted into the passenger seat of her old Ford. She didn't really remember the drive home, but suddenly, Kathleen was there, opening the door and taking her arm to guide her up the porch steps and into the house.

Despite Louisa's objections, Kathleen led her up the stairs to her bedroom, where she slipped Louisa's shoes off and pushed her back onto her pillow. She found a crocheted throw and drew it up to Louisa's chin.

"You rest now," Kathleen said.

"I will. Thank you."

"We'll check in on you later." Kathleen backed out of the room, pulling the door partway shut, leaving Louisa alone.

She lay there and closed her eyes, tears running from her eyes into her hair. "Why now?" she whispered.

Chapter 14

THE BELL ON THE market's door rang almost non-stop as people came in and out all morning. Molly wondered how she could have lived on this island most of her life and never have known just how busy this store was during high season. Of course, it helped that it was the only place onisland to buy most of what Miranda and Tim stocked. The tourists needed snacks, drinks, replacements for the things they'd forgotten: toothbrushes, soap, shampoo, beach towels, over the counter medicines. And lots and lots of sunscreen and aloe gel. Even this far north, people managed to get sunburned. And the islanders needed everything else.

Allison and Rachel had the checkout counter under control, so Molly patrolled the aisles, helping people with their searches for this and that. When Terry Fahy came in, needing some lumber for a project at his house, Molly gratefully ducked out back with him, to the separate building that served as a kind of warehouse for the bulkier things the market stocked. She helped him load what he needed into his truck and wrote out a chit listing everything for him to sign.

"Tim will catch you later to settle this," she said. This honor system was one of the things she loved about living here. She was just heading back inside when her mom found her.

"There you are," Jenny said.

"How's Miranda doing?"

"She's tired, but good. The baby is adorable, of course," Jenny said wistfully. "And Ellis is so excited to have a baby sister. He keeps trying to put his toys in her bassinet. All of them."

Molly grinned. "You'll soon have one of those of your own to spoil."

"Yes, but they'll be on Big Sister, not here. It won't be the same." They headed toward the market's rear entry. "I'm going to help out here for a few hours. I know you've been here since opening."

"Speaking of Big Sister," Molly said, "Dad told me the Turners were interested in going over. Want to come along? I was going to ask them if tomorrow would suit."

Jenny's eyes lit up. "That would be wonderful. Early?"

"Yup, six-ish, if they'll agree to get going that early." Molly pulled her mom to a stop before they got inside. "Did you hear about Miss Louisa?"

"Yes." Jenny checked, but no one was within hearing distance. "Rebecca told me. Olivia and Mr. Woodhouse got left behind at the library when Kathleen drove her home. Rebecca brought the boxes to her later that afternoon. She said Louisa was odd, distracted. Didn't even remember she hadn't brought them home."

"I tried stopping by yesterday," Molly said. "She was out in the garden, wouldn't stop weeding. Wouldn't talk. Said she was busy. Almost asked me to leave." She glanced at her mother. "Do you think we need to try and get her to a doctor?"

Jenny scoffed. "You think she's likely to go?"

"No," Molly admitted. "I could arrest her. Make her go."

"Good luck with that."

"I'll check on her again. And speaking of weird, have you seen Aidan the last few days?"

"Not since the night of Kathleen's birthday."

"He hasn't been on the Little Sister run," Molly said, frowning. "I've been looking out for him. Bobby and Fred said he's been doing the Big Sister route. Did..." She hesitated a second.

"Meredith Turner?"

"Yeah." Molly sighed in relief. "You know?"

Jenny nodded. "Rebecca told me about that, too. What do you make of it?"

Molly shrugged. "Not sure what to make of it. There's something about those people. Aidan, Miss Louisa. Somehow, it's all tied together."

"Hmmm." Jenny gazed skyward.

Molly looked too, but the sky was clear. "Something coming?"

Her mom often had feelings, things about the island that she could sense, but now she shook her head. "Just can't tell."

⚎⚎⚎⚎⚎⚎

THE BOAT ROSE AND fell in a regular rhythm as it rode the swells. Overhead, a lingering rose hue tinted the clouds.

"Sorry it's so choppy," Molly called back. "You okay?"

Meredith glanced at her parents, but they looked as excited as she was. "We're fine." She leaned forward to make herself heard over the wind and the steady hum of the boat motor. "Are you sure we're not taking a spot from Kathleen? We could have gone on a different day."

Molly grinned and shook her head. "She has a deadline, and had to work today, no matter what. Besides, this way, the dogs can tussle and play together all day."

151

Jenny bent down to a basket at her feet. "Coffee? Muffin?"

Roy accepted only a muffin. He'd brought a travel cup of Wilma's coffee. But Irene and Meredith both took cups from her.

Meredith sat back, snugging her hood a little more tightly around her neck. "Do you mind talking while we ride?" she asked Jenny.

"Not at all." Jenny helped herself to a blueberry muffin and sat back.

"Big Sister isn't like Little Sister? I read that land was sold way back when, and that's why it's built up so much."

She saw Molly turn to share a quick glance with her mom before Jenny said, "That's right. There aren't many island families left on Big Sister."

Irene, apparently as interested in this as Meredith was, said, "But it's only island families on Little Sister. We asked about houses for sale, and there aren't any. Not even for rent."

Jenny seemed to stall by taking a bite of her muffin and then reaching down for a drink. "We don't sell houses on Little Sister. Or land."

Irene and Meredith, both ready to ask more questions, paused at this bit of news.

"Ever? I mean, how do you…?" Meredith couldn't conceive of not selling real estate.

Jenny smiled. "Our ancestors took precautions. Even though the Irish were desperate to own land, they came from a system where they couldn't. So, when they were rescued by the First Ones, who couldn't fathom chopping land into bits that someone could claim as their own, they realized the wisdom of that. No one claims land any more than we claim sky or sea. It's been that way ever since. Houses and land get passed down in families."

"Wow." Meredith sat back.

That explained, kind of, the almost tribal feel of Little Sister's islanders. The way they looked out for one another, like the rotating schedule at the market to help the owners there.

When at last Big Sister came into view, Irene's gasp was audible over the other noise.

"Those are some big houses," Roy commented.

"No way we could afford to live here," Molly said over her shoulder.

Even from a distance, the vast expanses of glass and the colossal size of the houses were overwhelming. The marina, as Molly steered them among the boats anchored there, was like a yacht showroom. Their modest boat was one of the smallest. Molly tied up to the dock and steadied the launch as the Turners climbed out. Meredith was surprised to see a ferry already docked as well.

"Why is the ferry here so early?"

Jenny chuckled. "Big Sister has four or five ferry runs a day in season. Most people are just day trippers, here for a few hours of shopping or dining and then back before nightfall."

"This is delightful," Irene said, taking in the array of shops spreading out beyond the marina. She hooked an arm through Roy's. "Come on, honey."

He paused. "Wait, we don't want to keep the Coopers waiting. What time should we meet you back here?"

Molly glanced at her watch. "How about in four hours?"

"Sounds good." Roy allowed himself to be pulled along. "See you in four hours."

"You know where I'll be," Jenny said, hurrying off in the direction of The Lobster Pot and Brandi.

"You're not going with?" Molly asked Meredith.

"I know where they'll be," Meredith said with a half-laugh. "Mom will go into every gallery, and Dad will want to talk to every bartender about brewing."

"Where to?" Molly asked.

"I don't mean to invite myself along with you," Meredith said. "I can wander around and occupy myself."

"Come on." Molly leaned her head in the direction of the ferry. "Just want to check something."

Meredith followed, her heart pounding more as they neared the ferry, bigger than the one that had brought them to Little Sister. Apparently all the cars had departed. A few marina workers were using forklifts to transfer cargo on and off the ferry. Molly went to speak to one of them and returned a moment later.

"We'll come back in a few hours," she said. "Let me show you around."

They wandered the village, already crawling with people, most of them tourists, judging by the shopping bags dangling from their hands. Molly led them out of town, to a row of the gargantuan houses they'd seen on their approach to the island.

"How much would one of these go for?" Meredith asked.

Molly snorted. "More than I'll make in my lifetime, probably."

Meredith's head swiveled as they walked. "It really is different here, isn't it?"

"Yeah. A day on this island, and I am so glad to get back to Little Sister."

"Molly," Meredith said, "on the way here, your mother said houses and land aren't sold on Little Sister."

"Yeah."

"So, if someone else, someone not from there, wanted to live there, how could they?"

Molly didn't answer immediately. Meredith kept pace with her, studying her profile, wondering for a minute if she was going to answer.

"You can't."

"Can't what?"

Molly slowed and faced her. "Only people from island families can live on Little Sister. Others can visit, but that's all."

"Oh." The crush of disappointment in Meredith's chest was unexpected. And strong. "Oh." She nodded.

"I'm sorry, Meredith."

154

"No, no I get it," Meredith said quickly. "I was just wondering. I mean we live clear across the country. It's..."

She forced a smile and walked on. "I think I saw something about a lighthouse?"

They spent a couple of hours hiking out to the lighthouse, wandering back toward the village through some of the residential areas—not quite as grand as the houses along the coast, but still way bigger and more expensive than anything on Little Sister.

Molly knew a lot about the island's history and kept up a running commentary. She told Meredith about Little Sister's quest to become green and self-sustaining, with their push for solar and wind power.

"I wish Big Sister would do the same, but I don't think the people here are willing to sacrifice or invest in it."

They arrived back in town in time to see another ferry chugging into the marina. Meredith followed as Molly jogged toward it. When she saw Aidan Cooper striding down the gangplank, his arms loaded with crates that he added to a stack already sitting on the dock, she hung back. She watched as Molly flung herself into her brother's arms, pounding him on the back.

Molly looked around and found Meredith, waving her forward. "Come here."

Meredith's feet obeyed, but her mouth was dry as she found herself looking up into Aidan's eyes.

"You two met the other night," Molly was saying. "Meredith is visiting from Oregon. Can you grab a bite?"

Aidan glanced over his shoulder. "Uh, I should—"

"Let him do the unloading," Molly said, pointing to the teenager running the forklift. "You don't have to shove off again for two hours. I checked."

Without giving him time to argue, she took him by the arm with one hand, Meredith with the other, and led them away from the commotion at the dock.

Molly let them go as the crowd thinned. They followed her as she wound her way down an alley, off the main drag, to a much quieter street.

"We can talk easier in here," she said, pointing to a small place Meredith wouldn't have given a second glance to.

Inside, it was dark and cool, a trio of ceiling fans stirring the air. There were only a few other people here, mostly workers, Meredith guessed, judging from the lack of expensive logos on their shirts and the absence of shopping bags.

Meredith took a seat across from Aidan, who seemed to be looking anywhere but at her.

"What are you doing on Big Sister?" he asked, and Meredith realized he hadn't said a word in her hearing the night of the birthday party. His voice was softer, quieter than she'd have guessed, and still had a bit of the lilt she'd picked up in the Little Sister islanders' speech patterns.

"Mom wanted to visit Brandi," Molly was saying. "And the Turners wanted to look around." She reached up and brushed her fingers over his jaw. "What happened to the beard?"

"Too hot. I'll grow it again in the winter."

A waitress appeared at their table. "Hey, Aidan," she said, flashing him a smile. "Molly." She nodded at Meredith. "What can I get you?"

"Iced tea and a double-decker BLT," Aidan said.

"Coke and a single-decker for me," Molly said.

Meredith tilted her head in Molly's direction. "Same."

"Be right up." The waitress stuck her pencil behind her ear and went to the bar to get their drinks.

An awkward silence settled over the table.

"How many runs a day are you doing?" Molly asked at last.

"Three if I do Big Sister," he said.

"Why aren't you doing ours?" Molly asked. "Thanks," she said when the waitress brought their drinks to the table.

Aidan shrugged. "Bobby likes doing the Little Sister run, and Tony's father passed away. He needed to take some time off, and this route needed to be covered."

"Well, Mom would like to see you more often, so trade off, if you can."

"Will do," he said. Raising his eyes to Meredith's, he asked, "Are you enjoying the island?"

"Big or Little?" she asked.

His mouth quirked into a grin. "Both, I guess."

"Big Sister is nice. Everything is beautiful and spiffed up, but," she tugged a paper straw free from its wrapper, "I like Little Sister more."

He gave her a small nod, and she was dismayed to feel a flutter somewhere in the vicinity of her stomach. Molly asked if he'd seen their other brothers. While they talked, it gave Meredith a chance to study him more closely. He was dark, like Molly, with a couple days' stubble covering his jaw. His lips curled up a little at the corners, but, judging by the frown lines between his brows, it looked as if he didn't smile often. She'd seen how strong he was down at the marina, but it was the strength of a man who worked for a living, not muscles groomed at a gym. There was something else about him, not physical, but more a shyness that was totally at odds with his physical strength. She couldn't put her finger on it, exactly, but it intrigued her.

She was startled when their food arrived and Aidan caught her watching him. She diverted her attention to her sandwich.

"How much longer are you staying?" Aidan asked.

It took a second for Meredith to realize he was speaking to her. "Oh," she swallowed quickly, wiping a bit of mayonnaise from the corner of her mouth, "we don't have any definite plans. I'm off until September, and my parents are retired now, so... we're flexible. I'm hoping we'll stay the rest of the summer."

What made you say that? she asked herself but, as she saw the unexpected flicker of a smile on Aidan's face, she lowered her eyes, enjoying the warmth spreading inside her.

A STEADY RAIN THRUMMED on the roof, pattering against the windows. Kathleen lay nestled in Molly's arms as they listened to it.

"Isn't this better than being out there?" Kathleen asked.

Molly pressed her lips to Kathleen's forehead. "Yes, but it's not helping me get the McKinnons' house painted. Right now, it's two-tone, and the clapboards will have to dry for a few days before I can get back to it."

Kathleen snuggled into Molly's neck. "The house isn't going anywhere, and two-tone might become an island fashion."

Molly snorted. "Maybe you're right."

Kathleen listened to the beat of Molly's heart. "I saw Aidan again yesterday. Third time this week. He's doing the Little Sister run again?"

"I think Meredith Turner might have something to do with that."

"Can't believe you hijacked both of them for lunch that day."

Molly's laugh vibrated in Kathleen's ear. "I can't believe I did, either. But I swear, if they hadn't been dragged together, the two of them would never have talked."

"You think there's something there?"

"I don't know."

Something in Molly's voice made Kathleen shift to look at her. "Do you want there to be?"

Molly didn't answer immediately. "I don't know," she said again. "I want him to be happy, and I hope that means being with someone some day. But I don't want him to fall for her if the Turners are going to head back to Oregon in a few weeks."

"Has he ever had a relationship?"

"Not that I know of." Molly rubbed her cheek against Kathleen's hair. "When you went back to the mainland last year..."

"To take care of Susannah?"

158

"Yeah. Aidan told me he didn't think he could ever let himself love someone. He said he wasn't strong enough to need someone else."

"But that's so wrong. He's such a great guy. It makes my heart hurt to think of him being alone always."

"I know." Molly paused. "But it would be harder for him to let someone in, and then, if it didn't work out..."

They lay quietly for a few minutes.

"What do you think of the Turners?" Kathleen asked.

"What do you mean?"

"Well, you spent a lot of time with them the day you went to Big Sister. You were the one who invited them to dinner. You like them, don't you?"

"I do. Not sure why. I don't connect to other tourists, but there's something about them."

"Irene is talented. We went sketching last week. I took her to the cemetery and the stone circle."

"Really?"

"Molly, she connected to the place." Kathleen sighed. "I could see it on her face. Standing among the stones, inside the circle. It spoke to her."

"Meredith asked about houses for sale."

"They couldn't do the Passing," Kathleen reminded them both. "There's no connection to the island. No matter how much we like them, there's that."

"I know. It's the first time I've ever wished we didn't have those traditions."

Molly's stomach growled loudly.

Kathleen patted it. "Time for breakfast. Come on."

A few minutes later, seated at the table over a bowl of oatmeal, Kathleen said, "I think I'm going to visit Miss Louisa today. I haven't seen her since that day at the library."

"I tried," Molly said. "But she's been very strange."

"I know." Kathleen reached for her coffee cup. "Rebecca said Louisa almost threw her out when she went by with some soup she'd made. It's just not like her."

When she was finished, Molly stood with her bowl and cup and bent down to kiss Kathleen. "Let me know if you figure anything out. Since I can't work outside, I'll be down the marina with Dad."

Kathleen quickly did the dishes. She cut part of the loaf of orange cranberry bread she'd baked the day before and wrapped it. As soon as she reached for her rain jacket, Blossom was at her side.

"Today, we drive," she told him, plucking the car keys out of the bowl on the table. "We can't be dripping water all over Miss Louisa's floors."

The rain had slowed to a light drizzle, and it looked as if the sky to the east was lighter. Without even realizing it, she'd developed the unconscious habit of reading the island's weather patterns—changes in wind direction, the look of the clouds approaching the island, even the smell of the air. She remembered when she'd automatically reached for the weather app on her phone that was always in her hand or pocket, the same phone that now lay in a drawer somewhere, unused these days.

When she parked next to Louisa's sedan, she saw that the front door was open, so no worries that she might not be up. Most of the islanders were early risers, but still.

Blossom bounded after a rabbit grazing in the yard and then came trotting back, his tail waving a like a victory flag for having chased the varmint away. They climbed the porch steps, and Kathleen was just getting ready to call out and knock when she heard a voice. Thinking Louisa might already have company, she paused.

"Be quiet!"

That was definitely Louisa's voice. Worried now, Kathleen listened again, wondering if Louisa needed help.

"Leave me alone."

"Miss Louisa!" Kathleen banged loudly on the screen door, and there was sudden silence from inside the house. "Miss Louisa, are you okay?"

She was just reaching for the handle when Louisa appeared on the other side of the screen in her robe and slippers, her hair hanging down around her shoulders.

"Katie, what are you doing here?"

"I came by to see how you're doing, and I heard you. Are you all right?"

"I'm fine," Louisa said, her fingers fumbling with the sash of her robe. "I was just..."

"May I come in?"

"You don't—"

"Miss Louisa," Kathleen said firmly as she pulled the screen door open. "I'm not going away until I know you're all right."

Kathleen stepped inside. Even Blossom entered quietly as if he knew something was wrong. Up close, she was startled by Louisa's appearance. Her eyes were sunken, with dark circles under them, and her hair was lank, as if it hadn't been washed in several days. It was hard to tell under her robe, but she looked even thinner than normal.

Kathleen smiled and held up her parcel. "Look, I made some of your special orange cranberry bread. I thought we could have some over a cup of tea."

Without giving Louisa time to argue or try to get her to leave, Kathleen strode through to the kitchen. On her way, she glanced around. Everything looked the same, except, "Where are Mr. Woodhouse and Miss Olivia?"

Louisa, looking even more flustered, waved a hand vaguely in the direction of the stairs.

Kathleen's brain worked furiously as she filled the kettle and put it on to boil. "Have you had any other visitors lately? I know Rebecca came by. How was her soup?"

"No," Louisa said, standing in the middle of the kitchen, watching Kathleen cut slices of bread. "No other visitors. And the soup was fine. It was nice of her to do that."

Louisa began to sound a bit more like herself.

"Would you get us some cups for the tea? I remember the day I first tasted your orange cranberry bread. It was my first day back at Nanna's house. Remember? You and Miss Olivia came by to welcome me. You spent nearly the entire day helping me to clean the cottage, get it ready to be lived in."

She placed the bread on plates and carried them to the table, relieved to hear Louisa chuckle.

"I do remember. We didn't know then how territorial and protective you were, Katie. We just barged in and took over, didn't we?"

The kettle began to whistle.

Kathleen had to laugh, too. "Yeah, I guess I was wound a little tighter in those days. Had to be in control."

Louisa poured two mugs full of hot water and brought them to the table, sitting opposite Kathleen. Kathleen selected a tea bag from the tin on the table and set it to steep while she spread some butter on her bread.

"Well, from the way your life used to be, with that other girl, it's understandable. You had to find your own way, set your life up the way you wanted it for a change."

Louisa's voice hitched on those last words, and she crumbled, burying her face in her hands, her frail shoulders shaking with her sobs.

Kathleen shifted to the chair beside her, wrapping an arm around her. She let Louisa cry until it began to slow. Tugging a napkin loose from the holder, she offered it. Louisa blotted her eyes and blew her nose.

"I'm so sorry," she said. "Here you came to visit, and look at me."

Kathleen took one of Louisa's bony hands in hers. "Miss Louisa, I know I'm not your peer, but I hope you think of me as a friend, even if I'm only the granddaughter of one your closest friends."

Louisa gave her a tremulous smile. "Katie, you are so like Maisie. I... I haven't had anyone to tell..."

"To tell what? You can tell me anything. You know all my ugly secrets."

Louisa smiled again and patted her cheek. "Go sit and drink your tea while it's hot. Let me see where to begin."

Kathleen stayed where she was but pulled her mug and plate to her, listening.

"I told you once," Louisa hesitated a moment, her cheeks flushed, "that I'd had a... that there'd been someone, when I was in college."

"I remember. That was the day you told me you thought Olivia might have been gay. You said your relationship was with one of your professors."

"Willem Gephardt. My classics professor." She gave Kathleen an embarrassed look. "He was very handsome, and he immediately noticed my work. He began asking me to come by his office to discuss literature, and... things eventually became romantic between us."

She paused to eat a bit. Kathleen waited.

"I also told you, I eventually discovered that there'd been others." Louisa's lips tightened. "And I also found out he had a wife and five children."

"I'm sorry." Kathleen reached for her hand again. "Did you love him?"

Louisa nodded. "I did. Desperately." Her brow creased. "That's a good word, isn't it? How deeply can any nineteen-year-old love? It was desperate. Especially when..."

Her eyes filled again, and her chin quivered.

"Especially when what?" Kathleen prompted gently.

"Especially when I found out I was pregnant," Louisa whispered.

Kathleen gasped. She couldn't help it. Louisa withdrew her hand, but Kathleen took it again. "No, no, no. I'm not judging. I just never expected... What did you do?"

"I did what most girls in my situation did in those days. I went away somewhere—there were lots of homes for girls like me—to hide away from society until my time came, and then give the baby up for adoption."

"Oh, Miss Louisa. You never told anyone about this, did you?"

Louisa shook her head. "Not Ollie. Not even Maisie. And we told each other everything." Louisa raised her eyes. "You asked me to tell you about Maisie and Séan's bonding. I can't. I wasn't there. I said I had to stay and take classes that summer, but that was the year... No one understood why I wasn't there, and I couldn't tell anyone."

Kathleen tried to imagine what that must have been like. "So you were all alone, through all of it?"

"Yes," Louisa said. "And, in those days, they took the baby immediately. You never even got to hold it, because they were afraid, if you did..."

"You wouldn't give it up," Kathleen finished for her.

Louisa nodded again. "All I know is, it was a girl. Born August 12th, 1960. In Bethlehem, New Hampshire."

It took several seconds for this information to click in Kathleen's brain. When it did, her mouth gaped.

"New Hampshire. You think... It can't be."

"I don't know what to think, Katie. The dreams they've been having, finding Little Sister, coming here. Irene said she was waiting to hear if she'd been adopted in New Hampshire."

"But that might mean... Miss Louisa, you might not be the last of your line. They might be able to Pass."

Louisa shook her head. "No, no. It would mean everyone would have to know. I couldn't."

Kathleen gazed at her sympathetically. "I really don't think anyone would judge you. We all love you. And if you're not the end of the Woodhouse line—"

Louisa gripped Kathleen's wrist. "Promise me you won't say anything. Not even to Molly. Not until I'm ready. We don't even know if Irene could be the one."

Kathleen hesitated, loath to make such a promise, but Louisa fixed her with such a pleading expression. She sighed. "I promise."

Chapter 15

MEREDITH SWIRLED HER GLASS, the ice clinking rhythmically as she stared out the window of the diner. Several cars crawled up the hill, making their way slowly through the few pedestrians strolling into the village from the direction of the marina.

"Refill, dear?"

She jumped a little and found Wilma standing beside the table, a pitcher of iced tea in her hands.

"Yes, thank you."

Wilma poured. "He should be heading up this way soon."

"Who?" Meredith felt the heat in her cheeks.

But Wilma only smiled, moving on to the next table, leaving Meredith to stare after her. Her heart did skip a beat when she saw Aidan striding up the hill from the marina. He couldn't have been more different from Grant. Where appearance was everything to Grant— the right clothes, the right car, *the right girlfriend*, she thought wryly—

167

so far, nothing about Aidan indicated he cared at all about those things. She tried not to look like she was waiting for him, but she couldn't help it. When he entered the diner and saw her, he hesitated a moment and then changed direction.

"Mind if I join you?" he asked.

"I was hoping you would," she said. A part of her brain kicked her for being so transparent, but, somehow, with Aidan it seemed stupid not to be.

Without asking, Wilma brought another iced tea, giving Meredith a small wink. "We've fresh chicken salad today."

"I'll have that, not a sandwich. Just on a plate, please," Meredith said.

"Make mine a sandwich, Wilma," Aidan said.

"Be right up." Wilma bustled away.

Meredith pointed through the window. "Looks like you had a full load today."

He nodded. "We did. Nice day, people want to go for a cruise." He glanced around the diner. "Where are your folks?"

"They decided to go for a bike ride." Meredith chuckled. "I haven't seen my dad on a bike since he took the training wheels off mine."

She watched Aidan squeeze the lemon into his tea. "How long have you been a ferry captain?"

"Not long at all as captain. Just a mate before that." He thought. "Not even a year."

"What did you do before that?"

He snorted. "What just about everybody here does. Fished. Fixed boats." He shrugged. "It's the island life."

"You didn't like fishing?"

"It's a good life," he conceded. He nodded his thanks to Wilma when she brought their meals. "A hard life, though. You set your own hours, you have some freedom, but you're at the mercy of the sea and the catch. Always chasing the catch."

He tore a big bite out of his sandwich.

She regarded him as she scooped some chicken salad onto her fork. "You sound almost wistful, like you miss it."

A corner of his mouth quirked into a reluctant grin. "I suppose. I miss spending time with my brothers. Ferrying is long hours, regular pay. Stability. I needed that."

"Why?" At the frown that creased his brow, Meredith immediately apologized. "I'm sorry. I'm asking too many questions."

He shook his head. "Not too many. Just questions I don't always think about." He looked at her and quickly lowered his eyes. "I drank. Too much."

She glanced around to see if anyone was within hearing distance, and he laughed out loud, but it was a harsh, angry laugh.

"It's a small island. There's hardly a soul lives here that didn't pick my drunk ass up one time or another. Molly hauled me home more times than I can count."

He took a bite and chewed slowly. "Had to do something different. Kathleen helped me see that."

Meredith paused with her fork halfway to her mouth. "Kathleen? What did she have to do with it?"

His mouth tightened into something that might have been a smile, but he shook his head again. "That's her tale to tell, if she chooses."

Meredith felt like a fool. She busied herself with her lunch while he finished his sandwich. There were tons more questions just ready to burst from her mouth, but she held them back.

"I hear you and your mom have a story of your own to tell," he said. "Something about a dream?"

"Yeah." Relieved to have something else to talk about, Meredith said, "We both had the same dream. Of a shipwreck and being rescued."

Aidan pushed his plate aside and rested his elbows on the table. Meredith watched his hand, strong fingers wrapped around his glass, so unlike Grant's soft, manicured hands.

"But you had a different dream," he said, snapping her attention back to the present. "At Bealtaine."

For long seconds, she stared into his dark eyes, searching them. "Did you have the same one?"

"Not sure. It wasn't a dream for me, exactly. I wasn't asleep. We're all used to... seeing things during the island festivals. I was at the beach, and suddenly, you were there. On the other side of the bonfire, just like you were real. I thought..." He ran a hand through his thick hair. "I didn't know what to think. Figured it was just the... And then you were here."

She leaned forward. "You figured it was just what?"

This time, he was the one to glance around. "You can't live on this island and not realize that some things happen that can't be explained. We mostly accept it. Keep it quiet."

"I believe it," she said fervently. "How else could I explain the shipwreck dream, and seeing you, and everything else that led us here?"

That led me to you.

But as Meredith gazed into Aidan's eyes, she couldn't say that. Not yet.

⬚⬚⬚⬚⬚⬚⬚⬚⬚

LOUISA COCKED AN EAR, listening, but the only sounds were the birds and the occasional car, probably driving a group of tourists around the island's ring road. She bent to her garden, plucking weeds and picking a few early green beans for dinner. In the next row, she tugged some of the carrots loose from the rich soil, dropping them into her basket.

A light gust blew up, and she clapped a hand to her head to keep her floppy hat from sailing away.

"Figures," she muttered, working her way along the row, "first I can't shut you up. Now that you know, you won't talk to me."

It had been a week. A week since she'd told Katie Halloran what she'd never told anyone. She'd been waiting for Ollie to say something, but there'd been not a peep.

When they were girls, there had been times when they'd argued and not spoken, but it had never lasted longer than a couple of days before one or the other of them couldn't stand it any longer and they made up.

She stood with a groan, rubbing her low back. Carrying her basket, she made her way to the back porch where she stepped out of her Wellies and into her slippers. She hung her hat on a peg inside the kitchen door and dumped her vegetables into the sink. She thought briefly about sitting to rest, but dinner wouldn't fix itself.

"Work first, rest later." Sometimes she was afraid, if she let herself sit, she'd stay there until she just dried up and blew out to sea on the island winds. All in all, it wouldn't be a bad way to go, she supposed.

With a pan of water heating on the stovetop, she snapped the ends off the beans and, once the water was boiling, dropped the beans in to blanch for a few minutes. When they were drained and set in the refrigerator to keep for the night's dinner, she poured herself a glass of lemonade and went out to the front porch carrying an old shoebox she'd discovered deep in the cupboard under the stairs.

The boxes of ashes were sitting in the windowsill, where Daddy and Ollie could enjoy the nice breeze blowing through the screen.

Louisa rocked and sipped her lemonade, watching a few bicyclists roll by and wave. It pleased her that Katie seemed to have kept her word. Down the library with the children yesterday morning, Rebecca hadn't said anything about Louisa's... indiscretion, and Louisa knew her well enough to know that if Rebecca had anything to say, she'd say it.

But keeping it quiet didn't fix what to do about it. If Irene really was the baby she'd given up for adoption... Louisa pressed her hand to her heart, her eyes closed. *Don't be ridiculous. It just can't be.*

Sniffing, she lifted her reading glasses from where they hung around her neck and opened the shoebox on her lap. Inside were dozens of photos, some curled and yellowed. She leafed through them, chuckling at some of the images. There was one of her and Maisie and Ollie when they were little, all bundled up, being pulled on a sled by Daddy, the snow up to his knees. Mama must have taken the photo. There were so many—Christmases, Bealtaines, winter solstices. Those had been some of the best, her sitting in Mama's lap, Ollie in Daddy's, listening to the island's shipwreck story, every year, all the islanders gathered in the stone circle in the dark on the longest night, waiting for the dawn to come. She'd loved those nights better than any. They'd made her feel a connection to the island that went to her soul. It rooted her here, no matter how far away she'd tried to go.

She came upon a handful of photos that were taken when she was teaching, surrounded by the island's children. She clapped a hand to her mouth. Several of the teenage boys towered over her, accentuating her petite size, but the dark hair she had back then, her eyes laughing at the camera—the resemblance to Irene and Meredith was unmistakable. For several minutes, she sat, transfixed by the images.

She dug deeper into the box and found a sealed envelope. Prying the brittle flap loose, she discovered another bunch of photographs. She leafed through them. Olivia was in most of them, but so was a girl Louisa had never seen.

She adjusted her glasses and squinted to read the date in tiny print in the photos' white border—*July 1960.*

The summer she'd been in New Hampshire.

She stared harder at the images, Ollie laughing, her arm around this other girl, a tomboyish girl with a short haircut. It was hard to tell in the black-and-white photos, but it looked as if she was maybe a redhead with blue eyes. Louisa flipped the photos over and saw, scrawled in Olivia's handwriting, *Mary Dale Loughlin.*

Mesmerized, Louisa shuffled through the photos, studying each one. There, on her sister's face, was an expression Louisa had never seen. *Ollie was in love.*

She sat in her rocker, feeling a surprising mix of happiness and melancholy at the realization that she and her sister had each kept secrets from the other.

"Why didn't you tell me?" she murmured.

"Same reason you didn't tell me, I expect," came the reply she'd known would come now. "Shame."

"But you had nothing to be ashamed of," Louisa said. "You know the First Ones always had some who loved the same gender. No one here would have cared."

"But Mary Dale wasn't from here, and her people didn't feel that way. Even she was ashamed. That made me ashamed, even though I was never so happy. She wanted me to lie, and I couldn't."

Louisa gave a half-laugh. "No. You were always a horrible liar. You couldn't have done it." Her expression sobered. "Wouldn't have done it."

"But you. You had a baby, Lou. A baby. And you never told me."

Tears streamed from Louisa's closed eyes. "I couldn't. I tried to forget, but I couldn't do that, either." She covered her face with her hands. "I never..." she gasped in between sobs, "never even got to hold her."

"You could now."

⬚⬚⬚⬚⬚⬚⬚⬚⬚⬚

IRENE SAT AT THE far end of the hotel's veranda with a large pad in her lap—part of a stash of art supplies she'd purchased at the market— as she sketched the village's main street for a watercolor. Roy sat in a nearby chair, baby Charlotte sleeping in his arms.

Meredith, breathless from a kind of walk/jog with Jasper, climbed the hotel's steps, standing on the edge of one to stretch her calves. Her mouth gaped when she realized what her father was holding.

"What are you doing?" she asked her father.

He raised a finger to his lips. "Babysitting," he whispered. "She was fussy when I went into the market, and Miranda was trying to wait on some people. I took her, and she fell fast asleep."

Jasper came over for a sniff. His nose must have tickled because Charlotte gave a little squirm. Satisfied that this thing was safe, he flopped down on his side, panting.

"Miranda and Tim just let you take her?"

"They know where to find her. Not like we can go anywhere." He smiled down at the little bundle. "Reminds me of when you were this size."

"You never held Meredith when she was that size," Irene corrected him. "You thought you'd break her."

"Well," he said with a grin, "I've grown wiser in my old age. Sure would be nice to have one or two of these of our own."

"Oh, God, don't you start," Meredith said, now bending over to stretch her tight hamstrings.

"Where'd you go?" Irene asked.

"Out to the beach and back," Meredith said. "Too many people there."

Irene chuckled. "You sound like an islander."

The same thought had struck Meredith as she said it. She knew the tourists had to be considered a bit of a nuisance to the islanders, even if they depended on them. It was just hard sometimes to remember that she and her parents fit into that nuisance category.

She dropped into a rocker beside her father. "This has been the best summer."

"It has," he agreed. "I fully expected to go crazy on this little island, but it's been refreshing to slow down."

Meredith watched her mom working, her dad rocking, and wished there was a way they could stay, but she understood the island's rules.

From inside, the hotel's telephone rang, and she heard Wilma answering. A moment later, she opened the screen door.

"Oh, there you are, Mrs. Turner."

"Wilma, please call me Irene."

"You have a phone call, Irene."

"Me?" Irene lowered her pencil. "Who would call me here?"

"Well," Roy said, "you could go see."

Irene jumped up to follow Wilma inside. Meredith listened, but couldn't make out individual words, only her mother's excited tone. She glanced questioningly at her dad, but he just shrugged.

They both turned when Irene rushed through the door onto the porch several minutes later.

"That was Art," she said, brandishing a paper.

"Why was Art calling you here?" Roy asked, half-rising from his seat. "Is the house—"

"Everything is fine," Irene said, her cheeks flushed, eyes bright. "He and Kenny have been collecting our mail."

Meredith huffed impatiently while her mother repositioned her chair to face them, but she recognized the expression on her mom's face. Whatever Art had told her was big, and Irene had to present it as such.

"Yesterday," Irene said, laying the paper on her knees and spreading her hands over it, "an envelope came. From New Hampshire."

"Your birth certificate?" Roy asked.

Irene's head gave a spasmodic nod, but she couldn't seem to speak now.

"Well?" Meredith burst out. "Don't keep us in suspense. What did yours say?"

Irene held out the paper. "Art faxed it here."

Meredith took it and held it for her father so they could both read it.

"Then you are adopted," Roy said.

"Mother's name, Mary Flannery," Meredith read. "Father, unknown."

Irene's eyes glimmered with tears. "Why didn't Mom and Dad tell us about this?"

Roy handed the baby to Meredith and went to kneel in front of Irene and hold her. "We'll search all of their papers again, now that we know what we're looking for. Maybe we'll find something."

"How's Art?" Meredith asked. "He was so upset before we left."

Irene sat back, dabbing at her eyes, and Roy took his chair again. "I think he actually feels a little better now."

Meredith nodded. "It's not just him."

"Yes." Irene smiled tremulously. "I thought I knew how I'd feel, but... it does feel unsettled to know you weren't wanted. Were given away."

"Mom, no," Meredith said, shifting the baby in her lap. "Don't think of it like that. If she was unmarried in 1960, there's no way she could have been a single mom, not without a horrible stigma. Granddad and Grandma were great parents, weren't they? They were ready for a family. They chose you. Both of you."

"You're right, honey." Irene's chin quivered. "It's just going to take some time to get used to the idea."

※※※※※※※※※※

SOMEDAY, MOLLY THOUGHT AS she hauled her scull out of her parents' garage to load on top of her Toyota, she should get around to building a shed or garage at the cottage. Kathleen wouldn't mind, and then she could bring her indoor rower and other exercise equipment to the house she actually lived in.

"Mo!"

She paused when Jenny hurried over with a basket draped with a towel.

"I made some banana walnut muffins for Joey and your father this morning," Jenny said. "Take some home with you."

"Thanks, Mom."

"Sometimes I think if it weren't for you having your boat here, I'd never see you at all." Jenny gave her a kiss on the cheek. "You and Kathleen come by one evening for supper."

"We will," Molly promised. "Any word on Brandi?"

"Any day now. Her mother promised to call when she goes into labor."

"Keep us posted."

Jenny peered at the eastern sky, glowing a brilliant crimson. "Probably have a blow later today. Be careful."

"That's why I want to get out now. Tell Dad I'll check on the power station later this morning."

Molly slid her oars into the SUV's cargo hold and waved to her mom as she pulled out.

When she got to the beach, she navigated the 4-Runner down the rocky track near the sea wall. She was surprised to see a dog running on the beach and, for a moment, thought Kathleen and Blossom had come this way on a walk. Kathleen had said she was too busy to take a walk this morning, but maybe she'd changed her mind. Molly carried the scull toward the water and realized the dog wasn't Blossom.

"Hi, Jasper," she said when he came bounding over. She set the scull down and saw Meredith strolling in her direction. "Morning."

"Do you always row this early?"

Molly checked the sky. Still crimson, but the storm wouldn't be here for hours yet. "Calmest time of day. What're you doing out so early?"

"Couldn't sleep. Decided to go for a walk." Meredith pointed at the ocean. "Thought I might swim around the island."

For a moment, Molly tried to decide whether Meredith was serious. She pointed at a dilapidated NO SWIMMING sign. "Wouldn't recommend it. It's not deep around Little Sister, but there are fierce currents. You'll be halfway to Nova Scotia before you know it."

"Just kidding. I never swim in my patch of the Pacific. Way too cold. Some do go out in wetsuits."

Molly went back to the Toyota for her oars and carried them to the scull to lock them in.

"Beach is a long way from the hotel," Molly observed. She looked more closely at Meredith. "You okay?"

Meredith nodded tightly, kicking at the sand. "I wanted to see..." She pointed to a dark shadow on the sand further down the beach. "Is that where you guys had the bonfire?"

"Yeah. Why?"

But Meredith didn't answer. She gazed out to sea. "What happened to him? He says he drank and that Kathleen had something to do with him stopping." She turned to Molly. "What happened?"

Shit.

"Meredith..." Molly began.

"I'm not trying to pry," Meredith cut in. "Well, I guess I am, but not out of curiosity. When I look at him, I can see... something in his eyes. Something he hasn't forgiven himself for."

Molly stared at her for a long time, searching her face. "When Aidan was fifteen," she said at last, "he challenged Kathleen's brother to a race." She pointed to her scull. "In one of these. A storm was brewing. Aidan made it back, barely. Bryan didn't."

"Oh, my God." Meredith pressed a hand to her mouth. "And he blames himself."

Molly clenched her jaw at the memory. "There was a lot of blame to go around."

This time it was Meredith studying Molly. "What about the shipwreck? The one that brought your ancestors here."

Molly, who'd been expecting more questions about the accident, was startled. "What about it?"

"Where did it happen?"

"From the records we have," Molly said, extending an arm in the southeast direction, "it went down out there. It took the First Ones a long time to row through the storm to get to the wreck. By the time they arrived, the ship was on her side and going under. Survivors were clinging to debris in the water. They brought them back here."

When Meredith stood, frowning in the direction Molly had indicated, Molly asked, "What is it?"

Meredith bit her lip for a moment. "You were born here. You're an islander. Do you ever dream about it? The shipwreck?"

"I can't say I have."

"Then why did my mom and I?" Meredith's eyes filled with tears. "If it didn't mean something, why did it happen?"

Molly could only shake her head. "I don't know."

Chapter 16

B LOSSOM SNORED SOFTLY, HIS head resting on Kathleen's foot as she bent over one of the genealogy books, tracing a line back with one finger, while her other hand marked a place on the tree of another book. There, four generations ago, the Ahearns and the Woodhouses shared a common ancestor.

"So," she breathed, sitting back, "Jenny's side of the family, not Joe's. And far enough back to not be an issue."

She caught herself. *An issue for what? They're not islanders.* She kept reminding herself of that, but was it true? If Irene was the baby Louisa had given up, didn't that make her part of this island lineage? She'd been scouring the books to find any other examples of an adoptee returning to Little Sister, but there just weren't any.

"This could shake things up around here," she muttered, her head propped on her hand as she stared at the pages.

When she'd finally found the third recorded island tremor, in

January 1863, there'd been a lot of conjecture about its meaning. The most obvious, as Kathleen had pointed out, was that the country was in the middle of the Civil War, but not everyone agreed. "That didn't impact us at all," Louisa had pointed out, since Little Sister hadn't sent any islanders to take part in any conflicts until the Great War. "But there were submarines in the Civil War," Rebecca had mused. "The old fishermen have always told tales of seeing strange things in the waters around here. Maybe one came this far north." In searching the death records, they'd also found that two island fishermen had died in an autumn storm. In the end, they still didn't know for certain what the quake signified.

"What are you studying?"

She and Blossom both jumped at Rebecca's unexpected entrance. "Oh, you scared me."

"So I see." Rebecca's eyebrow ticked up in an expression Kathleen had learned to recognize. "What are you looking for?"

Kathleen cursed the flush she felt creeping from her neck into her cheeks. "Nothing—" she started to say, but heaved a sigh. "I can't say. Not completely."

She closed the books as Rebecca took a seat across from her. "Can I ask you a question, knowing I may not be able to answer yours in return?"

Rebecca's eyes reflected her curiosity, but she said only, "Of course."

"Have you ever... has there ever been a Passing of someone not knowingly from a Little Sister lineage?"

Rebecca sat back, looking somewhat nonplussed at the wording of the question. "Why would someone even attempt a Passing if they weren't from one of our family lines?"

"Well..."

"Good morning!" came a voice from the front.

Kathleen closed her eyes for a moment. "Be right there."

The children and their parents began stomping into the library for their reading group. Louisa entered with a child clinging to each of her hands.

"Such wonderful news about Brandi!" she said, beaming. "I'll bet Jenny is over the moon."

"She is," Rebecca said. "Joe took her over to Big Sister yesterday morning when they got the call. The baby was born about four o'clock, but Matty almost didn't make it. Their boat had engine trouble, and he and Joey were stuck for a few hours, trying to repair it. Got there just in time. Benjamin Ahearn Cooper. Jenny's going to stay the week, help out at the restaurant."

"I can't remember the last time we had two newborns on the island so close together," Louisa said.

"Technically, Benjamin isn't a Little Sister baby," Rebecca reminded her.

"Stuff and nonsense," Louisa said stoutly. "He'll always be a Little Sister baby."

Kathleen seized on this. "Even if he's not raised here?"

"Well, you weren't raised here, were you?" Louisa pointed out. "If you're one of ours, you're always one of ours."

Kathleen felt Rebecca's probing gaze but refused to meet her eyes. "Looks as if you've got a full house here this morning."

The kids milled around, some of them searching for the books they'd been reading the last time they were there.

"Need any helpers?"

The door opened again, and Meredith and Irene Turner entered the library. Jasper trotted in and greeted Blossom.

"Two teachers here, if you could use us," Irene said.

"That would be wonderful," Rebecca said.

Kathleen immediately focused her attention on Louisa and caught her staring at Irene for a moment.

"Miss Louisa," said a little redheaded boy with a vividly freckled face who was tugging on her skirt. "Miss Louisa!"

"Yes, Jonah," Louisa said. "What is it?"

"Today's my birthday!"

"Is it?" Louisa sat down and picked him up to sit on her lap. "And how old are you?"

He held up five fingers.

"Five!" Louisa exclaimed. "I remember when you were this many." She formed an O with her fingers. "I saw you when you were born."

"Meredith," Kathleen said casually, "we know your birthday is May first, but Irene, when's yours?"

"August twelfth," Irene said.

Hating herself for doing it, Kathleen said, "And what year were you born, if you don't mind my asking."

"I don't mind. 1960." Irene pulled out a chair while most of the kids began to settle on the floor, a few of them curled up with the dogs. "My brother just sent me a copy of my birth certificate. Turns out I was adopted, from Bethlehem, New Hampshire. My birth mother's name was—"

"Mary Flannery."

Louisa said it so softly, in sync with Irene, that Kathleen seemed to be the only one who heard it. Louisa kept her eyes downcast.

"Pick a book, Jonah," she said. "Let's read."

<hr />

WITHOUT REALIZING SHE WAS doing it, Meredith had drifted into a routine of walking or bicycling early—exploring the island that could never be home. She'd found the cemetery and the stone circle. Wandering among the grave markers, she recognized many of the island names. She found Kathleen's grandparents' graves, and several Coopers. Creeping into the stone circle, she'd stood, eyes closed, absorbing the energy of the place. She knew Jeanette and Barb would probably tell her the spirits of the place were speaking to her. The idea of that was somehow comforting rather than something to be scoffed at.

She and Jasper had always spent their summers getting out early to walk on the beach or go for a hike, but in Pacific City, the marine layer was unpredictable and cold. Here, even when there was fog, it burned away to reveal glorious mornings, the sunlight shimmering on the waves.

Most days, by the time she got back to the hotel and showered, her dad was babysitting. He was spending hours with Charlotte and Ellis.

"I'm not sure who's going to miss this more when we leave," Irene had said.

The thought of leaving—though she knew it was inevitable—made Meredith long to freeze time. It was already mid-July, and time was the very thing that was flying by way too fast. Time on the island, time with Wilma and Nels and the Coopers and Kathleen and... Aidan.

He was piloting the Little Sister ferry nearly every day, and today, as most days, she eagerly waited for it to dock. Aidan had to see everyone off the ferry and usually had to help with unloading the cargo before he could come find her. She paced along the porch, searching for him.

"You're going to wear out those floorboards, dear," Wilma said with a chuckle. She handed Meredith two glasses of iced tea. "Take this down to him, why don't you? It's a hot one today."

Wilma laughed to herself as she went back inside. Meredith blushed at the realization that she was being so obvious, and she wondered if she shouldn't make herself so available. She'd never been like this with Grant, never waited breathlessly for the next time she could see him, be with him. Lunches with Aidan meant more to her than whole nights with Grant ever had. They didn't talk about anything deep. He wanted to know what life in Pacific City was like. He asked about her work, and told tales of growing up on Little Sister, some of the pranks he and his brothers had played. Even she was surprised at how much she looked forward to their conversations.

It was crazy to feel this much this soon, but, "Screw it."

She hurried down the hotel steps and descended the hill to the marina.

Fred, when he saw her, called out, "Hey, boy! Your girl's here for ya!" before he bent over, laughing, when Aidan swore at him.

"What if I'm here for you, big boy?" Meredith asked in her best Mae West imitation.

Fred's face froze mid-laugh. Meredith smiled and handed him one of the glasses. "Wilma thought you two might need something cold to drink in this heat."

"Close your mouth, fool," Aidan said, striding over to take the other glass from her, his fingers closing around hers for a moment as his eyes raked her face with such obvious pleasure that Meredith's heart skipped a few beats.

He raised his other arm, swiping the sweat dripping from his chin with his sleeve. "Thank you."

She nodded and stepped back. Fred gulped his tea and handed the empty glass back to her.

"Thanks, gal. Tell Wilma we'll be up soon for more."

"See you in a few minutes," Aidan said.

She took his glass also and returned to the hotel, refusing to turn around to see if he was watching.

She had a table waiting when Aidan and Fred entered the diner. Fred, as always, headed to the counter. Aidan held up a finger to her, disappearing for a few minutes. When he reappeared and approached the table, she saw that he'd rinsed his face and changed into a clean shirt.

"You didn't have to do that," she said as he sat.

"I couldn't stand myself," he said with a self-conscious smile.

For several seconds, they stared into each other's eyes while Meredith searched for something to say.

Wilma bustled over with two fresh glasses of tea. "Hot day out there, Aidan. You cool down a bit."

"That's not likely," he muttered.

Meredith choked on her tea.

"Sorry, what was that?" Wilma asked.

"Nothing," he said quickly. "I'll have whatever the special is today."

"Me, too," Meredith said.

"Mmm hmm." Wilma stuck her pencil into her bun. "Two crabcake sandwiches, coming up."

"Sorry," Aidan said in a low voice.

Meredith couldn't hide a smile. "No apology necessary."

"Can I ask you something?" Aidan asked, leaning forward, his elbows braced on the table.

"Of course."

His mouth opened and closed a couple of times before he blurted, "Why aren't you with someone?"

"Oh." Meredith blushed, wondering why she hadn't seen this question coming. "I was. Until a few months ago."

He studied her. "What did he or she do?"

Meredith paused, her mouth open to answer, as it hit her how he'd phrased the question. *Only a man from here would ask it that way,* she thought.

"He. And he cheated."

"Stupid guy, to let you go."

She shrugged. "I'm allowed to think that."

"And I'm not," he said with a grin.

Wilma arrived with a tray and the pitcher of tea. "Here are your crab cakes, topped with Nels's special sauce."

"Thanks, Wilma." Aidan gave her a nod as she refilled their glasses.

Meredith waited until Wilma had moved on before saying, "You

187

should be wondering if he made the right decision."

Aidan shook his head. "Cheating isn't right, no matter what. If you're ready to move on, be honest and move on."

She took a bite before asking, "What about you? Why isn't there anyone?"

"Too busy." He took a bite of his sandwich. "Most days are sixteen to eighteen hours."

"Aren't you lonely?" she asked.

"Sometimes," he admitted. "But it's good to be busy."

"Kathleen's brother."

He looked up sharply.

"I asked."

They ate in silence for a few minutes, other people coming and going from the diner.

"It's a long time to punish yourself," she said quietly.

"Actions have consequences," he retorted. "Even fifteen-year-olds should know that. There is no time limit on some things."

"Aidan," she said, reaching out to take his hand. She thought he might jerk away, but he gave her fingers a squeeze, staring down at their intertwined fingers.

"I'm working on it," he murmured.

She released his hand reluctantly and let him eat. He only had a short break for lunch and then had to get back to work, loading the ferry for the return voyage.

When they finished their lunch, she walked him out onto the porch. He stood one step below her so that they were about eye level.

"Will I see you tomorrow?" she asked.

For a moment, she thought he was going to kiss her. Then Fred stomped through the door.

"Let's get'er loaded, boy."

Aidan turned to follow Fred down the stairs, but looked over his shoulder. "Tomorrow."

THE BREEZE BLOWING THROUGH the screens was warm, fluttering the pages of the novel lying open on Louisa's lap. Her focus, though, wasn't on the book. She stared out the window, her fingers tapping her lips.

"You know what you need to do."

Louisa waved an annoyed hand. "Don't tell me what to do, Ollie."

"I'm not telling you. You are. You don't want to listen. You never did."

"That's not so."

"Is, too. People always said I was the stubborn one because I spoke plain. But you, just because you come across sweet and use big words, they don't realize you're more stubborn than I ever was."

Louisa had to snort. "That's true, I suppose."

She got to her feet and paced restlessly. She went into the kitchen, thinking she might make a batch of cookies or a cake, but she got no further than getting the canister of flour out. A few minutes later, she was outside, wandering toward the garden. There were a few late strawberries left to be picked, along with more green beans, but she only stood, staring at everything.

Listlessly, she returned to the house. She unfurled the hose to water the flowers growing around the porch before climbing the steps to sit in the rocker there.

"Ask Katie to go with you," Olivia suggested.

Chewing on a fingernail, Louisa considered. "That... that might help. I just don't know how to tell them."

"They love you, sister. Trust that. Tell them."

Louisa closed her eyes for a moment and then pushed to her feet and hurried inside to the telephone.

"Rebecca? Is Jenny back?"

"She got back last night," came Rebecca's voice over the phone. "Why?"

"We need to call a meeting. Today, if possible."

"Why?" Rebecca demanded.

"I'll explain when the council's together. Can you call the others?"

Rebecca was silent for a moment, and Louisa knew she was bursting to ask more questions, but she said only, "I will. An hour? At my house."

Louisa hung up and stood, still clutching the handset. Picking it up, she dialed again. "Katie? Are you busy?"

Half an hour later, wearing a clean change of clothes, her hair brushed and retwisted into her usual bun, Louisa was waiting outside when Kathleen drove up to the house.

"Where are we going?" Kathleen asked, backing around.

"To Rebecca's house."

Out of the corner of her eye, Louisa saw Kathleen turn to her.

"Do you want Mr. Woodhouse and Miss Olivia to come along?"

Louisa gave a tight shake of her head. Kathleen only took Louisa's hand. Louisa squeezed hard and felt her own trembling.

Molly's SUV was already there when they arrived at Rebecca's cottage. Rebecca was waiting for them.

"Come in. Jenny came with Molly. Joe's going to pick up Wilma on his way. Patrick couldn't get away from the pub."

The others were gathered in the living room. Curiosity as to why the island council had been summoned was plainly written on their faces, but no one asked questions. When Joe and Wilma arrived, Rebecca got everyone seated with extra chairs pulled from the kitchen. They glanced around from one to the other. Molly stared at Kathleen, who had seated herself beside Louisa, but Kathleen only gave a tiny shake of her head.

"Miss Louisa," Rebecca began, "why did you call this meeting?" Her gaze flicked in Kathleen's direction. "And, technically, Kathleen isn't part of the island council."

"Because I need to tell you all... a story." Louisa reached for Kathleen's hand. "And because Katie already knows."

In a halting, stumbling narrative, the story slowly spooled out—*every humiliating bit of it.* When she faltered, Kathleen squeezed her hand, offering her strength to help keep Louisa strong enough to do what had to be done. When at last, Louisa finished, the room was filled with a ringing silence.

Jenny leaned forward. "So, you're telling us that Irene Turner is the baby you gave up for adoption?"

Louisa nodded.

Beside her, Kathleen gasped. "That's why they looked so familiar to me when they first got here! She and Meredith look like you."

Louisa tried to smile. "Like I used to. When she told us what her birthdate was and then, the name on her birth certificate, I knew for certain."

Joe frowned. "But—"

"I used my mother's name," Louisa said quickly. "Or, at least, an Anglicized version. Mary Flannery."

"Then that means they are an island family," Kathleen said.

"What?" Rebecca's voice whipped like a lash. "No, it doesn't."

"Whyever not?" Wilma asked. "She's Miss Louisa's daughter, isn't she?"

"Maybe she is, maybe not," Rebecca insisted. "But she has no connection to the island."

"Her dreams are a connection," Jenny said. "It's blood memory. You would accept that as the explanation if any of us had dreams like hers."

Wilma leaned toward Molly and whispered, "What dreams?"

"Tell you later," Molly whispered back.

Rebecca shot to her feet. "This isn't, it can't..." She rounded on Jenny. "We can't do a Passing on this basis!"

"Whyever not?" Wilma asked again.

"It's never been done!" Rebecca's jaw set in a mulish expression.

"Rebecca," Louisa said firmly. "Please sit down."

Rebecca, whose mouth was open to argue, did as Louisa asked. Louisa folded her hands.

"I am not asking for you to make a decision one way or the other, but the council can't make a fair decision without knowing the truth. All of it. It's not fair to Little Sister, and it's not fair to the Turners." Her chin quivered, but her voice was steady. "That's why I told you what I've only ever shared with Katie."

She stood. "Katie and I will leave you now, and I'll abide by whatever decision the council makes."

She held her head high as she left them to decide what to do with her secret.

Chapter 17

THE WIND HAD SHIFTED. Meredith stood beside the hotel with Jasper, sniffing, listening to the change in the distant sound of surf crashing against the island's granite core. The marina and little harbor were more sheltered, but she could tell a storm was approaching. No ferry today.

The depth of her disappointment caught her by surprise. She'd never felt the need to see Grant every day. In fact, she was fairly certain they'd never have lasted five years if she had seen him daily. But the thought that she wouldn't see Aidan...

This is ridiculous. You've only known him for a month. You haven't even kissed him yet. How can you be—

Her brain stopped before it could complete that thought. She cleaned up after Jasper and went back up to her room to wash and let Jasper eat. In the diner a little bit later, Wilma had a cup of coffee waiting for her at her usual table beside an open window. Jasper stretched out under the table, his back pressed against her leg.

"The usual, Meredith?"

"I think I'll do something wildly different today." Meredith considered. "I'd love your husband's waffles this morning."

Wilma chuckled. "My Nels is a wonderful cook, if I do say so. Be right up."

Meredith gazed out the window, a breeze fluttering the corners of the folded napkins anchored by silverware. She jumped when her mom pulled out the chair opposite and sat down.

"Morning." Irene smiled when Wilma appeared with coffee. "Just eggs and toast for me this morning, Wilma." She gave a wave to the locals at the counter who nodded in their direction.

"Getting to be part of the gang here?" Meredith asked.

"I guess so." Irene sounded kind of wistful. "It's going to be hard to go back," she said, giving voice to the growing dread inside Meredith.

"Yeah."

They sat, sipping their coffee, watching some of the early traffic out on the village's main street.

"How's Dad feeling about being here? He sure seems to be taken with Miranda's baby."

"I know," Irene said. "I was worried he'd be bored silly after three days, but he has surprised me."

"What about you?" Meredith studied her mother. "I hardly see you, except at dinner. You've been out sketching and painting almost every day."

Before Irene could reply, Wilma brought their breakfast plates on a tray, refilling coffee cups while she was there. She hovered for a moment, looking down at both of them.

Meredith and Irene exchanged a puzzled glance. "Anything wrong, Wilma?" Irene asked.

"No, no. Nothing a'tall," Wilma said with a secretive smile. "I'll leave you to your breakfast."

They thanked her as she moved off to check other tables.

"So," Meredith said, getting back to where they'd left off, "how are you?"

"Oh, honey, I love it here." Irene's face lit up. "I haven't felt this much creativity in years. Decades. I didn't tell you or your father..." She checked, but no one else was listening. "Siobhan saw a couple of my watercolors and asked me if I wanted to place a few in her shop."

She grabbed Meredith's arm. "They sold! All of them."

"Mom, that's fantastic." Meredith spread butter over her waffle, making sure to get some into each square.

"I think you missed one," Irene teased. "Kenny sent an email. He and Art have booked a room here for two weeks in early August. They want to see what all the fuss is about."

"Really? I've missed them. It'll be good to have us all back together again."

"I think Art is still coming to grips with the whole adoption thing." Irene dipped a corner of her toast into her egg yolk.

"What about you?" Meredith asked as she poured syrup over her waffle.

"It's an adjustment," Irene conceded. "To think one thing all our lives and then find out it wasn't so. It makes you look at your life differently."

They both ate for a few minutes before Irene said, "Speaking of looking at life differently, you and Aidan have been spending a lot of time together, or at least as much as his schedule allows."

Meredith's fork hung suspended over her plate, syrup dripping in a thick thread from the chunk of waffle speared on it. "What about it?"

"Do you think that's wise, given that we're leaving in a little over a month?"

"Mom—"

"I know you're old enough to manage your own business, Meredith," Irene cut in, looking embarrassed. "It's just that, it hasn't been all that long since Grant, and, well, I can't help but wonder if you're trying to fill some kind of gap..."

Meredith laughed. "Mom, you're so cute. I'm fine. Breaking things off with Grant was the smartest thing I've done in a long time."

"Really?"

"Really. I told you what he did. I'm not missing him. Honest."

"What about Aidan?" Irene frowned. "Do you really want to start something that can't go anywhere? I just don't want to see you hurt."

Meredith paused for a second, trying to think of something flippant to say, but she couldn't. "How long did you know Dad before you knew he was the one?"

Irene set her fork down, a startled expression on her face. "You think Aidan is the one for you?"

Meredith met her mother's eyes and felt the truth settle over her like a warm blanket. "I think he was the one for me before I ever knew he existed."

⬛⬛⬛⬛⬛⬛

KATHLEEN LAY, STARING AT the moonlight spilling across the bed, across the empty place where Molly should be. And wasn't.

"I can't believe you didn't tell me!" Molly had exploded the moment she got home after Louisa's revelation.

Hours after. So Kathleen knew the council's debate had been heated, and apparently, without coming to a decision. She still didn't know which side of the argument Molly fell on, because they hadn't spoken for three days.

It was so unlike Molly to stay angry. *That used to be me*, Kathleen thought now, resting her hand on Molly's pillow. *The suspicious one, the one who couldn't trust.*

"I promised I wouldn't," she'd tried to explain over and over. "Louisa asked me to keep it from everyone, even you, until she was ready."

196

But all Molly could see was that Kathleen had held back something so important from her—"We don't keep secrets anymore, remember?" she'd accused. "And something like this! Did it occur to you that this was what the island was warning us about this spring?"

At that, Kathleen had fallen silent. She'd almost forgotten the quake they'd all felt, the impending sense that something important, probably something bad, was coming.

"I thought you liked the Turners," Kathleen had countered.

"Liking them or not liking them is beside the point," Molly insisted as she stomped around the kitchen. "Our job—my job—is to protect the island. And this..." She'd raised both hands to clutch at her hair, but Kathleen had flinched at the sudden movement.

In an instant, the atmosphere in the kitchen changed, crackling with tension.

"Did you... do you really think..." Molly couldn't finish the thought as she slowly lowered her arms.

"No, no!" Kathleen fought desperately to explain. "I know you would never. It was just instinct, just a reaction. It didn't mean anything."

Only it did. Kathleen closed her eyes now at the memory of the hurt in Molly's eyes. She rolled onto her back, and tears leaked from her eyes into her hair. All those years, living with the constant shadow of Susannah's abusive father, that pattern of dealing with conflict always simmering just under the surface in any argument she and Susannah got into. She'd never actually hit Kathleen, but she'd come close. *And I practically cowered in front of Molly.*

Molly hadn't yelled anymore. She hadn't said anything. She was sleeping down the hall in Kathleen's old room from when she was a girl—rising early and coming home late. *To avoid me. At least she didn't run to her parents' house.*

Kathleen was determined to wait this out, to give Molly time to get over her hurt and anger, to find a way to make this better.

Blossom was confused, clearly torn between the two rooms. Kathleen heard his nails clicking on the wooden floorboards every time he went from one room to the other, the doors partially closed—*but no slamming, no locking.* Kathleen chose to take that as a good sign that she and Molly could fix this.

She rolled over onto her other side and slept fitfully, pursued by bad dreams in which the islanders forced all three Turners onto the ferry. "You, too," Rebecca said to Kathleen, pointing. "You don't belong here. Not really." Aidan and Fred called to her that she had to hurry, they needed to get underway.

She sat bolt upright, gasping. Blossom jumped up from his bed and placed his front paws on the mattress, nosing her.

"I'm all right," she whispered, hugging him until her racing heart slowed.

She went down the hall and peeked into the other room. Molly was gone. She went to the bathroom to brush her teeth and try to do something with her hair.

Downstairs, Molly had put the extra coffee in a Thermos to keep it hot for her. She poured a cup and forced herself to eat a bowl of cereal while she weighed her options. She had a new book to edit and really should get to work on it, but that dream... *Maybe I should talk to Rebecca, explain why I kept Louisa's secret.*

She quickly finished breakfast and cleaned up before heading out the front door, only to realize the wind had picked up. To the west, the sky was nearly black with roiling clouds. A big one was blowing in and would arrive within a few hours.

Blossom looked up at her, clearly asking whether they were going or staying.

"We'd better stay here. Get the computers backed up and unplugged. You go hurry up. I'll fill the oil lamps."

Blossom leapt off the porch as if he understood and sprinted into the trees.

Kathleen went back inside. "Later," she muttered. "I'll talk to Rebecca later, after the storm blows over."

<hr>

THE WIND HOWLED FOR a third straight day, and whitecaps tossed spray as intrepid gulls flew drunkenly through the gale. The few passengers who got off the ferry were all kind of green around the gills.

"They look a little wobbly in the legs," Molly commented to her dad.

Joe chuckled. "Poor buggers. Ferry's not going back today, that's for sure."

They zipped and snapped their rain jackets, their hoods cinched down over ball caps to partially shield their eyes while they gave Fred and Aidan a hand unloading the cargo. The market went through more merchandise in the high season, so they received a pallet of goods two or three times a week. The island's recycling and trash bins also filled more quickly in the summer and had to be off-loaded weekly.

Even with their rain gear, the four of them were soaked through by the time they finished.

"What isn't wet from the rain is drenched with sweat," Molly said under the cover of the boathouse as she flapped her wet jacket.

"Thanks for your help," Aidan said, taking his dripping ball cap off to comb his hand through his hair. "We wouldn't have chanced it today, but the storms the last couple of days kept us on the mainland. Knew the island needed this stuff."

Fred retrieved two oilcloth duffle bags from the ferry and dropped one at Aidan's feet. "Here ya go, boy. Go home, get a hot shower and dry clothes. I'm gonna see if Patrick can put me up at the pub."

"A hot shower sounds really good about now," Aidan agreed.

"I'll drive you home," Molly offered. "Mom will be glad to see you."

They both pulled their hoods back up and splashed up the hill into the village, where the Toyota was parked. Aidan paused.

"Give me a minute, will you?"

He handed Molly his duffle and dashed across the street to the hotel, bounding up the steps two at a time. Taking care to stay outside on the porch as he dripped water all over, he peered through the glass into the diner. A moment later, Meredith Turner stepped outside to speak with him. Molly scowled, watching them as the wipers slapped back and forth. She saw Meredith nod and smile, and then Aidan ran back through the deluge, hopping into the Toyota's passenger seat.

"Got a date!" he said, shaking droplets of rain everywhere when he flipped his hood back.

Wordlessly, she put the 4-Runner in gear and drove.

"What's the matter with you?" Aidan asked.

"Don't know what you mean." Molly squinted through the streaky windshield. "Why don't I ever remember to put new wipers in when it's *not* raining?"

"I may not live with you any more, Mo," Aidan said, "but you're still a terrible liar."

Molly pulled over. "Aidan, what the hell are you doing with Meredith Turner? She's an offlander. Gonna be leaving in a few weeks. And what do we really know about them? Why would you set yourself up for—"

She stopped. "Sorry. It's none of my business."

"No, it isn't," he said coldly. They sat for a minute, listening to the steady thrum of the rain on the SUV's roof. "There's something about her, Molly. Something that's never been there with anyone else. Ever."

One look at his face, and all of her arguments died on her lips. *Who are you to tell him not to do this? When you aren't even taking care of the relationship you have. And if what Louisa had told them was true...*

"What?" he asked, staring at her quizzically.

"Nothing." She pulled out onto the road again and dropped him off at their parents' house.

"Thanks for the lift," he said, pulling his hood up again. "And for, you know."

She gave him a light punch in the shoulder. "See you."

He got out and sprinted up the back porch steps. Through the kitchen window, Molly watched their mom hurry over to greet him. She put the Toyota in reverse, pausing at the end of the drive, trying to decide which way to go.

Her first instinct was always to be suspicious of people, to question their motives instead of just trusting. She'd done it with Kathleen. She was doing it now, with the Turners, even knowing what she knew about them. With a heavy sigh, she turned toward home.

Blossom's head appeared behind the screen door before she even got out. He danced around when she came inside and hung her dripping jacket on a peg.

"Where's your mom?"

He raced up the stairs, and Molly followed. Before she got to the top of the stairs, Kathleen emerged from her office, standing silently, her eyes puffy and bruised looking.

"I'm sorry," Molly said.

Kathleen moved into her arms, holding her tightly, her face burrowed into Molly's neck.

"I'm sorry, too," Kathleen whispered. "I love you."

"And I love you."

Blossom squeezed in between them, his tail thumping on the floor.

"I'm getting you wet," Molly said.

"I don't care." Kathleen's arms tightened. "I never meant to deceive you. And—"

"I know. I'm so sorry." She breathed in Kathleen's scent.

"Get out of these wet clothes," Kathleen said. "I've got a pot of potato soup on the stove."

"Oh, that sounds good. Be down in a minute."

Before Molly could get her damp jeans off, she heard a familiar pop as the electricity went off. The lamp on the dresser flickered off and then back on as the batteries kicked in. She finished changing and clicked the lamp off before hurrying downstairs.

"Did you have your computers unplugged?"

"Yeah. Everything is safe. Batteries are low after so many rainy days with just the wind turbine, so I've been only using what power I need to." Kathleen ladled two bowls of soup. "Glad I had this already made. Can you pour the coffee?"

They sat down with an oil lamp providing warm light.

"This smells wonderful." Molly reached for Kathleen's hand. "Thanks."

Kathleen smiled, bringing Molly's hand to her lips. "Eat."

They turned their attention to the meal.

"Ferry got here?" Kathleen asked.

"Yeah. Aidan said he wouldn't have chanced it except they couldn't get here Monday or Tuesday. Won't be leaving today, though."

Molly spooned up some of the thick soup. The warmth felt wonderful as it slid down her gullet. "Gosh, that's good."

She frowned as she stirred her soup. "You believe Miss Louisa? About Irene being her daughter?"

"Yes." Kathleen swallowed quickly. "Don't you?"

"I want to, but..." Molly dropped her head to her hand. "How can we just let outsiders in?"

"I was an outsider once," Kathleen reminded her quietly. "Even you thought so."

"I know." Molly twirled her spoon. "And I was wrong. You were part of an island family, and I shouldn't have—"

"What made me part of an island family?" Kathleen pressed. "I hadn't been here in almost a quarter century. So it wasn't my physical presence here."

"You know the answer to that," Molly said, picking her head up. "You were born into your right to be here. That never goes away."

"Irene can't help the circumstances of her birth."

Molly opened her mouth to argue further, but she couldn't think of a valid argument to that. "Aidan is going to see Meredith this evening."

Kathleen took a sip of her coffee. "Is that a problem?"

Molly ran her hand through her damp hair. "I don't know. I like her, but what happens to him when they leave?"

Kathleen reached for her hand. "Maybe a better question is, what if they don't leave?"

⬛⬛⬛⬛⬛⬛⬛⬛

AGAIN, MEREDITH'S HOTEL BED was layered with the nicest of the clothes she'd brought. When she and her folks had packed for a two-week vacation, they hadn't considered they'd need to do laundry for an extended summer stay. When they'd asked Wilma a few weeks ago where the island's Laundromat was, she'd burst into laughter.

"Land sakes!" she said when she could speak. "We don't have one of them here. You just give me what needs washing, and I'll take care of it."

She was as good as her word. Everything they gave her was clean and neatly folded on their beds when they got back to their rooms.

Meredith sighed now. She'd also never considered she might be going on a date. And she had no idea where she and Aidan would be eating. The pub served a few fried things to make the beer go down easier, but there weren't any restaurants on Little Sister besides the diner, so she'd supposed that was the default until Wilma pulled her aside almost as soon as Aidan had asked her.

"You two won't have any privacy a'tall with these big ears trying to listen to every word you say."

Meredith hadn't asked how Wilma knew Aidan had invited her to dinner, but, "We'll arrange something more private," Wilma had promised.

"What do you think?" She held up first one top, then the other for Jasper who glanced up from his bowl of kibble and then went back to eating. "You are no help at all."

She finally decided on her fallback outfit of capris with a sleeveless blouse. At the last minute, she also layered a light sweater over top. The storm had brought cooler temperatures with it as it blew through.

She quickly hung up the rest of her clothes and went to her parents' room. "You sure you don't mind keeping Jasper with you this evening?" she asked when her father opened the door.

"We don't mind." Roy bent down to scratch Jasper's neck. "You have a good time."

"Thanks."

She hurried downstairs to find Aidan waiting for her. It was the first time since the night of Kathleen's birthday that she'd seen him out of his work uniform. Not that he was dressed up, but she thought he looked wonderful in jeans and a button-down, the sleeves rolled up to his elbows.

"Hi," she said a little breathlessly.

If she'd wondered if she looked okay, her answer was in his eyes.

"I hope you don't mind a picnic," he said.

Her eyes flicked to the scene outside. The rain had finally stopped, but the wind was still fierce.

"Here you go," Wilma said, scurrying to them with a picnic hamper in her hands. "You two have a good time."

Aidan took the basket from her. "Thanks, Wilma."

He held the screen door for Meredith and pointed to a pickup. "We're in the Chevy."

He hurried down the steps ahead of her to get the door and give her a boost up into the seat. On the driver's side, he stashed the basket in the jumpseat and climbed in behind the wheel.

"Um, where are we going?" Meredith asked, her mind churning through all the places she'd been on the island, wondering where on earth they could picnic in this gale.

But Aidan only shook his head with a grin. "You'll see."

He drove out of the village. The trees whipped in the wind, and a few birds tried to make headway without much success. He wound around the island on the ring road, pulling at last into the cemetery.

"We're eating here?" she asked dubiously.

He grinned again. "Not quite." He retrieved the basket as she climbed out of the truck.

He led her on a winding path through the headstones, reaching back for her hand. They made their way to the small building at the rear of the cemetery. Aidan pushed the door open and stepped back to allow her to enter first.

In the dim light coming through the windows, she looked around. "Is this a chapel?"

"Yep." He set the basket down and pulled out a lighter. Moving around the chapel, he lit several candles sitting on stone ledges all around the space.

With more light, Meredith saw a scattering of pillows and cushions as well as benches serving as pews. Aidan gathered several of the cushions and created seating for them, placing the basket in the middle. He took her by the hand again and led her to a stack of cushions.

"We're out of the weather," he said. "We're alone. And we have some great food."

She giggled, but immediately clapped a hand over her mouth. "Are we allowed to talk in here?" she whispered.

His roar of laughter filled the space. "This chapel serves lots of purposes. It's where we gather for Christmas, and we do hold some funerals here. Some come here to meditate or pray." He sat cross-legged and looked around. "I haven't actually been in here for a very long time."

He opened the basket and pulled out sealed containers along with plates, napkins, and utensils. He popped the tops off two Cokes and handed one to Meredith.

"What's for dinner?" Meredith asked.

"No idea. Wilma said to leave it to her, so I did."

They took the lids off the containers and found a smorgasbord of Nels's cooking: crab cakes, fried chicken, pasta salad, green bean salad.

"And apple pie for dessert," he said, opening the last container.

They dished some of everything onto their plates. Meredith looked around, taking in the plain granite slab serving as the altar.

"Do you have a priest or minister on the island?"

"Well, my aunt is an ordained minister, but she only uses that title for offlanders who want to get married here. For us..." His eyes met hers. "Her role is different for us. Different ceremonies."

"Different how?" Meredith asked, cutting into a crab cake.

"Our ceremonies are ones handed down. Most of them are combinations of traditions we inherited from the First Ones and the Irish who stayed here."

Meredith thought about what she'd learned from Jeanette. "What tribe were the First Ones?"

He speared some pasta salad on his fork. "We don't really know. Maine has lots of Native tribes, but from what I remember, the First Ones didn't identify themselves as a specific tribe. Of course, they couldn't understand each other's languages at first, so maybe the Irish didn't understand, but they seemed to be a mix of a few tribes."

He raised his eyes to the trees beyond the windows, blowing in the wind. "I do that voyage almost every day, and it takes me almost three hours, with an engine. They couldn't have known what they'd find when they left the mainland. Kind of like the Polynesian is-landers, setting off across the Pacific. I guess they found Big Sister first, and then were able to make their way here."

"So what ceremonies?" Meredith asked as she reached for a drum-stick.

"We have naming ceremonies for babies instead of baptisms. We celebrate the Celtic festivals."

"Like Bealtaine?"

Their eyes met, and she knew they were both remembering what they'd seen that night. He nodded.

"What about marriage?" she asked, and she noticed her heart was thumping in her chest.

He lowered his eyes. "We don't get married."

She choked on a swallow of Coke. "What," she gasped when she stopped coughing, "do you mean? Your parents? Molly and Kathleen? Wilma and Nels? I thought they were all married."

He shook his head. "They're bonded. I mean, they get married, too, so it's legal everywhere else, but for us, we bond."

"Bond." She tried to remember whether she'd heard anyone else mention this. "What does that mean?"

He raised his eyes to hers. "It means more to us than marriage," he said solemnly. "The ceremony bonds us not only to each other, but to the island, to everyone connected to Little Sister."

She tried to look away but couldn't. It seemed his eyes bored into hers, locking her in place.

"There is no divorce for us once we're bonded." He gave a little sideways nod of his head. "Sounds weird, I guess, to other people. But... we don't bond until we know."

Meredith's heart beat painfully. "Know what?"

"That it's forever," he said quietly.

He took her Coke from her and set it down, leaning toward her to meet her lips with his. He tasted of the spices from the food. She returned the kiss, tentatively at first, but he was gentle, almost shy. When he began to pull away, she pressed forward, her mouth opening to his. He raised a hand to her head, fingers twining into her hair to cradle her, drawing her to him. Her body responded with a quivering deep in her belly, a longing stronger than any she'd ever felt before.

She didn't remember much of the rest of their dinner. She wondered vaguely if it was as hard for him to eat as it was for her. When at last they packed up and carried everything out to the truck, they stood under the stars and kissed again, long, lingering kisses, their bodies pressed together.

Back at the hotel, Aidan walked her up to the lobby and handed the basket to Wilma with his thanks. When she took it and disappeared into the kitchen, Aidan cleared his throat.

"Well, I guess—"

But Meredith reached for his hand. He hesitated, and she stepped closer to him, brushing his lips with hers. With a smile, she tugged on his hand and led him up the stairs.

Chapter 18

ONE OF THE THINGS LOUISA had always loved about summers on Little Sister was the way everything gleamed after a storm blew through. In the slanting sun of the early morning, each leaf, the trunks of the trees, every flower and blade of grass, it was all sharp and pristine, as if a camera had found the perfect focus. She stood on the porch in her robe, breathing deeply of the summer morning. Long shadows rippled across the yard from the oak tree. Off to the side, the garden looked as if had doubled in size after the rain, the plants heavy with produce. She'd be out there this afternoon, but first...

"You aren't going to let the kids down, are you?"

"Don't be silly, Ollie." But Louisa didn't move to go inside and get dressed.

"You're worried about seeing Rebecca."

Louisa frowned. "I haven't seen or spoken to her since... I have no idea what the council decided."

"Won't know if you keep hiding out here."

"I am not hiding out!"

"Are so. You haven't left the house for days."

"It was storming, in case you couldn't tell."

"Sister," Olivia said more gently, "you'll have to live with their decision, either way it goes. At least you told them. You don't have to hold it inside anymore."

Louisa heaved a sigh. "You're right about that."

It did feel lighter, having told her secret. Like lancing a boil that had been festering for a long time. Hurts like the devil while it's being done, but the relief after is worth it.

"Who's going to tell the girl?"

Louisa started. "Girl?"

"Your girl. She deserves to know the truth."

Her throat was suddenly tight as Louisa pressed a hand to her heart. "My girl. And my granddaughter. Oh, Ollie, can you believe it? We have family. More to come after us."

"You'd best get going."

By the time Louisa had had her breakfast and got dressed, the sun was much higher and the focus had softened a little. She drove to the library but sat in her car for several minutes before finally getting out. She was early, but she wanted time to speak with Rebecca before the children arrived.

Stepping onto the porch, she heard raised voices. Rebecca and... Katie?

"Hello?" she called out as she pulled the screen door open.

The voices immediately quieted. Rebecca emerged from the back room.

"Good morning, Miss Louisa."

Louisa's eyes went to Kathleen, standing behind Rebecca and looking upset. "What's going on?"

When neither of them answered, Louisa drew herself up. "This is about me, isn't it?"

"No," said Rebecca at the same time that Kathleen said, "Yes."

Louisa simply raised her eyebrows.

"We were discussing your... revelation," Rebecca said.

"And?" Louisa braced herself.

"That's not all we were discussing," Kathleen said.

When Louisa only waited, Kathleen said, "I wanted to know what would happen if my cousins—assuming I have any—suddenly showed up here."

"And I told you, that is a ridiculous comparison," Rebecca snapped.

"It isn't," Kathleen insisted. "When I came here, I was able to Pass, even though I didn't know anything about the island's traditions."

"But you have your roots here," Louisa pointed out. "Summers with Maisie and your brother."

"I know," Kathleen said. "Which is why I asked about cousins."

Louisa frowned in bewilderment. "You mean your Aunt Moira? She hasn't been here since she finished school and left Little Sister. Does she have children?"

"No idea," Kathleen said. "But that's beside the point, or maybe, it is my point." She cast a glance in Rebecca's direction. "If she does, and they've never been to Little Sister, but they showed up unexpectedly, would they Pass?"

Louisa and Rebecca stared at each other for a moment.

"Has that ever happened before?" Rebecca asked.

"Not that I know of," Louisa said. "Would they?"

"Maybe," Rebecca grudgingly admitted. "But it doesn't mean they'd be entitled to live here. Unless," she turned to Kathleen, "you were willing to share your cottage."

"But," Kathleen held up a triumphant finger, "if I were willing, they'd Pass, and they'd be allowed to stay."

Rebecca scowled. "I suppose so."

"Even though it's never been done before," Kathleen pressed.

Rebecca didn't answer immediately. Finally, "It doesn't seem to break any of the rules of the island's charter."

"Then how is that any different from Miss Louisa's connection to Irene and Meredith?"

Rebecca's mouth opened and closed a few times, but she couldn't seem to find any words.

Louisa's hands were clenched together as she asked the question she'd been dreading. "What was the council's decision?"

"We couldn't come to a decision," Rebecca said. "We decided to table it for now." She frowned in Kathleen's direction. "But maybe we should reconvene."

Voices outside signaled the arrival of the children. Louisa gave a tight nod and pasted a smile on her face.

❧❧❧❧❧❧❧❧❧❧

KATHLEEN SAT BACK, FROWNING at the image on the monitor. She was working on a new cover for a cozy mystery, part of a series, and something about this one just wasn't working. The font was a given, as it needed to match the other books, but maybe in a different color. When Blossom jumped up at a knock on the door, she was almost relieved to leave it.

He raced her down the stairs, his tail wagging madly as he bounced around in front of the door.

"Meredith, hi," Kathleen said. She pushed the screen door open, and let Blossom out to romp with Jasper. "Come on in."

"Are you sure?" Meredith asked. "I hate to just drop in on you."

"I'm sure." Kathleen led the way back to the kitchen. "I needed a break. Something to drink? Iced tea? Lemonade? Coke?"

"Lemonade would be wonderful, thanks." Meredith looked around as she followed. "Your house is really cute. Aidan pointed it out to me."

212

"Thanks. It was my grandmother's."

"And all the Hallorans before that."

Something in her tone made Kathleen stop and glance at her. "Yeah." She poured two glasses of lemonade and joined Meredith at the table.

"Where's Molly?" Meredith asked.

"She's probably patching someone's leaky roof or repairing someone's rotted deck boards. Lots of maintenance on island houses. I had a lot to learn when I moved here."

"I never thought about that." Meredith stared into her glass, giving Kathleen a chance to study her more closely.

She looked tired, upset. Surely Molly would have said if the council had reached a decision over the last few days since the scene at the library. *Or if Miss Louisa decided to tell them.*

"Everything okay?"

To her shock, Meredith's eyes filled.

"I'm so sorry," Meredith said, her voice cracking. "I don't mean to... I just don't have anyone else I can talk to here."

Kathleen leaned forward. "What is it?"

"Have you—" Meredith swiped at her eyes. "Aidan and I had dinner together last week, when the ferry had to stay overnight. We... actually had more than dinner."

"Oh. Ooooh." Kathleen thought back. Molly had dropped Aidan off at the Cooper house that day in the storm, but, "I haven't been in the village much the last few days. What's going on?"

"I was kind of hoping you knew. Aidan hasn't been piloting the ferry since they left that next day. I keep looking for him and—"

She pressed her fingers to her eyes. "God, I sound like some lovelorn teenager, don't I?"

Kathleen stalled by taking a drink. "How do you feel?"

When Meredith didn't answer, Kathleen asked, "Do you love him?"

Meredith surprised her again by laughing. "You sound like my mother. And I know, I'd probably be asking the same thing if I were listening to me. I've only known him for a few weeks, and of that time, I get to talk to him for about thirty minutes a day! It is crazy."

A low woof at the back screen door gave Kathleen the excuse to get up and let the dogs in. They both lapped water from the bowl on the floor, leaving a sloppy trail of drops when they flopped down under the table, panting.

"How long did you and Molly see each other before you knew you were in love with her?" Meredith asked.

Kathleen thought back. "It was a couple of months, but we didn't really date. It was more like we kept getting thrown together. But when I think about it, not that much longer than you've known Aidan."

"But that's the thing," Meredith said, leaning forward, her eyes burning into Kathleen's. "I may have only met him six weeks ago, but I feel I've known him all my life."

Kathleen didn't know what to say. "Maybe you have."

Meredith's eyes narrowed, and it was Kathleen's turn to laugh.

"I'm not teasing you," she said. "Molly told me that Aidan saw you at Bealtaine. Maybe there is a connection between you that goes beyond the time you've been onisland. Or beyond your time together in this life."

This was so hard, having the knowledge of Meredith's true connection to the island, but not being free to say. Instead, she said, "My first Samhain here, I had a vision. Of my grandmother and my brother. I learned early on that things happen here that can't always be explained."

Tears shimmered in Meredith's eyes again. "Then why is Aidan avoiding me? He got what he wanted and now—" She stopped, lowering her eyes in embarrassment. "TMI. Sorry."

"Meredith, I told you Aidan has battled his demons. He blamed himself for my brother's drowning. He drank too much until... until he decided to stop. But I've never known him to use women that way.

In fact, now that I think about it, I've not known Aidan to be involved with anyone at all."

"Just one-night stands, like me?"

"That's not what I mean."

"What do you mean?"

"I think the thought of loving someone scares Aidan to death. If he does feel something for you, and if he's avoiding you, it's not because he played you. It's because he's terrified."

Meredith sniffed and sipped her lemonade, thinking about this. "You really think so?"

"Yeah, I do."

Meredith gave her a tremulous smile. "Thanks, Kathleen. I know it's kind of silly, but I felt like you and I connected right away. It's nice to have a friend here."

Kathleen had to bite her lip for a moment to keep from blurting out what she knew. "I think you have more friends here than you know," she finally said.

"I wish that were true," Meredith said wistfully. "I know the rules, and I understand them, I just wish..."

"What do you wish?"

Meredith met her eyes, and Kathleen saw the internal struggle taking place.

"This island has felt like home almost from the first moment I set foot on it," Meredith said. "I just wish there were a way I could stay."

<hr />

FOREVER AFTER, MOLLY REMEMBEREd that day, that conversation with Meredith—"that I wasn't even part of," she would point out frequently—as the start of a kind of conspiracy.

"And you were the ringleader," she accused Kathleen on more than one occasion.

If Kathleen felt any embarrassment or regret, she never let on. As soon as Molly got home the afternoon that Meredith had been there, Kathleen was waiting with a cold Harp's to tell her all about Meredith and Aidan.

Before she knew it, Molly had been wrangled into taking Kathleen to Big Sister—"I checked," she'd said before Molly could argue, "Aidan is piloting one of the Big Sister ferries. We need to talk to him."

"We can't get involved," Molly had protested in horror at the mere thought of getting in the middle of her brother's love life.

But no matter how awkward it might be, Molly couldn't shake the memory that it had been Aidan who'd come to her after he took Kathleen back to the mainland when she left to go take care of her ex; Aidan who encouraged her to go after Kathleen and tell her how she felt; Aidan who had confessed to Molly that he wasn't strong enough to let himself fall in love.

She watched Kathleen, determined to try and help if she could, and she knew she couldn't walk away from a chance to help her brother find the happiness she'd found with Kathleen.

So a couple of days after Meredith's visit, they were up at dawn, packing for a day offisland. Blossom, reading the signs that something exciting was happening, bolted down his breakfast and positioned himself where he could watch both doors, just in case they tried to leave without him.

"Hope you don't mind," Molly said as they put their backpacks into the back seat of the Toyota, "but we can't go to Big Sister and not invite Mom to come along and visit with Brandi and Benjamin."

"Of course I don't mind." Kathleen let Blossom hop in the cargo area and closed the hatch. "As a matter of fact," she said when she got in, "I think we may need your mom's help."

They drove to the Cooper house, where Jenny was waiting with a basket packed with snacks.

A light fog lay over the marina when they parked. Another boat was chugging out of the harbor, its engine coughing occasionally.

"Is that Joey?" Molly asked when Joe came out to greet them.

"Yeah." He held the boat steady for Kathleen while Blossom hopped in. "I've been after him to switch out that fuel pump, but he hasn't done it yet." He gave Jenny a kiss before helping her into the idling boat. "Got the launch all fueled up for you. Should get you there and back, no worries. Give my love to Brandi and Benjamin."

He untied the line as Molly stepped into the boat.

"Gonna be chilly until this burns off," Molly said. "Be sure to put your jackets on."

Kathleen tugged her windbreaker out of her backpack, and Jenny snugged a hat over her head.

"See you tonight, honey. There's stew in the fridge if we're late," Jenny said, settling into one of the seats.

Kathleen folded a blanket for Blossom to curl up on and made sure the life vests were within reach.

When she caught Molly watching her, she said, "I'm fine. Really. Just being prepared."

"Good idea," Molly said, hiding a smile. It hadn't been all that long ago that the thought of being on a boat terrified Kathleen. Not all that surprising considering how her brother died, but damned inconvenient if you lived on an island.

She snugged her hoodie around her neck and slowly pulled away from the dock.

As expected, the sun had risen and burned off the mists by the time they were halfway to Big Sister. The windows of the enormous houses glinted, reflecting the light as they approached. She eased the launch up to a slip in the marina and climbed out to tie it to a cleat.

"Oh." Molly paused with her sweatshirt half pulled over her head.

"What is it?" Kathleen asked. She peeled her jacket off and folded it into her backpack, untangling Blossom's leash to clip to his collar.

"The Capri." Molly pointed. "The one I restored this past winter." She gazed longingly at the little beauty, bobbing on the water, her brightwork gleaming in the morning sun.

Kathleen and Blossom led the way toward the island's main street, but Jenny held Molly back.

"Mo, I got a call yesterday," she said in a low voice. "From Monty, here on Big Sister. He said to tell you they're ready. Whatever that means."

"Really?" Molly glanced in Kathleen's direction, grateful for her mom's discretion. "Thanks. And don't say anything."

"Figured." Jenny gave her shoulder a rub. "It had 'secret' written all over it."

Molly grinned. "Yeah."

The shops were just opening, but the first ferry of the day hadn't yet arrived.

"I'll meet you both at The Lobster Pot," Molly said. "But first, I'll just check on which ferry Aidan is piloting today."

When Kathleen hesitated, she said, "I won't talk to him without you, but there's no sense hanging out here for hours if he isn't due in on one of the early boats."

Appeased, Kathleen went with Jenny. Molly went to the marina office and learned that Aidan had been assigned to the ten o'clock ferry the last few days. When she left the office, she checked to make sure Kathleen wasn't in sight before darting down one of the side streets.

The jewelry store wasn't officially open yet, but when she tapped on the window, the owner unlocked the door. "I was hoping I'd see you soon," Monty said. "I think you'll be pleased."

When she got to the restaurant a little while later, her backpack was a tiny bit heavier and her bank account a lot lighter. But it was worth it.

She climbed the stairs to the small apartment above the restaurant and found her mom bouncing Benjamin on her knee, his chubby hands flailing as he gurgled happily. Marriage and motherhood seemed to agree with Brandi. Molly had to admit, Matty had made a good choice. She picked up a framed photo. They made a beautiful family.

She and Kathleen visited for a while, taking turns holding Benjamin until it was time to go. "See you soon," she said to Brandi. "Mom, meet us down the marina by three."

The day was getting hot and humid on the hike back to the marina. They arrived just as the ferry was pulling in. They waited until the cars had offloaded, along with about a dozen pedestrians. When Aidan saw the two of them standing there, Molly read his lips as he mouthed, "Oh, shit."

The cargo to the island had apparently come on the first ferry, so he had no excuses when Molly wrangled him to accompany them to the same small bar they'd gone to with Meredith. The dark interior was cooled somewhat by the ceiling fans whirring on high like plane propellers.

The same waitress as before came to their table with three iced teas. "These okay?"

"Perfect, Sherry. Thanks." Aidan squeezed the slice of lemon into his tea.

"Double-decker BLT, Aidan?" she asked.

"Yeah."

"Same for me," Molly said.

"I'll have a tuna salad sandwich," Kathleen said.

"Be right up."

Aidan sat back with a resigned sigh. "Out with it."

"Okay," Molly said. "What's up with you and Meredith Turner?"

"Butt out, Mo."

Unperturbed by his glower, she said, "Can't do that, Aidan."

"Aidan," Kathleen said in a gentler tone. "How do you feel about her?"

"Seriously?" He glanced around, but the guys sitting at the bar were busy talking. No one else was near enough to overhear. "You're asking how I feel about a woman?"

"Not just a woman," Molly said. "You saw her. The island gave the two of you a connection. And now," she leaned closer, "you sleep with her and then take off?"

"Shit." He raked his hand through his hair. "She told you that?"

"She told me," Kathleen said. "She doesn't know what to think, Aidan."

The conversation was interrupted by Sherry returning with their sandwiches. When she left, Aidan stalled by sprinkling some salt and pepper on his BLT.

"Meredith?" Molly prompted.

Aidan's response was to stuff his mouth with a huge bite. Kathleen shook her head when Molly started to harangue him. They focused on their sandwiches for a few minutes.

"Do you love her?" Kathleen asked, timing the question for when Aidan couldn't avoid answering.

"Jesus," he muttered.

"I don't think he'll help dig you out of this," Molly said.

"Aidan," Kathleen said, laying a hand on his arm, "we're not trying to interfere. Too much," she added when he glared at her. "But it really seems like there's something between you and, if there is..." She glanced questioningly at Molly.

"There's something you should know," Molly finished for her.

He forgot to eat while they told him the story of Louisa's pregnancy and giving the baby up for adoption.

"Miss Louisa," he said in disbelief. "And she's kept that secret all these years?"

"Yeah. The Turners don't know yet," Kathleen said. "But it looks as though Irene is that baby."

He choked on his tea. Molly gave him a couple of whacks on the back.

"And the council hadn't decided what to do about it," Molly told him. "So, don't say anything to Meredith yet."

"But they could be an island family." He took another bite, chewing absently as this new information sunk in.

"That's what the council has to decide," Molly said. "Rebecca isn't so sure."

"The point is," Kathleen said, "if you do love Meredith, you need to know all of this."

"Aidan," Molly said, "you helped me figure things out when I needed to tell Kathleen how I felt. It's my turn to return the favor. If you love her, don't be afraid of it. Tell her. If you don't, if you let her go back to Oregon without being honest with her, you'll always regret it."

Chapter 19

EVEN ON LITTLE SISTER, summer heat waves were becoming
more common. Since no one on the island had air conditioning, that meant fans were running to keep the air in the
buildings moving. Outside, the wind that remained constant and
powered the turbines was sticky and muggy.

The islanders simply accepted this as another of the things life
brought in its seasonal cycle. The tourists grumbled; a few cut their
vacations short, checking out of the hotel early to catch the next ferry
back to the comforts they were accustomed to.

With or without them, there were still fish and clams and lobsters
to catch, gardens to harvest and preserves to put up for the coming
winter, house repairs to finish before the autumn storms and cold
weather arrived.

For eighty years, Louisa had lived this cycle. It was as natural to
her as breathing. She did miss having Olivia to help pick and can the

produce from the garden. She stood in the middle of the tomato plants, a bushel basket at her feet nearly full.

"Good morning, Miss Louisa."

"Katie! What are you doing here?" she asked, lifting the droopy brim of her straw hat.

"Came to help you, of course." Kathleen carefully stepped through the beans and carrots. "Always seems once the tomatoes start, it's a tidal wave of them."

Louisa chuckled. "It is that."

"I'll carry this into the kitchen," Kathleen said, picking up the full basket. "Be right back."

They worked their way through the plants, picking everything that was ripe or nearly ripe. Inside, Louisa set a few aside for tomato sandwiches later, and they washed the rest, setting a couple of big pots on the stove to boil. Kathleen washed the jars and lids while Louisa placed the tomatoes in one pot long enough for the skins to split and peel away.

"Have you heard anything more from the council?" Kathleen asked.

"Not a word." It came out a bit sharper than Louisa had intended. "I suppose," she added more gently, "it is a big decision."

She transferred the scalded tomatoes to another pot for a cold-water bath to stop them cooking any further. "But I've reached my own decision."

Kathleen paused her drying of the jars. "What's that?"

"I've decided I'm going to tell Irene and her husband and daughter."

Kathleen's mouth fell open. "Are you really?"

Louisa nodded, continuing to cycle tomatoes from boiling water to cold bath to a separate plate to dry. "I am. Regardless of what the council decides, Irene deserves to know the truth."

Kathleen wrapped an arm around her shoulders and gave her a squeeze. "If it matters, I think you're doing the right thing."

"Of course it matters!" Louisa glanced up at her. "In fact, I'd like to do it soon, and I'd like you and Molly and Jenny and Joe to be here."

She noticed when Kathleen's eyes flicked in the direction of the wooden boxes on two of the kitchen chairs. "And it's time Daddy and Ollie met them."

"What about Rebecca?" Kathleen asked, dropping her arm to go back to her jars.

Louisa hesitated. "I don't know."

"She hurt your feelings, didn't she?"

Sudden tears blurred Louisa's eyes as she began chopping and crushing some of the tomatoes. She swiped her forearm across her face. "She's Keeper. She has a job to do. The island is more important than any one of us."

"I suppose." Kathleen plucked a clean towel from a drawer and began wiping the lids.

"Make sure those are completely clean and dry," Louisa reminded her, "or they won't seal."

They worked in silence for a few minutes.

"You know," Louisa said, "if you become Keeper after Rebecca, you may have to make hard choices like this, too."

"I know." Kathleen slid a sideways glance in her direction. "Did you know that Meredith and Aidan have... they've been seeing each other?"

Louisa's head snapped up. "They have?"

Kathleen nodded. "I looked up your family tree and the Coopers, to make sure there wouldn't be any connections too close for them to... you know."

Louisa chuckled. "So you are learning." She narrowed her eyes as she thought back. "But I don't think we have any connections for a few generations."

"Four," Kathleen said. "And it wasn't with the Coopers; it was with the Ahearns."

"Oh, that's right," Louisa recalled. "I think my great-grandmother and Jenny's great-great-grandfather were siblings. Or something like that."

Kathleen began measuring a little lemon juice into each of the canning jars. "How do you remember so much? I have to look it up every time."

"Told you, I've a head for dates. And names." Louisa followed, carefully spooning the tomatoes into each jar. "It was part of what I enjoyed about teaching."

She concentrated on what she was doing, and Kathleen came along behind her to wipe the tops of the jars and screw the lids into place.

Using large tongs, Louisa lowered the jars into the other pot of softly boiling water. "Set the timer for twenty minutes, Katie."

Together, they cleaned up. When the timer went off, they set the jars to cool, listening for the telltale "pop" as each jar sealed itself.

"Time for lunch," Louisa said. "You toast the bread, and I'll cut the tomatoes."

Kathleen put four slices of bread in the toaster and got plates from the cupboard.

"You heard that Meredith is a teacher, too," Louisa said quietly.

Kathleen paused as she opened the refrigerator for the mayonnaise. "You think Little Sister could have its own teacher again?"

Louisa lifted one shoulder. "It would be nice to have an option. Not all the children would have to board on the mainland if we did."

She looked askance at Kathleen. "You think I'm silly, don't you?"

"No," Kathleen said quickly. "Not silly." She grinned. "Maybe overly optimistic."

Louisa laughed. "You might be right. Just an old lady, wishing for what was."

Kathleen spread mayonnaise on each slice of toast. "Here's to wishing for what might be."

XXXXXXXXXX

JASPER'S TONGUE LOLLED AS he loped beside Meredith. Her legs churned up a rise in the ring road. Between walking and biking, the two of them had put a lot of miles on their legs the past several days.

After her talk with Kathleen—the memory of which made her cringe in humiliation every time she thought about it—she'd been determined not to be in the village when the ferry arrived.

"I will not waste the rest of my summer, sitting around and waiting for him to show up," she panted.

She'd bought bread and sandwich fixings at the market—"no need to keep paying for lunch at the diner every day," she'd said to her parents—and packed lunch and water for herself and Jasper. Together, they'd been exploring more of the off-road parts of the island. She'd wandered up to the Head, gazing at the enormous wind turbines swooshing in the ever-present wind. She'd explored the stone circle behind the cemetery, though she'd avoided going back into the chapel. She wanted no reminders of that night with Aidan.

She'd also begun exploring some of the trails that veered into the woods. Even if she got lost, she figured it was only a matter of time before she emerged near some house or landmark she recognized. She'd found some breathtaking vistas in all directions—literally breathtaking, as she'd had to bend over, hands braced on knees to catch her breath after some of the hillier hikes. But that was happening less and less.

"We're both getting in shape, buddy," she said to Jasper, noting his leaner build under a glossier coat. "This place has been good for us."

But that realization only made her sadder that they'd be leaving soon. Art and Kenny were due next week. With their arrival, and the start of August, it seemed her days here were numbered.

"Who am I kidding?" she asked Jasper, stepping over some roots in a trail. "They were always numbered. We were never going to belong here, were we?"

Jasper glanced over his shoulder, urging her on as they followed a new trail they'd never been on.

She gasped again, but in wonder this time, when they emerged at a rocky outcropping that seemed to jut over the ocean. She called Jasper back from the edge, afraid he'd go over. She clambered onto the rocks, making her way cautiously toward the precipice. Down below, waves pounded against the island's base.

They both flopped down on the rocks. Meredith poured water into a collapsible bowl for Jasper before tipping the bottle up to her own mouth.

She sat, staring out at the ocean, feeling the faint tremors of ocean pounding against bedrock. It felt as if she was linked to the island's core, to the water swirling after it crashed against her, to all the life clinging to this rock in the middle of all of the ocean's immensity.

Slowly, her breathing calmed and she lost track of time. There was just the sunlight and Jasper and the birds soaring lazy circles on the air currents.

A noise behind her startled her, and she nearly jumped out of her skin.

"I'm sorry," said Rebecca, stepping out of the woods. "I didn't realize anyone was here."

Meredith scrambled to her feet. Jasper jumped off the rocks to trot over and say hello. "I shouldn't be here," Meredith said.

"Why not?" Rebecca climbed onto the rocks to stand beside her. "It's a good place. I often come here to pray."

"Pray." Meredith turned back to the ocean, wondering if that's what she'd been doing.

"Meditate. Ponder. Pray. It's all the same." Rebecca took a deep breath. "It allows us to connect."

Meredith thought of what she'd been feeling a little bit ago and nodded. "That's it."

Rebecca studied her. "That's what?"

"Nothing," Meredith said with a self-conscious laugh.

"I don't think it was nothing," Rebecca pressed. "Tell me. Please."

"Well, today's the first time we found this spot." Meredith indicated the rocks. "We were sitting, feeling the beat of the ocean against the island, and it was..."

"It was what?"

"It was like my roots went all the way down, and I felt the sea and the island and..." She laughed again. "Silly, I know."

But Rebecca wasn't laughing. She frowned and lowered her head.

"Anyway," said Meredith. "We've had this place to ourselves long enough. See you later."

Rebecca didn't seem to have heard at first. Her head snapped up when Meredith and Jasper hopped down off the rocks. "Later."

Meredith took her time wandering back out to the ring road and around into the village. When she got to the hotel, her mother was pacing on the porch.

"Where have you been?"

"Why?" Meredith asked. "What's wrong?"

"Nothing's wrong, but we've been invited to dinner. Tonight. Go up and shower."

But Meredith hung back. "To dinner where?" Her face darkened. "The Coopers?"

"Not the Coopers, but I think some of them will be there." Irene's face lit up. "Louisa Woodhouse has invited us. She called the hotel and asked Wilma to extend the invitation."

She gave Meredith's butt a swat. "Now, hurry and shower. I'll go ask Wilma and Nels what we can bring."

Meredith's mind was racing as she hurriedly showered and changed clothes. She wished she could stop sweating, but her skin had a light sheen again by the time she got downstairs. She found her mom out on the porch with a bag in her hand as her father pulled the Subaru up.

"I asked Nels for a big batch of his pasta salad," Irene said, indicating the bag. "This should go well with anything being served for dinner."

"Crank the air conditioning, will you?" Meredith asked her dad when they got into the car.

Meredith remembered which was the Woodhouse place, directing her father from the back seat, next to Jasper who had his head hanging out the open window, despite the AC.

She recognized Molly's official sheriff SUV along with another that she didn't know. Kathleen came out to greet them.

Blossom immediately dropped into a play bow, an invitation Jasper took him up on as they zoomed around the yard in a game of chase.

Off to one side, Joe Cooper and Molly were busy at a smoking grill.

"Hope you like barbequed chicken," Joe said.

"We like anything," Roy replied, veering off to join them.

Meredith followed her mother up the porch steps to enter the house. It was charming—dozens of framed paintings covering most of the walls, more photos sitting about on the tables and the piano. She dallied, bending over to scrutinize some of the black-and-white images, and, as she gazed at one, her breath caught in her throat.

"Meredith? Where are you?"

"Coming, Mom." She hurried through into the kitchen, where Louisa was chopping vegetables for a large salad.

Kathleen had the refrigerator open. "Beer? Wine? Tea?"

"I'll have a beer," Meredith said, while her mother opted for wine.

"Make mine wine, too, Katie," Louisa said.

Jenny, busy checking a pan of potatoes roasting in the oven, turned to smile over her shoulder. "You've been getting plenty of exercise lately, Meredith. I've seen you walking everywhere."

If Jenny knew that it was to avoid having to see her son, she diplomatically kept that part quiet.

"Just trying to take advantage of the island while we're here," Meredith said.

"My brother and his husband will be arriving next week," Irene said. "We were so enthusiastic about Little Sister that they said they had to come and see for themselves."

Meredith caught Louisa staring almost hungrily at Irene. Shaken, she went out onto the back porch to take in a gulp of air.

"Are you all right?" Kathleen asked, following her outside with two bottles of Guinness in her hands.

Meredith nodded weakly. She met Kathleen's eyes.

"You know," Kathleen said quietly.

Meredith could only nod again, blinking back tears. It was a few seconds before she could speak. "The photos and, just now, the way Louisa was watching my mother."

Kathleen passed one of the bottles to her. "You probably need this."

Meredith drained half the bottle and raised a trembling hand to her mouth. "How long have you known?"

Kathleen led her down the stairs to where they could speak without being overheard. "Not long. When your mom mentioned she was born in New Hampshire, Miss Louisa suspected, but she'd never told anyone. She kind of blurted it out to me one day when we were alone. And then, when your mother told us that morning at the library that she'd received her birth certificate and learned her biological mother's name was Mary Flannery—that was Louisa's mother's name that she used at the maternity home."

"But," Meredith turned to Kathleen, her eyes bright with hope, "this means—"

"We don't know what it means yet, Meredith," Kathleen cut in. "I'm sorry. I don't know what to say, except nothing like this has ever happened before, and the island council doesn't know how to handle it."

The hope that had sprung up so violently inside Meredith crumpled, leaving her feeling numb.

"Chicken's ready," Joe called out, Molly and Roy carrying two platters up the back steps into the kitchen.

Meredith followed Kathleen inside and went through the motions of filling a plate and forcing herself to participate in the conversation. She tried to pay attention, but kept finding herself staring at Louisa.

She's my grandmother. Now that she knew, the resemblance was unmistakable. *This is what Mom will look like.* She was more startled when she realized, *This is what I will look like.*

At one point during the dinner, while Irene was talking to Jenny about something, Louisa turned before Meredith could look away. Frozen in that moment, their eyes met, and Meredith demanded the truth.

Louisa gave the tiniest nod. "Everyone," she said, silencing the various conversations around the table, "I have a story to tell you."

※※※※※※※※※

LATER THAT NIGHT, MOLLY lay side by side with Kathleen, the sheet folded across the bottom of the bed, the ceiling fan whirring above to cool their naked bodies.

"Holy cow, that was a dinner to remember," she murmured.

Kathleen nodded. "I'm so glad it's over, though. Everyone knows now. I hated knowing something so huge and not being able to tell anyone. First you, then the Turners. It felt like a lie to be running into them and keep them in the dark."

"Irene took it well. She seemed thrilled. It must be weird, though."

"How do you mean?" Kathleen turned on her side, nuzzling against Molly's shoulder.

"Well, here's your mother, but not. She didn't raise you. Doesn't really know you. You've got this connection, but it's based on... basically an accident. How do you build a relationship on that?"

"*Do* you build a relationship on that?" Kathleen echoed. "I know some people who were sorry they ever sought out relatives based only on biology."

"Yeah, but Miss Louisa is great."

"She's great to us because she's ours," Kathleen pointed out. "Meredith didn't seem as happy as her mom."

Molly thought about that. "No. She seemed almost angry."

"I don't think that had anything to do with Miss Louisa."

Molly rolled her head toward Kathleen. "What do you mean?"

"We were talking outside, and she'd just realized the truth. She immediately jumped to their connection to Little Sister. I had to shut her down on that."

"Oh."

"I keep trying to put myself in her place, knowing you want to be here, but not being allowed to stay."

"But that's different—"

"I know," Kathleen interrupted. "But not by much. Think about it. I was gone for almost twenty-five years. Instead of us knowing her as someone who's never been connected to Little Sister, think of her as someone who's been gone for thirty-five years."

Molly pressed her lips to Kathleen's forehead. "When you put it like that..."

"Exactly."

"Damn."

Chapter 20

T HE NEXT FEW DAYS were so busy with a hard deadline looming that Kathleen had no time to spare to think about Miss Louisa or the Turners. She barely had time to think about Molly.

It was late one afternoon when she heard clattering downstairs and realized Blossom was no longer with her. She groaned a little as she stood up and marched in place a few times to get the blood flowing in her legs before she braved the stairs. In the kitchen, she found Molly getting dinner ready.

"Thank you," she said, taking her glasses off to knuckle her tired eyes. "I think this edit is going to kill me."

"Bad writing?" Molly asked from where she was making a salad of tomatoes, peppers, and onions. "Can you get the Italian dressing out of the fridge?"

"Not bad," Kathleen said in reply to Molly's first question as she opened the refrigerator. "But it's a time travel story, and the loops are making me dizzy. If such and such happens in the second or third loop, does that mean so and so couldn't have happened in the first or second? I had to make a schematic for myself, trying to keep it all straight. Let's not ever time travel."

"What if suddenly there are two of me?" Molly asked, grinning.

Kathleen wrapped her arms around Molly's neck and kissed her. "I think one of you is all I can handle."

"Oh?" Molly paused her work to kiss Kathleen back, her mouth and tongue seeking. Kathleen responded. Molly pulled away to look into Kathleen's eyes. "Think of what two of me could do to you."

"Keep that up and we're never going to get to dinner."

Molly turned back to her salad. "I am hungry."

"You're always hungry." Kathleen gave her another light kiss on the cheek. "We'll save it for tonight."

She got a bowl of chicken salad out of the refrigerator and poured water for both of them. "I love cold dinners in the summertime."

As they ate, Molly told her about her day fixing a stone chimney for one of the islanders Kathleen knew only by name. "Reminds me," Molly said, reaching for her glass, "I want to clean our chimney soon, make sure it's safe for the winter."

They quickly washed the dishes, and Kathleen's gaze was pulled upward.

"No," Molly said firmly. "No more work tonight. Come on."

She took Kathleen by the hand and led her to the front door. Blossom skidded behind them, his tail wagging. "Don't worry, you're coming." She grabbed the car keys on their way out.

"Where are we going?" Kathleen asked.

"You'll see. Get in."

Molly drove them into the village where several people still roamed the streets. The stores that catered to them were open late, taking advantage of the activity. There were still another couple of hours of daylight, but parts of the street were in shadow. Molly parked and pointed to a little shop with a steady line.

"Ice cream."

Kathleen laughed. "I haven't had an ice cream cone in forever. Oh, a hot fudge sundae. That's what I want. With extra hot fudge."

"Extra hot fudge. Check."

Molly got in line, and Kathleen peeked into a few store windows. Siobhan was doing quite the business. Kathleen tilted her head, studying a few new watercolors in the window.

"Beautiful, aren't they?" Siobhan asked, stepping outside.

"They are." Kathleen leaned closer. "Nice technique."

"Irene Turner."

Kathleen straightened. "Really?" She glanced around, but no one who would understand was nearby. "Any word from the council?"

Siobhan shook her head. "Rebecca has asked us to meet next week. I suspect that will be the topic of the meeting. I understand Miss Louisa told them."

"She did." Kathleen gazed toward the hotel. "I should check on Meredith."

A tiny line creased Siobhan's brow. "There's been a change in her energy the last few days."

Three years ago, Kathleen would have scoffed at such a statement, but now, she listened, feeling a twinge of guilt. "I've been busy. I should have checked on her sooner."

Siobhan laid a hand on Kathleen's arm. "I think she could use a friend." She smiled when Molly approached, her hands laden with treats. Blossom followed hopefully, almost tripping her.

"See you both soon," Siobhan said, going back into her shop.

"Hot fudge sundae, extra fudge." Molly handed Kathleen her bowl. "Banana split for me."

They wandered the village as they ate.

"It's kind of fun, playing tourist," Kathleen said. "Let's head over to the hotel."

They crossed the street, mostly empty of cars, to where several people were rocking in the chairs on the hotel's porch.

"Molly, Kathleen." Irene jumped up when she saw them. "Let me introduce my brother, Art Millward, and his husband, Kenny Emmart."

They shook hands all round, and Kathleen wondered how Irene and Art could have ever thought they were siblings. He definitely looked more Mediterranean, with his olive complexion, and a prominent brow and nose giving him a more hawkish profile.

"We just got here today," Kenny said. "What a charming place."

"We like it," Molly said tightly.

Kathleen recognized her protective tone and quickly said, "We're glad to have you on Little Sister."

She scanned the porch. "Where's Meredith?"

Roy waved an arm. "She took Jasper for a walk. I think she said something about the beach."

Kathleen nodded. As far as she was aware, it was still Bobby who'd been piloting the Little Sister ferry. No sign of Aidan.

Sudden raised voices from the direction of the marina caught their attention.

"I'm going to see what that's about," Molly muttered, heading down the hill.

Kathleen made small talk, asking Art and Kenny about their trip and the ferry crossing. "Well," she said when she felt she could politely say good-bye, "I'm sure we'll see you around. Night."

She and Blossom hurried to the marina in time to see Joey fling his yellow oilskins into the marina office.

"I told you, I'll get to it!" He stomped past Kathleen without a word.

"But—" Molly started, but Joe laid a hand on her shoulder.

"Leave it. He'll have to learn the hard way," he said.

With a nod to Kathleen, he picked up the oilskins and hung them to dry.

"Come on," Molly said. "Let's go."

She and Kathleen walked back to where the Toyota was parked.

"What was that about?" Kathleen asked.

Molly's nostrils flared as she turned the ignition. "That fuel pump. We've been after him for weeks to replace it. He barely made it in today. He and Matty have already broken down three times, and they just keep patching it. Told him I'd stay tonight and help, but... you heard him."

She continued to fume on the drive home. "You never do that," she said, pounding the wheel. "You never go out with gear that's not working. First rule Dad taught us."

Joey had never struck Kathleen as particularly hard-working or enterprising. Not like Molly, who was always busy, nor like Aidan, who had taken the initiative to begin training to get his captain's license. Even Matty, used to being the baby of the family, was looking more responsible now that he had a wife and baby to support.

"Like your dad said," she pointed out, "maybe Joey has to learn things the hard way."

Molly pulled up to their cottage. She blew out an exasperated breath. "Sorry. It was a nice evening. I don't want to spend the rest of it thinking about what a jerk my brother is."

They got out, standing under the inky sky while Blossom trotted into the trees. Kathleen wrapped her arms around Molly's neck.

"I think I remember where we left off while dinner was being prepped," she said coyly.

Molly smiled. "Oh, yeah? Where was that?"

Kathleen kissed her, a deep soft kiss, her body melting into Molly's, her hands pulling Molly's hips into hers.

"Remember now?" Kathleen murmured.

"Oh, yeah..."

LOUISA CARRIED A WICKER basket of wet sheets out to the line. The heat had continued, sticky with humidity. It would take a little longer for the sheets to dry, but no one on the island used dryers when the clothesline would do.

She felt lighter than she had in weeks. *Maybe years,* she thought. After the first year or so, the pregnancy hadn't been something that stayed on her mind constantly, but every now and again—*and every August*—she wondered where her baby was, what had become of her, hoped she was happy and well. It sometimes seemed too much to believe that Irene was actually here.

"My daughter," she whispered, shivering a little.

"Not really your daughter, though, is she?"

Louisa sighed. "You always have to spoil everything, Ollie."

"Do not."

"Do so. Can't you let me have this, be happy with it?"

"Just don't want you to be disappointed, sister. Best to be realistic about things. You didn't raise her. She had a mother and father."

Louisa reached for a couple of clothespins. "I know." She pursed her lips for a moment. "But we have family, Ollie. Flesh and blood. With blood memory. People to come after us."

"That is something, Lou. We never thought we'd see that. What do you think the council will decide?"

Louisa straightened a wrinkle in one of the sheets. "I'm not sure. Rebecca seemed dead set against them."

"You should take advantage of the time they're here. Have them to the house again."

Louisa's head lifted. "I could do that. For supper, maybe."

"Go call them."

Louisa hurried inside. Wilma quickly found Irene, who eagerly accepted the invitation but told her that their number had grown by two. She insisted they bring dinner. With that settled, Louisa began dusting and cleaning.

By six that evening, the Turners had arrived, carrying several containers of food from the diner, along with drinks from the market.

"Thank you so much for the invitation," Irene said. She introduced Art and Kenny.

Louisa invited them all inside, where she had fans going to keep the air moving.

"What a charming house," Kenny said appreciatively.

"Thank you," said Louisa, feeling the scrutiny she was receiving from Art. Meredith, she noticed, hadn't said a word.

Louisa filled a bowl with cold water for Jasper. She set it on the floor for him, giving him a pat when he came over to lap a bit of it.

Roy and Art laid out containers of fried chicken, a few different kinds of salads, and some of Nels's crab cakes. Irene and Meredith poured wine for everyone while Kenny helped Louisa set out glasses of ice water.

Louisa had already set the table. "Sit down, please."

An awkward silence fell over the gathering at first, broken when Kenny asked how old the house was. As Louisa talked—"something you never have trouble doing," she could hear Ollie say—the tension eased.

Art wanted to know more about the island's history, and Louisa settled into teacher mode, entertaining her guests, almost forgetting why she'd invited them.

Every now and again, Louisa glanced at Meredith, who'd kept her eyes downcast, eating without saying a word.

Finally, when Louisa asked Art what he did for a living, Meredith slammed her fist on the table. "Are we really going to sit here and pretend this is a normal get-together?"

"Meredith!" Irene's lips compressed into an expression that Louisa recognized only too well. "We are guests in this house!"

"And we're guests on this island!" Meredith reminded them. She pointed at Louisa. "You may have been born to an islander, but we're not welcome to stay here."

"Now we're getting to the meat of it," Kenny said in an undertone.

Art leaned forward, his gaze intense. "You really are Irene's biological mother?"

"Based on her birthdate, on where she was born," Louisa said calmly, "and the name on her birth certificate, which is the name I used when I went to New Hampshire, I believe I am."

Meredith pushed up from the table and stalked out of the room, only to return in a moment with a photo. "There. You want proof? Look at this. Who does that look like?"

Kenny leaned nearer to stare along with Art. "Oh, my God." He glanced from Louisa to Irene. "You're the spitting image of—"

"Don't say her mother," Meredith spat.

"Meredith," Irene's nostrils flared, "why are you being like this?"

"Why?" Meredith's eyes filled. "Because our entire lives have been turned upside-down by that damned ancestry test you insisted we all take. Because we have biological connections to the Woodhouse family and this damned island, but we're not family. Because—"

Her voice broke, and she ran from the house, Jasper on her heels. "Meredith!"

Irene started to rise from her chair, but Roy, who hadn't said a word thus far, pulled her back down. "Let her go."

"Usually I'm the drama queen," Kenny said, but the joke fell flat.

Louisa shook her head. "I don't blame her." She looked in the direction Meredith had fled. "She feels a connection to the island, but she doesn't know where she belongs."

"Oh, it's more than that," Roy said quietly.

␢␢␢␢␢␢␢␢␢␢␢

THE SKY SLOWLY TRANSITIONED, like one of those mythological images of Nyx, pulling the shade of night across the sky. Overhead, daylight gave way to starlight, and still, Meredith sat on the bluff, her arms wrapped around her knees as she stared out at the sea, listening to the crashing of the waves far below. The wind cooled a little as it lightly buffeted her. Jasper lay beside her, his warmth welcome.

It was humiliating to think about her meltdown at Louisa's house. She lowered her head to her knee.

"Maybe we should just go home and forget about this place," she whispered.

Jasper whined and sat up to nuzzle her cheek.

She wrapped an arm around him. "But it's not just this place, is it?" She pressed her face into his fur, trying not to think about Aidan and the hole in her heart that she knew only he could fill.

"We should go," she said at last. "They'll be getting worried."

She got stiffly to her feet and clambered down off the rocks. They made their way along the now-familiar path through the woods toward the ring road that would take her back to the hotel, back to her parents and uncles, back to... what? Her life on the other side of the country. She was almost startled at how hard it was to try and remember her small house in Pacific City, her job teaching at Nestucca Valley, Jan and Barb and all of her other friends there. It felt as if that was the part of her life she'd only seen in dreams, and this part, here on Little Sister, was the part that was real.

No cars passed as she walked. The islanders were probably either at home or at the pub, in which case, they'd be driving home later. The houses she walked by had one or two windows illuminated against the falling darkness. They should have looked warm and inviting, but she only felt shut out.

She reached down to scratch her fingers through the thick fur on Jasper's neck. "We don't really belong anywhere."

Chapter 21

A COLD RAIN SPATTERED the 4-Runner's windshield—swiped clean with new wipers—as Molly drove to the market. She needed some lumber and shingles for a roof job. She couldn't do it until the rain stopped, but she wanted to make sure Tim and Miranda had everything in stock. If not, the job would have to wait until he could get a new shipment over on the ferry.

She parked and pulled her hood up before trotting to the market. Miranda had the baby in a papoose thing strung over her shoulders.

"How's the little one?" Molly asked, giving Charlotte a finger to grasp in her tiny fist.

"She's wonderful," Miranda said, beaming. "She sleeps through the night, hardly makes a fuss. But she's very independent. I think she's going to be a Charlie, not a Charlotte."

Molly grinned. "Charlie. I like that. Have you set a date for her naming?"

"We're working on it."

Molly wriggled her finger out of the baby's grip. "Where's Tim?"

Miranda nodded toward the back. "Greenhouse. Picking lettuce."

"See you later." Molly wove her way through the tourists cluttering the aisles.

"Molly."

She stopped and turned at the sound of her name. "Art. How are you?"

"Good." He had a basket full of cookies and bags of chips. "Just stocking up on essentials for a long day of games. Seems we brought our weather with us."

"We've been known to have rainy spells, with or without visitors from the Pacific Northwest." She glanced out the window at the downpour. "But the forecast does call for a few days of this, some of it stormy. Sorry you won't see the island at her best until this moves out."

She began to move by him, but he quickly shifted to block her. "Reney seems to love it here. Roy, too. I'm surprised by how content they seem. Surely there's some way they can rent a house or something. I mean," he said with a smug smile, "money is no object."

Molly pasted a polite smile on her face. "Then I suggest they look around on Big Sister. There's probably something available there." She stepped around him. "I've business..."

Without a backward glance, she hurried through the store to the greenhouse out back. There, she found Tim, the lettuce forgotten, having a hose fight with Ellis.

"Hey, I'm wet enough." She jumped back when one of the hoses sent a wild spray in her direction.

"Sorry, Mo." Tim laughed and turned the water off. He and Ellis were both sopping wet. "What can I do for you?"

"I have to replace Willie and Orla Walsh's roof. Need about a dozen sheets of three-quarter-inch plywood and new shingles. Do you have that in stock?"

"Pretty sure we do. I'll check and let you know."

"Thanks. I'll let you get back to your water battle."

She left the greenhouse, but opted not to return through the store. "Money is no object," she muttered darkly. People like that thought money could get them anything they wanted, and they never understood that, here, their money didn't mean squat.

She splashed back to the Toyota and got the wipers going just in time to see Kathleen in her Nissan, driving out of the marina parking lot.

"What the...?"

She turned the ignition off again and sprinted down to the marina office, flapping her jacket as she stepped inside.

"Hey!" Joe said, wiping drops off his ledger.

"Sorry." Molly stopped her flapping. "What was Kathleen doing here?"

"Huh?" Joe turned his back on her, opening a file drawer. "She wasn't here."

"But I just saw—"

"Hey, got a call from Bobby," Joe interrupted. "Laurie has to have surgery tomorrow, so he's taking a couple of weeks off. Aidan will be piloting the Little Sister ferry for a while."

"Wait," Molly said, her mind racing to process this new information. "Okay, I need to talk to Aidan anyhow, so I'll be glad to see him, but what kind of surgery? Is she okay?"

"Yeah." Joe looked embarrassed. "Woman stuff. Ask your mom."

"I will." Molly stared at him, but he kept turning away, pretending to be busy with paperwork. "What about—"

"Oh," Joe said, cutting her off again, "I want to do some maintenance on the generators next week. You free?"

"Yeah. I can be. Just let me know when."

"Okay. Gotta get to..."

He yanked a jacket off a hook and hurried out of the office, leaving her standing there with her mouth open.

She stomped through the rain to her SUV and sat with the wipers going, the rain pounding on the roof. "Something's up."

She put the Toyota in gear and drove to her parents' house. One more time, she sloshed her way through the downpour to the back porch. Inside the kitchen door, she toed off her wet boots and left them on the tray with all the others. Her jacket, hung on a peg, dripped steadily onto the tray.

"Mo," said Jenny, entering the kitchen. "Thought I heard someone. Want some hot coffee?"

"Sounds good. Thanks."

Jenny scooped some coffee into the basket and got a fresh pot brewing. "This front looks like it's going to last a few days."

"Yeah," Molly said, sitting at the table. "Nice break in the heat. What's up with Laurie? Dad said she has to have surgery."

Jenny set a plate of muffins on the table. "She has to have a hysterectomy."

"Not cancer or anything, is it?"

"No. Just fibroids and lots of discomfort. Her doctor recommended it. But she'll be down for a few weeks. I offered to go stay with them, but Bobby said he'd take a couple of weeks, and then if she needs someone, I'll go."

"Rebecca could help."

"She would, I'm sure." Jenny poured coffee for both of them and joined Molly at the table. "But she's not such a caretaker. She'd be restless inside two days."

"Yeah."

"The council meets Thursday," Jenny reminded them both.

"Figure this is about the Turners. Whether we're going to consider them islanders or not."

Jenny cradled her coffee in her hands. "Have you decided?"

Molly picked a muffin off the plate. "Banana?" Jenny nodded. Molly broke it into chunks. A cat head immediately appeared at her thigh. "Weird cat," she said, offering Minnow a bite. When her mother just waited, Molly shrugged. "I think I've decided, and then I change my mind. It's happened about twenty times. But then Kathleen compared herself to Meredith, made me look at things differently."

Jenny helped herself to a muffin. "I've gone back and forth, too." She slowly peeled the paper away. "I'm going to vote to accept them. Maybe it's never happened this way before, but they descend from an island line. And I think it would mean a lot to Miss Louisa. One mistake at such a young age shouldn't mark her life forever. And it resulted in a new life, a new family. How can we not honor that?"

"I think Meredith has been having a hard time." Molly stole a glance at her mother.

Jenny was watching her with that knowing gaze. "Have you talked to him?"

"How do you always know?"

A tiny smile played upon Jenny's lips. "It's my job. Have you?"

"Yes." Molly popped a big piece of muffin into her mouth and chewed. "Kathleen and I corralled him over at Big Sister, tried to talk some sense into him. He's running scared."

"I know. Maybe now that he'll have to come back here, they'll at least talk."

Molly huffed. "Or maybe I'll just arrest him and haul both their asses in. Sometimes I wish we had a jail."

<hr />

"NO, THANKS." MEREDITH SHOOK her head when Kenny held up a deck of cards.

She'd played enough gin rummy, chess, Monopoly, poker, and Trivial Pursuit the last two days to last her the rest of her life. The weather was forecast to worsen later in the day, but already, the wind gusts were strong enough to send the rain sideways. The boats in the island's small harbor bobbed wildly. The ferry had had engine trouble and hadn't come at all yesterday. She'd heard Wilma telling someone it was coming today, come hell or high water, but would most likely have to overnight.

Kenny pulled a chair up beside her, and they sat gazing out the window at the dreary scene beyond. Jasper lay curled up at Meredith's feet.

"Charming."

"You being sarcastic?"

"Don't get your hackles up. I mean it. This place is charming. More than I expected. I can see why you love it."

"Sorry." She smiled. "Being here has forced us to slow down. Look at things differently."

"And what are you seeing differently?"

She bit her lip for a moment. It seemed her stupid emotions were constantly ready to brim over. Of course, her hormones weren't helping. "Everything," she said at last.

"Art tried to bribe that cute sheriff, you know."

She turned to him. "What?"

Kenny raised one shoulder. "He figured this story about no houses to rent or sell to outsiders was bogus. He thought they were just trying to up the ante, so he decided to see if he could push it a little."

Meredith sat up, her heart beating faster. *Maybe...*

"No such luck." Kenny chuckled. "He said Molly's eyes blazed a little. He had the feeling she wanted to tell him to go to hell, but she just said to go to that other island instead."

Meredith sagged back against her chair again. She felt Kenny's eyes on her. "Stop poking."

"Quite the coincidence," Kenny said, changing topics, "your mother finding her biological mother, hidden away here in this remote little place."

"I don't think it was coincidence," Meredith said.

Kenny didn't reply immediately. "No. Those dreams Irene told us about. You were led here. But now what?"

Now what? How could Kenny know that Meredith had asked herself that very question at least a thousand times.

"Are you going to try and contact any of the other possible relatives the DNA kit listed?"

Meredith glared at him. "No," she said flatly. "I think this is all the new family I can handle."

Jasper sat up, and Meredith took the opportunity to escape any further interrogation.

"Need to go out?" she asked, getting to her feet.

"In this?" Kenny asked in disbelief.

"Unless I can train him to use the toilet," she said, forcing a grin.

She went to get her rain jacket, though she doubted it would offer much protection. Tugging the cords on her hood, she snugged it tight. There was no need for a leash for Jasper, who didn't really like going out in the rain.

"You go hurry up," she said to him, pointing to the large patch of grass beside the hotel.

He gave her a sullen look and slunk out to the yard. A sudden gust of wind threatened to tear her hood free, and she reached up to grab the visor. Rain dripped from her hand inside the cuff of her jacket, worming its way along her forearm. She put her back to the wind, impatiently waiting for Jasper to pick the exact right spot and see if he was going to do anything she needed to clean up. He just peed—a very long pee—and trotted back to her, rubbing his wet face between her knees to dry off on her jeans.

"Come on," she said. "We'll go dry both of us off."

She turned and nearly ran into someone standing behind her. Squinting against the rain to see who was under that rain slicker, her mouth fell open. "Aidan."

He stared down at her, his dark eyes fierce. "We need to talk."

For a moment, they stood there staring at each other, the curtain of rain making it seem the rest of the world had disappeared.

"Okay," she managed to say.

He took her by the elbow to steer her toward the sheltered side of the hotel where the wind and rain were a little less blustery.

"Meredith, I—"

"Aidan!"

They both looked for the source of the shout. Joe pounded through the rain, no rain gear, water sluicing down his face.

"What is it?" Aidan yelled.

"Matty, Joey," Joe said, holding one hand up to shield his eyes from the stinging raindrops. "They're down, twelve miles out. Can't get the engine going. We gotta go after them."

Aidan spared a few seconds to look back at Meredith. "Coming!"

She nodded, and he pelted after his father, down to the marina.

⬛⬛⬛⬛⬛⬛⬛

KATHLEEN TRIED TO SETTLE in her chair and read, but the wind whistled around the cottage, and it seemed to her that there were voices trying to be heard in the gale. It was a day like this—a storm like this—when Aidan and Bryan were racing, when she and Nanna had waited for hours, when Bryan didn't make it back.

She gave up and went to the kitchen, Blossom almost glued to her leg. She put a kettle on but almost immediately turned the burner off.

Ever since Molly's curt phone call a few hours ago, telling her that Joey and Matty were stranded and that she was going out with her father and Aidan to get them, she'd been trying to quell the panic that threatened to drown her. For just a moment, Molly had stayed on the line, and Kathleen knew they were both torn. Saying "I love you" felt like a good-bye, so Kathleen had blurted, "Come back to me."

"I will," came Molly's staticky voice over the line, and then she was gone.

Kathleen tried not to remember what it felt like, the night of the storm, when searchers had found broken splinters of Bryan's scull, but not his body. Not until the next day, when it washed up.

She pressed her hand to her chest. *Breathe,* she reminded herself. *You can't fall to pieces again.* Not like the night she'd tried to run from her memories of her mother wishing it had been her and not Bryan who'd died.

"You're one of ours now."

She'd clung to Rebecca's words before when she needed them, when she needed to believe that she belonged to this island and its people.

Grabbing her rain jacket off its peg, she and Blossom ran to the Nissan. She might have to wait for Molly, but she didn't have to wait alone.

She almost cried with relief when she saw the lights burning in the Coopers' kitchen windows. Blossom raced her up the porch steps. Climbing the back steps after him, she peered through the kitchen door. Nearly every surface was covered with food: cooling racks with cookies and a couple of pies; a slow cooker on the counter; another pot on the stove.

When she knocked softly and opened the door, Jenny's head snapped up, her jaw tight, as she kneaded a large mound of dough.

"Get in here," she said. "Pour us both a cup of coffee."

Kathleen grabbed an old towel lying atop the boots and scrubbed Blossom partially dry before he could shake. Her own dripping rain jacket she hung over the boot tray next to the door. The radio had been moved to the table. It gave a burst of static, but then nothing.

The familiar—the aroma of the baked goods, the scattered jars of spices, canisters of flour and sugar, the pungent scent of whatever was bubbling in the pot—it immediately soothed some of Kathleen's jangled nerves. She didn't need to ask Jenny why she was doing this.

She poured two mugs of strong coffee and, for a moment, worried about the caffeine. A giggle burst out of her before she could stop it. If Jenny wondered what that was about, she didn't ask.

"What can I do?" Kathleen asked, setting one mug near Jenny's floury work surface.

"Melt a stick of butter?"

Kathleen got the butter out of the fridge and cut a stick into chunks, dropping them into a small saucepan. Every time the radio belched a spurt of static, they both paused, but there was nothing.

"Have you talked to Brandi?" Kathleen asked. *Have you told her her husband might die at sea today?*

Kathleen's hand trembled so violently that she splashed some of the melted butter onto the stovetop. She quickly wiped it up.

"About an hour ago," Jenny said. "The Coast Guard has been called. They've got a cutter and a helicopter out, helping to search. Phone lines were getting iffy. She has her radio set to the same channel."

They worked in silence for a while, Jenny rolling out the dough, Kathleen helping to brush the melted butter over top of it before Jenny sprinkled a cinnamon-sugar mix on top of that. She rolled the whole into a log, cut it into one-inch discs, and set them aside to rise again.

Kathleen went to the sink to wash her hands and stood, staring out at the rain.

"I should have gone with them." She turned to Jenny. "Why are we just standing here, waiting like good women are supposed to?"

Jenny fixed her with a steely gaze. "I did that once, early on. Ronan and Tommy Callahan got caught in a storm like this. I went with Joe and a few others to rescue them. I grew up on the water, but I'd never been out in waves like that. Joe was so worried about me that he nearly got washed overboard because he wasn't paying attention to what he needed to. I was a distraction. That's what you would have been."

Kathleen stared into her eyes and knew it was the truth. She was less experienced than Jenny or any of the others when it came to boats and how to maneuver through rough waters. Molly would have been so distracted, trying to keep her safe, that she couldn't have done her job.

"It has nothing to do with us being women. Or being too weak to go out. It's about knowing our limitations and letting them do what they know how to do."

Kathleen nodded. "You're right."

She ran hot soapy water in the sink to help clean up. Another screech of static from the radio made them both jump. Kathleen quickly turned the faucet off, and Jenny stood frozen, her hands full of flour she was swiping off the table.

"Nothing yet..." came Joe's voice. "Will..."

The transmission stopped.

"Will what?" Kathleen whispered, but Jenny glared at the radio, demanding it speak to them again.

"...Coast Guard..."

"What?" Jenny whispered this time. "Coast Guard what?"

But there was nothing further. The radio went silent.

Woodenly, Kathleen turned back to the sink. Jenny dumped the used flour in the trash and gathered the canisters to take them back to the pantry.

Kathleen flinched at the sound of glass breaking, followed by another sound. She found Jenny sobbing in the pantry, a broken jar of preserves shattered on the floor.

She wrapped her arms around Jenny as she shook. Strangely, no tears came to her own eyes. When Jenny's tears slowed, Kathleen guided her to the kitchen and sat with her at the table.

"I have to clean—"

"I'll do it," Kathleen said. "You stay here."

She picked up all the broken glass and mopped up the sticky strawberry preserves with a bucket of water and wet rag. When she returned to the kitchen, Jenny had calmed down. She held a fresh cup of coffee out to Kathleen.

They sat, staring at the radio, willing it to speak again, to give them the news they prayed for.

"Don't tell anyone about that," Jenny murmured.

"I won't." Kathleen gripped her coffee mug. "How do you—"

"I have to," Jenny said. "I have to let them go. They couldn't do what they need to if they worried about me every time they go out. It would be as big a distraction as being in the boat with them. They can't have half their minds on us."

Kathleen nodded, silently sipping her coffee. Blossom whined and sat with his head resting on Kathleen's thigh.

Outside, the trees groaned in the storm, and wind whistled through windows as an early twilight fell.

More bursts of static came from the radio, with unintelligible voices. Jenny twiddled a knob and there was a sudden "—got them."

She snatched up the microphone. "Come again."

"We've got them," came Joe's voice through the static. "On our way home with Coast Guard escort."

Kathleen reached for Jenny's hand, both their knuckles white as they squeezed. Sudden tears filled Kathleen's eyes.

"Don't tell Molly."

Jenny nodded. "Our secret."

<hr/>

WILMA WANDERED THE DINER, refilling coffee cups, though the diner would normally have closed an hour ago. "We'll be here as long as it takes," she said when Roy asked if she wanted them all to leave.

Several locals occupied the stools at the counter, where a radio sat. The tourists were subdued and respectful as they all waited for word. When Art came in, his voice had seemed unnaturally loud as he asked, "What's going on?"

Irene hurriedly whispered to him, and his eyes had immediately sought Meredith.

Her food lay untouched. She longed to leave the diner, be away from everyone, the occasional probing glances cast in her direction. But the radio was the only lifeline to what was going on.

Every time the static broke through, everyone immediately ceased talking, listening hard. And every time it turned out to be nothing, her hopes fell a little more.

Meredith caught whispers, "all the Coopers except Jenny" and "reminds me of the night Bryan Halloran died" and "has anyone checked on Jenny?" until she thought she might scream from the tension.

What if they don't come back?

She squeezed her eyes shut, trying to stop that voice inside her head. "I'll be outside. Let me know if—"

"We will," Roy said. "Go."

Jasper followed her out to the porch where she had room to pace. Some rain blew in with each gust of wind, but she didn't care. She couldn't remember the last time she'd prayed, and she didn't know now whom to pray to. But she knew where she wanted to be. For a moment, she thought about going upstairs for her car keys and finding the Subaru in the hotel's parking lot, but this felt like something of a baptism.

Squinting her eyes to shield them from the sting of the rain, she set out, Jasper at her side. Together, they made their way out of the village, following the ring road. She didn't pass any cars. Some of the houses had lights on; others were dark. She hoped she would know when she reached her destination, but everything looked different in the gloom and rain.

When she reached the cemetery, she left the road, wending her way among the stones. Belatedly, she wondered if the chapel had a lock. To her relief, it didn't. She ran a finger down Jasper's back and got him to shake outside, before they stepped through the door. Her own clothing was so thoroughly sodden that she left a wet trail as she crept toward the big slab of granite, carefully feeling her way in the gloom. There, she found a book of matches and lit several of the candles.

Shivering, she sat down on one of the wooden benches—figuring a wet bottom wouldn't do any harm on that surface—and closed her eyes. She opened her mouth, but didn't know what to say. Or to whom she should say it. She'd grown up in the Presbyterian church, but hadn't attended for years. The people here on Little Sister believed in such a blend of things that she didn't know what to think.

All she knew was that, for her, trying to imagine the world without Aidan Cooper in it was impossible. At last, she whispered, "Please, if you're listening, if you exist—in any form—protect them. Bring them all back to us." She hesitated. "All I ask is for Aidan to be safely with his family. I will leave here, if that's how it must be, but please keep him safe."

Jasper rested his head on her foot as she sat, whispering the same words over and over.

She had no idea how much time had passed when the chapel door opened suddenly, and she and Jasper nearly jumped out of their skins. In the wildly flickering light of the candles, Meredith stared at a figure standing there in a hooded slicker. When the hood was lowered, she found herself gazing into Louisa Woodhouse's eyes.

Meredith rose to her feet, uncertain if she was breaking another Little Sister rule by being here. Maybe this chapel was for islanders only.

"Thought I might find you here," Louisa said. She flapped her jacket and approached.

"I didn't mean to intrude," Meredith said.

"You're not intruding, dear." Louisa pointed to the bench. "May I?"

Meredith nodded and they both sat, Louisa patting Jasper's head. "Why did you think I might be here?" Meredith asked.

Louisa didn't answer immediately. "It's hard, the waiting. Hard no matter who it is, but even harder if someone you care about, someone you love, is out there."

She closed her eyes for a moment, and she seemed older, more fragile than Meredith remembered.

"I've been through more vigils like this than I care to remember," Louisa said quietly. "It's part of living here, but it never gets any easier."

When she opened her eyes, she fixed them again on Meredith. "I would never presume to think of myself as your grandmother, Meredith, but you don't have to wait alone. You have people here, people who care about you."

All the emotion, all the tension—not just of this awful night, but of the past weeks—it all came crashing down, and Meredith found herself sobbing in Louisa's arms.

"Shhhhhh," Louisa murmured, rocking her as if she were a little girl with a skinned knee.

Meredith let go of everything she'd been holding in—her longing for a home here, her anger and resentment that it couldn't be hers, her frustration at loving a man who wouldn't love her back. When at last her crying slowed and she extricated herself from Louisa's arms, she was mortified.

"I'm sorry," she hiccupped. "I don't usually..." She wiped her eyes with her fingers, but her nose was running, and she didn't even have long sleeves.

"Here." Louisa pulled a folded tissue from the pocket of her slicker.

Meredith took it and blew her nose. "Thank you."

The door burst open for a second time.

"Miss Louisa, I saw your car—" Rebecca stood there, the rain blowing in behind her. Her sharp eyes took in the scene. "Oh. I didn't realize. They found them. They're on their way back."

Chapter 22

XCEPT FOR THE CONTINUED howling of the wind and breaking of waves, sending spray and foam over the deck, the ride back to Little Sister was silent. The Coast Guard cutter stayed to their leeward side as much as they could. Molly heard her dad on the radio with the cutter now and again as she held the wheel, trying to maintain as steady a course as possible through fifteen-foot swells.

Behind her, Aidan kept an eye on Joey and Matty, both of whom were battered but not seriously injured.

Joe had left a GPS beacon on the fishing boat. In the faint hope that it wouldn't be swamped and sink, they might be able to find it and either repair it or tow it back.

It had been hairy, trying to pull up alongside their boat and get both the boys dragged onto the launch as the boats pitched. A few times, Molly had been sure the launch was going to be rammed and take on water. At that point, the cutter was too far away to get to them if they went down.

She was so furious with her brothers that she couldn't even speak to them. The hours dragged on interminably, and with no break in the storm, no stars to guide them, it seemed to take forever to get back.

Finally, the hulk of the Head came into view. The Coast Guard accompanied them around to the island's northern exposure. With a blast of its horn, the cutter veered off when they could finally make their way into harbor.

Only when the launch was securely tied to a slip in the marina did Molly let herself relax. The hours of adrenaline left her ready to collapse now, but she'd be damned if she'd let her stupid brothers pick her ass up in such a humiliating way after putting them all through such a night.

Still, her legs were wobbly as it seemed the entire island descended on them, crowding onto the dock, pounding them all on the back, shaking hands, giving hugs. She lost track of who she was even greeting. There was only one person she wanted to see.

The mob surrounded them and herded them back up to the diner, its lights beaming like a lighthouse to welcome them home. The Coopers were soaked to the skin, even under their rain gear. Their slickers were tugged off them and replaced by warm blankets wrapped around their shoulders.

Nels was busily dishing out five steaming bowls of thick potato and clam chowder while Wilma fussed and got them all seated at a table in the middle of the diner, with cups of fresh coffee plunked down in front of them.

The islanders all wanted an account of what happened. Molly crammed some soup into her mouth to keep herself from having to speak. Her eyes scoured the faces around her as Joe and Matty filled everyone in on the night's events.

One of the hotel guests produced a laptop with a camera and a spotty Internet connection so that Matty could see and speak to Brandi, who broke down in tears upon seeing him safe and sound.

Nearby, Molly gradually became aware of Irene and Roy Turner, along with the brother and brother-in-law, but she didn't see Meredith. Aidan, across the table from her, looked as wiped out as she felt. He sat with his hand propping his head up as he stared into his coffee, his chowder mostly untouched.

A funny kind of buzzing filled Molly's ears, and it seemed as though she was watching everything around her through some kind of gauzy filter. The voices in the diner might have been coming to her from underwater, the way they gurgled and echoed.

A bone-deep fatigue filled her, a weariness so profound, it was almost painful. When the diner went quiet, she wondered for a moment if she had fallen asleep, but then the crowd parted, and her mother was there. Joe got to his feet and held her for the longest time. Behind her, Molly at last saw the one person she'd been looking for. Kathleen stood there, her eyes burning into Molly's, though she didn't move or say a thing. Vaguely, it registered for Molly that Miss Louisa and Rebecca were standing behind Kathleen with Meredith, but her brain was too tired to wonder why that was.

When her mom and dad finally let each other go, Jenny turned to the table. "Boys, home. Now."

A groundswell of laughter filled the diner until the men were guffawing and whacking her brothers on the back. Relief made it possible to laugh for most, but not for Molly. She pushed to her feet, and was grateful when Kathleen went before her, leading the way outside and sparing them the spectacle of having to greet each other with everyone ogling them.

In the car, Kathleen only gave a tight nod. Blossom, in the back seat, was ecstatic to see Molly, nuzzling her ear and whining. Not a word was spoken as they drove home. Kathleen parked, and Molly got out. Only then did they fall into each other's arms, Kathleen propping Molly's wobbly knees.

"You came back to me," Kathleen managed to say through her tears.

"Told you I would." Molly tried to hold Kathleen tightly, but her arms—her whole body—was so wiped out that she couldn't stop trembling. "Come upstairs with me. Now."

Up in their room, she tugged out a drawer in her nightstand, nearly panicking when she couldn't find what she was looking for.

"No!" She dropped to her knees and opened the next drawer down.

"What is it?" Kathleen asked, but Molly didn't answer, tossing murder mysteries and tool catalogs on the floor as she dug.

"Got it," Molly said shakily, retrieving a small box.

She sat cross-legged on the floor, and Kathleen sat facing her, a bewildered expression on her face.

Molly raised an unsteady finger to the diamond shooting stars suspended from Kathleen's neck. "I gave you this to show you how much I loved you, but I wanted us both to have something, something that confirms our bond to everyone else."

She held the box out. Kathleen took it and pried the top open.

"Oh, Molly," she breathed. "How...?" She gasped. "Your mysterious errands on Big Sister."

She lifted out one of the two rings inside, examining it. "A Celtic hound?"

Molly tilted her head. "Couldn't leave Blossom out."

At the mention of his name, Blossom squirmed closer, looking expectantly from one of them to the other.

Molly took the ring from Kathleen and slipped it onto her left ring finger. "All I could think of," she started, but her voice cracked. "These were here, waiting for the right time, and I almost didn't get to give it to you."

Tears streamed down her face. Kathleen leaned forward to brush them away. She took the other ring from the box and slid it onto Molly's finger.

"I didn't need this, Molly Cooper, but I love that you did."

They gazed down at their clasped hands.

"For a while," Molly whispered, "I wasn't sure I'd be able to keep my promise. I've never been out in a storm as bad as that."

Kathleen rose to her feet and pulled Molly up after her. She helped Molly undress and got them both into bed.

Under the covers, she held Molly close. "You're here now, safe in my arms."

※※※※※※※※※

REBECCA, LOUISA MUSED WITH a smile, had always had the ability to surprise her. She'd been wicked smart as a girl, excelling in every lesson Louisa taught, impatient even then with her slower classmates. Unlike some of the others—like Jenny and then Molly—when Rebecca left Little Sister to go to college, Louisa had been certain she'd return. Little Sister was a deeper part of Rebecca's soul than most.

Even as a girl, she'd connected instinctively to the island's spirits, its rituals. She'd dogged Naomi Greatneck, the Keeper back then, incessantly asking questions about the island's families and traditions, studying the books as a youngster. In college, she'd studied philosophy and religion, had become ordained as a non-denominational minister, all in preparation for her life's calling. She'd been born to be the next Keeper after Naomi, to Wilma's great relief, as she had no desire to follow in her mother's footsteps.

To most, Rebecca was intimidating. She could be—and usually was—acerbic, sarcastic, and abrasive. But, to those who knew her, her gruffness hid a kind heart and an intuitive ability to see beyond the obvious.

So Louisa wasn't entirely surprised when, upon Rebecca's finding her and Meredith in the chapel, she'd invited them to come home with her to wait.

"Shouldn't we go to the marina or hotel?" Meredith had asked.

"You can," Rebecca had replied with a shrug, "if you want to sit around with everyone for hours." She'd waved an arm overhead, where the wind howled through the trees around them. "They can't make way quickly through this. It's going to be a long night."

At her cottage, Rebecca had found a dry robe for Meredith to change into, as her clothes were still cold and wet. Rebecca had tossed them in the dryer while Louisa got a kettle heating on the stove. Rebecca had folded an old blanket on the floor to make a warm place for Jasper to curl up.

Once they all had cups of hot tea and a plate of shortbread to help soothe them, Rebecca had plied Meredith with questions to keep her occupied and distracted.

The girl had talked about her home on the Pacific coast and her job teaching high schoolers. Both Rebecca and Louisa had been fascinated by her account of Barb's ability to see her Native blood, and even more fascinated by the story of her visit to Barb's grandmother. Rebecca had had several questions about the hypnosis and wanted to know more about the dreams both Meredith and Irene had had.

"Tell us more about Bealtaine," Rebecca had prompted. "Your birthday. You really saw Aidan?"

In halting words, Meredith described the scene, the dancing around the bonfire, the sound of the waves in the background. "He was in between Jenny and you that night. I remember that now that I know both of you, but it was him I focused on. It was like he could see me, too."

"You and my nephew," Rebecca murmured, sitting back to study Meredith.

"But..." Meredith stammered, "I don't believe in things like destiny.

And Aidan, he doesn't... I don't think he does, either. He's made it pretty clear he doesn't really want anything to do with me."

Rebecca had waved an impatient hand. "That boy hasn't known what he wants for a long time." Her eyes narrowed as she sipped her tea.

At last, word had come that the rescuers were nearing the island. Rebecca drove Louisa's car into the village, though she grumbled about driving such a short distance. When they'd arrived at the diner, Joe and the kids were already inside, with just about the entire island gathered to welcome them home.

When Jenny shooed the boys home, Louisa had turned to look for Meredith, only to see her disappearing upstairs to her hotel room.

Rebecca was watching, too, with an expression on her face that Louisa knew only too well. Rebecca Ahearn was fighting a battle with herself, and Louisa knew from experience that she was best left to fight it out alone. Without a word, Louisa made her way back to her car and drove home for some much-needed sleep.

▨▨▨▨▨▨▨▨

WHEN MEREDITH EMERGED FROM her room about ten a.m., bleary-eyed and groggy, one look at everyone else told her she was in good company.

"That was quite a night, wasn't it?" Kenny asked, pulling a chair out for her at the table where he sat with Irene and Art.

"Gives you a better idea what life here would be like," Art said with a shake of his head. "And they said that ferry only runs once a month in the winter! How can anyone live like that?"

I could.

But Meredith didn't say it aloud. She nodded her thanks when Wilma brought her a cup of coffee, laying a warm hand on her shoulder.

"Pancakes, dear?"

"Yes, please." Meredith glanced around. "Where's Dad?"

"Not sure," Irene said.

For the first time, Meredith noticed her mother's red eyes. "What's wrong?"

"The island council meets tonight," Irene said quietly.

"And we keep telling her, the sooner she gets this crazy idea out of her head, the better," Art said, a dark expression on his face.

"It's not crazy," Irene said tartly.

"What idea?" Meredith asked.

Irene leaned nearer. "What if, if the council decides to accept us as part of Little Sister, what would you think about..."

Meredith frowned. "About what?"

"About moving here."

Meredith's breath caught in her throat. A month ago, she would have given almost anything for her parents to be considering this, but now... She couldn't.

"No."

"No?" Irene sat back, her eyes wide. "I would have thought you'd jump—"

"You were wrong." Meredith pushed to her feet just as Wilma came around the counter with her breakfast. "Sorry, I—"

She almost ran out of the diner, Jasper's nails scratching on the linoleum as he scrambled to go with her. Shoving the door open, she flung herself straight into Aidan's arms. He grabbed her by the shoulders, her hands trapped against his chest. For a moment, they stared into each other's eyes before she pushed back, out of his grasp.

Her brain whirled, trying to think of something to say. "How are your brothers?"

"They're tired, but fine." He nodded toward the marina. "They got a signal from the fishing boat, so they're going out with Dad to try and repair her."

His eyes raked her face. "Do you have a few minutes?"

She gave a half-laugh. "A few minutes. Yes, I have a few minutes."

His face reflected his confusion, but he held an arm out toward a truck. "Can we...?"

"Just a second." She took Jasper back inside to her mom. "Hold him. I'll be back soon."

Aidan tried to get the truck door for her, but she pushed his arm away, yanking the door open and slamming it closed as he went around to the driver's side. She didn't say anything on the way out of the village, up the ring road. She thought he might be planning on going back to the cemetery and the chapel.

I swear I will slap him if he does.

She had no idea where this anger had come from, but she grabbed onto it, holding it to her like armor.

To her relief, he drove past the cemetery to a place where the road was wide enough to pull off and park on the side. She got out and followed him into the woods, along a trail that merged with others she soon recognized. They stepped out of the woods onto the rocky bluff she'd discovered a while ago.

To look at the incredibly blue sky and calm water, no one would ever know that the storm had even been there. The beauty felt like a taunt and made her even angrier.

The ever-present wind tossed her hair across her face. Impatiently, she reached up to tuck it behind her ear. "Well?"

Aidan was clearly set off-balance by Meredith's attitude. "What's wrong?"

This time, she laughed heartily, but there was no humor in it. "What's wrong. Let's see. We sleep together, and then that's the last I see of you for weeks. I learn that Louisa is my biological grandmother—I"

She stopped and nodded when the shock of that revelation was not reflected on his face. "You knew, too. So did everyone else on Little Sister, it seems. Everyone except my mother and me. Apparently, we're part of a Little Sister family, but we're bastards, so no one really knows whether we fit in here or not."

She turned her back on him when she felt tears sting her eyes. "I finally find the place I've been searching for my entire life, but I don't belong. And—"

His hands grasped her arms again, but tenderly this time. Damn it, she didn't want tenderness, and she really didn't want to cry in front of him.

"Don't—" she started, but he turned her around, crushing his lips to hers.

She tried not to kiss him back, tried not to want his arms around her, tried to hate him, but she couldn't do any of those things. Her arms wrapped around his neck, her body responding in ways that pissed her off even more.

When he lifted his face from hers, it was to tuck her against his chest, holding her so tightly, so tightly...

"I've spent every minute of every day trying not to want you, not to think of you," he said.

She pushed away so she could look at him. "Why? What is wrong with me?"

He gaped at her. "Nothing! Nothing is wrong with you."

She climbed onto the rocks and stood facing the ocean. "You don't do that to someone you—someone you care about," she said over her shoulder.

He stepped up to stand beside her. "You do if all you've ever done is run and hide so you don't have to face things that might..."

She refused to look at him. "Might what?"

He was quiet for several seconds. "Might hurt you. If you let them in. But then I hurt you. I'm sorry."

She bit her lip and waited.

"I don't want to use what happened to Bryan as an excuse. It's not. But I wasn't strong enough to deal with it without... without doing stupid stuff to avoid letting myself feel it. I've never let anyone else close enough to hurt that much if I lost them."

At last she turned to look at him.

"I'm not brave enough," he confessed in such a low voice that the wind took the words away before she was certain she'd heard them.

"But you are," she said. "Look what you did yesterday."

He shook his head. "That's different. That was for family. I can do it for others when the worst that could happen is I die."

She thought she understood. "It's harder to live." She thought about her own fears and took a step to him. "Aidan, I love you."

He raised his eyes and stared at her.

"One of us has to be brave enough to say it. I love you more than I ever thought I could love anyone," she said simply. "And it terrifies me to feel that way about someone I may leave in a few days and never see again. Because if I go, I won't be back. I won't spend my life in some half-existence, neither alive nor dead, not happy or sad. It sucks to be in this... this in-between place where you can't live, but you can't heal, either."

She forced herself to smile. "I love you too much to let it twist into something that I hate to feel."

His eyes shone with tears, but he didn't speak.

"I understand," she said, "if that's more than you wanted. More than you can handle. But I had to tell you the truth."

She turned to leap down off the rocks, but he caught her hand.

"It's not."

She frowned. "What's not...?"

"It's not more than I wanted. It might be more than I can handle." He pulled her closer and laid a gentle hand on her cheek, his thumb tracing the corner of her mouth. "You are all I want, Meredith. If you'll have me, I will try to be strong enough to love you."

Gazing into his eyes, she saw the hesitation, the fear that he might not be able to measure up. She raised up on her toes to brush her lips over his.

"I've never done this, either, Aidan. Not like this. Body and soul. We'll find a way to be strong enough. Together."

Chapter 23

MOLLY TRIED TO READ but couldn't concentrate. She lowered her book, staring at the dark fireplace while she chewed her nails down to nubs.

"You know," Kathleen said, taking her hand, "I would love to take advantage of all the things you could do with these shorter nails, but if you nibble them down any further, you're going to be bleeding."

Molly grinned up at her. "Maybe later tonight you can tell me all the things you'd like me to do." She kissed Kathleen's hand. "Diner should be closed by now. Patrick'll have a harder time getting away from the pub, but the whole council has to be there for this."

She pushed out of her recliner. "Don't know when I'll be home. This could take a while."

Kathleen led the way to the door. "I'm going with you."

Molly grabbed Kathleen's hand. "You know I love you, and I realize you're training to be the next Keeper—"

"But I'm not a member of the council," Kathleen finished for her. "I know that. And I won't stay long. But I have something to say. And the council is going to hear it."

"Okaaaay." Molly let go of her hand and followed her and Blossom to the door.

"We'll walk home."

"No, let's take your Nissan, and I'll get a lift home from Mom and Dad."

They drove to the library, where a few vehicles were already parked, including Louisa's old sedan.

"Is Louisa going to get a vote?" Kathleen asked.

Molly shrugged. "She's still a member of the council, so I suppose so, unless she abstains."

Obviously, Wilma, Patrick, and Siobhan had walked, as they were all gathered in the library's back room, along with Jenny, Rebecca, and Joe. They all looked around in confusion when Kathleen accompanied Molly through the door.

"Don't worry," Kathleen said. "I'm not staying. But I wanted to say something to all of you before you deliberate this situation with the Turners."

Molly took a seat at the table, but Kathleen remained standing.

"I realize," Kathleen began, and Molly heard the slight tremor in her voice, "that Little Sister has never dealt with a situation like the one we find ourselves in. And I know that my story isn't the same as Miss Louisa's and the Turners', but it's also not that different."

Kathleen stared over their heads. "My estrangement from the island was absolute and complete for almost a quarter-century. When I came back here, it was with virtually no knowledge of island traditions. I didn't know that Nanna leased the cottage. I didn't know about the Passing. In so many ways, I was no more an islander than Irene and Meredith are now. Miss Louisa did probably the hardest thing any woman can do in giving Irene up for adoption when she knew she wasn't ready to raise a baby. Living with that decision has been punishment enough. Neither Miss Louisa nor her daughter or granddaughter should be punished any longer."

Molly's heart swelled with pride.

"I'll leave now," Kathleen said. "Thanks for listening."

She patted her thigh for Blossom and gave Molly a parting glance as she closed the door behind them.

Molly shifted her chair around to face the others gathered around the table. "Who wants to go next?"

An uncomfortable silence filled the room.

Rebecca cleared her throat. "I suppose I should speak."

It was nearly midnight when Molly was dropped off at home. "Night," she said sleepily to her parents.

She let herself in as quietly as she could. At the top of the stairs, Blossom was waiting for her. She brushed her teeth and undressed in the dark.

"Well?" Kathleen whispered when Molly slid under the sheet. She shifted closer.

Molly rolled to face her. "There was a lot of back and forth, not only about the Turners, but about the meaning of the island quake."

It took Kathleen a minute. "I'd almost forgotten. What was the discussion?"

"Most felt it was foretelling us almost losing the boys."

"But we didn't lose anyone."

"And that was the argument. My mom and dad, Wilma, most of the council felt that was what the island was warning us about."

"But not everyone."

Molly shook her head. "I don't think Siobhan and Rebecca were convinced that was it."

"What do you think?"

Molly rubbed the heel of one hand against her eye. "I think I'm tired of thinking about it. If the island has something to say, let her just come out and say it."

Kathleen ran her hand up and down Molly's back. "And? What about the Turners?"

"They're part of the Woodhouse clan, if they want to be." She waited a beat. "And Miranda and Tim have asked Roy Turner to be Charlotte's *athair inis.*"

"Her—" Kathleen raised up on her elbow. "Really? And who's the *máthair inis?*"

"Brandi."

"Wow. That's brilliant. If that doesn't convince Brandi to embrace Little Sister, nothing will."

"I think that's the general idea. Maybe she and Matty will want to do the same for Benjamin some day. And asking Roy to do this kind of cements the Turners as part of the island. Even Rebecca couldn't think of anything to say."

Kathleen leaned down and kissed her. "Thank you."

"What are you thanking me for?" Molly asked, combing her fingers through Kathleen's soft hair. "You did most of the convincing."

"I doubt that." Kathleen nestled close, wrapping her arms around Molly.

"Mmmm," Molly mused. "I do think Rebecca had already started to have a change of heart. That surprised me. Figured she was dead-set against them."

Kathleen's hand slid under Molly's T-shirt. "Know what would surprise me?"

Molly's mouth tugged into a grin when Kathleen's hand moved around and cupped her breast. She gave a sharp intake of breath. "What?"

"You show me how creative you can get with those fingers of yours."

"Oh," Molly said, shifting to lie atop Kathleen. "It won't be just my fingers."

MEREDITH WAS UP BEFORE the sun. She went to the window and breathed deep of the sea air flowing through the screens. Dressing quickly, she laced up her walking shoes and headed out with Jasper.

The village, nestled around the marina on the island's north side, was still sleepy. A couple of fishermen strolled to the marina. Her heart gave a quick jolt when she recognized Joey and gave him a small wave.

She wanted the beach to herself this morning, and hoped no one else had had the same idea. The morning was cool, clear. She broke into an occasional jog, while Jasper darted into the woods to chase a few rabbits, re-emerging farther ahead on the road, checking to make sure she was still coming.

When she got to the beach, her heart sank. Molly's SUV was there. But when she clambered over the rocky sea wall, she spied Molly in her scull already far out to sea.

"She must have been relieved to get here without me or any other annoying tourists," she said with a chuckle.

She wasn't even an islander, but Meredith could appreciate how intrusive it must feel to have strangers like herself invading spaces the islanders normally had to themselves. She took off her shoes and socks to walk through the surf, washing onto the sand in a ceaseless rhythm. It was gentle this morning, but what was calming and beautiful now could be fierce and vengeful. She hadn't been out on the ocean in that storm the other night, but she'd seen what it had done to the Coopers. That was another reality of life on the island. The people who chose to live here were constantly caught in that dance, that balance between beauty and isolation on the one hand, and the harsh reality of what it cost to eek a living out of the ocean on the other.

The water was icy and took her breath away for a moment. Jasper chased some sandpipers, who circled and immediately landed again as soon he galumphed away.

She stood, her feet in the water, watching as the orange disk of the sun broke over the horizon, its light washing over her. Molly was a tiny speck on the water now.

Molly and Joey. Aidan's family.

For a while—a very short while—she'd been ecstatic just to know that Aidan loved her, too. But then reality had set in. Where would they live? She supposed she could just move to Maine and live with him on the mainland, as his ferry job had him returning there every night.

But, she thought, even as she felt guilty for thinking it, *I want to live here.*

And not just live here as Aidan's spouse or mate or whatever. She knew it was her pride speaking, and it shouldn't matter, but she didn't want to slide sideways into being an islander only by marriage.

She pondered the dilemma as she walked, occasionally bending to pick up and examine a shell. Some creature's house for a time. Now abandoned for a new one. *A house is just a house, isn't it? It's who you share it with that matters.*

So immersed was she in her own thoughts that she didn't realize Molly was rowing back until she dragged her scull onto the sand.

"You're up early," Molly said, breathing hard as she climbed out and unlocked her oars.

"Same." Meredith gestured toward the scull. "You really like that."

"It's heaven to me." Molly leaned on her oars, letting her breathing slow. "Just me and the ocean. And an occasional pod of dolphins."

"Really?"

Molly grinned. "I love it when they race me."

She looked so like Aidan when she grinned like that.

"Might have to try that some day." Meredith's throat tightened as she wondered when exactly that might be. *Not likely to be here, is it?*

She felt Molly's gaze nudging her, but she couldn't meet it.

"Guess I should get back," she said, walking with Molly to where the Toyota was parked. She sat on a rock to brush the sand off her feet and put her socks and shoes back on while Molly loaded the scull onto her roof rack, securing it with thick bungee cords.

Molly hooked a thumb at the SUV. "Want a ride?"

"No, thanks. We need the walk."

"Okay. Have a good day, Meredith. I'll see you later."

Meredith gave her a wave and whistled for Jasper, who came bounding in her direction, wet and sandy.

"Oh, you're not going to be welcome in the hotel, old man."

They made their way back to town, several cars and trucks now on the road. At the side of the hotel was a hose. Meredith used it to sluice the sand and saltwater out of Jasper's coat, and then, between his shaking and her hands to scrape as much water out of his fur as possible, he was partially dry. Wilma must have seen, because she met them on the porch.

"Land sakes, looks like he had a good romp. Here's an old towel to rub him dry with."

"Wilma, why are you—" Meredith found it hard to speak past the sudden lump in her throat. "Thanks."

Inside the diner, she found her mom and dad digging into big breakfasts.

"You're up early," Roy said, eyeing her closely through his glasses.

Meredith nodded. "Thanks," she said to Wilma when she placed a cup of coffee and a plate heaped with eggs, bacon, and toast down in front of her.

"Now, you're going to need a good meal to get your day going, so you eat every bit of this, hear?"

Meredith stared after her. "What's that about?"

"Not sure," Irene said. She gestured at her own plate. "But we got the same."

Roy leaned near and whispered, "Are they fattening us up for some kind of sacrifice to the island gods?"

Meredith nearly snorted coffee out her nose. She struggled to swallow and had to cough. She hadn't expected to have much of an appetite after her sobering thoughts at the beach, but she was ravenous.

A shadow fell over the table as she dug into her food, and she looked up to see Rebecca Ahearn standing there.

"Take your time, but when you're done eating, we'll get started."

She walked away to the counter, where she and Wilma put their heads together.

"What in the world is that about?" Roy asked.

Irene shrugged, but Meredith thought she knew. And she was afraid to hope she might be right.

✳✳✳✳✳✳✳✳✳✳

KATHLEEN PACED AROUND AND around the library, threading a figure-eight path between the tables in the front room. Blossom, clearly puzzled by his human's odd behavior, followed at first, but then lay where he could keep a protective eye on her.

The windows were all thrown open to the August morning, as was the front door. The breeze blowing through the screens smelled of the geraniums that Rebecca had growing along the porch. She caught occasional snatches of conversations as tourists walked or bicycled by, but, as the library was tucked back off the village's main street, it didn't get much traffic. The children's reading group had ended last week, and the kids would be heading back to the mainland for school in just a few weeks. This summer felt as though it had flown by.

Blossom's ears suddenly pricked, the tips flopped over. Kathleen stopped her pacing and waited. Voices drew near and, a moment later, Rebecca stepped inside with the Turners and Jasper. Blossom got up to greet his buddy, and Meredith let both dogs out to play.

"Kathleen," Irene said. "What are you doing here?"

"What are *we* doing here?" Roy asked.

"Follow us," Rebecca said in reply.

She led the way to the back room, where Kathleen already had an old leather-bound book laid ready on the table in front of Rebecca's chair.

"Please," Rebecca said, gesturing to the three chairs lined up along one side, while she and Kathleen took the two on the other side.

The Turners sat, Irene and Roy looking in bewilderment at each other, but Meredith, Kathleen noted, stared only at the book. *She knows.*

"You have learned," Rebecca began, "that the island has rules about its families, about who can live here." She folded her hands over top of the book. "You also know that your situation has never before presented itself. Being born of an islander, but not of an island family, is something we'd never had to consider."

Irene reached for Roy's hand, squeezing it tightly.

"The island council met a few nights ago," Rebecca continued.

Kathleen had to bite the inside of her cheek to keep from blurting out the news. Rebecca was clearly enjoying the suspense.

"It wasn't easy for us to change our thinking, but a few things persuaded us." Rebecca slid a sideways glance in Kathleen's direction. Kathleen hid a smile. "We've decided that you are part of the Woodhouse family. You are part of Little Sister and her evolving history."

Meredith sat like a statue, barely seeming to breathe. Her eyes raised at last to Rebecca and Kathleen. "We're here this morning to do our Passing."

Irene frowned. "Our... what?"

"This," said Rebecca, "is the ritual that records your branch of an island lineage. The Keeper of the Record does this for everyone who comes from an island family."

"I did mine when I came back to live," Kathleen said.

"Those of us who grew up here did this as teens." Rebecca slid the book to Kathleen.

"What? Me?" Kathleen sputtered.

"You've been training to be the next Keeper, haven't you?" Rebecca tapped the book. "Time to do your first Passing."

Kathleen's fingers fumbled as she opened the Woodhouse book, flipping through pages until she found the one she needed. Unscrewing the top off the inkbottle, she hoped desperately she could make this nibbed pen work without leaving a huge blot on the page.

"Irene," she said, "you were born to Louisa Flannery Woodhouse on August twelfth, 1960." She paused with the pen hovering over the page. "Hey, your birthday's tomorrow."

Carefully, she extended a line from Louisa's name and wrote *"Irene Woodhouse–"*, but then she paused and turned to Rebecca. "Her adopted name?"

"I think so."

Kathleen leaned over the book again, adding *"Millward"*, the metal nib making a scratching sound as it was dragged along the thick paper.

"What about her biological father?" Roy asked. "Do we even know his name?"

"I do," Kathleen said with some hesitation, but Irene's expression was curious, not guarded. "Willem Gephardt."

"Well, now we know where the German in your DNA came from," Roy said wryly.

Kathleen looked to Rebecca for guidance, but Rebecca asked, "What do you think?"

Kathleen stared at the page for a moment. "I think we should include him in the bio but not in the tree."

Rebecca nodded. "Make it so."

It took a few minutes for Kathleen to scratch out the additional information on another page, continuing where Miss Louisa's biography had left off.

Turning back to the family tree, she recorded Irene's marriage to Roy, with the date, and then added Meredith. "Born May first, 1984, right?"

When everything was written—*with no blots and no errors*, Kathleen noted proudly—she closed that book while Rebecca opened another.

"I'll do this part," she said drily. "Or we'll be here forever."

"What's this then?" Irene asked, leaning forward to peer at a page of varied signatures with dark blotches beside them.

"This is the book that records the lessees—the caretakers, if you will—of the Woodhouse home. You know by now that no one on this island owns the land or the houses. This is how we do it. And I realize technically, Miss Louisa still holds the lease, but you will follow someday if you choose to live here, so…"

"Wait a minute," Roy cut in. "How much is this lease?"

"A dollar a year," Kathleen said. "But Miss Louisa is paid up for this year."

The argument ready on Roy's lips apparently vanished. He closed his mouth.

"But now," said Rebecca, "we need your signatures and a drop of blood, please."

Irene and Meredith looked quizzically at each other. "Blood?" Irene asked.

"Yeah," Kathleen said with a mournful shake of her head. "That's the part that always gets me."

"Something you'll need to get over." Rebecca held out a pen and a pocketknife.

First Irene and then Meredith pricked their fingers and pressed them to the page alongside their signatures.

"I know you've been here for a couple of months," Rebecca said, closing the book, "but welcome, officially, to Little Sister."

Kathleen peered at Meredith, trying to read the emotions crossing her face, but she couldn't be sure what she was seeing. Relief? Questions?

Rebecca stood to put the books away, but Meredith's hand shot out. "May I study them?"

"Of course." Rebecca set the books in front of her. "Miss Louisa asked us to tell you that she's expecting all three of you for lunch at her house."

Irene looked torn as she glanced from Roy to the books. "I'd love to study them, too, when we have more time."

She scooted her chair away from the table, but Meredith sat with her hands reverently placed on the book.

"I'll meet you at the hotel in a little bit," she said. When Irene opened her mouth, Meredith quickly said, "I won't lose track of time. I'll be there soon to shower."

After her parents left, Meredith looked to Rebecca and Kathleen. "Is there any record in any of these books of a girl, a survivor of the wreck, named Ida?"

Kathleen shared a startled glance with Rebecca. "Yes. Ida Sullivan, fifteen years old." She leaned over the table and opened one of the books, flipping to one of the first pages.

"Ida Sullivan," Meredith breathed.

⬛⬛⬛⬛⬛⬛⬛⬛

THE TABLE WAS SET with a red-checked gingham cloth, plates and silverware all gleaming. Glasses were lined up on the counter, ready to be filled with the variety of drinks chilling in the refrigerator. The food was all prepared: chicken salad, a sweet and sour cucumber salad—"don't add too much vinegar," Ollie had volunteered—tomatoes still warm from the sun-kissed garden, sliced thick and juicy.

And still Louisa fretted. "They know now," she said as she checked the table one last time.

The wooden boxes already occupied two of the chairs at the table.

"Do you think this will change things?"

"I don't know," Louisa admitted. "I think..." she said slowly, "Irene and Meredith have accepted their connection to me. But I don't know how they feel about being Woodhouses."

"Who wouldn't want to be a Woodhouse?"

Louisa couldn't help smiling at Olivia's indignation. She glanced around. "I don't know, sister. If it comes with this old house, all the work it needs. Will they want it?"

Ollie didn't answer. She'd worried as much as Louisa about all the things they hadn't been able to keep up with.

She heard car doors and hurried out to the porch. The dog trotted to her and sat politely so she could pat his head.

"Come in, come in."

Irene carried another container of food from the diner. "I hate arriving empty-handed, but without a kitchen..."

"You didn't need to do that, but thank you." Louisa led the way. "Roy, would you pour the drinks?"

As they seated themselves around the table—"don't sit on Daddy," she said to Meredith—Louisa anxiously kept on eye on their reaction, looking for any hint that anyone needed for anything.

"Miss Louisa," said Roy with a warm smile, "this all looks wonderful. Thank you for inviting us."

"Yes," Irene said quickly. "We were delighted to get your invitation."

Meredith had yet to speak, Louisa noticed, though there was no air of hostility radiating from her.

"Well, there's plenty of everything," Louisa said as she pulled out a chair, "so don't be shy."

Once the dishes had been passed and their plates were full, Louisa said, "You had a big morning. Your Passing."

"It was fascinating," Irene said. "The way you've kept track of every member of every family. Does it go all the way back to the shipwreck?"

"Almost." Louisa cut a slice of tomato. "I think it took about a decade after the wreck for things to settle and the islanders to realize they needed to memorialize what had happened and begin recording their new life."

She let them eat for a moment before saying, "I hope your brother and his partner weren't offended that I didn't invite them as well, but I needed to speak to the three of you."

The air around the table changed immediately.

"Now that you've been accepted by the council, and you've done your Passing, you need to know what that means." Louisa paused to take a long drink of tea, wishing she had something stronger. "This house, if you want it, will pass to you."

"How does that work?" Meredith asked, speaking for the first time. "Houses stay in families, don't they?"

Louisa nodded. "They do. Often more than one generation lives together, like Joe and Jenny still sharing their house with Joey. Some families have had three, even four, generations living together. I'm obviously all alone here, so after I'm gone—"

It sounded so strange to be talking about this, but with Daddy and Ollie's boxes of ashes seated at the table, it was time to face the inevitable.

"After I'm gone, you will have the right to take over the lease, should you choose to live here full time."

Roy sat forward, lifting his glasses higher on his nose. "What would have happened if your connection to Irene hadn't been discovered?"

"If there's no known family—and that's part of why we keep such careful records—then the house is put up for a lottery right away. Any other islander can submit their name, and the council will draw. Houses have passed out of family lines that way in the past. If there is family, they have a year to claim the house before it goes to lottery. That's what happened with Katie Halloran."

"But what—" Meredith began, but stopped abruptly.

"But what, dear?" Louisa said.

Meredith's cheeks were flushed, and there was a determined light in her eyes. "What if we don't want to wait? What if we wanted to be here now? With you. In this house. How would that work? And would you be willing?"

Louisa's mouth opened, but no words would come out. She thought she might have heard Ollie hiss, "Say something!"

"You... you would want to live here, with me?"

"I know you're used to having this place to yourself," Meredith said quickly. "And I wouldn't want to intrude, but..."

"Meredith!" Irene's lips compressed. "We can't impose—"

"I know," Meredith cut in. She returned to Louisa. "And if it is an imposition, you have to say so. You have to tell us."

Louisa's heart was thumping so loudly she thought certainly they must be hearing it. "Sure I can't think of anything I would love more than to have you—all of you—living here, if that's what you want."

A ringing silence followed her words.

"Now, you must understand," she said quickly, "island life in winter is not like you've experienced this summer. It gets wicked cold, with the winds off the ocean. This house is old. There are more projects than I've been able to keep up with. I don't know how serious you are..."

"We're serious," Meredith said. "At least, I am."

She looked to Irene and Roy.

"I... I don't know," Irene said, eyes wide. "We've talked about different places we might live, now that Roy is retired."

"What?" Meredith demanded. "You never said—"

"And we do love it here..." Irene continued, ignoring Meredith. "We actually started to daydream about what it might be like to live here."

"What about Art and Kenny?" Roy asked.

"They make more money than all of us put together," Irene said with a wave of her hand. "They can come visit any time they want."

Roy glanced upward. "Miss Louisa, are you sure this house is big enough for all of us? What if we get sick of one another?"

"Well," she said with a chuckle, "it wouldn't be the first time this house has had squabbles and arguments. My sister was very stubborn."

She was certain she heard an echo of, "Was not."

"As for the rooms, Daddy and Mama's room sits empty. So does Olivia's. And there's another room besides mine. We've plenty of space."

The Turners all took turns staring questioningly at one another.

"Let us talk about it," Roy said.

"I don't need to talk," Meredith said breathlessly. "I'll need some time to sell my house and most of my stuff." She reached for Louisa's hand. "Are you sure? I couldn't stand it if this wasn't real."

Louisa smiled through her tears. "I'm sure. It's real."

Chapter 24

IT ALWAYS AMUSED KATHLEEN how quickly news spread among the islanders. There was a low buzz of conversation that she noticed as soon as she and Blossom stepped inside the market. Since it was just past six a.m., and Miranda had unlocked the door a few minutes ago, it could only be islanders. No tourists were usually up at this hour.

She found Miranda nose to nose with Jenny Cooper.

"What's up?" she asked.

"Have you heard?" Miranda said before Jenny could get a word out. "The Turners are moving in with Miss Louisa!"

"What?" Kathleen wasn't certain she'd heard correctly. "They just did their Passing yesterday morning. How do you know?"

"Irene came in here last evening," Miranda said. "It seems they had lunch with Miss Louisa and the whole thing just kind of happened."

Kathleen looked to Jenny for confirmation. Jenny nodded.

"Wow." Kathleen couldn't think of anything else to say for a moment. "Life is going to change for Miss Louisa."

"I hope it'll be a good change," Jenny said.

"Why wouldn't it?" Miranda asked.

Jenny gave a half-shrug. "They're still new. Haven't been through an offseason, have they?"

"But how soon is this going to happen?" Kathleen asked. "They all have houses and jobs—at least Meredith does—in Oregon to deal with."

"Don't know." Miranda reached for Charlie, who had started to fuss from the infant beanbag-like thing behind the counter. Bouncing the baby on her hip, she said, "They sound like they're serious."

"I hope they are, if they started this," Kathleen said. "I'd hate to see them get Miss Louisa's hopes up and then dash them."

One look from Jenny confirmed that she had the same worry.

"Wow," Kathleen said again. "Happy birthday, Irene."

"What?" Jenny asked.

"Today is Irene's birthday."

All three of them gasped at the same time.

"Her *tar abháile!*" Kathleen stared at the other two. "Would it be done this soon?"

"Well," Jenny said slowly. "It's traditionally done the first birthday after coming of age here, or after coming back to live, like yours. I'll talk to Rebecca."

She jabbed a finger at Kathleen. "You find out what they're doing tonight. But don't say anything just yet."

Jenny hurried from the market.

"What did you need?" Miranda asked.

Kathleen had almost forgotten that she'd actually come in here to buy a few things. She quickly did her shopping and checked out.

"Good luck with your sleuthing," Miranda said as Kathleen gathered her tote bags.

290

Outside, she placed the bags in the baskets that straddled either side of her rear tire and pushed the bike over to the diner. Peering through the window, she saw Meredith alone at a table, jotting something on a sheet of paper, with Jasper at her feet.

She lowered the kickstand and went inside, Blossom on her heels. "Mind if we join you?"

Meredith looked up in surprise. "Not at all."

The two dogs sprawled under the table.

Meredith reached for Kathleen's hand, turning it so the light glinted off the ring. "Is this new? I noticed it yesterday in the library."

"Yes. Molly had them made on Big Sister. We didn't do rings when we got bonded, but she wanted us to have something." Kathleen's throat suddenly felt tight. "She gave it to me after the big storm."

Meredith released her hand but gazed at her with a knowing expression.

"Thanks," Kathleen said when Wilma appeared with a mug of aromatic coffee.

"Any breakfast, Katie?"

"No, thanks."

"Let me know if either of you needs anything."

They both watched Wilma moving among the tables, topping up coffee mugs and picking up empty plates.

"She's been so sweet to us all summer," Meredith said.

"She was pretty wonderful to me when I came back, too." Kathleen studied Meredith's face as she sipped her coffee. "I understand congratulations are in order."

Meredith stiffened. "*Are* you congratulating me?"

"Shouldn't I?"

"You aren't afraid we're taking advantage of Miss Louisa?"

Kathleen smiled. "Miss Louisa is sharper than most people give her credit for." Her smile faded. "But I think she has been lonely since

291

Olivia died. It would break my heart to see her get used to having people in the house again and then it not work out."

"Why wouldn't it work out?" Meredith asked with a slight frown.

"Relax, I'm on your side," Kathleen said. "But I arrived here in October with no clue what it was going to be like. Winters here are brutal and long. If you want a word of advice..."

Meredith's guarded expression clearly reflected her doubt that she did want advice.

Kathleen chuckled. "Buy an electric blanket. Best investment ever."

Meredith relaxed. "Thanks. Guess I'm just feeling a little over-whelmed now that the reality of moving here is starting to sink in." She glanced down at the paper before her. "I was just making a list of everything I need to do back in Pacific City."

"Have you told your employer?"

Meredith shook her head. "Without cell service, I was debating asking Wilma if I could place a call later today. They'll need time to post the position. School starts in just a few weeks. They're going to be pissed."

"Have you thought about what you'll do here?" Kathleen won-dered if Meredith had considered what had already occurred to her.

"Well," Meredith checked to make sure no one else could over-hear, "I had wondered how the islanders would feel about having a teacher here again. What do you think?"

Kathleen fought to maintain a neutral expression. "I think most would like that. It's too late to change plans now. Take this year, get through a winter. If you still want to teach, bring it up to the island council early next spring."

"Good advice."

"What are you guys doing for your mom's birthday?"

"Um, I suppose celebrating here tonight. Art is having a hard time with our decision."

Kathleen regarded her. "He'll miss having your mom closer?"

Meredith nodded. "Especially now, since learning he was adopted, he's kind of needed family more. That's the only part of this that I regret. I don't want to hurt him."

Kathleen considered. "How about you and your family all come to our house tonight? Dinner and birthday cake. Say six o'clock?"

Meredith's mouth fell open. "Really? You're sure?"

"I'm sure. And you don't need to bring anything." Kathleen got to her feet and patted her thigh. Blossom scrambled out from under the table. "See you tonight."

THE NEW COPPER FUEL line wasn't at quite the right angle to meet the fitting on the burner. Molly tweaked it just a bit and tried again.

"Don't give me a hard time," she crooned, testing the nut carefully. The threads met. "Yes!"

She hand-tightened the nut as far as she could and then used a wrench to snug it a little more. She flicked the furnace's on switch, coughing when a cloud of black smoke belched from the beast, as it burned off some of the sludge that had clogged up the old line. She watched carefully for any leaking oil between the tank and the burner. Nothing. With a satisfied nod, she turned the furnace off and bagged up her tools.

Outside, she lowered the cellar's door and latched it securely. She quickly hooked up the hose from the truck and pumped a hundred gallons into the tank. When she was finished with that, she wiped her hands clean and went to the front door.

Knocking, she stepped inside. "All done, Sarah."

"Oh, thanks, Molly." Sarah McGovern came out of the kitchen with a crying two-year-old clinging to her leg.

Molly squatted down and handed him a six-inch length of the old fuel line she'd cleaned up. He immediately stopped crying and began playing with the nut that twirled freely on the copper.

"That nut won't come loose."

"It'll keep him busy for a while," Sarah said gratefully. "Thanks for getting out here."

"Thanks for calling early," Molly said. "Every year, it's the same. Most folks wait until we get our first hard frost and then realize their tanks are empty and the furnace won't start. So much easier to get it tuned up before they need it."

She backed out to the porch. "Just stop by the marina and settle with Dad whenever you're in town."

"Will do."

Sarah waved her off as she backed the truck around.

Molly muttered to herself on the drive back to the village. "Fix things when they start to go bad, instead of waiting until you're stuck miles out to sea..."

She was still furious with Joey and Matty. They'd replaced the fuel pump—"the one that needed replacing for three months," she hadn't been able to stop herself from pointing out—on the fishing boat once they'd located it, but she hadn't forgiven them. The two of them had always been lazy, but Molly and Aidan had covered for them time and again, always taking the responsibility of keeping the boat engines tuned and in good repair. With Aidan now a ferry pilot and Molly busy with her own life, the work had fallen on the two youngest.

"And they failed," Molly had reminded her dad. "Spectacularly. And they almost took us with them."

Just that morning, she'd stalked wordlessly past Joey into the marina office to get the keys to the truck and fill its tank with heating oil.

She waved at a group of tourists on bikes, all laughing, carefree, clearly enjoying their vacation. She glanced at the ring gleaming on her finger and wondered if she and Kathleen should go somewhere.

After Labor Day, after the tourists mostly cleared out. It was kind of ironic, she supposed, that they would take a holiday away from the place others came to for a holiday.

"Maybe Nova Scotia," she pondered aloud. "Someplace she's never been."

At the marina, she parked the truck in its reserved spot where the tank could easily be filled. As she climbed out, she saw Joey chugging up to a slip, towing a tarp-covered boat behind. He nodded in her direction, but she turned on her heel.

Scowling, she stomped to the office to fill out the ledger of her time, parts, and the amount of oil she'd delivered.

When her father came in, she whirled on him, her finger jabbing in the direction of the boathouse. "If he thinks I'm going to take on some kind of rebuild or restoration after what—"

"Easy, Mo." Joe held up both hands. "It's nothing for you to worry about."

Her mouth was already open to argue, but she foundered. "Oh. All right, then."

"Your mother called and said I'm to tell you that you and Kathleen are hosting the birthday dinner for Irene Turner this evening, and you're supposed to pick up some hamburger and chicken."

She frowned. "For how many?"

Joe shrugged. "No idea. But you'd best hurry if you're going to get home in time to shower. You smell like an oil furnace."

Lifting her arm, she pressed her nose to her T-shirt sleeve. "I guess I do." She tucked the ledger back in its drawer.

"And Mo," Joe added, stopping her before she left the office. "Take it easy on Joey. He knows he screwed up."

Her face darkened. "I'll believe that when he shows he'll take care of things before they're a problem."

She made her way to the market. As soon as she stepped inside, Miranda called out, "Got it all bagged up for you, Mo."

She reached into the drink cooler and handed Molly a heavy tote bag. Molly peered inside.

"How many people are we having?"

"Not sure," Miranda said. "But Kathleen asked for five pounds each, plus a few other things. I'd say you're having a *céilí!*"

"Okay." Molly hefted the bag. "Here's to... whatever."

⬙⬙⬙⬙⬙⬙⬙⬙⬙⬙⬙

IT WAS REALLY SWEET, Meredith thought, of Kathleen to have put together this impromptu birthday celebration for her mom. Irene was thoroughly enjoying her sixtieth birthday party. When they'd arrived here in June, Meredith hadn't even thought ahead to the fact that they might still be here for this. She didn't really have anything for her mom, and felt horrible about it. But her mom was more familiar than she was with the gifty things in the market or in the island's shops.

"I don't need anything," Irene had said when Meredith voiced her dismay. "Just being here with you and your father and uncles and..."

She didn't say "Louisa", but Meredith knew she felt a connection with her biological mother that she was hesitant to voice. Especially around Art.

He and Kenny were charmed by the quaintness of Kathleen and Molly's cottage. Molly showed them all the upgrades she'd done in terms of solar panels and a small house-sized wind turbine.

"We really need to look into this when we get home," Kenny said.

"Yeah," Art said sarcastically. "Because we're just brimming with sunshine."

"More wine?"

She looked up to see Kathleen standing there with a bottle. "Sure." She waved at the crowd of people gathered in the yard. "This is really nice of you. I know my mom appreciates it."

"Our pleasure," Kathleen said, a mysterious smile playing on her lips as she moved on, refilling other glasses.

Meredith had half-hoped Aidan would be there, but she was sure he couldn't take another night off. When he'd piloted the ferry in earlier, he'd been so busy that there hadn't been a chance to say more than hello. But the look her gave her was enough to let her know his feelings hadn't changed.

There had been such a whirlwind of happenings the last couple of days—the Passing, lunch with Louisa and the invitation to live with her, now her mom's birthday. It felt to her as if she were caught in a hurricane or tornado, with scenes from the last few days swirling around her so fast, she couldn't line them up properly. She still couldn't believe they were going to move here. She was almost afraid to wake up and find it had all been some kind of dream.

Louisa had engaged Art in a spirited conversation, judging by his hand gestures.

"I think he's in love," Kenny said, joining Meredith.

Meredith snorted. "She's a pistol." She studied them for a few minutes. "Is he going to hunt for his biological parents?"

Kenny swirled his beer around the inside of the bottle. "I don't know. He talks about it one minute, then says he doesn't want to know the next." He fondly watched his husband, now being lectured to about something by Louisa. "If he knew he'd find someone like her, he would. Maybe he'll just ask to be adopted as a Woodhouse."

Meredith leaned her head against his shoulder, and he in turn wrapped a protective arm around her. "You know," she said, "the both of you will always be welcome here."

He kissed the top of her head. "I know," he said softly, "but it won't be the same. Nothing will. I just can't believe your grandparents kept such a huge secret from the two of them."

"I know. I keep wondering about that."

"What about you?"

She raised her head to look at him. "What do you mean?"

"You and Aidan. What's happening there?"

"Oh," she said with a half-laugh. "I think we might be setting a course toward a future together."

"Listen to you, getting all nautical." He gave her a squeeze.

"I'm not sure what that will look like, since he has to drive the ferry back to the mainland every night, but... he assured me he feels the same way I do."

Kenny took her by both shoulders and stared full into her face. "And this feels like the real deal? Not like that pompous ass you were with before?"

She let out a full belly laugh this time. "The real deal. And not like Grant at all. God, what was I thinking?"

"Honey, that's what we wondered." Kenny clinked his bottle against her glass and drank. "Here's to real."

Kathleen and Jenny called everyone to fill their plates. Dinner was kind of raucous, with lots of talk and laughter and teasing. Even Rebecca was smiling and having a good time. Meredith found herself studying everyone, wondering if life could really stay this good.

When dinner was done and most of the birthday cake had been consumed, Rebecca stood.

"It's time."

The Turners wore confused expressions, but the islanders all got up and headed toward the drive.

"Just get in," Molly said to Meredith, holding the Toyota's back door open and giving Louisa a hand up to climb in as well.

A few moments later, a caravan of cars and SUVs pulled up at the cemetery as dusk fell. Bewildered, Meredith followed everyone as they made their way among the grave markers, past the chapel to the stone circle. Ducking under the low stone lintel, they all gathered inside. Louisa and Rebecca pulled Irene into the center of the space while most of the others lit candles and encircled them.

"What's going on?" Irene asked, wide-eyed.

"It's your *tar abháile*," Rebecca said. "Your homecoming. Traditionally, this is done when we come of age—"

"Too late for that," Art muttered to a scattering of laughter.

Rebecca smiled. "Or the first birthday after one of us decides to return to Little Sister to make a life here." She gazed at Irene. "Is that your intention?"

Irene nodded wordlessly.

Meredith watched, fascinated, as Rebecca took a candle from Kathleen and held it for Louisa, who ignited a small pine branch, letting it flame brightly so that the ashes dropped into a wooden bowl held in Rebecca's other hand. Louisa mixed the ashes with some substance in the bottom of the bowl.

"As..." Louisa hesitated for a moment, "as the one who gave birth to you, and the oldest remaining member of our family, it is my honor to do your homecoming back to Little Sister."

Rebecca passed the bowl to Kathleen and tugged her knife out of her pocket. Unfolding the blade, she said, "I need a few drops of blood."

Irene hesitantly held out her hand. Rebecca stabbed her finger, letting the blood drip into the bowl where it was mixed with the ashes.

Louisa dipped her thumb into the mixture and anointed Irene's lips. "May you speak only truth."

Louisa smeared a bit of oily ash on each of Irene's eyelids and intoned, "May you see only beauty."

She moved to Irene's forehead and then her chest, with blessings at each for Irene to know her soul's purpose and lastly to know and receive love.

Rebecca squatted down to dig a hole in the earth floor of the stone enclosure. Louisa scraped the remains of the blood and ashes into the hole, where they were buried to become part of the shrine— part of Little Sister.

Meredith's face was wet with tears at the beauty and the simplicity of the ceremony, and knew, without any doubt, that she wanted the same, come next Bealtaine.

Chapter 25

A THIRD STRAIGHT DAY of heavy rain had most of the islanders hunkering indoors. No winds, no huge waves. Just dark clouds that made for constant twilight and dreariness. The ferry had been able to get to the island each day, but with such lousy weather, there'd been few people willing to travel the extra distance to Little Sister just to walk around in the rain. Art and Kenny had left a couple of days ago, according to Wilma, but the Turners were planning on staying on until after Labor Day.

"You know," Kathleen had said over breakfast when Molly was fretting about not being able to finish the roof on the Walsh's garage, "the beauty of living on an island and working for ourselves is we can take a day off when we want to. I think this is a perfect day to stay home. Read. Drink tea. Bake something really decadent and get fat. Together."

At the mention of baking, Molly's arguments had evaporated midprotest. "Bake? Maybe orange cranberry bread?"

"You're so easy," Kathleen had said with a snort.

She'd put Molly to work chopping cranberries and zesting a couple of oranges while she mixed the other ingredients. Before long, the cottage was filled with the aroma of the baking bread.

Kathleen glanced over now from her chair, her feet propped on the ottoman to where Molly was stretched out in her recliner, half-asleep with her book splayed across her chest. "Ready for another slice?"

"I've had three already," Molly said, picking up her private detective novel to mark her page. She lowered the footrest of the recliner. "But who's counting?"

She got up to cut another slab of bread for each of them, "accidentally" dropping a small chunk on the floor for Blossom to snatch. She carried Kathleen's plate over to where she was sketching.

"Me?" She leaned closer to look at the pencil lines depicting her, stretched out, book in hand.

"You're so seldom still for more than five seconds," Kathleen said. "I just like to do quick studies. Maybe it'll turn into a painting one day."

She raised her face for a kiss, which Molly delivered before going back to her recliner. But when she pushed back to elevate the leg rest, she didn't open her book up again.

"What do you think of the whole Woodhouse/Turner thing?"

Kathleen chewed thoughtfully. "I haven't seen Miss Louisa this happy since before Olivia died."

"I know." But Molly frowned as she broke a piece of bread off and popped it into her mouth.

"What's wrong, then?"

"Well, these folks come here for the first time, no knowledge or experience of the island. Now, they're planning on moving in to a ready-made house, basically free to them. They're going to be selling two houses back west and... what? Just waiting for Louisa to die?"

Kathleen shifted in her chair, curling her legs under her. "I don't think it's like that. I heard Roy talking to Tim at the market a couple of days ago, asking about how we get things like water heaters and washers and furnaces."

"There's nothing wrong with that furnace," Molly bristled.

"I know," Kathleen said quickly. "The point is, he's looking at what might need to be updated, replaced, fixed around that house. You told me you keep patching the roof and the wooden shingles, a few at a time, and you never charged the sisters for your work. What if they finally had the whole house done, properly?"

She hid a smile when Molly's eyes slid out of focus and a dazed look settled across her features.

"I've dreamed of what that house could look like if everything was fixed up. A new roof and a good coat of paint or sealer to protect the siding."

"Sounds like it might have a chance now, if the Turners will have the money and time to make it happen. And think how many new jobs you'll have. You won't be free for the next five years."

Molly grudgingly raised one shoulder. "There is that."

Kathleen laughed but then her smile faded. "What about Aidan?"

Molly turned to her. "What about him?"

"Have you talked to him? What's happening with him and Meredith?"

"No idea." Molly frowned again. "When Bobby came back after Laurie's surgery, he took over the Big Sister route, and Aidan kept this one. But when I'm in town, it seems he stays busy with the ferry. Wilma told Mom they're not having lunch together every day like they were for a while. Something changed after the storm. Not sure what."

"Maybe it's time someone talked to him."

Molly narrowed her eyes. "You mean, maybe it's time I talked to him."

"Yeah," Kathleen nodded. "That."

"You ply me with food and then trick me into stuff."

Kathleen smiled sweetly. "And it works every time."

⬧⬧⬧⬧⬧⬧⬧⬧⬧⬧

"WHAT DO YOU MEAN there's no cell service here! It's the twenty-first century, for God's sake. I have business calls to make! Meetings I need to Skype into!"

Meredith sat rocking on the hotel's front porch, biting her lip to keep from laughing at the irate man inside. She heard the teenage girl at the desk stammering an apology.

"I don't need your goddamned apology!" he shouted. "I need a cell signal! And look at this Internet connection. I can't keep it for more than twenty seconds before it goes dead!"

At that, Meredith shoved to her feet and stormed inside, only to find that her father had beaten her to it. He must have been reading in the hotel parlor.

"Tara," Roy said, and Meredith realized with some surprise that they already knew the names of all of the teens helping out at the hotel and most of the shops, "why don't you go find Wilma. She may be able to help this gentleman."

Tara scurried off upstairs, where Wilma was probably helping to strip sheets and clean rooms.

Roy turned to the red-faced man standing with his phone in his hand. "Sir, I understand you're upset, but that is no reason to speak to that girl in such a manner."

"Who the hell are you?" demanded the man. "Her father?"

"No, just a hotel guest, like yourself," Roy said calmly.

"Then piss off!" The man looked around for someone else to yell at.

A pretty woman descended the staircase accompanied by two boisterous boys who looked to be about five and seven, roaring past her down the stairs.

"Phil?" she said. "I could hear you all the way upstairs. What's wrong?"

"What's wrong?" he growled. "You and your bright ideas." Putting on a high voice, he said, "The other island will be just as charming."

The boys stormed, yelling, out onto the porch.

"Boys," she called, "you stay out of the rain." Turning to her husband, she said, "But we couldn't get a reservation on Big Sister. You waited too long—"

"Oh, so it's my fault we're stuck for a week on a rock that's too primitive to even have a goddamned cell tower."

His face was so red, he looked to Meredith as if he was going to burst a blood vessel.

"I have meetings, Rhonda. Phone calls. I can't be out of communication for an entire week!"

Rhonda cast an embarrassed glance in Meredith and Roy's direction. "Phil, please."

"You know, Phil," Roy said genially, "We felt just like that when we got here, but you might find it's kind of relaxing to slow down a little. Spend some time with your boys. They're at a fun age, but they'll grow up faster than you can believe, and memories like this will mean a lot."

Phil stared open-mouthed at Roy. "Who the hell *are* you?" he repeated. "Get away from me."

Rhonda laid a restraining hand on his arm, but he shook her off and stomped out onto the porch, holding his phone up over his head as if he could locate a cell signal that way.

"I'm sorry about that," she said. "He's not normally like this. He just has a big business deal he's worried about."

"Well, throwing a tantrum and cussing at the staff isn't going to get him cell service," Meredith said tartly. She pointed skyward. "And until the clouds clear, there won't be any consistent satellite service for Internet. It's just the way it is here, so he might as well relax."

Rhonda tucked her blonde hair behind her ear. "I don't think Phil knows how to relax." She gave them another murmured apology and went out to join her family.

"Great," Meredith grumbled. "And they're just off the boat. An entire week we get to listen to the loud family."

Her dad wrapped an arm around her shoulders and gave her a squeeze. "Take your own advice and relax. I think I heard Nels saying something about sending lunch down to a hunky ferry pilot hanging out at the boathouse."

"Hunky?" Meredith couldn't hold back a giggle. "Dad, have you been reading romances again?"

He grinned. "Limited selection of reading material here. Have you read them? Some of them are pretty steamy."

She held up her hands and closed her eyes. "I can't even—"

"Go see Nels."

She almost ran to the kitchen, as much to get away from her father as to see if there really was anything to take down to Aidan and Fred. She'd been trying not to crowd Aidan by expecting to spend every lunch break with him. She figured it was better to leave him wanting more time with her than less.

"Hey, Nels." Peeking through the swinging door into the kitchen, she wondered if the man ever got to leave.

His fair head popped up from where he was checking something in the oven. "Hiya, Meredith."

"I heard you've got something for the ferry boys?" She realized what she'd just said and almost giggled again. "Sorry, that didn't come out right."

But Nels apparently thought it was hilarious. He laughed so hard, he had to bend over and brace his hands on his knees. She glanced at his teenage assistant.

"Garrett, is he okay?"

The gangly redhead with the vivid freckles just nodded. "He's been in a really good mood. We've been working on his new recipe for a cinnamon and cardamom bread with a weird name." He reached for a large paper bag. "We've got lunch all packed up for Aidan and Fred."

"I'll take it down to them."

The bag was heavy, and she needed to keep one hand under it to support it. Too late, she realized her rain jacket was upstairs. She changed direction to go back to the hotel lobby, but her dad appeared, holding her jacket.

"Thought you might need this."

She frowned skeptically at him. "What are you up to?"

"Nothing," he said with a too-innocent expression on his face.

She slipped the jacket on and flipped the hood over her head before picking the bag up again and using her backside to push the screen door open.

She nodded to a few familiar faces on her way down the hill to the marina. The ferry was docked, but seemed to only be half-unloaded with no sign of Fred or Aidan. The boathouse sat on the other side of the marina office. A broad wooden structure, it had been pounded by decades of storms and salt air, weathering the boards to a dove-gray. She made her way along the dock in that direction to where a side door was ajar. From inside, voices carried.

"She was beautiful once."

That sounded like Fred.

Aidan's voice she recognized as he said, "You can still appreciate her curves."

What the—

Then Joe said, "Wait till you see the size of her—"

Meredith yanked the door open, startling all three. "Gentlemen."

The men jumped guiltily, instinctively moving to shield her view of a boat bobbing in the water behind them.

"It's you," Joe said in relief. He squatted down to tug a blue tarp back in place, covering the boat again.

"I brought lunch," Meredith said, shaking her head.

Joe pointed at the boat. "Don't say anything about this, will you?"

"Don't worry." Meredith hid a smile. Joe must have bought it without telling Jenny. Men and their toys.

Fred, though, was all about the food. He shifted a toolbox off a workbench and unloaded the cartons of Nels's food from the bag.

"I'll let you guys eat," she said, catching Aidan's eye before she turned toward the door.

"Meredith, wait." Aidan took her by the elbow and guided her outside to an overhang where they were mostly shielded from the rain. "I..."

He paused and reached up to push her hood back, brushing his fingers along her hair. "You are so beautiful."

She laughed, pleased but embarrassed. "So are you."

And he was, with his black hair gleaming and wet, his dark eyes focused so intently on her. She raised up on her toes to kiss him, lost in the sensations he brought out in her.

When he pulled away, she cleared her throat. "You were saying?"

"Oh, yeah. Almost forgot." He gave her a lopsided smile. "I took this weekend off and—"

"The whole weekend?" she interrupted.

"Yeah. We're celebrating Mo's birthday this weekend, so it'll be a big thing. Matty and Brandi are boating over with the baby."

"Oh." Meredith's face fell. "You'll be busy with your family."

"No. I mean, I will, but I want you to be there. And I want some private time with you, too." He tucked her hair behind her ear. "More than just a few minutes over lunch with Fred as our chaperone."

As if in response to his name, Fred hollered from the boathouse, "Aidan? Boy, if you don't get in here, I'm eatin' your lunch, too."

"Be right there," Aidan called while Meredith snorted. "See? Anyway, will you be available? I don't want to assume that you are, just because I'm finally around."

"I'll check my calendar and get back to you," she said. "I've become quite the social butterfly on Little Sister."

He grinned. "From what I hear, you and your parents have been shaking things up quite a bit."

Her smile faltered. "Is that a good thing? Are we upsetting people? Because—"

"Relax," he said. "No one is upset. And from what I hear, Miss Louisa is ecstatic. That's part of what I want to talk to you about."

"What?" She frowned. "We shouldn't have taken her up on her invitation to live with her?"

But he only shook his head. "This weekend. We'll have plenty to talk about."

He leaned down for another kiss. "Gotta go. See you in a few days."

She pulled her hood back up and stepped out into the rain. "Can't wait."

PLUCKING ANOTHER RIPE TOMATO, Louisa raised it to her nose. Oh, how she loved that smell, the succulent redness, warmed by the morning sun. She placed it in her basket with the others. She bent to pick a few weeds and tugged an onion out of the earth, rubbing the dirt off with her thumb.

"You'll go nicely with a hamburger for supper."

Her head tilted at the sound of singing. Lifting the tattered brim of her hat, she peered in the direction of the road and smiled. Aidan. She'd recognize that rangy stride anywhere. She couldn't remember the last time she'd heard him sing.

He loped into her drive and waved when he saw her, veering in her direction. "Good morning, Miss Louisa."

He took her basket for her without asking. "Need anything more?"

She had to push her straw hat back on her head to see his face. "Depends. Are you joining me? I fancied tomato sandwiches for a late breakfast. Or an early lunch. These days, I eat when I've a mind to."

"I'd love to join you."

She quickly picked two more tomatoes. He held out the basket and offered her a hand to climb out of the squash vines wrapped around her feet.

"Gonna be a hot one." He kept her hand in his as they strolled to the house.

"That's why I'm out here on the early side."

He gave her a hand up the back porch steps into the kitchen. They both knew she was perfectly capable of getting up and down those stairs on her own, but she accepted graciously.

She put him to work toasting some bread while she sliced the tomatoes. "Still have some iced tea from yesterday. Want me to pour it?"

"No thanks," he said. "Just water now. I left Fred to unload, stopped by to see my folks, had some coffee with Mom and Dad before he headed back down the marina."

"And now you're here."

He shrugged. "And now I'm here."

She didn't probe with any more questions for the time being. He'd come around to it when he was ready. She laid out the mayonnaise, salt, and pepper, along with two icy glasses of water.

When the toast was ready—"let it cool a bit, so it's not steamy," she'd instructed—they sat at the table to construct their sandwiches.

"Hope you don't mind just tomato, without bacon or lettuce," she said, spreading a thick layer of mayonnaise on her toast.

"Reminds me of summers when we were kids." He shook his head. "Don't know how Mom kept enough food in the house to feed us. Seems we never stopped eating."

She laughed. "I suppose with three boys, and Molly trying to keep up with you, Jenny had her hands full. Ollie was a big eater."

He raised his eyebrows at the thick sandwich she'd put together. "You may have been fooling all of us."

She took a bite, savoring the tangy flavor, and had to wipe the tomato juice dripping down her chin. When she could talk, she said, "I'm just better at hiding it."

The amused smile crinkling her eyes faded. She lowered her gaze as she swallowed. "I suppose I've been good at hiding a lot of things."

"My mistakes were right out in the open for everyone to see," Aidan said matter-of-factly. "You had to hide yours. Must have been hard."

She forced herself to meet his eyes. "The hardest thing I've ever done."

"But it was the right thing," he said earnestly. "You gave her the best chance you could."

Sudden tears stung her eyes. "I've always hoped so. The island would have accepted us, but the outside world wouldn't have. Not in those days." She dabbed at her eyes. "And I wasn't ready to come back. Not then."

He studied her for a moment. "I know this probably wasn't what you wanted from life, but I don't think you know how much you gave to the island. To me."

She waved a hand at him, and one heavy slice of tomato promptly slid out of her sandwich. "You hated school."

He snorted. "Yeah, but I loved you."

Those darned tears sprang to her eyes again. Refusing to look at him, she busied herself stuffing her tomato back inside the toasted bread. "Well..."

"You cared enough to ride me," he added. "Hard. Especially after... after Bryan died."

She blinked fast to clear her eyes. "You had a rough time after that. We didn't know how to help you."

"But you did," he insisted. "Just knowing that you expected more of me. I know I never showed how much it meant, but sometimes, I deliberately acted up, just to see if you cared enough to reprimand me." He paused. "You never let me down. Neither did Mom or Dad. Or Mo. Through all the stupid sh—stuff I pulled, you all stood by me. And I want you to stand by me now."

Her head snapped up. "What do you mean? Stand by you how?"

He set his sandwich down and fixed her with an intense stare. "I mean to ask Meredith to bond with me."

"You—" Louisa didn't even notice when her sandwich fell apart again, the tomatoes squishing out to plop onto her plate. "Bond? You mean it?"

"I do," he said solemnly. "I know I haven't known her long, and we haven't really spent much time together, but when I saw her—in that vision or whatever it was—at Bealtaine, I knew she was for me. I don't know how to explain it better than that. The time I have spent with her this summer has only made me realize how much I need her in my life."

"Oh, Aidan, I so want you—and Meredith—to be happy."

"But I also want to ask if you'll stand for me."

Louisa was speechless for a long moment. "Me?" she croaked when she could speak. "Wouldn't you want your mother or father?"

"Mom got to stand for Mo when she and Kathleen bonded. And I know, if Matty ever talks Brandi into doing it, he'll ask Dad." He leaned his elbows on the table. "And I realize, technically, you're Meredith's biological grandmother, so maybe she should have first dibs, but..." He reached for her hand. "I can't think of anyone I'd rather have at my side."

"Aidan, I'd be so honored. Yes, of course, I'll stand for you." A thought occurred to her. "But what about the ferry? Will you live on the mainland?"

He grinned. "That's the best part. I've been keeping track—ever since this crazy idea popped into my head—of how many day passengers we have on the ferry. For the last eight weeks, there've only been five. So I talked to Bobby, and together, we went to our supervisor. We're looking at changing the schedule, so the ferry arrives here at four or five, overnights, and then leaves again in the morning."

Louisa's face lit up. "So you'd be home every night? Here, on island."

He nodded. "It's not a for-sure thing yet, but I'm hoping."

"I'm so happy for you."

"Thanks, but..." He took a deep breath. "That's not all I wanted to ask you."

Chapter 26

EYES SCREWED SHUT AGAINST the fine dust and cobwebs covering her face, Molly squirmed farther under the crawl space. She swiped a hand over her eyes to clear them, and squinted at the pipes, looking for any sign of a leak. Her headlamp's beam cut through the darkness, illuminating more spiders than she really cared to think about, but everything looked dry.

"Are you sure, Lena?" she called back toward the crawl space entrance. "I don't see anything."

Lena Clearwater crouched outside, peering in to where Molly lay on her side. "I know I heard the sound of water running or dripping or something, under the kitchen. Further in."

A curious chicken squawked, trying to see what all the excitement was.

"Oh, no you don't, Petunia," Lena said, grabbing the hen and shoving her aside. "Molly doesn't need your help."

Cursing under her breath, Molly wriggled her way deeper into the space, sharp rocks scraping her ribs. "Damn!"

"What was that?" Lena called.

"Nothing," Molly grumbled.

Some days, she wondered why in the hell she did this. This was not how she wanted to spend her Saturday morning. Or her birthday. She pulled away thick insulation that rained down itchy fiberglass bits onto her sweaty neck, and finally found the kitchen water and drain pipes. Again, it all looked dry. No puddles, no wetness on the pipes or the insulation.

"Go run some water in the kitchen sink."

She waited, listening to Lena's footsteps as the floorboards above her creaked, sending a fresh sprinkling of dust down onto her. She heard the water run through the pipes and gurgle down the drainpipe, out toward the septic tank. Tugging a flashlight from her belt, she aimed its beam in addition to her headlamp, tracing the pipes from tank to sink. Nothing.

Just to be sure, since she was under here and filthy, she checked out the plumbing under the bathroom, too. It all looked fine.

Squirming back toward the entrance, Molly finally escaped the dark confines into fresh air. She ripped her headlamp off and reached for a towel Lena held out to her, scrubbing it over her face and hair.

"Ugh," she said with a shiver. "No sign of any water, but you've got a bumper crop of spiders down there."

Lena laughed. "Well, who knows what I heard. Thanks for checking, Molly. Want a glass of water? Or tea?"

Molly nodded as she rubbed the towel over the back of her neck and down her arms. She followed Lena up the back porch steps, but stayed outside.

"Hey, Harry," she said to the six-year-old sitting there, whittling a stick. She sat down next to him. "Nice knife."

He proudly handed her the pocketknife. "Got it for my birthday. I'm making a sword. Just a play sword."

"Wow," she said. "I think I was ten before I got my first knife. You know how to close it safely, right?"

He nodded. "And always cut away from me."

"Yeah." Molly made a fist and showed him a white scar across her knuckle. "This is what happens if you don't do that."

His eyes got big. "Did you need stitches?"

"I did." Molly kept a straight face. "My dad had to use fishing line to sew it up for me."

Harry's eyes got even bigger, and he glanced down at the blade when Molly handed the knife back to him, handle first.

Lena stepped back outside with a tall glass of cold water. "Here you go."

"Oh, thank you." Molly swished the first mouthful around and spit it over the side of the porch. "Just to get the spiders out." She quickly gulped the rest down. "That was good."

"How much do I owe you, Molly?" Lena asked.

"Nothing. Didn't find anything to fix, did I?"

"But you spent time checking."

"No worries." She handed the glass back and descended the stairs. "See you, Harry."

He brandished his sword. "See you tonight, Molly."

"Shhhh." Lena bent down and whispered in his ear.

Molly chuckled to herself. Harry was only the latest of several people who'd let slip little hints that something was happening later this evening. The fact that it was her birthday didn't require much sleuthing to figure out that someone was planning a surprise. Make that someones. She'd caught Kathleen in whispered phone conversations, and she suspected the guilty party on the other end of the line was her mom. Aidan's mysterious weekend off was another clue, but she had a strong feeling she was only a small part of his reasons for being here.

She started the Toyota and waved as she pulled out. She knew, on the mainland, any repairperson would have automatically charged just for coming to the house, before any work was done. Still, she always felt weird doing that if she didn't actually fix anything. But sometime in the next week, a dozen eggs or a cake or big batch of cookies would show up the house. Lena and the rest of the islanders always showed their appreciation in some way. It was just how they did things here. She'd never get rich, but "we don't need much, do we?" she and Kathleen often reminded each other.

It had taken Kathleen a long time to lose that drive, that need to get ahead.

"Get ahead of what?" Molly used to ask. "Passing someone on the ring road here just means you're going to get back where you started sooner."

She loved the pace of life on Little Sister, and couldn't help but wonder if the Turners were going to be able to make that adjustment. She really hoped so, mostly for Miss Louisa's sake.

She drove over to the power station. Might as well do some maintenance on the diesel generators while she was dirty. Then she'd go home and clean up for whatever Kathleen had planned.

⚒⚒⚒⚒⚒⚒⚒⚒⚒

THE ENTIRE COTTAGE WAS filled with the aroma of the applesauce cake baking for Molly's birthday dinner. Kathleen's mouth watered as she opened the oven to check on it. She'd never made it before and had almost begged off when Molly requested it. She found the recipe in one of Nanna's old cookbooks, the pages yellowed and brittle. To her surprise, the cake was turning out better than she'd hoped. Now, for the frosting. She wanted to have this done before Molly finished up at the Clearwater place. Lena had conspired with her to keep Molly occupied for at least an hour.

Jenny was taking care of dinner. Matty and Brandi had promised to bring Benjamin for the weekend. The plan was for dinner first, then drag Molly down to the marina, where the entire island would be gathered to surprise her with her new boat. Kathleen had been afraid it was a little too rough, too big a project, but Joe had assured her that Molly had taken on worse. For her to get to finally restore a 1937 Runabout that she could keep for herself, well, Kathleen hoped it was going to be as good a present as she'd envisioned.

She was unwrapping a block of cream cheese when Blossom leapt to his feet, head tilted as he listened to something she couldn't hear.

"What's wrong?" she asked when he started whining.

He danced in circles, whining more frantically.

"Blossom?"

Kathleen stood there with half the ingredients for the frosting plopped into the bowl, but Blossom began barking and running from the back door to the front. She set the cream cheese on the counter, wiping her hands on a towel and heading to the front of the house in time to see him jump up on the front screen door, hitting the lever with his paws so that it sprang open. He bolted outside.

"Damn!"

She hurried to the door, calling after him. "Blossom! Blossom!"

But he raced to the edge of the yard and disappeared into the woods. She ran to the kitchen and yanked the cake out of the oven, remembering to flick the dial to turn the oven off. She sprinted from the house to the woods and followed Blossom's trail as quickly as she could.

She knew this trail—it was the same one she'd stumbled down in the dark her first Yule onisland, the night she'd fallen into a ravine and hit her head. She was careful not to trip or fall today—Blossom's agitated behavior worried her, and she wanted to get to the trail's end in one piece.

As she descended, she heard a commotion. She stopped for a few seconds to listen. Blossom was ahead, barking in a way she'd never heard before, and then she heard screams.

Though she was gasping for air, Kathleen charged down the last part of the trail where the woods thinned above the beach. A small crowd had gathered around a panic-stricken woman. Kathleen didn't recognize any of the people. No islanders.

"My boys! My boys are out there!"

Blossom bounded into the surf, still barking. It was past high tide, but the water was still washing halfway to the sea wall before receding, wave after wave.

"Blossom!" Kathleen called, but he was swimming, rising with each incoming wave, and then moving farther away. She surged into the water, as deep as her hips, but she was no strong swimmer, no match for the ocean and the tides. She strained her eyes and thought she saw two small dots, bobbing far out on the water.

The mother was still screaming, "Someone call 911!"

"There is no 911 on Little Sister," someone else said.

Kathleen waded out of the water onto the beach. "Are you sure they're out there? How old are they?"

The woman was almost incoherent. "Yes! I only looked away for a few minutes! They're only babies. Five and almost eight. Someone do something!"

"Who's here with a car?" Kathleen asked, spying three cars parked near the beach.

"I am," one man said.

"Me, too." A woman raised her hand.

"You," Kathleen pointed at the man, "drive to the village and sound the alarm at the marina. They'll need boats."

"You," she said to the woman, "go to the nearest house, tell them to call around and find Molly, the sheriff. She was at Lena Clearwater's house. Hurry!"

"Molly, Lena Clearwater," the woman repeated over and over as she ran to her car.

They squealed away in a cloud of dust as the others stood helplessly on the beach, a few people trying to console the mother, who was still wailing.

Kathleen walked away from the group before she slapped the careless woman. But she knew it was old demons driving her own panic. She fought to subdue them. "Please bring them back," she prayed. "Bring them all back."

⬚⬚⬚⬚⬚⬚⬚⬚⬚⬚

THE MEWING OF GULLS was the alarm clock when Meredith had awakened to find Aidan lying on his side, watching her sleep.

"How long have you been awake?" she'd asked drowsily.

"A while." He'd combed his fingers through her hair, sifting the strands through his fingers. "Thinking about how much I like waking up with you."

His fresh breath indicated he'd already been up.

"Me, too." She gave him a quick kiss and slipped out of bed to the bathroom, self-conscious at padding naked across the room with him watching her.

A few minutes later, bladder empty and teeth brushed, she'd returned to bed to find him as eager as she was for another round of lovemaking.

She lost track of time, but it seemed much later in the morning when they lay side-by-side, both wonderfully tired and content.

"This is a little weird," he said, still panting. "With your parents next door to us."

"I know, but I think they figured it out when I asked them to keep Jasper with them last night. They'll have to get used to it."

He grinned. "Will they?"

She rolled onto her side, resting her hand on his stubbly jaw. "Yes."

His grin faded. "About that..." He sat up. "I wanted to talk to you—"

321

His head snapped up, and Meredith sat up at the sudden shouting coming from several places at once. Someone was yelling down below, maybe in the hotel lobby, with more bellowing and the frantic clang of a bell coming through the open window.

They both leapt out of bed. Aidan dragged his jeans on, slipping barefoot into his boots and reaching for his shirt. Checking quickly that Meredith was partially clothed in her T-shirt, shorts halfway up, he yanked the door open and hurtled down the stairs, leaving her to follow.

When she got to the lobby a few seconds later, it was to find that annoying man, Phil, hollering incoherently about the Coast Guard as Wilma tried to calm him. Meredith left them to run out onto the porch and down the stairs toward the marina. She got there in time to see Aidan jumping into a boat with his father while a couple of other men started a second boat.

"Go to the beach!" Aidan hollered back at her.

She sprinted back up the hill toward the hotel to find her parents and Jasper there. "What's going on?"

"I think there are kids swept out to sea," Roy said.

Meredith glanced toward the lobby. "Oh, shit."

She grabbed one of the bicycles in the hotel's bike rack. "Going to the beach. Meet me there."

Jasper accompanied her as she pedaled, her legs soon burning with the unexpected effort. By the time they got to the beach, she was gasping for air, and Jasper's tongue was lolling. She saw the knot of people gathered around the woman, Rhonda, from the hotel.

"So it is her kids."

Kathleen was standing off to herself, staring out to sea. Meredith went to her.

"What happened?"

Kathleen opened her mouth to answer, but Jasper shot by them, leaping into the waves until he was swimming.

"Jasper! Jasper, come!" Meredith shouted, running into the surf. But he kept dog paddling, beyond where she could get to him.

"Blossom swam out, too." Kathleen's voice cracked.

Meredith waded back to her, watching helplessly as her dog disappeared from view each time a wave surged, only to see his head bobbing again when the surf receded.

She took a quick look at Kathleen and was struck by the ashen color of her face. "Are you okay?"

Kathleen's chin quivered, but she couldn't reply. Meredith almost kicked herself when she remembered—*Kathleen's brother and then that stormy night not so long ago.*

"They'll be all right," she said, wrapping an arm around Kathleen's shoulders. "A couple of boats went out to come around and help search. Aidan and Joe and others. They'll find them."

She forced herself to believe her own words.

More people arrived until the small beach was packed with onlookers, even though they couldn't see anything from this vantage point. Behind them, Meredith heard Rhonda's continued sobbing and occasional shrieking.

"There you are." Irene and Roy appeared beside them, Irene peering anxiously out to sea.

"Anything?" Roy asked.

"Not yet." Meredith said, clasping her mother's hand.

"Where's Jasper?" Irene asked, looking around.

Wordlessly, Meredith pointed.

Her mother's sharp intake of breath echoed Meredith's own barely controlled sense of panic. Movement off to her side caught her eye. She saw Kathleen moving toward the woods at the edge of the beach, watched her begin to climb a faint trail.

"I'll meet you back at the hotel," Meredith said to her parents.

She wove her way through the throng and followed Kathleen, trotting to catch up to her once she was in the trees.

"Sorry," Kathleen said over her shoulder. "Just can't stand being in the middle of all those people. It's like some kind of spectacle for them, a great, tragic story they can tell about their holiday on Little Sister."

"Do you mind if I come with you?"

"Come on."

Kathleen clearly knew where she was going, so Meredith trailed her. Eventually, they stepped out of the woods near the bluff.

"I know this place," Meredith said.

But they weren't alone. Rebecca was already there, binoculars in hand. She waved them up onto the rocks.

"Can see a lot more from up here," she said.

Kathleen and Meredith joined her. From their vantage point, they watched two boats, moving slowly, hundreds of yards apart from each other. A third boat came zooming in their direction.

"Aidan went out with Joe," Meredith said. "And I saw a couple of other guys getting into a second boat, but who's in that third one?"

Rebecca raised the binoculars, taking a moment to focus them before saying, "Molly and Joey."

Kathleen shielded her eyes from the sun. "Was she at Lena's?"

Rebecca shook her head, slipping the lanyard from around her neck and handing the binoculars to her. "She'd already finished there. No one could find her for a while. She'd gone to the power station. Someone saw her SUV and told her what was happening."

Kathleen placed the binoculars against her eyeglasses for a few seconds but then handed them to Meredith, saying, "I can never get these things to focus."

Meredith swept the binoculars over the scene below, looking for any sign of the dogs. "I can't see anything on the water. No dogs, no kids."

"Dogs?" Rebecca asked.

"Both dogs went into the water," Kathleen said, her voice tight.

Molly's boat pulled up next to one of the others. Meredith twiddled the dial on the binoculars. It was Joe and Aidan. They spoke for a moment and then she and Joey pulled away.

From their elevated position, the observers watched as the boats moved farther apart, covering a broader search area. They sat on the rocks, silently surveying the search until even the boats were nothing more than small specks on the water.

Rebecca touched a hand to Meredith's shoulder, nodding in Kathleen's direction. She looked as if she was fighting tears.

"Let's go your house," Rebecca suggested. "We can't see anything now, and they'll radio as soon as they have news."

Kathleen didn't argue as Meredith gave her a hand up. Silently, they descended the trail, taking forks Meredith had never explored until she saw a flash of blue through the trees, and they approached Kathleen and Molly's cottage from the rear. They climbed the back porch steps into the kitchen.

"Pour us all something to drink," Rebecca said while she picked up the phone and dialed. "Jenny? I'm with Kathleen at her house. Meredith is with us. Any word?" She turned her back and lowered her voice. "Tell them the dogs went after the boys."

Kathleen robotically reached for the cream cheese that was sitting on the counter and placed it in the refrigerator. She poured three glasses of lemonade as she and Meredith listened.

Rebecca hung up. "Nothing yet."

Kathleen served the lemonade, and they all sat at the table, but Kathleen took her glasses off and pressed a napkin to her eyes.

"Sorry," she whispered. "I know he's just a dog, but..." She couldn't continue.

"He's not just a dog," Meredith said staunchly. "If anything happens to Blossom or Jasper because of those careless people, I'll..." Her stopped when her own throat got tight.

"Blossom saved you," Rebecca said to Kathleen. "Before you had Molly, before you felt at home here, you two saved each other."

"But why did he and Jasper go into the water?" Kathleen asked. "They never did before."

"Because they knew the boys were in trouble," Rebecca said as if this should be obvious. "They dove in where no other humans were willing to go."

Kathleen dropped her head to her hand. "If we lose them, my heart will never be the same."

Meredith couldn't bear to let herself dwell on that possibility. "Is life on this island always so tragic?" she asked bitterly.

Rebecca regarded her. "Life here is no more tragic than elsewhere. It's just more condensed. When you know everyone, when it involves visitors to your home, when things threaten your home, you feel them more deeply than when it's just something you hear on the evening news."

She gave Meredith a grim smile. "Life here has never been easy. Disease, death, accidents, storms. Not everyone is suited for it. Beauty isn't one-sided. Sometimes it comes with a terrible cost. If you've made up your mind to live here, you'll have to get used to that."

▓▓▓▓▓▓▓▓▓▓

EVEN WITH POLARIZED SUNGLASSES and a ball cap pulled low over her eyes, Molly's head was pounding. She'd been staring at the waves for so long that the sun's reflections were seared on the back of her eyeballs. The wind had stirred up a low chop to the ocean that cast constant shadows, and she was starting to see things on the water where there were none.

"Let me drive for a while," Joey said, taking the wheel.

"Thanks." Molly took a long swig of water, closing her eyes for just a moment before hanging her sunglasses from the keeper around her neck and raising the binoculars.

There was no chatter, no noise other than the hum of the motor and an occasional burst of static from the radio as the three boats signaled that none of them had seen anything. No kids. No dogs.

Molly's breath had caught when they got word that the two dogs had launched themselves into the water. If they didn't find Blossom... She really couldn't think about it.

Little Sister had never had to do a search like this. She and her dad and brothers had participated in searches off Big Sister over the years—they had so many more people who insisted on wading and swimming despite the warnings. Tourists who were used to beaches along the coast didn't understand how treacherous the waters around the islands could be—swirling undertows and deviously fast currents could carry someone miles in a very short amount of time.

She glanced at her brother, steering the boat while scanning the water around them. This was the most time she'd spent with Joey since the night they'd had to go rescue them. He seemed different. More serious, more responsible. Joe had told her that Joey had taken the time to do a full tune-up on the fishing boat. She couldn't remember the last time he'd done any regular maintenance on it. She knew he and Matty put in long hours just with the fishing and lobstering, and by the time he got back to the marina, it was late and he was tired. But you couldn't rely on something like a boat, miles out to sea nearly every day, and not put in the time to take care of her. Sooner or later, something was going to break down, and experience had taught her that it always happened at a really bad time. *Maybe he's finally learned that.*

She returned to searching the water, her eyes sweeping in a wide arc, looking for something, any—"There!"

"Where?" Joey turned in the direction she'd pointed, spinning the wheel to bring the boat about.

A dark silhouette, too misshapen to be a boy or a dog, Molly thought. Her heart thudded as they drew up to it. Joey threw the boat into neutral and helped her haul two sodden lumps up and onto the deck.

"Blossom!" She dropped to her knees. Joey untangled the arms and legs of the boy who was clinging to him. "Is he...?"

"He's breathing," Joey said. "How's the dog?"

Blossom's tail gave a weak thump.

"Radio the others," she said.

While Joey communicated their find, she reached for a pile of blankets and quickly got the dog and boy wrapped warmly, rubbing them both to stimulate circulation. The boy came to enough to vomit up the saltwater he'd swallowed. Then he started crying.

"Shhh," she said. "We've got you. You're safe now."

That made him cry harder for his mother, which prompted another bout of vomiting, mostly clear liquid. Blossom was no longer responding at all. They both seemed to be beyond what Little Sister's meager health care could handle.

"Joey," she called. "We've got to get them to Big Sister. Radio again. Tell them where we're going."

She sat between them, chafing Blossom and praying. She heard Joey talking to someone on Little Sister, giving them an update and asking them to get the parents of the boy over to Big Sister.

He pushed the engine as fast as he could go given the steady chop, but it still seemed to take forever before Big Sister's beach mansions came into view.

A group of medical staff was waiting at the marina to take the boy into their care. Joey went with them to provide as much information as he could until the parents could get there, while Molly gathered Blossom in her arms and rushed him the few extra blocks to the vet clinic, where they were also waiting. Two vet techs took him from her, promising that Dr. Steve would give her an update as soon as he had one.

She watched them disappear through a swinging door. Dropping into a chair, she took her sunglasses off and pressed her fingers to her eyes.

"Do you need anything, Molly?" the receptionist asked.

"Water and ibuprofen, if you have it, Sonya."

Sonya went into a back room and returned a moment later with a bottle of cold water and three tablets. "Here you go."

"Thanks." Molly gratefully tossed the pills into her mouth and chugged half the bottle.

"Can you tell us what happened?" Sonya said.

Molly explained what she knew, which wasn't much, considering all her information was second-hand.

"Sounds like Blossom saved that little boy's life," Sonya said sympathetically.

Molly could only nod, wondering about Jasper and the brother.

She had no idea how long she sat there before the vet came out. She jumped up when she saw him. "Steve, how is he?"

"I think he'll be okay," he said. "We induced some vomiting and got him on an IV to dilute the saline in his system, but he was severely hypothermic and just played out. I don't think he could have lasted much longer, Molly. Good thing you found him when you did." He laid a hand on her shoulder. "Want to see him?"

She followed him back to where Blossom lay on an exam table, wrapped in blankets under a warming lamp, with an IV line inserted into one foreleg.

"Can I stay with him?"

"Sure."

One of the techs brought a chair over. Molly sat with her hand on Blossom's ribs, feeling his shallow breaths and his continued shivering.

"Hang in there, little man," she murmured. "Your mother needs you. We both need you."

She lay her head down on her other arm, keeping one hand on him.

She must have dozed off, because she was startled awake by sudden commotion. The door to the exam area burst open, and Aidan entered, carrying a large bundle in his arms. He set his burden down on an adjacent table.

"It's Jasper," he said, glancing in Molly's direction. "We found him, holding onto the other boy's rash guard, trying to keep him afloat."

He and Molly moved out of the way as Steve and the techs took over with Jasper, doing much the same as they'd done with Blossom.

Molly's question was in her eyes. Aidan shook his head. "But if Jasper hadn't held on, we might never have found his body. We brought them both here."

She nodded, numb. "The docs at the clinic will have to call it. I'll have to write up a report."

"There's nothing we could have done, Mo. Nothing you could have done."

Another set of voices came from the direction of the waiting room and, suddenly, Kathleen and Meredith were there. All Molly knew was the warmth of Kathleen's arms as they wrapped around her. Out of the corner of her eye, she saw Aidan holding Meredith.

"I'll... get some more chairs," Sonya said.

Chapter 27

THE NEXT FEW DAYS were a blur. Matty and Brandi, who had just boated over to Little Sister with the baby, returned to Big Sister, where Brandi's family insisted on hosting the Coopers, along with Kathleen and Meredith, in their home near the restaurant. Molly spent most of Sunday with her counterpart on Big Sister, getting details to fill out the accidental death report to be filed with the proper authorities on the mainland. The parents of the two boys were naturally distraught. Molly told Kathleen that had been the hardest part, having to question the mother about what had happened for their report.

"That marriage is going to have a hard time surviving," she confided. "He was blaming her for not watching them, and she was blaming him for putting his work ahead of his family."

As sorry as Kathleen was for the two parents, her heart ached for the younger brother, the survivor. Molly must have seen something in her face, because she wrapped her arms around her and said, "He'll be okay."

Aidan was moody, irritable, mostly choosing to stay on the periphery of the subdued conversations. Kathleen found him pacing with a cup of coffee around and around the deck of The Lobster Pot Sunday morning after Molly had left.

"You okay?"

He gave her a surly look. "No. I took this weekend off so I could talk to Meredith about..." He brandished his mug, sloshing a little coffee over the lip. "But we never got to, and now, I've got to go back this afternoon. And next weekend is Labor Day, and she'll be going back, and..."

"Hey," Kathleen said, daring to give his shoulder a rub, though she wasn't sure he wouldn't tell her to go to hell. "What else is it?"

He leaned against the rail but wouldn't meet her eye. "The kid," he finally admitted in a low voice. "When we dragged him and the dog out of the water, for a minute—"

His voice broke and he turned away.

"Bryan." She nodded. "I know."

Because she did, he let her lean against him as they stood together for a long time.

Bobby and Fred, when they brought the Sunday ferry in to Little Sister, had worked with Wilma to collect the family's luggage from the hotel and had driven their car onto the ferry, with permission to make an unscheduled passage to Big Sister.

"I don't think they'll ever want to set foot on Little Sister again," Bobby told Molly when they chugged in and anchored to the Big Sister dock. "Glad we were able to do it this way."

They pulled out later Sunday afternoon, now loaded with a small casket, quickly constructed by a local woodworker, in addition to the mourning family. Joe and Joey went back to Little Sister, too, with a promise to return if they were needed.

With Molly busy with official duties, Kathleen and Meredith spent hours at the vet's office, where Blossom and Jasper were both recovering. Jasper was having a harder time, due to the fact that he was ten years old and had been in the water longer. Meredith had been able to call her parents at the hotel to give them regular updates.

Finally, on Monday morning, Dr. Steve pronounced both dogs out of danger. "Keep them quiet, though," he advised. "No running or exertion. Bland diet. Lots of rest."

Kathleen didn't think that would be a problem as they slowly walked the dogs to the marina—both of them still looking a little wobbly—where Joe had left one boat waiting. Both Blossom and Jasper looked apprehensive when it came time to get into the craft. Molly picked Blossom up and stepped into the boat, then took Jasper from Meredith's arms. They got both dogs lying comfortably on folded blankets.

"We'll be back over this weekend," Brandi promised, holding Benjamin and waving them off.

Kathleen and Meredith settled into seats as Molly eased the boat away from the slip.

She glanced back. "Why are they coming again? I mean, it's great to see them, and Mom can't get enough of the baby, but...?"

Kathleen's throat got tight. "We were supposed to celebrate your birthday, and never got to."

A heavy silence settled over the boat. It seemed a lifetime ago she was worried about an applesauce cake and keeping the antique boat a surprise.

"Will you, still?" Meredith asked hesitantly. "After all this?"

Kathleen watched Molly's shoulders stiffen, and she thought of all the years when it felt like her own life was subsumed by Bryan's death.

"Yes," she said with conviction. "When I had my first birthday onisland—my *tar abháile*—it was my first birthday celebration since the day my brother drowned on my tenth. Jenny said to my—" She stopped short, remembering that Meredith didn't know the whole ugly history of her family's dysfunction. "She said we could celebrate life even while we honor someone else's memory. We need to do that."

Molly's shoulders relaxed. When she glanced back, Kathleen didn't need to see her eyes behind her sunglasses to know what was in them.

The ride to Little Sister was uneventful, except for the crowd waiting for them at the marina.

"Brandi must have called Mom," Molly said as she tossed a rope to her dad, who tied it to a cleat.

The folks gathered there applauded and cheered as the dogs were handed up to those on the dock. Irene rushed to embrace Meredith, then knelt to hug Jasper.

"We're so glad you're all back, safe and sound."

Two of the kids from the reading group hung colorful ribbons with handmade medals around both dogs' necks amid a fresh round of applause. Blossom and Jasper both wagged their tails, looking somewhat bemused by all the attention.

Jenny was there, too. "Our dog heroes need to rest. Doctor's orders. We'll celebrate more later."

"Thanks," Molly muttered as her mom shepherded her and Kathleen and Blossom toward the Toyota. "We'll call you later, okay?"

Kathleen helped Blossom into the rear seat and watched Irene guiding Meredith and Jasper up the hill to the hotel. Meredith gave them a wave. Kathleen waved back and got in.

The cottage was just as Kathleen had left it—the unfinished cake sitting on the counter, the ingredients for the frosting sitting half-mixed in the bowl. For a moment, Molly stood, looking at everything before she moved into Kathleen's arms, shaking with the tears she hadn't let herself shed until now.

"Jeff," she whispered when she could speak.

"What?" Kathleen said.

"His name was Jeff Dixon."

"I didn't know," Kathleen murmured.

What she did know was that Jeff Dixon would forever be part of Molly's birthday just as Bryan was part of hers.

※※※※※※※※※

TIME MOVES DIFFERENTLY HERE, Meredith mused as she sipped a large mug of coffee. She watched Jasper, sound asleep on the dog bed she'd carried to the hotel porch, next to her rocker. No long hikes or bike rides for them. Not yet. She smiled watching him sleep, but the smile faded when she remembered how close she'd come to losing him. His muzzle was almost white. *How did I not notice that before?*

He'd been her companion almost her entire adult life, since she passed a "Puppeys 4 Sale" sign on her move to Pacific City. New job, new house. Why not a new dog to go with? Together, they'd explored the coast, weathered storms—literal and otherwise—as boyfriends came and went from Meredith's life.

She'd spent nearly a third of her life with this dog, the most constant thing in her life besides her parents and uncles. *A third of my life,* she thought. *But it all seems like yesterday.*

Rebecca's words kept playing through her mind as well, and they rang true. How many nights had she caught the news on TV over dinner, hearing about a massive pileup on some far-away interstate, or a mass shooting at a school or mosque, or some new weather disaster somewhere? It was always there, but not. Tragic stories, but because they were far away, because they didn't involve people she knew, those things hadn't touched her in a real, visceral way. Yes, she felt and grieved for the people who'd suffered those losses, but it was always filtered by distance.

Then two little boys, brought into this small, insular world of Little Sister, had touched and changed her life forever. Though she barely knew them, their presence—and sudden absence—had caused a shift in the atmosphere here.

There'd been a quiet, almost a pall over the island the last few days, since they got back from Big Sister. She wondered if it had felt like this after Kathleen's brother drowned. Probably more, she realized, because Bryan had belonged to Little Sister. Life here *was* more condensed, as Rebecca had said. One summer on this island had changed her life completely.

A few of the locals exited the diner, on their way to the marina. They nodded and tipped their caps in her direction. The sky was getting lighter, and the day's wind was just beginning to pick up, swirling in gentle breaths against her skin. A few gulls circled over the marina, their mewing adding to the sounds of morning. Over at the market, lights were on as Miranda and Tim served some of the islanders who liked to shop early before the tourists got in the way.

I'll do the same, when I live here.

That thought made her stop rocking. It still felt a bit like a fantasy, the whole "I'm quitting my job to go live on an island I dreamed about" thing. She knew her uncles didn't believe her parents would do it. Would her mom and dad really uproot themselves, sell their house and say good-bye to friends and family to do this? Or when they got back, would that resolve disappear? Like waking from a spell after they'd escaped the enchanted forest.

She knew her own choice had been made. Sometimes, she felt it had been made for her, centuries ago. The practical thoughts of moving were still daunting. Sell her stuff or move it? Say good-bye to her friends, coworkers, neighbors—people she knew she'd probably never see again. Jan and Barb might travel out this way if she pushed hard enough. She'd written both of them, but there was no way to express in letters how this summer, this island and its people, had changed her life. That would have to wait until she saw them in person. Maybe she could get them to come here next summer. But she also knew, from previous coworkers who'd retired or taken different jobs, promises to stay in touch too often never materialized.

The screen door opened, interrupting her train of thought.

"There you are."

She raised her finger to her lips. Her dad stepped carefully over Jasper and took the rocker next to her. For long minutes, he just sat beside her and rocked.

"Ready to go back?" he asked at last.

Meredith's breath hitched. Did he mean, just go back?

"I've been thinking," he said. "We'll have a lot to do. Been in that house a long time. We've accumulated a lot of stuff. Makes my back hurt, just thinking about the attic."

She turned to him. "You mean it? You're still ready to move here, for good?"

One corner of his mouth lifted in his crooked smile. "You think we'll change our minds? Decide this was all some fantasy and come back to earth once we're home?"

Meredith wondered why she'd ever thought he was always too caught up in his absent-minded professor projects and theories to see things clearly. She swore he was reading her mind now.

He must have read that, too, because he chuckled. "I haven't seen your mother this excited, this alive since we first met." He sighed and rocked and gazed around. "I have to admit, this place gets under your skin. I've been making a list. When I get home, I'll make a spreadsheet of everything we need to do."

Meredith snorted.

"What?"

"Nothing, Dad." She reached for his hand. "Nothing."

HOLDING UP A FADED flannel shirt, Louisa pursed her lips as she tried to decide whether it was good enough to donate. "Elbows are thin, but the rest is in good shape."

She folded it and placed it on the smaller pile on the bed. A separate pile consisting of threadbare undershirts and old dungarees with back pockets half ripped away and more flannel shirts too far gone to be worn was considerably larger.

"They'll make good rags," she said, though it pained her to think of her daddy's clothes being cut up into rags.

"Sorry you have to do this alone."

Louisa shrugged. "Neither of us could bring ourselves to do this after Daddy passed. We always said we'd get to it one day."

"One day never came. Not while I was alive, anyway."

Louisa opened another drawer and tugged out a handful of colorful socks. "Why in the world did he like such garish socks?"

Ollie chuckled. "He did, didn't he? Used to love it when people stared at his socks."

Louisa added them to the donate pile. "Someone may like them."

"You know, you're going to have to do the same with my room, sister."

Louisa didn't reply. She kept sorting, one drawer at a time.

"No one needs a house full of dead people's things, Lou. If they come, they'll have things of their own, and they'll need empty closets and dressers."

"I suppose," Louisa whispered through a tight throat.

"Does make you realize, though..."

Louisa straightened. "Realize what?"

"That I lived a whole life on this rock on this planet and left nothing behind, nothing that will last now I'm gone. Just old clothes that no one wants."

A long silence followed.

"But that's not true for you, is it?" Olivia added. "You will leave something behind. Not just your students and all that you did for them, but now, family. It's good, Lou. Embrace it. It's good."

Her heart somewhat lightened, Louisa finished emptying out her father's room and bagged up the piles on the bed. She carried it all out to the car and then came inside to whip up a batch of potato salad. When it was done and chilling in the refrigerator, she brewed a fresh pitcher of iced tea and placed it in the fridge, too.

Upstairs again, she changed into a linen tunic and loose trousers and brushed her hair before twisting it back into its bun. Downstairs, she gathered up the two wooden boxes and took them out to the car, where she seatbelted both of them securely in the front passenger seat.

"We can't have you eavesdropping, now, can we?"

She made one last check of the house to be sure all was in order before going to the refrigerator to get the potato salad and make the short drive to the Cooper house.

"Jenny?" she called out as she let herself in.

"In here," came Jenny's voice from the kitchen.

Louisa put her bowl in the refrigerator, adding it to the others crammed in there. "What else can I help with?"

She was happily making deviled eggs as others began to arrive: Rebecca, Brandi and Matty with little Benjamin. Joe and Joey already had the grill going. Kathleen and Molly came with Blossom, who seemed to have recovered from his adventure, judging from how focused he was on trying to get Minnow to play with him.

"Happy belated birthday, Mo," Jenny said, giving Molly a hug. "We didn't get to celebrate last weekend, so..."

Louisa glanced up and did a double take at the dark expression on Molly's face. "Molly," she said. "I forgot to bring Daddy and Olivia in from the car. Would you mind?"

"Thanks," Kathleen said in a low voice when Molly left the kitchen. "She really wasn't too keen on this."

"All the more reason to do it," Jenny said firmly. "And thank you all for agreeing to a mid-day celebration."

"Aidan will be able to come, won't he?" Louisa asked. "He tried to make the time last week, but..."

When Aidan did arrive, he had the Turners and Jasper with him. Jasper flopped down in the living room, where Blossom gave up on trying to convince Minnow to crawl out from under the sofa and lay down beside his buddy instead.

"Come in, come in," Jenny said to them. "Help yourselves to drinks. We've just about got everything ready."

Molly's mood seemed to lighten with the laughter and conversation around the table. For her part, Louisa reveled in it. She knew Irene and her family would have to go back west in a few days. She tried not to dwell on how long it might be before they could sell their homes and move to Little Sister for good. She'd become accustomed to being alone in that house, but, oh, how lovely it would be to have others with her again.

"You okay?" Aidan asked, eyeing her closely.

"I'm fine," she said, patting his hand. Conversations swirled around them as everyone talked at once. She crooked a finger, and Aidan leaned nearer.

"Later, when we go to the marina, you take Meredith to the house. You can talk privately there."

His eyes widened, and she patted his hand again. He gave a nervous nod.

⁂

AIDAN SHUFFLED HIS FEET nervously when Meredith joined him on the front porch of the Woodhouse place.

"We could have walked here," Meredith pointed out, wondering why they were here, alone, when the rest of the party was back at the Coopers.

Aidan shook his head. "I don't have that much time." He gestured to the two chairs on the porch.

340

Meredith took one while he took the other. She waited, but he could only stare at the floorboards and couldn't seem to say whatever was on his mind. Her heart pounded, but it did so from somewhere down near her stomach. He'd brought her here to break up. *Can you break up with someone you've never really been with?*

But, in her mind, in her heart, she had been with him. More than she ever had with Grant. Still. If this was what he was here to say... might as well get it over with.

"Aidan, what's wrong?"

"Nothing—" He lurched to his feet and started pacing, raking his hand through his hair. "Meredith, do you remember, the night we had dinner, at the chapel, and we talked about bonding?"

"Yes," she said slowly.

"And I told you we don't bond young. Or quickly, because it's forever."

"Yes."

He paused his pacing and returned to the chair beside her. "I know this may seem quick, cause we haven't known each other very long, but, will you bond with me?"

Before she could answer, he blurted, "I never, ever thought I'd meet anyone... I never saw this in my future, but you've changed everything I used to think. I want to spend the rest of my life with you."

Her heart was beating again, but now it had jumped into her throat, blocking any words, almost choking her. She could only nod. He leaned over for a kiss. As she met his lips, her mind raced with a million questions, and, as they clicked through her brain, her heart plummeted again. She pulled away but kept hold of his hand.

"Does this mean we'd live on the mainland?"

"I think I've worked it out so that I can be onisland every night."

"Really?" Her face lit up, but then the next question pushed its way through the crowd. "Where would we live? I thought I'd be living here with Miss Louisa, but..."

341

"We will. If you want. I spoke with Miss Louisa already. I'll become a Woodhouse."

Completely flummoxed now, she sat back, staring at him. "Become a Woodhouse."

He grinned. "Hasn't anyone talked to you about Little Sister traditions?"

She thought through her many conversations with Kathleen and others. "Several of them. Which are you referring to?"

"When offlanders bond with islanders, they take the island name. Even men. Nels is a Greatneck because Wilma is a Greatneck. Same with Tim and Miranda. She's a Shannahan, so he is, too. The First Ones traced their lines back through their foremothers, so if the woman is the islander, that's the family name they go by. That way, the island's family lines continue."

Meredith was still confused. "I don't get it. You're a Cooper, and I'm not a Woodhouse."

"But you are. As far as the island is concerned, you're part of Miss Louisa's lineage, and that makes you a Woodhouse. As for me, Matty already has a child. Don't know if Mo and Kathleen have any plans, and I don't see Joey ever growing up, but the Cooper line will continue."

His expression sobered. "When Miss Olivia died, Louisa believed she was going to see her family line die with her. Then you and your mom showed up, and all of that changed. If we..." He paused, looking embarrassed. "If we have children, I'd like them to be Woodhouses."

The riot of questions churning in Meredith's head quieted. She still needed answers to many of them, but she knew all she needed to for now.

"Yes, I'll bond with you. Yes, I'll become a Woodhouse. And yes, we'll have more Woodhouse children."

He bent to kiss her. "We'll not just have them; they'll be part of the island."

"What do you mean?"

But he shook his head. "You'll see tonight. I can't stay, but you'll be there."

⬚⬚⬚⬚⬚⬚⬚⬚⬚⬚⬚

A FULL MOON ROSE, casting her light over the stone circle, the trees, the stones in the cemetery. The moon shadows rippled and shifted as the wind rustled leafy branches where a group of people gathered under one of the oldest oak trees.

Kathleen nervously ran through the ritual again in her mind, wondering if she really wanted to become Keeper after all.

"I think everyone is here," said Rebecca. "Miranda, Tim." She indicated where they were to stand. "Brandi, you and Roy here."

Matty took Benjamin while Brandi moved to stand beside Roy.

"This naming ceremony is one we hold dear," Rebecca said. "Our ancestors knew that our children needed to be rooted here, one with our mother, the island. Not all partake of this ritual now, but it is a way of joining a life—at birth and again at death—to the island. For we know, everything that is born, dies and is reborn again."

She gestured to Kathleen, who stabbed a shovel into the earth to dig a hole at the base of the tree.

"That's deep enough." Rebecca withdrew her knife from her pocket. "Tim?"

He stepped forward, holding something wrapped in paper. Kathleen tried not to gag when he handed it to her.

"Oh, hush," Rebecca hissed as she slit open the paper and peeled it away. "It's frozen."

She took Charlotte from Miranda and handed her to Roy. "You agree to stand for this child as her *athair inis*—her island father. And you," she looked to Brandi, "as her *máthair inis*? To help raise her if anything should happen to Miranda or Timothy."

343

"We do," they said in unison.

"As all of our traditions, this is a sacred blood pact, between you and this child and the island. Hold out a hand."

She quickly scored each of their thumbs, holding them so that the blood dripped onto the parcel that Kathleen held. "Your blood, mixed with the placenta of this baby, links you and links her to the island forever."

She nodded at Kathleen, who was only too ready to place the frozen placenta in the hole she'd dug and cover it with the loose dirt.

"What is the baby's name?" Rebecca asked.

Kathleen thought this was a strange question to ask, as they'd been calling the baby by her name for over two months.

"Charlotte Olivia Shannahan," Miranda said.

Miss Louisa gasped, and Kathleen glanced over to see Meredith wrap a supporting arm around her shoulders.

"Charlotte Olivia Shannahan," Rebecca repeated with a smile, "we honor you." She took first Brandi's, then Roy's hand, smearing a bit of blood from each on Charlotte's forehead. "Bright blessings on you, always."

Chapter 28

MOLLY DUCKED INTO THE boathouse, trying to avoid Fred, who had been on a tear lately about politics. Not that she didn't like a good political argument, but she generally had to have a couple of beers in her system first.

She squatted down at the edge of the dock where the boat bobbed on the water and tugged the tarp off the Runabout. She couldn't wipe the grin from her face. All these years restoring and repairing antique boats for others, she'd never seriously thought about getting one for herself. The island couldn't have given her a nicer gift. She knew Kathleen had chunked in the biggest part of the purchase price—"Don't ask how much it was," Kathleen had said. "We wanted to do it." But the fact that everyone else wanted to pitch in touched Molly deeply.

A sudden flapping of wings announced company. "Hey, Cap'n Jack. Been waiting for you." She leaned over to the workbench where she'd stashed several cans of tuna and pulled the top off one. "Got some lunch for you."

The gull hopped nearer on his one leg to pick the tuna neatly from the can. As he ate, he watched her step gingerly onto the Runabout. She made mental notes about all the things the little boat would need, what she'd have to order and what she could do herself. The driver's seat was rotted, the leather brittle and torn, but she sat anyhow, running her hands over the wheel, imagining the roar the rebuilt engine would make when she adjusted the throttle.

With a sigh, she climbed out and threw the tarp back over her new toy. This work would have to wait until things slowed down in a few weeks. Labor Day was the official end to the season, when the kids went back to the mainland for school, but the tourist traffic would continue through most of September. Once that tapered off, she'd have more time for projects of her own.

A sudden burst of sunlight momentarily blinded her when the boathouse door opened. Molly squinted and threw a hand up until the door closed again.

"Sorry." Aidan stepped inside.

Cap'n Jack squawked and flapped up to perch on the workbench, where he could keep a wary eye on the newcomer.

"Pet of yours?"

Molly moved the tuna can to the workbench so the gull could finish his snack. "More of an occasional visitor."

Aidan pointed at the boat. "That was a nice gift."

"It was. Nicer than anything I ever expected."

"You do a lot for folks here, Mo. They wanted to let you know how much they appreciate you."

Aidan shuffled his feet, a sign that he wanted to talk. Molly overturned two five-gallon buckets and sat on one. Aidan took the other. Knowing her brother as she did, she waited, watching the reflections shimmering on the pilings.

"Labor Day this weekend," he said at last.

"Yeah."

"Turners will be leaving in a few days."

"Spect they will." She eyed him, but he was staring at his boots. "But they're still planning on coming back?"

He nodded. "That's what they say." He took in and expelled a deep breath. "I asked Meredith to bond with me."

If Molly hadn't been sitting, she would have fallen over. "Say again?"

He straightened and met her eyes. "I asked Meredith to bond. With me. And I'm going to take the Woodhouse name."

This time, Molly's jaw dropped.

Aidan snorted. "Close your mouth before something flies in."

She shut her mouth. "Hells bells, Aidan. Bonding *and* taking the Woodhouse name?"

"Yep."

"Have you told Mom and Dad?"

"Not yet."

Tons of questions churned through her head, but all that came out was, "Wow."

"I talked to Miss Louisa first, to see how she'd feel about it."

"I'm sure she's thrilled. The Woodhouse line will go on."

"Exactly." Aidan leaned closer, elbows on knees. "Don't know what you and Kathleen are planning, but Matty already has a child who can carry on the Cooper line."

"You left out Joey," Molly said with a wry smirk.

Aidan roared with laughter. Cap'n Jack flapped his wings at the unexpected noise. When the laugher faded, Aidan wiped his eyes.

"Do you think Mom and Dad will be upset?"

"I doubt it," Molly said. "You know they just want you to be happy. Me, too." She paused a moment. "Are you?"

He looked at her with shining eyes. "I am, Mo. You know," he scrubbed his hand over his bristly jaw, "I feel like I've been living in a storm ever since the night Bryan died. Maybe even before that. I think some people need the storm, they need that rush of constantly fighting to stay afloat. For years, I was like that, but now I know, it was only because I was afraid of the calm. In the calm, there's nothing to fight, no waves battering you from outside, trying to sink you. The calm forces you to listen, to look at your own reflection. And I never liked what I saw."

She tilted her head to study him, and she finally saw what she hadn't been sure she ever would. "Meredith is your calm," she said, understanding completely.

"She is. I see myself through her eyes." He gave her a sheepish smile. "And I finally like what I see."

"Well, damn, Aidan." Molly's throat got tight. She reached over and punched him in the shoulder.

※※※※※※※※※※

LABOR DAY WAS ALWAYS a mixed-up holiday on Little Sister, Kathleen was coming to realize. It was the last hoorah for the businesses that depended on tourists, but it was always tinged with a little sadness that it was also a farewell to the island's kids, who would be leaving with the coming week's ferry to return to school on the mainland.

This year, Louisa hosted a picnic to celebrate Aidan and Meredith's announced bonding—though it wouldn't happen for months—and to say a temporary good-bye to the Turners.

As always with these get-togethers, there was more food than they could possibly eat. Kathleen sat on a bench in the shade of Louisa's big oak tree with a glass of Guinness, watching Blossom, down in a play-bow, begging Jasper to chase him. The older dog complied for a bit, but then came back into the shade to plop down on his side, letting Blossom wrestle with him.

At the picnic table, Louisa was talking with Irene and Roy, looking happier than Kathleen had seen her in a long time. The resemblance between Louisa and Irene was still a little startling, and Kathleen wondered again why she hadn't seen it right away.

With that uncanny ability to say what Kathleen was thinking, Rebecca sat down beside her and said, "Like mother, like daughter."

Kathleen thought about those terms, how everyone assumed there was some kind of natural link between parent and child that was always there. "Giving birth to someone doesn't make you a mother."

She felt the weight of Rebecca's gaze scrutinizing her.

"Are we still talking about them?"

Kathleen avoided replying by taking a long drink.

"I don't think Louisa will try to take that place in Irene's life," Rebecca said. "She knows another woman stood in that role for her and Meredith. But she is getting a second chance to be in her daughter and granddaughter's life in a meaningful way. That's something."

She gave Kathleen's knee a squeeze and went inside, leaving Kathleen to wonder where in the world that reaction had come from. She'd barely thought of her mother for months, let alone pondered their non-relationship.

Blossom, giving up trying to get Jasper to wrestle with him, flopped down in the grass beside his chum. They lay side-by-side, tongues lolling and eyes half-closed.

"Hey."

Kathleen looked up to see Meredith standing next to her.

"Mind if I join you?"

"Not at all." Kathleen patted the seat beside her. "Congratulations. Aidan's a good guy."

"It still feels a little surreal," Meredith said, swirling her wine around the inside of her glass. "Go on a quest to find the mystery island you've been dreaming about, then find your dream-man and decide over the course of less than three months to spend the rest of your lives together."

Kathleen chuckled. "Well, when you put it like that..."

Meredith's face turned serious. "Were you nervous? To bond with Molly? The whole 'forever' thing?"

"I was, a little." Kathleen smiled wistfully at the recollection. "But I was more worried that she might want to back out."

"And the ceremony...?"

"Uh uh." Kathleen shook her head. "I'm only going to tell you what I was told. It involves nudity and blood. Like most of the rituals on this island."

Meredith groaned. "Really? Nudity?"

"See, I was more worried about the blood. Look at you. You have nothing to worry about."

"Well, I am worried about a couple of things," Meredith said slowly.

Kathleen shifted to face her. "Like?"

"Well, Aidan did tell me someone has to stand for you during the ceremony. I don't really know anyone here that well, but..." She looked at Kathleen. "You were the first to welcome me here. And word has it that it was you who intervened on our behalf with the island council. So, I wanted to ask if you would stand for me?"

Kathleen's mouth opened and closed a couple of times. "I don't know what to say."

"Yes would be good."

"Are you sure? You don't want... I don't know—"

"I'm asking the person I want."

Kathleen's heart swelled. "Meredith, I'd be honored. Thank you."

Meredith embraced her. "Thank you." She took it all in, the people laughing and talking. "It's going to be hard to leave, even for a couple of months."

"It will," Kathleen agreed. "I had to leave, in my first year back here. To help take care of... of a friend who was sick. It wasn't even two weeks, but it felt like forever."

Meredith ran her hand over the weathered bench. "My principal is not happy with me, quitting with such short notice. But I don't think they'll have any trouble finding someone to replace me. It's a nice school system. Someone will want my position."

"Aren't there people you're going to miss?"

"Yeah. I hope they'll come to visit. Two of them I'd really like you to meet."

"You said there were a couple of things," Kathleen remembered.

Meredith's eyes filled with sudden tears as she watched the dogs. "I have a huge favor to ask of you. And Molly."

"What is it?"

"Jasper's really not bouncing back like I'd hoped after..." Meredith's voice broke and she had to stop. "I think two cross-country trips, hopefully only a month or two apart, would be too much on him. He gets along great with Blossom. Would you guys mind keeping him for me? I'll pay Miranda in advance for food and treats and anything else he might need."

Kathleen's own throat got tight as she imagined how hard it would be to leave Blossom, even for a little while. "We'll take care of him until you get back here."

Meredith nodded through her tears and walked away. Kathleen watched her go, wondering at how different life on the island would be next year.

"You look pensive." Molly sat next to her.

"I like this." Kathleen leaned her head on Molly's shoulder. "All I have to do is sit by myself and I get a whole parade of visitors."

"I was getting kind of jealous," Molly teased, wrapping an arm around Kathleen.

"I keep thinking."

"About?"

"That quake thing the island did in April." Kathleen lifted her head so she could look at Molly. "Was it warning us about the boy?"

"I've been thinking about it, too," Molly said, gazing up at the clouds. "I'm not so sure it was meant to be a warning of something bad. Think how much has happened. Miss Louisa has family she didn't know about, and now they've decided, not just to live here, but to bond and become part of the island. And the boy's drowning. And Aidan coming back. Maybe the island was just letting us know change was coming."

Kathleen thought about that. "Oh, there's going to be another change. We're adopting."

Molly actually leaned away from her with her mouth open.

"Wish I had a picture of that reaction," Kathleen said with a big grin. "Only temporarily, so maybe I should have said fostering. We're going to be keeping Jasper for Meredith, so he doesn't have to be dragged cross country twice more."

Molly heaved a sigh of relief. "I know we talked some about this a few months ago..." She narrowed her eyes. "When you said Aidan was your type."

Kathleen chortled. "I forgot about that. I guess he's taken now. What about it?"

"Well," Molly said with a wag of her head. "With talk of babies and family lines continuing and, you know, the way some women talk about their biological clocks, I just wanted to... you know, I thought we should talk again."

"No." Kathleen kissed her cheek. "No ticking clocks for me. All I need are you and one or two fur-kids."

As MUCH AS SHE wished her last few days on Little Sister could last forever, Meredith found time jumping in fast leaps. Labor Day weekend was over before she knew it, and then she and her parents watched from the hotel as island parents brought the kids to the marina to leave for school on the mainland with lots of hugs and a few tears.

"Maybe that will be different next year," Irene said. "If you decide to teach here, they won't have to leave."

Meredith nodded. "I expect some will go, even if it works out here. Either they won't trust me to stay or they won't want to lose the contacts they've made on the mainland. Still, I hope some will want their kids to stay on Little Sister."

She kept Jasper with her, enjoying every minute she had with him. She'd made arrangements with Miranda to bill her credit card for anything Kathleen and Molly purchased for Jasper or Blossom.

"And don't let them argue about it."

"Promise," Miranda had sworn, hand up.

The Turners settled with Wilma, though they'd been paying weekly.

"We'll sure miss you around here," she said. "But you'll be back, soon enough. Remember to check the ferry schedule, too. Come next week, it'll only run weekly, and might be monthly by the time you return."

Irene left a few last paintings with Siobhan, but packed up the rest to give to her friends in Portland. "So they'll know where we're going."

"One good thing," Roy grunted when he carried the suitcases downstairs to the lobby, "you both know how little you can get by with now. Remember that when it comes time to sort through things back home."

It was true, Meredith thought, as she drove to Kathleen and Molly's cottage on the day they were to depart. She'd learned a lot about herself this summer. Not that she'd ever set a lot of store by things, but her closet and dressers were stuffed with way more than she needed. There'd be lots of donations to thrift stores and charities as she packed up her house.

When she pulled in to their drive, Blossom was waiting. Jasper hopped out of the car to greet him.

"Are you sure you don't mind?" she asked when Kathleen stepped outside.

"We don't mind at all." Kathleen carefully avoided looking at Meredith. "Are you sure? About leaving him with us?"

Meredith nodded tightly. "It's best for him. And I don't want him to watch me sail away without him."

Her voice broke. Kathleen rubbed her shoulder and helped carry Jasper's bed and food into the house.

"I know. I felt the same way, having to leave Blossom behind when I left. Jasper will miss you, but we'll take good care of him."

"Thank you." Meredith flung her arms around Kathleen. "Thank you for everything."

"I'm so glad you found us."

"Me, too." Meredith stepped back, swiping her eyes. "Come here, old man."

Jasper trotted to her for a final hug.

"You be good," she whispered into his ear. "I'll miss you."

She hurried to the car, afraid if she lingered or looked back, she'd never be able to leave him.

The ferry had arrived while she was gone, and her heart gave a flutter when she saw Aidan unloading some big crate with the fork-lift. He gave her a wave.

At the hotel, her dad had the luggage out on the porch, ready to load.

"I think he drew up a schematic for how to load everything in the most efficient way," Irene said.

"I heard that." Roy glanced at them as he lifted the rear door of the Forester. "As a matter of fact, I do have a plan that takes into account what we'll need for the nights we're on the road. That, my dear, is based on forty years of having to completely unpack the car

354

to find the thing you packed first, which, inevitably turns out to be the first thing you insist you need and, therefore, should have been the last thing packed."

Irene rolled her eyes while Meredith bit back a laugh.

She left her dad to it and sauntered down to the marina. "Hey."

"Hey, yourself," Aidan said, climbing down from the forklift to give her a kiss. "All set for the trip back?"

"I guess." She sighed. "Wish I didn't have to go back."

He wrapped his arms around her. "It won't be for long. By the time you're ready to be on Little Sister for good, I may be here with Miss Louisa. You've got our phone numbers?"

She nodded. "I'll miss you. And the island. And Jasper."

He gave her a crooked grin. "See, that's the part that makes me feel the best."

"Why?"

"Cause even if you decide, once you're back on the other coast, that you could live without me or the island, I know you'll always come back for him."

She laughed, though her eyes filled with tears.

He held her again. "And while I'm waiting for you to return, visiting him at Mo and Kathleen's will make me feel closer to you."

She lifted her face to him. "I love you. So much."

"I love you, too." He bent to kiss her again.

"Boy! Stop smoochin' that girl," Fred bellowed. "It's wicked hot and I wanna get this mess unloaded so's we can head back."

"Go," she said, giving Aidan a little shove. "We'll board as soon as you're ready."

She let him get back to work and climbed the hill to the hotel to find her mom in the diner.

"One last meal here before we leave?" Irene asked.

Meredith forced a smile, not sure she could eat, but she sat down. Her dad came in a few minutes later as Wilma brought drinks to all of them.

"Land sakes," she said, "this place won't feel the same without you. But you'll be back before we know it."

She took their orders and left.

"Mind if I join you?" Louisa asked, standing there with a faded canvas bag in her hand.

"Please." Roy pulled out the fourth chair at the table.

Louisa opened her bag and handed a cloth-wrapped object to Irene. "I thought you might like to have this."

Irene pulled back the cloth to reveal a framed photo—the one from the piano where a younger Louisa looked so like Irene, standing with her sister and their father. "Oh." She put her hand over her mouth.

"Just to remember the people you come from," Louisa said.

"Thank you." Irene grasped Louisa's hand. "For everything."

Louisa started to wave off her thanks, but Irene squeezed and said, "No, I mean it. You could have... ended it. Ended me. But you didn't. And you gave me my best chance. I'll never forget that."

Louisa seemed incapable of words. Luckily, Wilma's arrival with their lunches spared her the necessity of speaking.

"Brought you a tomato sandwich, Miss Louisa, just the way you like them, with extra mayo."

Roy steered the conversation to less emotional topics—namely his intention, when they returned, of crafting an ale good enough for Patrick to serve in the pub.

"And just where do you think you're going to do all this brewing?" Irene asked him.

"Sure you're welcome to use the cellar," Louisa said.

Roy beamed at her. "Thank you. If it takes off, maybe we can build a shed or something near the house."

Meredith knew this potential new project would now occupy his mind for the entire journey back to Oregon. She listened absent-mindedly while she watched people moving about in the village—Siobhan hanging a new flag from the pole on her shop; Miranda chasing Ellis who'd scooted out the door of the market; Joe fueling a boat for someone—all the scenes that would remain imprinted on her mind until she could return to this island and breathe again.

Before she knew it, it was time to board the ferry. After a last round of hugs, she followed Fred's hand signals as she drove the Subaru onto the ferry. Only one other car was departing with them. She joined her parents on the deck as the horn blasted and the ferry began to chug away from the island. Once they were out on open water, the engine picked up speed, churning through the waves.

Standing at the rail with the salt wind whipping her hair, she realized she stood between her two loves—Aidan before her up in the pilot house, and the island behind her, receding into the distance.

⬛⬛⬛⬛⬛⬛⬛⬛

LATER THAT EVENING, DINNER and dishes done, Louisa sat on the porch, listening to the sounds of the descending evening.

"Quiet tonight."

"Mmm hmm," she replied, rocking.

"You still have my room to clean out."

"I'll get to it. One day."

"Lou, there's no sense putting it off. Not like I can use those things."

"I know, Ollie. But I like having them around. Having you around."

For long moments, the only sound was the chirping of crickets.

"It won't be like this for long."

Louisa smiled. "So, I'll enjoy this while I have it. And then I'll enjoy the noise of family when they get back."

"Family. Who'd have thought, sister, at the start of this summer, that you'd be making room for a houseful of people."

"Young people and, maybe someday, babies. We'll go on."

"Never thought much about it when it was just the two of us, but it sounds nice. Going on."

"I did think about it," Louisa admitted, "but never dreamed this would happen."

She gazed up at the stars, an endless sky of them now that night had fallen, and it seemed to her that she could see eons past and future in those far-away points of light.

"What's it like, Ollie? Going on. Is it hard?"

"Not a bit. Mama and Daddy and Maisie—all of them are waiting for us."

"Why didn't you go with them?"

"Couldn't go without you, Lou."

"I might not be ready for a while."

"No matter. A day or a century. It's all the same here. Whenever you're ready, I'll be waiting for you."

Louisa smiled, comforted by that. "Life is a wonder, Ollie. I'd nearly forgotten. But life is a wonder."

THE END

About the Author

BESTSELLING AUTHOR CAREN WERLINGER published her first award-winning novel, *Looking Through Windows*, in 2008. Since then, she has published fifteen more novels, winning several more awards. Influenced by a diverse array of authors, including Rumer Godden, J.R.R. Tolkein, Ursula LeGuin, Marion Zimmer Bradley, Willa Cather and the Brontë sisters, Caren writes literary fiction that features the struggles and joys of characters readers can identify with. Her stories cover a wide range of genres: historical fiction, contemporary drama, and fantasy, including the award-winning Dragonmage Saga, a fantasy trilogy set in ancient Ireland. She has lived in Virginia for thirty years where she practices physical therapy, teaches anatomy, and lives with her wife and their canine fur-children.

Website: *carenwerlinger.com*
Blog: *cjwerlinger.wordpress.com*
Amazon: *www.amazon.com/Caren-J.-Werlinger/e/B002BOI2ZI*
Facebook: *www.facebook.com/CarenWerlingerAuthor*
Audible: *www.audible.com/author/Caren-J-Werlinger/B002BOI2ZI*

Made in the USA
Columbia, SC
16 September 2020